Midnight's Emissary

T.A. White

Chapter One

No matter how many times I visited the Book Haven, I always had trouble believing it was a hub of supernatural knowledge. It just seemed so unassuming. A book lover's paradise sure. With thirty two rooms crammed full of books, it was a maze that any Columbus dwelling book nerd would be overjoyed to disappear inside.

It was even popular with the out-of-town crowd since it was also one of the largest independent bookstores in the U.S. still in business. It didn't hurt that it had that old world charm that made German Village popular with tourists and hipsters. The building started life as a saloon before at some point being taken over by word loving entrepreneurs. Since then it had grown and assimilated the neighboring general store and cinema to become the unnavigable monstrosity that it was.

I nearly tripped on the uneven brick path leading to the alleyway entrance. The path was lined by bushes and trees. Spring had come early this year and some of the plants were already beginning to bloom way ahead of schedule. Daft things didn't realize in a day or two the weather would flip, as it always did in Ohio, and the frost would kill everything but the hardiest.

"Welcome to the Book Haven," a man greeted me as I stepped into the tiny nook serving as the store's entrance.

I waited as he checked out a woman and her two kids. Then I suppressed a sigh as a tall man in t-shirt and shorts stepped into the already cramped space. The guy looked like his frat days weren't far behind him.

The greeter looked at me expectantly as the woman and her horde filed past me. I gestured to the other man and said, "You can help him first."

"Are you sure?" the frat boy asked. He had blond hair, muscles bulging out of his body like they were trying to multiply, and towered over me by a foot.

No, I just said it because it's the exact opposite of what I want. I fought to keep the snarkiness off my face and nodded. Why do people always ask that? I wouldn't have offered if I wasn't sure.

I waited, semi impatiently as the man checked out, and stepped up to the counter as soon as he left. The cashier pushed a map toward me. I glanced at it briefly and smiled. Wasn't that cute? Not what I was here for but ok.

"I'm looking for the section on feline behavior," I said with the politest smile I could muster.

The man paused and looked me up and down, his thin face a little skeptical at what he saw.

At five feet seven inches, I was just above average height. My grayish, blue eyes, while not a common color, were not memorable enough to stand out. If a group of people tried to describe me later, half would say my eyes were blue and the other half gray. Dark brown hair with red undertones framed a face full of angles and hard edges. The uncertain description worked in my favor as I was trying to get into somewhere I wasn't exactly supposed to be.

I waited, hoping the code was still good from the last time I was here. Technically, I didn't have the credentials to get into the hidden sections of the bookstore. The parts the normal public didn't know about. The ones where people like me could find answers to their every question.

I knew I didn't fit the profile of someone who normally requested that room. For one thing, to most of the supernatural world, my aura was too closely aligned to that of a human's. Baby vamps barely registered on the power scale, and I was so new to the fanged ranks that I was practically in diapers.

I'd made sure to dress casually in jeans and a fitted blue t-shirt I'd gotten at a Colorado beer festival. My one nod to the slightly chilly weather was the rust colored leather jacket.

I arched one eyebrow at the man, letting him know I wasn't pleased with the delay. He gave me a sidelong, suspicious look even as he drew a map from under the counter and handed it to me.

Some of the tension gathering at the base of my neck leaked away.

I snatched the map and turned away, not bothering to thank him. People in this world rarely said thank you, and I didn't want to give him one more reason to think I didn't belong.

It worked. I couldn't believe it, but it worked.

I headed up the rickety, wooden steps and waited on the next landing until the couple descending had passed before heading up the next set of steps.

Despite the cool factor inherent in having a bookstore in a bunch of old buildings, it was a pain in the ass maneuvering through this place. I felt like an elephant in a china shop. The place was narrow, and in many spots you had to wait until oncoming traffic passed before proceeding.

Forget trying to sit in an aisle while you read. You'd be buffeted by the continuous coming and goings of every person tramping through this place.

A chain bookstore this was not. There were no comfy chairs to sit and peruse. No fancy coffee shop connected. And it smelled faintly of unfinished wood, mold and paper.

Still, it had been in business for a long time. Even longer if you took into account the hidden face of the bookstore. The one that served people like me. Or rather, people like who I was pretending to be. Powerful, connected, dangerous.

I took a look at the map and followed the blue line through one section after another until I stood in front of a roped off staircase. It had an exit sign that said "In case of emergency."

Got to hand it to these guys. They had a sense of humor.

I tucked the map into my back pocket and glanced both ways to make sure I wouldn't freak any unsuspecting normal out when I disappeared down the staircase.

Coast was clear. I threw one leg over the chain and stepped onto the top stair. Or at least that was my intention.

Instead I ended up tripping and falling when my foot landed much sooner than I expected. I ended up on all fours on the other side of the chain, staring down at red carpet with gold and cream detailing.

I climbed to my feet and looked around the cavernous room. It certainly wasn't the Book Haven, or maybe it was and the other place was just a pale imitation of this.

The ceiling towered several stories above me, so high that its depths were shrouded in shadow. Every wall was lined with row after row of book cases. So many and so high that there were ladders climbing the walls.

Unlike the normal store where the book shelves were fairly worn, thin scraps of wood only one step up from plywood, these shelves had the deep red gleam of high quality oak that had been cared for by overworked apprentices who'd no doubt spent most of their lives shining it until you could see your reflection in the wood's depths.

It wasn't my first time visiting this place, but I'd never been in this room.

Normally someone like me, someone low on the totem pole wouldn't have even known this place existed, but Hermes, the courier service I worked for, had sent me on several deliveries for the hidden bookstore.

The entrance to this place changed constantly. As far as I could tell this place existed in some kind of pocket realm. That's why I needed the map. It was the only way I could find a way inside.

The only thing I hadn't been sure of was the code phrase. It seemed to change every time I came here. My last delivery to the caretaker was four days ago so I figured it would be good still. And I was right.

My footsteps were muted as I moved into the depths of the bookstore. It was like walking through a tomb and reminded me of some of the battlefields I'd visited with my parents as a child. It had that same quiet that seemed to shout without ever making a sound. The kind that said you were risking life and limb bringing the noise of the living into a place where only the dead should walk.

I rubbed my arms, suddenly freezing. This place hadn't had this kind of unsettling feeling the last time I was here, or any of the times before that. It was like it knew I wasn't supposed to be here. I pushed forward, telling myself that I was letting my imagination run away with me.

The only thing this place seemed to have in common with the human side was the maze like labyrinth that its rooms formed. The passageways twisted and turned, narrowing unexpectedly before opening up into great rooms full of books and other items.

I paused by a table with a gold shield displayed on it. There was a great oak tree embossed on the metal, the fine detailing catching and sending the light rippling along the branches.

I drew closer, wondering what type of tools the maker used to give it such a lifelike look. I reached out to touch, almost anticipating the feel of live wood under my fingers.

"I wouldn't," a voice said next to my ear.

I jumped and snatched my hand back, straightening from where I'd bent closer to examine the shield. I hadn't realized I'd crossed an entire room to examine it until now.

"That thing has a habit of bespelling people. It's quite dangerous. If it likes you, it'll draw you into its internal world. If it doesn't, you'll just stand there and starve yourself to death. End result is the same either way. You die."

A man with curly brown hair and skin the color of walnut gave me a friendly smile as if he told people about the dangers of the homicidal shield all the time.

I stepped back from the item in question, not wanting to test my luck.

The man watched me with a bland gaze. Friendly, but not too friendly, as if he had all the time in the world to wait for me to do whatever it was I was going to do.

"Do you work here?" I asked. "I've never seen you before."

"Nor I you."

There was an awkward pause. Awkward on my side at least. The silence didn't seem to bother him in the least. It was like being watched by a cat, one that was utterly disinterested in your future or past because your actions had no bearing on its feline superiority.

"Um, I'm looking for something. Perhaps you could help me."

The man waited.

This guy was definitely a little weird, but then I was in a supernatural library with a moving entrance. I couldn't really expect anything less.

"I'm looking for a book."

The man smiled, his light brown eyes warming with laughter. "Well, we are in a bookstore."

Ah. That's right. Stupid statement.

Looked like the guy had a sense of humor. It was a relief actually. Made him seem slightly more human, which when standing in a supernatural bookstore next to a shield that ate people was surprisingly reassuring.

I gave him a strained smile. "I'm not really sure what I'm looking for. I mean I don't have a name or anything to give you."

This was a lot harder than I thought. For some reason, I thought I could just waltz in, find what I was looking for and then waltz out. No interaction with other people necessary and no one would be the wiser about my visit.

That hadn't happened and now I was awkwardly explaining myself to the man with the enigmatic gaze.

I took another step away from the shield. You could never be too careful with magical artifacts that might eat you. I meandered toward another table, taking the time to get my bravado back.

This plan would work or it wouldn't. If it didn't, they'd throw me out of the store. Probably ban me for life, which would affect any runs that might end here. They'd probably let my boss, Jerry, at Hermes know, in effect guaranteeing my subsequent firing.

I needed to stop thinking about everything that could go wrong. It was too late to turn back, and I didn't have time to have a panic attack now.

I met the man's eyes again, aware that they hadn't budged from me during my whole internal motivational speech. That was alright. It was creepy, but who wasn't a little creepy among the spooks.

"I'm hoping you can point me to a book that might have a rundown of who's who on the supernatural side of things. If it has anything to say about the inner politics of the different factions that would be great too."

"That's a big request."

Hence the reason I was essentially breaking into this place. I'd looked everywhere else. No one had anything that could act as a primer of the different species and factions making up this magically fucked up world. Or at least no one who was willing to deal with me, the no-power baby vamp who was marked by a sorcerer and at odds with the vampires.

"I'm aware."

He finally looked away, his focus turning inward as he sank into thought.

"There might be something."

Really? Hell yes. Maybe this hadn't been such a bad plan after all.

"That's great. Where is it? How much will it cost?"

I didn't have much money, but perhaps I could put it on a layaway plan or something.

His lips took on a sly quirk.

I paused, not liking the way he suddenly looked like the cat who caught the canary.

"The where is simple enough, you just have to find it. As for the cost, that's another matter. Some might say it will cost you nothing. And everything."

Was that a riddle? It certainly sounded like it. I hated riddles. My thought patterns were too linear, and I rarely guessed the correct answer. Maybe I should start looking for this thing on my own. No way did I want to accidentally promise my first born and be stuck in a Rumpelstiltskin situation. Not that, as a vampire, I could even have a first born, let alone a second.

"What would I do with a first born?" the man asked in a bemused voice.

I narrowed my eyes at him. A mind reader. Must be pretty powerful to get through my internal defenses. I'd thought they were pretty secure after the incident with the draugr. The one that landed me in my current situation.

Guess not.

In my distraction, had I dropped some of the layers?

The man gave no visual reaction at my reinforcing my mental defenses. Had what I done worked? I couldn't tell. I couldn't slam shut a door, effectively kicking the mental peeping tom out. The defenses were more organic and relied on confusion and misdirection as they created a mazelike forest in my mental landscape.

Aiden, a vampire I had met briefly during the incident, told me it was rare for someone to create a fortress based on nature. He said it like my mental forest made me rare, the kind of rare that might be referred to as a freak in ruder company. But I might have been reading into that.

"Maybe this book isn't for me," I said.

His smile was sweet and innocent, not the sly one of before. No way was I buying what he was selling. This had devil's bargain written all over it. The last thing I needed was to get sucked into another situation that was well over my head. I was barely treading water as it was.

"It'd be a pity if you walked away. The piece I have in mind would be perfect for your purposes."

I gave him a tight smile. "Somehow I think the price is a little steeper than I want to pay."

"Hm," he said, his eyes blank.

I finally placed what it was about him that was making me uneasy. His expressions were only surface deep. As if someone had taken clay and begun to make the facial expression that matched the feeling but forgot to make the rest of the features reflect that feeling. His lips smiled but the skin around them stayed still, no dimples or wrinkles. The skin around his eyes and on his forehead remained smooth and unmarked.

Yeah. I didn't know what this guy was, but he definitely wasn't human.

Time to carefully extricate myself from this conversation and make my way towards the exit.

"The cost is not high."

I stuffed my hands in my pockets, fingering the silver knife hidden there. "You know what they say, 'beware things that sound too good to be true.'"

His expression registered only slight surprise, as if he was no longer making the effort to appear human.

He could definitely still read my mind, or else he was really good at reading the situation.

"I have never heard that saying before."

I bet he hadn't heard a lot of sayings.

"Not true," he said. "I've heard this one – 'There are more things in heaven and earth.'"

Shakespeare. Lovely. I hated reading that play in high school.

I opened my mouth to respond and stopped, studying his inquisitive expression. He seemed awfully invested in me taking whatever it was he was trying to sell. It put me even more on guard.

I wanted knowledge but not at the expense of my life.

"You're right. You do know human expressions, but I'm afraid I'm just not interested in this amazing book of yours." I pointed behind me as I backed up. "I think I'll just be going now."

I started for the door.

"But you haven't found what you were looking for yet."

This guy just wasn't giving up.

I gave him a strained smile, not pausing as I headed for room's exit. "Thanks, but that's life."

His lips frowned. I say his lips because the rest of his face didn't move. This was really starting to creep me out. I was beginning to realize why only certain people were allowed into this place. Only the powerful and dangerous could make it in and out without death stalking every move.

I tried not to think of the weapons I was carrying on me, not certain that I could fight him off if he attacked.

He started forward as I neared the door and I bolted, darting over the threshold and down one twisting hallway after another. I shot a glance behind me, cursing when I saw him keeping pace with me, not getting closer but also not falling further behind.

I had no idea where I was or how to get back to the entrance. This was bad.

I rounded the corner and stumbled over a book lying in the middle of the floor. I barely caught myself from falling.

"What are you doing here?" a querulous voice asked. The tone said the owner wouldn't accept any half ass excuses either.

I looked up to find a pair of bright blue eyes looking out at me from a face so lined with wrinkles that it was hard to believe the owner had ever been anything but ancient. He looked like a sharpei. Even his wrinkles had wrinkles.

"I'm not talking to hear myself speak," he snapped.

"Uh." I glanced over my shoulder to find the other man had disappeared.

"Oh, good lord, it's like talking to a brick wall. No, I take that back. A brick wall would have a more intelligent conversation."

My stomach sank. I recognized him. He was the shop keeper I usually dealt with when making my deliveries. Talk about out of the pan and into the fire.

"I was just trying to find the exit," I said. Maybe he wouldn't recognize me. It's not like we'd had a lot of conversations in the past. He'd barely deigned to acknowledge me on the rare occasions I stopped by. "Your other shop keeper was showing me the way."

"Other shopkeeper? What shopkeeper? I'm the only one who carries that title." The man's eyes narrowed. "Wait a minute. I recognize you. You work for that upstart Jerry."

Damn. Guess he'd paid more attention than I thought.

"Yeah. You work for his little company. What was it called?" He looked around as if the name was just lingering in the air, waiting for him to see it.

"Hermes," I said. No point denying it now. If he knew Jerry's name, he'd eventually be able to tie it back to me.

"That's it." He pointed at me. "It still doesn't explain why you're inside the store."

I shrugged, feigning nonchalance. "I was looking for a book. Why else would I be here?"

His laugh was a cackle suited to any movie villain. "There are more reasons than there are stars in the galaxy. How did you even get in?"

"Same way most do."

"Be more specific. There are a million ways to gain entrance."

I'd really hoped to keep that part secret.

His eyebrows, two white caterpillars perching just above his sunken in eyes, rose in question as if to say 'today'.

"I asked the cashier at The Book Haven for a map to the feline behavior department," I admitted.

He harrumphed. "That shouldn't have gotten you inside. The code changed about five minutes after you dropped my package off last time."

I blinked. On one hand, his response shouldn't have been surprising. It was only good security to change passwords and codes once an unknown entity or hired errand girl was gone. I just hadn't expected it to be so instantaneous.

It did bring up the question of why the password had worked for me.

He shuffled over to a book case and pulled down a red leather bound book and flipped through its pages as he grumbled to himself.

He ran his finger down the page, pausing at one entry.

"Ah ha, I was right. The code changed three minutes after you left."

He peered back up at me, his eyes a bright spot of blue amidst his wrinkles.

I shrugged, not knowing what response he wanted from me. I couldn't change the truth.

"I don't know what to tell you. That's the code I used with the cashier. Maybe your system's broken."

"Impossible," he snapped. "It's never once had even a hiccup in all the years I've been the shopkeeper."

Judging by his wrinkles, that'd been a long, long time.

His eyes sharpened on the book at my feet. "What's that?" his voice deepened to nearly a growl. If I hadn't been staring at the old man in front of me, I would have sworn his voice was that of a young man.

I looked down at the book he was trying to incinerate with his gaze. Its cover was plain leather with the title embossed in it. It was a deep brown and the pages cream colored.

I bent down and picked it up. Out loud I read the words on the spine, "A study of the unexplained. The uninitiated's guide to the supernatural."

"Let me see it." He shuffled forward.

I held it out to him, but he didn't touch it, just peered at it like it was a snake preparing to strike.

"Well, that explains that," he murmured.

"Explains what?"

He gave me a gimlet glare. "Everything."

He turned around and shuffled away.

Well, that wasn't dire or anything.

"Are you going to follow me so I can show you to the exit, or are you going to stand there looking like a great lump of clay? If it's the second, you won't last long. Things roam these shelves looking for an easy target like you to consume."

I looked down at the book in my arms. "What do you want me to do with the book?"

"Bring it with you," he snapped. Under his breath, he mumbled, "It's not like it'd stay put anyway."

Pretending I hadn't heard that second part, I hurried after him, book in tow. Staying off the dinner menu worked well for my long term goals. The sooner I could put this place behind me the better. I never wanted to be this deep in the bookstore again.

He was mostly silent as he led me through the maze-like stacks of books. In contrast to the wide open rooms I'd wandered through before, he led me through hallway after small hallway of claustrophobia inducing spaces.

"Tell me about the other shopkeeper," he said abruptly. He sounded grim. Like he expected me to tell him the world was ending soon.

Seeing no harm in telling him about the creepy man I'd met, I said, "He had curly brown hair, brown eyes."

"Not that, you half-wit. I don't care what he looked like. Tell me what he said."

I pulled a face behind him.

"I can see you."

I paused, giving him a suspicious look. He hadn't turned, so unless he had eyes in the back of his head, I doubted that. Unless he was another mind reader.

I visualized burning the book in my hands, frowning when it pulsed with warmth against my fingers. If warmth was capable of giving off a feeling, this would have felt like indignation. I put that thought aside.

The old man failed to respond to my visualization, which meant he probably was not a mind reader. Good. Those guys always unsettled me. I don't like anybody knowing my most private thoughts. It's like having a peeping tom with x-ray vision spying on you in your most intimate moments.

The old man stopped and fixed a cranky stare on me.

"Right." What had the other man said? "He wanted to sell me a book."

"What kind of book?"

I debated how much to tell him. Couldn't hurt now. I was already in enough trouble. "A rundown of all the supernaturals and an insider's guide to the politics between the different factions."

He harrumphed again. "You wouldn't need such a thing if you would simply allow a clan to claim you. They would teach you everything you need to know."

Or only what they wanted me to know.

"Yes, yes. I've already been over this with the vampires. I don't need to go over it with a grumpy bookseller too."

He snorted. "Cocky and arrogant. What's wrong? Afraid of losing control of your life?"

I gave his back a searching look, not liking how closely he'd guessed my motivations. Even Liam hadn't hit the nail on the head so aptly.

Liam was a vampire I'd met last fall. The first vampire I'd met. Well, if you didn't count the bastard who turned me. I didn't. I tended to call him Jackass in my head. Liam was also the vampire who said he would teach me a little more about this world, and more importantly, a little more about what it meant to be vampire.

I hadn't heard much from him since that promise, which me to breaking into a restricted bookstore trying to bluff my way towards obtaining more knowledge.

"Sure, I guess you could say that." There was no point in denying it.

He gave me a gap toothed smile. "Good for you. Maybe you're smarter than you look."

We turned a corner and suddenly we were back in the cavern I started in. The man's head swiveled as he took in the expanse of books.

He cackled. "I haven't seen this section in a while."

How big was this place? Never mind. I didn't think my mind could handle the answer.

I tried to hand the book I'd been carrying to him. He waved me off and took a step back.

"What was the price you agreed to?" he asked.

"We didn't," I said. "He tried to tell me it was nothing and everything, but it sounded like it was too good to be true so I refused."

Well that and he had seriously creeped me out by that point.

I tried to hand it back to the shop keeper again. He refused to take it, his old man face frowning at me.

"Keep it. You've already paid the price, and it wouldn't stay with me anyway."

My hands hung in the air, holding out the book, while I processed what he said.

"No, I haven't paid anything or agreed to any payment."

He shrugged. "Doesn't mean it hasn't already been paid. Look, the price really is nothing."

"And everything," I protested. I remembered that part. It was the part that had tripped my internal alarms.

He waved my protest away. "That means nothing. No worries. The book is yours."

"But I don't want the damn book."

"Too late now." He waved his hand at the door to the human side. "Out you go."

"Wait a minute. You can't make me pay for something if I never agreed to the deal." I'd learned this much from the sorcerer at least.

My phone rang before the shop keeper could respond. I glanced down and pulled it out of my pocket. It said 'Hermes Calling.'

I looked up to find myself alone in the stacks of books. I spun around. Damn it, where'd he go?

The phone rang again.

I answered, "What?"

The person on the other end sucked in a breath. "Is that how you answer when representing the company?"

It is when they have possibly caused me to agree to a deal I had no intention of agreeing to.

"What do you want, Janice?"

"You know my name isn't Janice," Beatrix snapped.

I did, but she looked like a Janice so that's what I called her. It didn't hurt that I knew she hated it, which is why I did it.

"What do you want?"

"You need to come into the office."

"It's my night off. I have plans." I glanced around the empty book cases. Or at least I had before the book keeper left me standing holding a book I didn't pay for.

"Too bad. Jerry needs all hands on deck."

"Can't this wait until tomorrow?"

Even if my excursion hadn't gone as planned, I still wanted the rest of the night to figure out what to do next.

"It can. If you want to be fired." Beatrix's voice was smug over the phone. She knew I wouldn't risk that.

"Fine," I gritted out. "I'll be there in an hour."

"Make it twenty minutes."

"Twenty minutes? Are you crazy? I have to go home first and grab my shit before heading to the office. No way can I get there in twenty minutes."

"I don't want to hear your excuses; just get your ass here in twenty."

There was a click and then silence. I looked at my phone screen. That harpy had hung up on me.

Guess I shouldn't be too surprised. She had made no secret from the moment we met that she didn't like me.

I took one last glance around the empty stacks before glancing down at the book in my hands. It looked so harmless with its leather cover and simple design, but then I think most books had that in common.

What should I do with it? Leave it behind or take it with me? The shopkeeper seemed adamant that I take it, even going so far to say that whatever its price was had already been paid.

Might as well keep it for now seeing as there was no one to hand it off to. I could always come back later to try to return it.

I headed to the exit for the normal side of the bookstore. Making the meeting was not going to be easy.

Chapter Two

I was ten minutes late when I rode my bike up to the office of Hermes Courier Service. It was like any other building in the Warehouse District. It was three stories and made from the same red brick that a lot of the older buildings in Columbus were built from. It had the same warehouse windows laid out in the same small squares making up a larger rectangle. Parts of it had graffiti decorating the brick. Maybe a little run down and showing its age but otherwise there was nothing to set it apart.

Recently, the Warehouse District had undergone a sort of renaissance as people bought up a lot of the older warehouses and turned them into offices and luxury apartment buildings featuring the industrial look. It had given the area a breath of fresh air. Making it a place you could go after dark without worrying if you'd make it to your destination in one piece.

From the stories I heard from other couriers, Jerry had bought this place when it was first built. Some said even before it was built. Who knew if that was true? Jerry liked to play things close to the vest.

I propped my bike against the brick, took out my chain and locked it to the drain pipe running up the side of the building. I wasn't really afraid someone passing by would try to steal it as Jerry had enough magical security wrapped around this place to discourage that sort of behavior.

I was more afraid of what my fellow couriers would do to it. They liked to play pranks, especially if they felt you were getting the good gigs. I'd only had to walk out once to find my bike tied to the top of a lamp post before I started locking it up.

I detached the seat and put it in my messenger bag. It'd be just like these bastards to take the seat to mess with me.

Not wanting to waste any more time, I hit the intercom button, then kept hitting it when no one answered. Beatrix had neglected to send me the new passcode for the door. No doubt on purpose.

I held the button down for several long seconds, knowing that she'd eventually cave and buzz me through.

Sure enough, seconds later the door buzzed, and I yanked it open before heading inside.

The interior had changed again. Instead of a wide open, empty space, there was one hall with several doors opening off it. The floor was slate gray, polished concrete and the ceiling had all the pipe and metal work exposed.

Jerry seemed to change the interior based on whatever weird mood he was currently in. This was the fifth change this year, and the year was only four months old. Even for him, that was a lot. It made me wonder if this newest change had anything to do with why he'd called me in on my night off.

I headed for the stairs at the end of the hall and walked up to the second floor. The office door was nicely labeled Hermes making it easier to find than in the past. Once I'd had to open nearly every door in the place before finding the right office. I still had nightmares about what was behind some of those doors.

It was like any normal office, a secretary's desk sat next to the only other door and there was a waiting room with seating to my right. It even had those fake trees that were so popular in offices.

Beatrix looked up from the file in front of her, one eyebrow lifting imperiously before she looked pointedly at the clock next to me. By this time I was more like fifteen minutes late.

I shrugged. I didn't feel too bad about that, being called in unexpectedly and all.

"Oh look, she finally found her way here," a voice said to my right.

The gnome folded the newspaper and set it to the side. I grimaced. Great, Tom. This visit wouldn't be complete without him.

I ignored him, knowing from prior experience that engaging him just escalated the insults. Beatrix watched the two of us with a bland expression. If I looked closely, I thought I could detect a slight smug tilt to her mouth. She was probably enjoying this immensely.

"We shouldn't be surprised. Miss Vampire keeps her own schedule. Never caring if she's late or on time."

Not true. I'm usually tediously punctual. That, and early. I've never not made a delivery on time. Except that time with the werewolves, but even that would have been on time if the recipient hadn't already been dead.

Ignore. Ignore. You can't win. He's going to have an opinion either way.

He came to stand in front of me.

"I'm here, Beatrix. What's so important that you called me in on my night off?" I asked, ignoring Tom.

It wasn't too difficult. As a gnome, he only came up to my chest, but that didn't mean he was harmless. He was like a squat tank, short but with muscles that looked like someone had stuck a bunch of rocks under his skin. He could punch his fist through a car door and then yank that door off the frame. I knew, I'd seen him do it when one of his clients refused to sign the acknowledgement form. Cute lawn ornament he was not.

He wore a skull cap to cover his pointed ears and curly brown hair. If his face wasn't creased into a perpetual frown, I would have said he was cute, in a middle aged man sort of way.

"Hey, I'm talking to you." He poked me in the chest. "What makes you think you can just do whatever you want?"

"Are you talking to me or just accusing me of crap that's not true again?"

Sometimes it was harder than others to ignore the cranky bastard. This was one of those times I was destined to fail.

He frowned so hard that the skin on his forehead turned into a V.

"Self-entitled little brat," he said.

"Name calling, really?" I leaned down. "You'll have to do better than that. Shorty."

His face turned red as his oversized hands bunched into fists at his side.

I fought the urge to take a step back. I knew he was sensitive about his height but hadn't thought it would drive him to violence so quickly.

I touched the pocket with the silver knife in it for reassurance. If he swung at me, I was using my weapon. It wouldn't do much good considering he was technically part of the fae. Iron would work better or maybe wood. It's one of those gray areas that I haven't been able to get a lot of information on. Yet.

"Think you're so smart, don't you, fanger?" His voice was nasty as he stepped forward until he had to crane his head back to meet my eyes.

This had gone on long enough. I wasn't here to start trouble with my fellow couriers, even if they were itching for a fight. Mainly because I was pretty sure Jerry would frown on such a thing.

17

Couriers with broken bones couldn't make deliveries.

All of a sudden I was done with the petty scrabbling. I didn't want to spend one of the few nights I had off arguing with the gnome. It was exhausting, not to mention drama I didn't need or want.

"What did I ever do to you, Tom? Every time we're in the same room, you go out of your way to create trouble for me. I don't recall ever doing something to earn this level of enmity."

"Your existence is plenty."

What did that even mean?

"What does that mean?"

He scoffed. "Like you don't know."

"I don't. Believe me, if I did I wouldn't be asking."

My puzzlement must have gotten through to him because he stepped back and gave me an assessing gaze, as if he was trying to judge my level of sincerity.

I tried to show my confusion. It wasn't hard because I honestly didn't know what I had ever done to earn this level of hostility.

I've had my share of obnoxious coworkers who didn't like me, but usually I've done something to earn it. Like that time I tied every pair of a fellow soldier's boot shoelaces to another boot's shoelaces.

She had it coming though. She told my battle buddy she was going to Hell because she thought she was the reincarnation of a vampire princess. I might have thought my battle buddy was bat shit crazy but that didn't mean I'd let some stranger walk up to her and make her feel bad about it. Though, looking back I may have written off my battle buddy's claims as fantasy a little too quickly. Who knew vampires and all this other shit actually existed.

"My nephew was supposed to have a job here," Tom said abruptly.

I blinked. Tom had family. Who'd have thought?

"How am I involved in that?" Not like I went around bad mouthing his nephew to get him black listed.

"Your job. He was supposed to have your job," Tom said through gritted teeth. "After they hired you, they said there were no more open spots. If you hadn't had your little buddy pull some strings, he'd be able to work here and earn some money for the family back home."

That was the reason for all the grief he'd been giving me over the past few years? Really? Now I wish I hadn't even asked. The answer just pissed me off.

I started and stopped speaking a few times before I could

18

compose myself enough to ask, "Correct me if I'm wrong, but wouldn't your nephew have used the same nepotism you're accusing me of to get this job?"

He gave me a nasty glare before shouldering past me, making sure to knock into me before leaving. I turned to watch him go, not wanting to chance him taking the opportunity to stick a knife in my back or at the very least try to put his fist through it.

He slammed the door; the framed photos on the wall rattled before hanging firm.

I turned back to Beatrix who had watched it all with that same smug face.

I took another look around. "For all hands on deck, you seem to be running pretty light. Where is everyone? I thought you were calling everyone in."

She didn't bother answering, just pointed a long, bony finger at the uncomfortable looking chairs in the waiting room. Propping my hands on my waist, I looked from them to her, suspecting that the matter wasn't as urgent as she'd made it seem on the phone.

This was my night off. I wasn't going to spend it in a sitting room with my thumb up my ass because she was on another power trip.

Screw it. I was out of here.

I turned on my heel and headed for the door.

"Unemployment line," she said with glee in her voice.

I paused.

She didn't have the power to fire people. She was bluffing.

I took another step.

"Jerry said to tell you that if you leave before he meets with you, don't bother coming back."

Shit, she was serious. Beatrix, I'd learned in the seven months since I met her, had no problem fucking with me at any and every opportunity, but she wouldn't bring Jerry's name into it unless it was something he'd actually said.

My situation was tenuous. Job prospects were slim for someone with my special needs and as much as I would like to ignore it, this job gave me protection against the vampires or any other spook who'd like to take advantage of a baby vamp.

Guess that meant I had no choice but to stick around until I found out what he wanted.

I did an about face and walked over to Beatrix's desk before hopping up and planting my ass on the edge.

"What do you think you're doing, you obnoxious twit?" Beatrix's voice rose in outrage.

"I'm guessing nothing in his instructions said where I had to sit while I waited for him, just that I needed to stay put." I gave her a toothy smile.

When she looked like she wanted to spit venom, I knew I had won.

No one said I couldn't fuck back. You would think after all our interactions she would have learned that by now.

It might have been smarter to try to win her good will, but there was only so much turning the other cheek I could handle. She'd been after me since she showed up and I had no idea why. I figured it'd become evident eventually, and if it didn't, we would have our little skirmishes until one of us got tired of it or quit.

I pulled out my phone and started playing a stupid game where I had to match objects before they hit the bottom of the screen. I wasn't very good at it. The game was loud, obnoxious and distracting. It's why I had downloaded it, planning to use it in a situation exactly like this.

It was satisfying listening to Beatrix grind her back teeth, getting louder every time I died. And I died a lot.

"Would you please stop that? It's annoying."

"In a moment. There's a wand on the next level."

"You've died in the same place, on the same pattern, three times now."

I gave her a cheeky smile. "Guess I need to practice more then."

She made a noise of frustration and picked up the phone, murmuring into it before setting it down.

I kept my smile of triumph aimed away from her, not wanting her to know so she could sabotage my victory. Aileen one, Beatrix zero. It took a little of the sting out of all the other times she'd won our little skirmishes.

The intercom buzzed.

I was off the desk and opening the door to Jerry's office before she could even finish saying, "He will see you now."

Jerry was seated behind a mammoth desk, twice the size of Beatrix's. If you put the two desks beside one another, hers would look like something built for a child whereas Jerry's was built for a man-sized giant.

When a person saw Jerry for the first time, they were often struck dumb at his size. His muscles had muscles and one oversized hand could engulf my skull and probably crush it with barely a thought. He couldn't walk more than a few feet down the street without getting asked what NFL team he played for. People gave him crazy eyes when he acted like he'd never heard the acronym before.

His face and body weren't the type you'd want to meet in an alley after dark or in the day or pretty much anywhere for that matter. Despite a face that said he could rip out your spleen and feed it to you without ever losing a minute of sleep, he was attractive enough in an intense, could kill you by breathing on you, kind of way. His brown hair never looked brushed and stuck out in weird tufts from his head.

For all that he could kill with one frown, he was a good boss. Probably the best I'd ever had. I owed him, even if he didn't give me this job out of the goodness of his heart but as a favor to someone he owed. The result was the same. Protection from what would have been even more monumental changes to an already upended life and a paycheck, that while it wasn't going to have me rolling in luxury, at least allowed me to be independent and take care of myself. What more could you ask for?

"Sit," his deep voice rumbled.

I sat without saying anything. Jerry was a little intimidating at the best of times and judging from the tense set of his shoulder's this wasn't going to be one of them. It would be wise to walk softly until I knew a little more of what was going on.

He continued reading the papers in front of him, turning the page and carefully reading the next. My lips quirked at the sight of a pair of black framed glasses perching on his nose.

I practiced the patience I learned standing in countless formations while in the military. I held still, thinking about nothing in particular. That was the trick to waiting. You didn't focus, not on the time, the frustration or that itch that was nagging at the middle of your back. You just existed. The alternative was to compose mental lists of ways to escape your mom's attention on your failed career prospects. They both accomplished the task of taking you out of the endless tedium of waiting.

"I have a job for you," Jerry said, without looking up from his papers.

I figured. It's not like we got together outside of work and went looking for teenagers to mug.

When he didn't seem inclined to continue, I prodded. "And that job is?"

21

"I took a big risk when I pulled you into my company."

I digested that statement. It didn't tell me what he wanted from me. It also didn't give me warm fuzzies about this job, with him starting the conversation by mentioning the risks he'd taken to shelter me from the vampires finding out about my existence. That's the sort of statement you usually made when you were planning to call in a favor. Especially since I was supposed to stay off the radar. That went topsy turvy last fall.

We'd both been waiting with baited breath to see what the vampires would do once they found out a vampire who hadn't been through the one hundred years of indentured service to a clan was running around free and unrestrained. It definitely didn't help that they now knew I'd never received any training in how to curb my appetite for blood or deal with all the other challenges being of the fanged variety presented.

Liam, the enforcer who'd run across me in an investigation, had nearly blown a gasket when he discovered my existence. Evidently, the bite and run was frowned upon. My sire was in a lot of trouble if Sir Cranky Pants, the name I gave Liam, ever caught up to him. Or so I'm assured. Not sure how much I believe that, but I'm willing to keep an open mind until it happens.

"I'm aware," I finally said.

"Now that the vampires know of your existence, it changes things."

Hold up a minute. Was he firing me? That couldn't happen. That could NOT happen. I've never been fired before. Never. Not once. I wasn't prepared to be fired now. I needed this job to survive.

"Jerry, you know I appreciate everything you've done for me, and if it's the vampires you're worried about, I've got the sorcerer's mark to protect me."

"Only you would think a sorcerer's mark is there to protect you." He gave me a put out look from beneath his bushy eyebrows.

I gave a mental shrug, conceding his point. It might not have been placed there to protect me per se but I'd managed to manipulate events enough that the effect was the same.

"You may be protected, but everyone who gave shelter to you or hid your existence is not. The vampires could decide to claim recompense from myself and the Captain."

Yes, I could see how that would be worrisome to him. At the same time, he'd known the risks. Better than I did even.

This also still didn't tell me why he was bringing this all up now. Months after my run in with Liam.

He took a deep breath and slid a square piece of paper to me. "I have a job for you."

Puzzled, I took the post-it size piece of paper and glanced at the name and address on it.

Sunshine Diner

9:00 p.m. tomorrow night, third booth from the back.

Don't be late.

I didn't get it. What was all the seriousness about if this was just another job? There had to be something more.

"This run will require a little bit more from you. It's not the average pick up and drop off."

"What does that mean?"

He was silent, his face creased with lines. He seemed almost worried, which was a little scary. Jerry didn't get worried. For the most part he was as calm and steady as a rock. Nothing fazed him.

"You'll see when you get there."

His face dropped back into its normal impassive expression. I knew I wasn't going to get anything else out of him.

I stood as he turned back to his papers. Hesitating in front of him, I finally left when he didn't look back up.

It was almost eleven p.m. so the meeting wasn't until tomorrow night. At this point, there was no use worrying about this mysterious job and what it would entail until tomorrow.

Why did I have a sinking feeling this job had something to do with the vampires?

Chapter Three

Pressing lightly on the bike's brake, I turned into the parking lot, barely noticing the sharp jolt as my wheels fought for purchase on the broken pavement. There were so many cracks in the asphalt that it was practically gravel at this point. Weeds, some as high as my knee, had burrowed through those cracks and made the already treacherous ground even harder to navigate. Luckily, my apartment's parking lot was about the size of a postage stamp.

I threw one leg over the seat and stepped down while the bike was still moving, bringing the bike and myself to a gradual halt.

I rented a second story walk up in an old duplex, just outside of campus, that looked like it was built around the turn of the nineteenth century. The cement stoop to the downstairs apartments had settled since its creation and drooped forward and to the side like a drunken sailor on shore leave. The rest of the foundation had settled in the opposite direction at some point because the brick next to the windows looked like they were slightly off kilter.

Knowing the owners like I did, I doubted they'd mitigated any of the settling and it was likely this place was one crazy party away from folding like a stack of cards.

The wooden stairs leading up to my place were no less rickety and rundown than the rest of the building. Anytime anything larger than a cat used them, they shook and trembled like they were in the midst of an earthquake.

It was a slum, made acceptable by the fact that they mostly rented to college students who planned to vacate within a year or two of renting. In the mind of a college student, who cared if the place wasn't safe and the landlord took three months to get around to fixing the hot water heater. It was cheap and that was all that mattered.

It was also all I could afford right now. Sometimes you had to just deal with the hand you had been dealt.

Someone walked out of the downstairs apartment closest to the staircase. I paused, curious. I'd never met one of my neighbors before.

They were usually out when I left for the night or fast asleep when I got home in the very early morning.

The man hesitated when he caught sight of me at the bottom of the stairs, preparing to pick up my bike. He was taller than me, probably over six feet by an inch or two. He had shoulder length copper, brown hair and a face that was all hard plains. His nose was a little too long and his mouth a little too thin, but those imperfections helped give his face character and break it out of the too pretty mold it would have fallen into otherwise.

He gave me a nod before continuing to a truck parked in the lot that I just now realized was full of furniture and boxes.

I watched for a moment. Was I getting new neighbors? How had I missed the last ones moving out?

It was possible they'd moved out during the day when I slept or while I was away on a run. To tell you the truth, I'd just kind of assumed both apartments on the lower floor were empty since the occupants were so quiet. From my experience, students aren't normally silent on the weekends. Where were the parties and general shenanigans that typically happened when you're young and dumb?

I shouldered my bike and headed upstairs, not wanting to get involved in small talk with my new neighbor. If he was anything like the last ones I'd had, I probably wouldn't even know he was there.

Even though my apartment's exterior was the sort that sent most tenant's running screaming into the night, I thought I'd done a pretty good job of creating a cozy place to call home. Granted, ninety percent of the furniture was hand me downs or things I could scrounge from garage sales and resale shops, but it had its own style. Where I could, I added knick knacks collected during my childhood or while I was overseas with the military. It'd never be featured in Home and Garden, more like thrifter's anonymous, but it suited me and my personality, which was as tattered and cobbled together as this place.

I propped the bike against the entryway wall and set my helmet on top of it. Walking into the kitchen, I pulled off my light jacket and threw it on the table along with my keys. Since I never ate dinner there, it had become a catchall for my random odds and ends.

I opened my fridge, pulled out a wine bottle and grabbed a glass from the cabinet. The liquid I poured looked like any red wine except a little thicker and not made from grapes. When I'd filled it most of the way up, I capped the bottle and stuck it back in the fridge before grabbing my glass and heading back to the table where I'd set the book

25

earlier.

Now that the matter with Hermes was taken care of, I had the rest of the night to focus on my original plan. I sifted through the junk that had somehow accumulated on the old, beaten up wood.

Where was it?

I know I left it here. This was where I put everything. Especially when I was in a hurry.

I stepped back and lifted a jacket off the pile. No book was hiding under it.

Damn it.

I glanced around. Where would I have put it if not here?

Maybe the living room? I headed in that direction, stopping by the couch and lifting the blanket off it.

No. I didn't remember being in my living room before heading to Hermes.

I turned to leave, banging my shin on my coffee table.

"Son of a bumble bee." I grabbed the offending appendage.

I blinked at the coffee table in front of me. In the middle of it, like an offering, sat the book.

How did it get there? And why did I not see it when I was tearing the rest of the living room apart?

My hands were hesitant as they reached for it. Since becoming a vampire, I was much more attuned when unexplained or suspicious things happened, like a book appearing somewhere I did not leave it. Especially when that book had come to me under odd circumstances.

Nothing happened as my fingers brushed the cover. No tingle in my fingers. Nothing bad jumped out to eat me, and I wasn't magically transported somewhere new.

It was almost a letdown to have it act like a normal book.

I fell onto the couch and propped my feet on the coffee table.

The Uninitiated's Guide to the Supernatural.

Long title. Sounded more like a field manual than a book.

I thumbed through the pages quickly as I tried to determine what about this thing had caused the book keeper to give it to me for free.

It didn't seem like anything special. It was just a normal book. One that had slightly disturbing hand drawn pictures. I hesitated on one of a monstrous creature surrounded by a mountain of skulls and wearing a necklace of ears. That was disturbing.

I flipped past it and read the description for another creature, something called a yamabusa. Hm, I hoped I never had occasion to meet one of those.

Enough of this. Time to get to what I really wanted to know.

I flipped to the glossary section and turned to the v's and looked up the section I wanted, which was appropriately named blood drinkers, before flipping to it.

My heart sank as I realized that only a page was devoted to vampires.

I skimmed the section before tossing the book back on the coffee table in frustration, running my fingers through my hair. All that trouble and for what? Information I already knew. The book only recounted things I had already figured out myself.

Vampires drank blood. Check. Knew that. The sun was mildly irritating to most unless they had been starved or gravely injured or were newly turned. Knew that because of the draugr incident. Usually forced their newly turned, otherwise known as yearlings, into what amounted to an indentured servitude for the first one hundred years of their life.

Seeing the glass of blood next to the book, I grabbed it and chugged, not stopping to breathe until every drop was gone. I sighed as the parched feeling in my throat disappeared, and I got a nice boost of warmth as the blood started working its magic.

I carried the glass to the sink and washed it out, having learned the hard way that old blood stunk. It took forever to get the stink of it out too. Being a vampire also came with a slightly heightened sense of smell. Not as good as a werewolf's but good enough that the smell of old food drove me crazy after a while. That was something that they hadn't included in their little book.

Frustrated at the totally pointless risk I took in procuring a book with no new information, I spent the rest of the night watching Netflix until shortly before dawn. I shut things down and headed to my bedroom where I prepared for the forced rest I'd experience as the sun began its ascent across the sky.

As I had many times before, I held up a timer. Two minutes before sunrise was scheduled, I hit the start button and then stared at the alarm clock. I knew the moment the sun cleared the horizon as I could literally feel sleep sucking away my consciousness. As I had every morning since learning that vampires could be awake during the day, I fought against closing my eyes with everything I had, trying to delay my eventual loss by even a second longer than the day before.

Every sunrise felt like I'd spent an entire week awake. Like my eyelids had lead weights attached to them. I went crossed eyed as I fought to stay awake, my vision wavering.

Then it was lights out.

*　　*　　*

I woke to a trio of alarms blaring, going from dead to the world to awake and aware in less than a second. One of my favorite things about being a vampire was how clear headed I was when I woke. Well, as long as the sun had set.

I may have been able to stay awake for a few minutes in the morning, but I still couldn't repeat my success during the draugr incident of waking earlier than sunset. I wanted to replicate that trick when my life wasn't on the line, or when I got a big power boost from a clan elder. It'd be a nice thing to have in my back pocket if my life ever counted on it again.

Blindly, I groped for the alarm, my hand hitting nothing by air. With a growl, I lifted my head off the pillow and looked around. The alarm clocks were all on the dresser on the other side of the room.

How did they get over there? I usually had them on the nightstand next to my bed. Grumbling to myself, I lumbered out of bed and shuffled over to turn them off.

There was nothing in this world more annoying than the sound of an alarm clock. I'd picked the most annoying ones I could find in the hopes it would inspire me to wake before the sunset.

So far I'd been unsuccessful and it looked like today was a repeat of more of the same. The sun set three minutes ago.

I picked up the timer sitting by the alarm clocks, puzzled at how it'd made its way over here. Unless I somehow managed to sleep walk and didn't remember it. Possible, but I'd never done so in my previous experiments.

The timer said five minutes and thirty seconds. That was almost a minute better than my previous best time.

Nice.

I had plenty of time before I needed to be at the Sunshine Diner for my meeting to learn about the job that had a little 'more' to it.

My breakfast of champions, well vampire ones anyway, consisted of another glass of O negative and a Reece's peanut butter cup. I'd found, much to my relief, that the myths surrounding vampires were only half right. We needed to drink blood, but we could also consume real food in moderation. Most of our nutrients still came from the blood, but my stomach could still handle solid food in small portions. The best part was that I never gained an ounce. I chose to eat a lot of things I never did as a human for fear of blowing up like a balloon.

I set the glass down and turned away from the counter before tripping and falling into the wall. I turned and glared at the object that had nearly caused me to break my neck.

The book sat innocently on the old, cracked linoleum.

I sank back into the wall and gave serious thought to leaping over the island to get out of the kitchen. That thing moved, and not like I put it somewhere and forgot. I knew I left it on the coffee table last night. No, it somehow moved itself to its present spot in the kitchen. Worse, it did it after I was in here.

There was something magical to the thing. Whether it had benign or malevolent intentions was the question. From the way the shop keeper had reacted when I picked it up, I was willing to bet he knew exactly what this thing could do.

Now, I wasn't against magic per se. Just extremely cautious of it. I'd already been forced into a situation I didn't care for once by it. I'd rather avoid something like that happening again.

Until I knew more about the repercussions of using this thing, I wanted nothing to do with it. I didn't even want to touch it.

I gave the book another suspicious look before edging around it. The thing could stay where it was for now. When I had a moment, I'd talk to the shop keeper to see what I could find out about the book. I wouldn't accept any of his half-truths this time.

More and more I regretted the ill-conceived notion that had led me to the Book Haven. Too late now. Chalk it up to a lesson learned. For now I needed to get ready for my meeting with my new client.

*   *   *

The Sunshine Diner was a throwback to the diners popular in the fifties. It was nearly thirty years old and a staple in the neighborhood. It had much of the same décor as when it was built, but instead of seeming ancient and run down, it managed to seem charming, like it was something out of my grandparents' courting days.

During breakfast they were always packed. Arrive any time after seven and you were looking at an hour wait. Lunch and dinner were only slightly less busy. Their peanut butter s'more milkshake was impossible to pass up.

That held true this time as I sat in a cracked, red vinyl booth and gave my waitress my typical order of milkshake and fries.

I people watched out the window as I waited for my meal. I was a little early but figured I'd top up on my sugar habit if I had to deal with a problem client. Might as well kill two birds with one stone. Eat and make sure I was here in plenty of time to scope out the area.

A milkshake and plate of fries was set in front of me. I eyed it with the sort of lust a parched man eyes a glass of water after being in the desert for a few days. Sugar and artery clogging grease, two of the tastiest food groups.

I took the spoon and dipped it in the shake. It was so thick that a straw wouldn't cut it. You needed the spoon until the milkshake melted a little.

I closed my eyes in bliss at the first taste. Thank God being a vampire hadn't robbed me of this. I don't know what I would have done if I never tasted peanut butter and chocolate and fries again. Life would have been a lot bleaker.

A figure stood beside me when I opened my eyes. I started and nearly upended a spoonful of shake into my lap.

I looked up. Liam. Speak of the lying devil.

I should have let Jerry fire me.

He watched me with an inscrutable expression.

I frowned, unwilling to offer him a seat. There was a chance he wasn't here to meet with me. Maybe he'd been passing by for some other reason, saw me and stopped in to apologize for stringing me along and promising to teach me a little more about what it means to be vampire. Stranger things have happened.

He sat across from me.

Damn. I'd really hoped this had just been a crazy coincidence.

Liam always reminded me a little of a dragon, one that hadn't been fully tamed. Fierce, proud and more than a little dangerous. He looked perfectly capable of having a civil conversation with someone, right before incinerating them where they stood so he could enjoy their perfectly cooked remains as a tasty snack.

He appeared to be in his early thirties, though I suspected he was hundreds of years older than that. He was attractive if you could get past the crappy personality that made you just want to punch him in the face while screaming 'you're not the boss of me.'

With dark brown hair cut short above his ears, cheek bones that could cut glass and lips that practically begged to be kissed, he'd probably starred in many a woman's fantasies. He was a chick magnet, no doubt, but I preferred my men to be a little less capable of world annihilation.

I took a fry and dipped it in my milkshake, waiting for him to speak. In the slight chance that he wasn't my client and had only sat down to nag me about joining a clan, I wasn't going to give him any clues. Jerry took confidentiality very seriously, and I didn't want Liam to stick around to get a glimpse of the person I was supposed to meet.

I ate several more fries in the same way. The silence stretched between us as he watched behind a bland mask.

The minutes dragged on.

Maybe I should say something, if only to speed this along.

No. I didn't care, remember? Not about anything he had to say. Unless he was here as a client, in which case I did care, but only from the standpoint of my job.

He'd had his chance to press the vampire agenda. He went MIA instead. In the end that told me all I needed to know.

"I should apologize," he finally said.

I arched an eyebrow. "Oh? For what?"

He gave me a look that said that I knew perfectly well for what.

I gave him a sickly sweet smile that said I had no idea what he was talking about.

I'd learned during our previous meeting that Liam was very good at managing his facial expressions. You had to pay very close attention to the micro expressions to have even a small clue as to what was going on behind his electric blue eyes.

There was a slight tightening at the corner of his mouth that I read as annoyance or maybe regret. Naw, had to be annoyance.

"I meant what I put in that note. I have every intention of furthering our acquaintance and teaching you the basics of what you need to know."

"How indulgent of you."

"Business elsewhere required my attention."

I shrugged my shoulders. "Ok. No big deal."

It wasn't either. Yes, he'd said he'd help me. Yes, I was kind of counting on that help, but in the end it didn't matter. He had other things to do; I'd moved on. Yes, possibly not in the best direction since I had a book capable of moving itself from one room to another, but I'd take that over a possible indentured service to the vampires any day of the week.

"We can pick up now that I'm back."

Again I shrugged. "No need. I'm good."

"You're good?"

"Yup."

His eyes narrowed slightly. "Bullshit."

I dunked another fry in my milkshake and then swirled it around for good measure before taking a sharp bite out of it.

"Strong words for someone who hasn't been here for the past few months," I observed mildly.

He let out a sound that I would have called a growl a few months ago before meeting a werewolf, who actually could growl.

"Is that why you're eating fries and drinking a milkshake?" he asked.

What was wrong with my food? It was tasty. It was in no way healthy, but I was a vampire. Healthy food had no meaning to me anymore.

"What do you have against my food?"

"The fact that you have to ask that question tells me everything I need to know."

Since I had no clue what he meant by that, I decided to move on.

"What are you doing here?"

"Haven't you guessed?" His lips twisted in a half smirk.

I sighed, already knowing where he was going with this.

"I'm your new client."

Great.

Jerry's speech suddenly made more sense. In the entire time that I'd worked for him, we'd never accepted a job from the vampires. Partly because of my special circumstance, but mostly because of something that happened way before I was ever hired. I didn't know the details. Just that it was bad and resulted in the vampires being blacklisted.

Now it looked like that had changed.

"Oh goody," I said in a deadpan voice.

I slurped at the milkshake, making sure to make extra noise when I saw the way Liam eyed my sugary awesomeness with disdain.

"There's no need to prolong this then," I said, pushing myself up and throwing enough money on the table to cover my meal. "I have no intention of working with you. You'll need to find another courier for whatever job you have going."

"I don't think so," Liam said without moving a muscle.

I snorted. I didn't care what he thought.

Before I could get more than a few steps away, he added, "There would be consequences if you walk away now. For yourself. And Jerry."

I stilled, keeping my back towards him. Something inside told me to keep walking, that I would regret letting him draw me in, but a bigger part wanted to know what those consequences would be. Were they the sort that were annoying but didn't really affect your life, like not being able to enter any vampire owned territory? Or were they the life altering, world changing sort, like we'll kill your family if you don't do what we tell you to? They'd made that threat before.

I rolled my shoulders and adjusted my messenger bag. This was going to suck so bad. I just knew it.

"Let's get this over with then, shall we?" I slid back into my booth, not bothering to take the messenger bag off. I planned to jet out of here at the soonest opportunity. "Tell me about the job."

"Glad you saw it my way."

Yeah, yeah. He got me to do things his way again. His day was coming. I just had to figure out his weakness. We'd see whose way we followed then.

"Just get on with it. This isn't my only stop tonight."

"I assumed from my conversation with Jerry that this matter would have your full attention until its completion."

I bit down on the response about assumptions and concentrated on keeping all snarky comments locked inside. He was a client now, even if I'd rather stab him in the eye than work for him. Didn't matter anymore. I wouldn't act unprofessional just because I'd rather endure another bout of sun therapy than deal with vampire stuff.

"You'll have to take that up with him. I don't decide the assignments."

He frowned at me. I gave him the expression I used to give my commanding officer when they were being ridiculous. It was a combination of 'I'm too dumb to understand what you're saying' and 'I can't even fathom why you're asking this of me.' In my experience, people either got really pissed or they left me alone because they figured it'd be a waste of time dealing with my level of obstinateness. Sometimes it was a little of both.

He didn't have either of those reactions, just settled back in his seat and watched me with an unamused expression.

33

I slurped at my milkshake and was gratified when the skin around his eyes tightened.

"You going to tell me why I'm here?"

He sighed. "You're like a child."

Insults. I'd better be getting paid for this.

"Anything you say, grandpa."

His huff sounded almost like a growl this time. I smothered my smile, feeling a small thrill of victory that I was getting to him. He looked so serious. He needed to loosen up a bit, even if it was at his own expense.

"I've called you here to hire you for a job. It's for a sensitive matter."

That wasn't cryptic or anything.

"Oh?"

"There is about to be a conclave for a new leader of these territories."

My interest sharpened. This was the first I was hearing about any of this.

Our primary job was to act as messengers, picking up and delivering what our clients wanted. The other part of the job, the one that didn't have a formal definition, was to act as news distributers. We were the gossips that held this shadow world together. After all, the news sites weren't reporting when the dryads and the nyads had a throw down, drag out brawl at Griggs Reservoir or whether the necromancer's had managed to put down that zombie outbreak in the old graveyard near the river.

We would have heard news of this magnitude.

The sound he made was full of frustration as he ran his fingers through his hair, leaving it sticking up. It gave him a slightly rumpled look that would have been adorable if he wasn't a sanctimonious jerk.

"This would be so much easier if you knew anything about our world."

And whose fault was that? "Sorry that I'm so uninformed. It's too bad my sire ran off and his stand in took a vacation before he could teach me anything."

"I've already apologized for that."

"And yet you're holding my lack of knowledge against me when you're the one who dropped the ball."

"If you would just join a clan."

"That will not happen. Drop it and move on."

34

I'm sure the glare he shot me had quelled many a more dangerous foe with its subzero temperature, but I just lifted an eyebrow and took another bite of my fry.

"There are four applicants for the position, all of whom will do anything they can to obtain it. It is the most powerful position in this part of the country and the fifth most powerful in North America. Whoever succeeds in the nomination will have full power over those who live in their territory."

Wait up, that sounded like he thought anybody living in the territory would owe fealty or something. Like this was feudal England or something.

"You mean vampires would have to listen to this person, right?"

I assumed it was just vampires as I doubted this was a position any supernatural species could apply for.

"No, everyone— human, supernatural and otherwise would answer to this person."

"Does everyone else know this?"

His words were careful when he said, "It has been brought to their attention in the past."

My eyes narrowed. I wondered how many of those people were still alive today and whether their descendants would still agree.

"Why hold this in Columbus?"

I loved my city, and it just got better every year. We were considered one of the fastest growing cities in the U.S. and were popular with young professionals, but we were no New York or even Chicago for that matter. I could think of a dozen cities not more than six hours from here that would be more attractive for this kind of thing.

"There are several reasons."

My ears perked. Sounded like he was about to teach me something. Finally.

"The first is that several ley lines run through the city."

That was news to me. Mainly because I had no idea what a ley line was.

"This city has power. Much more than the average city. It's one of the reasons it has such a strong supernatural population. It's also located in the heart of the potential applicant's new territory. It's customary to hold a selection in the territory in question."

"So I'm assuming since this is such a big deal, you're concerned with selection tampering."

35

He gave a small nod.

"It has already taken place."

"Thought you just announced this conclave thingy recently."

"It's been expected for decades. The former leader made his intention to step down known to many. Some of the applicants took the initiative to start making moves against their competition."

How enterprising of them. Sounded like a plot from one of those Renaissance political dramas. The one with the family of the pope.

Another thought occurred to me. "You're not expecting me to provide security or something."

His scoff of derision stung a little – I had talents that had proven useful in the past – but not much given that these applicants would probably be pretty heavy hitters in the vampire world. I don't want to say they could squash me like a bug, but it probably wouldn't be much harder than that.

"So what do you want from me?" I asked, ignoring the lack of confidence in my security skills.

"There are several tests an applicant must pass to be chosen. Some are tests that every vampire passes at some point, while others are tailored to the selection."

Fascinating stuff, but not what I asked.

"Perhaps the easiest one to pass is the ability to prove you can sire another vampire."

He paused as the waitress stopped by our booth.

"Can I get you folks anything else?"

Liam shook his head.

I propped my chin on my hand and gave her a big smile. "Yes, my friend would like a milkshake, I think chocolate would suit him."

"Alrighty then, one chocolate milkshake."

She left, leaving him glaring at me.

"I don't want a milkshake."

I waved away his objection. "Nonsense. You can't come to a diner and not get something. You'll stand out."

He gave me a dry look. "Somehow I doubt that was your motivation for ordering me one of those things."

"So your applicants need to be able to sire a vampire. That doesn't seem too hard."

"It's not. Once a vampire hits a certain age and obtains a certain level of discipline."

I sucked down another sip of the creamy goodness. Somehow I

36

didn't think he'd brought this topic up for no reason. I was betting it had something to do with what he wanted from me.

"What's that have to do with me?" I asked, hoping to speed things along. My milkshake was melting and I wanted to be done with this conversation sometime in the next century.

"I think one of the applicants was hexed over a century ago to prevent him from siring other vampires."

"Again, what does that have to do with me?"

"I need you to either find the witch who placed the hex or one of the vampire's descendants."

Wait. Hold on.

"The hexed vampire's descendants?"

I received a nod.

"What makes you think I can do something like that? I know almost zero about investigating."

His lips quirked. "Your encounter with the draugr say otherwise."

I waved his comment away. "That was mostly luck and being in the wrong place at the wrong time."

That and relying on an old friend to do most of the researching. I didn't plan on telling him about her. He didn't need any more ammo to take out my vulnerable spots.

"You also seem to have an established relationship with several witches. Because of your job you have access to people from all parts of the city."

In other words, people wouldn't talk to him because he was a big, bad vampire, the bogey man of this shadow world.

I smirked at him. "So I guess my being clanless has some use after all."

"In very rare instances."

Heh.

The bell over the diner door rang and a dark haired man in a light coat stepped inside, looking around before spotting us. He walked our way.

My gaze landed on his silver gray eyes. I couldn't look away, the moment feeling like it was happening at a distance. I felt lightheaded, then hot and sweaty. In the next second, I was ice cold, my teeth damn near chattering.

This couldn't be happening.

How did Liam find him?

I never thought I'd see him again.

I reached slowly into my messenger bag, my hand closing on the grip of my gun. It was a revolver called the Judge, a .45 caliber long colt with a 410 round. It might stop him, but then again it might not.

"Thomas," Liam said, standing. "You're late."

Thomas was a few inches shorter than Liam and just as good looking. He had a strong jaw with stubble shadowing it. His eyes were bright and alert as he nodded at me. I knew those eyes. They haunt me every morning just before the sun sends me into the land of the dead.

"Is this her, then?"

Thomas didn't seem too impressed with what he was seeing. He also didn't look like he'd ever seen me before. Something I knew to be false.

I couldn't react beyond a slight tightening of my finger on the trigger. Under the table, it was now pointed at the two men.

I wanted to squeeze that trigger so bad. It would take less than six pounds of pressure to fire. It seemed so easy. Just a pop, pop.

I knew from a previous encounter with Liam and my last hand gun that it might not be as simple as I thought. It was the only thing keeping me from emptying the entire clip into the men in front of me.

"It is. Thomas, this is Aileen. She is the unclaimed vampire I told you about."

I bet he did. And here I was hoping he'd make good on his promise to teach me some things. Maybe show me vampires weren't so awful.

"This is your plan?" Thomas asked, arching an eyebrow as he looked me over.

I was going to need to count back from one hundred to keep from shooting this guy.

"She's more resourceful than she looks."

A compliment and insult all rolled into one. How lovely.

"Liam tells me you refuse to join a clan," Thomas said, finally directing his comment to me.

I hesitated. Is that all Liam had said? Not knowing what game these two were playing, I gave him a nod.

"Where's your sire?"

Sitting right across from me.

I clamped down on that thought and shored up my mental defenses, adding tree after tree and boulders and hills. If he was a mind reader, I didn't want him having access to such dangerous thoughts.

How could he not recognize me? Or had he attacked so many

women in the last year trying to turn one of them that he simply didn't remember the one he had?

I lifted one shoulder in a shrug. The werewolves were able to tell if someone was lying. I didn't want to chance the vampires having the same ability. It wasn't one I possessed, but then I seemed to be lacking many of the talents associated with my kind.

"Do you speak?" His tone had an arctic chill to it.

I narrowed my eyes and grabbed a French fry, dunking it in the milkshake and taking a bite, my teeth clacking together.

Did I speak? Who did this guy think he was?

Made me want to be silent for the rest of this meeting just to mess with him.

"Why is she eating?" he asked, bewilderment in his tone. Then to me, "Why are you eating?"

Again I shrugged, before taking another bite out of the fry.

"Stop that."

In a blur of movement that I only half caught, my plate and milkshake disappeared. I blinked down at the empty table. In the next moment, the fry I was holding was torn out of my fingers.

What the hell?

No, stay calm. Be professional.

"What the hell?" I asked. "That was mine. Give it back."

"She speaks," Thomas said with sarcasm.

I scowled at him.

"Food is toxic to us. It will delay your development."

I pointed at my face. "Look at my face. Does it look like I give two nickels about my development? You don't take other people's food and do whatever you did to it. It's just not done. Who does that?"

I was fixating, a red tinge creeping into the corners of my vision. Deep breath. Deep breath. Don't try to tear their faces off just because they touched your stuff. Control. I needed control.

My temper was rising, made worse by the unexpected arrival of my sire and the fact they touched something that was mine. They were both twenty times stronger than me and having a shit fit right now would just endanger myself and everyone around me.

I took another deep breath and let it out, focusing on the two in front of me.

"Being territorial is also a vampire trait," Liam said.

Thomas grunted. "I see you have a bit of our temper as well."

I bared my teeth in a smile that had more in common with a snarl.

I didn't want to hear about vampire traits right now. It just made me want to rip one of their limbs off and beat them with it.

"You sure have a funny way of asking for a person's help," I said when I had myself back under control.

"But we didn't ask, did we? You're our hired help," Thomas said.

I snorted. "What is this? The eighteenth century? It doesn't work like that. I can turn this job down, and right now that's almost a given."

"You do that and the people around you will face the consequences," Liam said coolly.

He'd been quiet for the most part, observing the interaction between Thomas and me. I didn't like that. He was smart and saw way more than I wanted. I didn't need him drawing any conclusions about Thomas and me.

"Careful, Liam. Remember what happened the last time you tried to use the people I loved against me."

I rolled up the sleeve on my left arm where the sorcerer had left his mark. A stylized lion wrapped in a vine full of thorns stared out at us. It looked like a tattoo, but it wasn't. At first glance it seemed almost silver but when you looked closer there were specks of purple running through it, almost as if someone had embedded metallic purple thread in the skin.

It was beautiful and tied me on a metaphysical level to the sorcerer.

Thomas's hand flashed out, pinning mine in place as he bent over it to take a closer look. I tugged but couldn't budge my arm. I doubted Thomas was even aware I was trying to pull away.

"It's embedded pretty deep," he murmured. "Looks like they didn't really know what they were doing. The magic is creating a feedback loop between the two of you. It can be reversed, but it'll take some doing and could wind up killing one or both of them."

He seemed almost as if he was speaking to himself, like he had forgotten the two of us were sitting right here.

He came back to himself and gave me a sharp glance. He reminded me of a sergeant, one who was questioning the level of intelligence in his soldier.

"What could have possessed you to allow yourself to be marked by a sorcerer, of all people?"

I looked at Liam. "I don't know. Why don't we ask Liam?"

He unfolded his arms and gave me a cold look. "She did it to get out of her hundred years of service."

"And to protect my family from your threats," I finished.

The corner of Thomas' lips turned down. "You're something of an idiot. The only person you're hurting is yourself."

I gave a shrug. "I've never been afraid to cut off my nose to spite my face if it got me what I wanted in the end."

"You'll do the job," Liam said, leaning forward slightly. "That mark protects you right now, but there are ways to sever the link, even if it leads to your death. Do you really want to push us until we think the cost is worth it?"

No, I didn't. Even with all the obstacles that came with being a vampire, I loved life. I didn't want to jeopardize it. This was not a battle I was prepared to wage. There would be other times, other battles.

Seeing the answer on my face, Liam continued, "As I said, we need you to either find the witch who placed the hex or locate Thomas's descendants."

I really wish I had my food right now. A slurp of the sugary goodness that was a milkshake would go a long way to taking the sting from having to play ball with these two.

"What's to say the witch you're looking for is even in this city?" I shot Thomas a skeptical look. "I doubt Thomas has spent his entire life in Columbus. He could have picked up the hex any number of places."

"We've managed to trace the timing to when he was visiting the city," Liam said.

"Seems a little thin," I observed, noting the tightening around Thomas's eyes. Neither one answered. I was already hating this job. I asked my next question, "I get why you want the witch, but why locate his descendants?"

Thomas gave me an arrogant look. "That's not information you need to know."

I opened my mouth to argue and then shut it again. Their faces were closed and guarded. They wouldn't tell me and pushing might make them do something I might regret. There were other ways to get the information.

"Let's just say that his descendants, because of their direct blood link to him, may provide a way to work around the hex," Liam said.

"Do you have a place to start?" I asked.

Thomas reached inside his coat and withdrew a stack of folded paper, setting it on the table. "This is what I have managed to locate. I know two of my descendants relocated to this city in the 1800s, but I

41

lost track of them after the turn of the century. The last page contains a list of witches who had a grudge against me and the talent to perform the hex."

I pulled the papers to me and flipped through them quickly. I paused when I saw Miriam's name on the list of witches.

"Do you see something?" Liam asked.

I folded the papers up and stuck them in my messenger bag. "Just checking the information."

"The selection takes place in five days. We'll expect results before then," Thomas directed.

Five days? I wasn't a miracle worker. If his descendants came to this area in the 1800s, there would be an avalanche of data to sift through, not to mention I had almost zero experience in an investigation like this.

That was assuming there was anyone alive to find. There was every possibility that his descendants had died out.

Thomas stood. "I'll be taking my leave now."

Liam and I watched him walk away.

Watching the door shut behind him, I said, "I understand his investment in this. What's yours? You're an enforcer. Shouldn't you be making sure the selection goes off without interference?"

Not that I really understood what an enforcer did. Just that they seemed pretty important in the hierarchy of the vampire world.

Liam watched me with a thoughtful expression, like he was deciding how much to reveal.

"The other applicants would not be a good choice for the position."

"And he is?" By their own rules, Thomas had broken the most basic covenant, providing support to the children he turned. He might appear not to recognize me, but that could be a deception perpetrated for his own hidden reasons. It would be easier if she could tell Liam, but she was afraid it would give them more of a claim on her. They already had enough as it was.

Liam didn't answer as he got up, somehow making sliding out of the booth seem graceful. I always looked like a wounded elephant trying to lumber my way out of these.

He hesitated once standing. "I look forward to working with you on this."

Working together? I really didn't think so.

I gave him a polite smile. "Hermes couriers work alone."

The smile he gave me was full of teeth. It was the type that said the lion thought its dinner was adorable.

"Jerry has made an exception this time. We'll be working very closely on this. I'll be in touch later tonight so we can map out our next steps."

He gave me a flick of the fingers in goodbye before following his friend.

I grimaced at his back. He'd be in touch. Not if I could help it.

Jerry and I were going to have a little talk. He let me walk into this unprepared so I could be ambushed. Oh yes, we were going to have a long, very loud talk, and I wasn't going to let the fact that he was my boss and very intimidating stop me. That's what phones were for after all. To give you time to hide when you poked the bear.

Chapter Four

Predictably Beatrix was the one to answer when I called Jerry's number.

"Hermes Courier Service. We'll come to you. How may I help?"

"Put him on, Janice."

"Aileen." My name was a curse.

"Now that we've established the obvious, put him on."

"Jerry's busy at the moment."

I bit back a growl.

"Put. Him. On."

"I'm sorry, but that's just not possible."

Deep breath. Threats of physical violence wouldn't work. I needed to be smarter than the obnoxious secretary.

"Janice, this is for a job. I need to talk to Jerry. If you keep stone walling me, I will be forced to use my own judgement. Do you really want me to do that?"

There was a moment of silence. Then a click and a slight buzz as the call was transferred.

I allowed myself a small moment of victory, which vanished the moment Jerry answered.

"Aileen." His voice was terse.

"Jerry. Is there a reason you didn't warn me?"

"I was told not to."

"Since when do you listen when clients tell you how to conduct your business?"

Hermes was notorious for blacklisting people if they got out of line. Jerry had always run his business in the way he saw fit. I've never heard of him bending to others wishes.

"Since the vampires said they'd put a kill order on any of my couriers running a job."

I was quiet. Yeah, that might do it.

I mentally bumped this selection thing they were talking about to a higher priority level.

"They have to be bluffing."

"That may be, but I wasn't willing to risk it. I'll go to war if necessary but not when it can be easily avoided by doing what we would do anyway."

Made sense. It was the same reason I hadn't pushed back on Liam when he threatened Jerry and Hermes. They might be bluffing, but it wasn't worth testing that assumption. Yet.

I pinched the bridge of my nose.

"Shit."

I had to do the job or at least give the appearance of doing the job.

"I'm sorry to do this to you. I know you wanted nothing to do with the vampires, but this is your mess. You can't keep running from them forever."

I never planned to run forever. Just the next hundred years or so. Maybe once I could protect myself, I'd feel safe interacting with them, though I doubted it.

"If I don't do the job?" I asked.

His sigh was heavy. "You'll be cut loose. You'll have no protection. It won't just be the vampires after you then. Any spook could come gunning for you. I don't think even the sorcerer's mark could protect you from all of them."

"Fine. I get it. I'll do the job."

I did get it. He had to look out for himself and his people. As much help as he'd given me, I wasn't one of them. Not really.

We hung up.

Despite what Liam had said, I still planned to do other jobs. Some of these had been on my schedule for weeks. No way was I letting another courier take over my routes. The bastards would refuse to give them back.

I couldn't stop a snort of laughter, thinking about what Liam and Thomas wanted. I needed to find Thomas's descendants. Well, shit.

The part that bugged me was how Thomas didn't recognize me when I was sitting across from him. You would think he would have leapt at evidence that his little performance problem was a thing of the past. He was the one who'd turned me after all. Instead he acted like he'd never met me before in my life.

*   *   *

My first run of the night took me to a bar just north of

Clintonville. The many bike paths the city had developed made short work of getting me to my destination. I didn't even have to brave many streets or their crazy drivers.

The brisk air felt nice on my face and helped clear my head of some of the negative emotions and thoughts from the meeting with Liam and Thomas.

The ride brought a few things into perspective. Just because I took the job with the vampires didn't mean I had to produce results. Nothing in my contract stipulated a penalty should I fail to find the descendants or the witch.

I checked the contract after my conversation with Jerry. No penalty clause had been added. That left me a lot of wiggle room to work with. As long as I made them think I was doing my best, I should be safe. Ish.

The bar I was supposed to meet my client at was a sad looking building with a bright sign out front saying the Blue Pepper. A sombrero perched on the P. Despite the general air of disrepair, the parking lot seemed full enough. People didn't seem to care what their watering hole looked like as long as it served good drinks.

Of course some of the draw may have been more magical in nature.

I propped my bike against a pole and wrapped my bike lock around it before heading around to the back.

The shadows were thick here. While the parking lot had adequate lighting, the owner never bothered to put more than one light out back and that hung over the door employees used to take a smoke break.

My contact stood under that light, puffing away on a cigarette as she stared into the shadows.

"How is that djinn cuff working for you?" she asked, without turning her eyes toward me.

I stopped besides her, not even questioning how she knew that I'd put it to use. "So far so good."

"You know, when I gave you that, I didn't expect you to turn around and use it on a sorcerer."

Neither had I.

Its use had been born partly from desperation and partly from impulse.

"You never said not to."

She snorted. "Of course not. I didn't think I had to spell out what a bad idea it would be to constrain a sorcerer. Kind of like I shouldn't have to point out the utter stupidity of pulling a tiger's tail." She took another puff of her cigarette. "You're lucky it was Barrett's former apprentice you used it on or otherwise you'd be dead by now."

Some luck. I was pretty sure he was going to kill me as soon as I took that thing off. Since I was indebted to him for the next hundred years, it wasn't like I could remove it and then hide until he forgot who locked him away from his power.

"What can I say, Dahlia? I like to live dangerously."

Not really. I preferred a life of peace but that never quite worked out for me.

"You're an idiot."

I grinned, not taking the words to heart. She'd called me an idiot nearly every time I did a job for her. I'd long since learned it was a term of affection.

Dahlia was a tall woman with almond shaped eyes and stick straight hair the color of the shadows she stared into. The mass fell in a sheet to the middle of her back. Her skin was a dusky gold that always made her look sun kissed. She was blessed with good bone structure, all graceful lines and delicate details. That delicacy was a lie though, I've seen her pick a man up and throw him out of her bar. Literally throw him out. I think he sailed six feet.

She was my first client after Hermes hired me and my favorite.

"You got my stuff?"

Of course I had her stuff. "Would I be here if I didn't?"

"Guess not."

I pulled my messenger bag around and dug through it until I found a parcel wrapped in brown paper and tied with twine.

She took the package and untied it, revealing several packets and what looked like dried up sticks. The smell told me they were spices, though none seemed familiar. I delivered this same package once a month, and it was always the same type of stuff.

"It's all here." She selected a stick and held it out to me. "Would you like one?"

This was the first time she'd offered me anything from the package.

"What is it?"

Her loose shirt slid to the side to bare the delicate bones of her collar bone and shoulder. She shrugged gracefully. "Try it and find out."

I shook my head and pulled my phone out of my bag, tapping on it to get to the appropriate screen. When I had her job pulled up, I held it out to her.

"Thanks, but I think I'll pass."

Her lips tilted in a sly smile as she pressed her thumb to the screen. It lit up green, showing that the package had been delivered on time.

"Maybe next time, then."

Not if I could help it. I've learned accepting strange gifts had a habit of coming back and biting me in the ass.

I took the phone and tucked it in my bag.

"Anything new?" I asked.

Dahlia's bar saw a lot of traffic of the supes who lived in the area. She heard all kinds of things and for whatever reason she was sometimes willing to share that information with me.

"Lots of things are happening." She slid me a glance. "Things like the selection."

I shifted uncomfortably. I got the feeling Liam and Thomas would prefer the rest of the supernatural community be kept in the dark about the selection and since I was technically employed by them, I couldn't talk about anything relating to the job.

"Don't worry, little vampire." She smiled at me. "I won't pry."

I gave her a small smile. For all that she was a client, I considered Dahlia a sort of friend. Or at least a friendly acquaintance. I didn't want to ruin that because of the bossy duo.

"I've been hearing things," she said, her face turning serious. "Things that, if true, are disturbing."

I held my silence, letting her work through whatever internal dialogue was going on in her head. She'd share or she wouldn't. Sometimes she'd start speaking and then just trail off, staring into the dark. No amount of pushing or prodding could make her talk again. I've learned that patience and silence work better to get her started again.

She puffed on her cigarette, staring into the dark while the smoke drifted into shapes.

Just when I thought this would be one of those times she disappeared into her own world, she said, "It might be better for you to see it yourself. I may be seeing things that aren't there."

I waited a beat. "Ok. Is there something you want to show me?"

"No, but he may."

She gestured with the cigarette, pointing into the night. I followed where she was indicating, not seeing anything at first.

My eyes adjusted quickly. Vampires had superior night vision so it wasn't difficult to see into the darkness.

I overlooked him the first and second time. He blended into the shadows quite well. If it hadn't been for the bright red shoes, I might have continued looking right past him.

He was the size of a child and dressed in jeans and a wind breaker. His bald head said he was an adult, not a child roaming without their parent's knowledge. His features were unfinished, like someone had started molding a sculpture before getting distracted half way through. His chin and cheekbones were blunt, his nose lumpy. His skin was gray with a waxy sheen to it.

I knew him. He was a hobgoblin and liked to play pranks on some of Dahlia's customers. The pranks weren't anything big or particularly vicious, just small things like switching their drinks with another's or stealing their keys and putting them back in the wrong pocket.

"Is that Rick?" I asked as I walked closer.

"Yes." Dahlia stayed in the bar's doorway.

"Hey, Rick. What're you doing out here?"

His eyes were dull. They had no life behind them. Any expression on his face had been wiped clean, as if it was a blank slate.

"Rick."

I touched his shoulder lightly. When he didn't respond, I shook him. Then shook him again harder.

"Rick, wake up," I said sharply.

"It's useless," Dahlia said, appearing at my side. "He won't respond."

"Is this what you were talking about?"

She made a hm sound.

I didn't know what that meant.

I frowned at Rick, not liking the total lifelessness of him. He might as well have been a statue. He was normally so animated, never able to stand still for more than a few seconds. His mouth always going a mile a minute. He considered silence the equivalent of torture and always felt the need to fill it.

This was disturbing. Anybody could walk up and kill him, and he wouldn't be able to lift a finger to stop it. A normal could stumble across him and decide he made a good lawn ornament.

"How long has he been like this?" I asked

Dahlia cocked her head, her eyes studying the hobgoblin.

I waited, somewhat impatiently this time.

"Dahlia?" I asked again. "How long has he been like this?"

Her eyes shifted to me. "A few days."

"And you left him out here where anybody could find him?"

I'd thought the two of them were friends.

She turned and walked back into her bar.

Well, that was helpful.

I turned back to the hobgoblin. This really wasn't any of my business. Rick, unlike Dahlia, had never been particularly friendly, but he also hadn't gone out of his way to make my life miserable.

I owed him nothing.

I made a sound of frustration and picked him up. What had this guy been eating? He must have weighed over a hundred pounds. Even with the increased strength vampirism gave me, I was sweating by the time I got him to the back door of the bar.

Maybe I could put him in the storage room and stack some boxes around him. It wasn't much, but it was better than leaving him out in the open.

As I finished placing the last boxes around him, Rick's eyes blinked once and then again. Holding one of the boxes, I stepped closer.

"Rick?"

His gaze focused on me. His mouth opened and a high pitched wail came out. I jumped back in shock. The boxes exploded outward, and a gray streak raced past me. He scurried across the room and huddled in the corner.

What the hell just happened?

One moment he was doing his impression of a statue, and then he was racing around the room like his hair was on fire.

I hesitated to approach, the sight of him muttering to himself and rocking back and forth like his world was about to end leaving me uncomfortable. Like I was the reason for his terror.

"Hey, Rick. Do you remember me?" No response came. "It's Aileen. We met a few times at Dahlia's bar."

"Dahlia." His voice was soft as he momentarily stopped rocking.

"Yeah. That's where we are right now. Dahlia's bar, the Blue Pepper."

"Blue Pepper."

Great, now I had a parrot on my hands.

"Yeah, the Blue Pepper. Do you remember how you got here?"

His hands came up to cover his head and his muttering got louder.

Ok, that was evidently a traumatic subject. I needed to find a way to calm him down so I could get some good information out of him. The problem was I didn't know him well enough to know what might help him focus on something non-threatening. I needed Dahlia.

"Hey, it's ok. You don't have to think about that right now," I tried. I was not the most comforting person. I've always been the one staring awkwardly when someone breaks down in tears while asking myself why they couldn't have picked a better place to have a meltdown. One that wasn't so public, or you know, in my vicinity.

Needed a distraction. What could I say?

"Oh, that prank you played on those annoying bankers was pretty funny. I wonder how long it took them to figure out you switched their wallets."

This had happened the last time I was in the Blue Pepper. A pair of men from the local office for a national bank had made asses out of themselves and heckled some of the regulars. Rick had switched their wallets, which happened to be identical. The two still hadn't figured out the switch by the time they stumbled out to their cab.

"Three days," he said.

"Whoa, that's a pretty long time. I bet they spent a little bit of each other's money before they figured out what had happened."

"The tall one spent over a thousand dollars before the short one got his card back."

Heh. That's a pretty big payday. Guess it paid not to piss off the regulars.

Now that his rocking had nearly stopped and he wasn't clinging to the wall like he was trying to pass through it, I decided to chance a couple of questions about his statue impression.

"Rick, do you remember how you ended up in the woods outside the bar."

I used the word 'woods' loosely as the area was more underbrush and young trees that had reclaimed the area.

"Don't remember."

"What's the last thing you remember?" I asked, trying another tack.

His eyes avoided mine as he stared into the corner. "Last thing. Last thing. I had just rewired that jerk's car horn to his lights."

"And then?"

His forehead wrinkled as he frowned. "I heard something."

We were getting somewhere.

"Do you remember what that was?"

He touched his ear. "It was something I'd heard before. Or maybe not."

Ok, that was a little less helpful.

"The dark." He latched on to my arm, dragging me closer. "It had eyes. Many, many eyes."

"Do you know who did this?" I asked again. I didn't know what to do with the dark having many eyes. Was that a metaphor for something? Was there more than one attacker?

His eyes shifted back and forth. They landed on me, terror building in their depths.

"I must go," he moaned.

"Go? Go where?"

"I must go. He will be displeased."

He started patting his head and rocking back and forth.

"Who will be displeased?" He moaned louder and started hitting himself harder. "Rick? Who will be displeased?"

"Now. I must go now. The dark will come back. The eyes will come back."

"What eyes? Who? Give me something, Rick."

He threw his head back and wailed.

"He will devour me." He came to his feet, baring razor sharp teeth. His eyes filled with madness and rage.

He was seriously freaking me out. I'd never associated the little hobgoblin with something dangerous before, but right now he had the look of a cornered animal ready to tear apart the predator threatening it. Somehow I had the feeling I was supposed to be that predator.

He leapt, sharp claws catching my jacket as I rolled to the side. He landed on a box in the corner.

I watched him for any sign of movement as I backed towards the only door in the room. If I could make it there, I could lock him in and get Dahlia. She had more of a history with him. Maybe she could talk some of the crazy out of him.

"Rick, I think it would be best if you stayed here."

"He calls. I must go," he seethed, his face twisting with fear and madness.

I took another step toward the door. How fast was a hobgoblin? I was fast, but was I fast enough? His display earlier didn't give me a lot of confidence.

"We can figure this out together."

"Lies. There is no safety, no light. Only him and darkness and death. He comes and the world will tremble before him." His voice rose to ear splitting levels.

He crouched. I turned and fled, leaping for the door. It slammed shut behind me. A thump hit it and then a voice rose in rage.

"So it is as I thought," Dahlia said from where she'd pulled the door shut.

I leaned against the wall and gave her an exasperated look.

"Thanks for the assist. Too bad you didn't come in earlier."

Yes, I responded with sarcasm when I had my life threatened by a person no taller than my waist. It was a flaw. Everyone had them.

"You seemed like you had it in hand," she said.

Really? In what way. The part where he was huddled on the floor like a trauma victim or the part where he tried to tear me apart with his claws and teeth? Because I wasn't seeing any way I had handled that well.

"Since you seem to know what this is, would you care to explain?"

There was another thump against the door.

"We'll leave him there until this has passed."

A black tendril of smoke wrapped itself around the door, shielding it from view. It faded away leaving nothing but a blank wall behind.

Handy trick, that. I needed to figure out how she did that. As far as I knew she wasn't a sorcerer. Or a witch. She had skills that often left me scratching my head. I didn't ask what she was, figuring she'd share in her own time, or I'd puzzle it out when I knew more about this world.

Dahlia headed to the bar.

I hesitated, asking, "We're just going to leave him in there?"

"He can't get out and most can't get in. He should be safe enough."

I gave the space where the door had been a skeptical look. If she said so.

I followed her, taking a seat. It was a slow night, and the end of the bar I'd claimed was empty. Only a few stools taken.

The bar was in the shape of an L. A big mirror framed the wall behind the bar where I sat and every type of liquor you could think of, and a few I'd never heard of, lined the shelves. Despite that, the clientele here mostly preferred beer so there were several types in the cooler and on draft.

The other walls had a maroon patterned wallpaper covered by framed sepia photos and one of a kind posters. It was part saloon, part watering hole.

The lighting wasn't the best. There was a smoky haze to the room as if people had lit up hundreds of cigars in here over the years until the haze became a permanent part of the décor. It didn't smell like smoke though. It smelled like broken dreams and desperation.

Dahlia poured me a lemon drop martini and a jack and coke for herself. She slid both across the bar and then walked around to join me on a stool.

No one blinked at the bartender taking a seat beside a customer. That was the kind of place this bar was.

I took a sip. That was good stuff. No one made a lemon drop martini like Dahlia. It was the perfect mix of sweet and tart. I don't know how she knew it was my favorite drink, but she made it for me every time I came in.

"Back to my question," I said, once I'd savored my lemony drink. "Do you know what caused that?"

She brought her drink up to her lips but didn't sip from it, instead staring unseeing at the bar top. She put the drink back down.

"I have a guess."

When no answer was forthcoming, I prompted, "And that is?"

"Have you talked to your werewolf friends lately?" she asked instead.

I fought my sigh, knowing it would be useless to give in to my frustration.

"What werewolf friends?"

As far as I knew, I had none.

She gave me a sidelong glance and quirked her lips.

I thought a second longer. She couldn't mean Brax and his crew of psychopaths, could she? Because they weren't friends by any stretch of the imagination. We'd worked together briefly during the draugr situation last year, but I hadn't talked with them since then. Mostly by choice. I had no wish to change that.

"Do they know you don't consider them friends?" she asked, her face still reflecting a sly amusement.

"I doubt they care one way or the other."

"Hm."

"What's that mean?" I asked.

She shrugged a bare shoulder. "Just think you might be wrong,

54

that's all."

I narrowed my eyes at her, swishing the liquid in my martini glass. She'd gotten me off topic, and now I wanted to know what all her questions were about.

"I don't see what any of that has to do with Rick and his impression of a statue."

Dahlia picked up her drink and stood. "You should talk to your friend."

She walked off.

"Wait. That's it?" I called after her.

That told me nothing about what was going on. Nothing.

I took an angry sip of my drink, giving a small hum of pleasure.

"Well this is a surprise. A vampire enjoying – what is that?" A woman with red hair curling in a mess of waves around her head reached past me and picked up my martini. She took a small sip and made a face. "A lemon drop martini? Really?"

"Really." I took my glass back from her, careful not to spill a drop.

I gave the woman me a once over, noting the feral air she had. She was in tight jeans and a black fitted shirt with the saying "keep it real." Her smile had a dangerous edge to it. She moved with lethal animal grace to take the seat Dahlia had vacated.

Now I saw why Dahlia was asking me about the werewolves. "Sondra."

"The sun fearing vampire." She shot me a wicked grin.

I rolled my eyes, while mentally shushing her. The fact that I was a vampire and a baby one at that hadn't made the rounds yet. I wanted to keep it that way.

Sondra wasn't my favorite werewolf. She'd once chased me around a kitchen trying to get me to sip blood from her wrist. Since I had never consumed live blood straight from the source, I refused. It took Brax, the werewolves' alpha, to get her to back off.

I looked around for Dahlia, but it seemed she had disappeared. Figured.

"What brings you here?" I asked.

She stole my drink and took another sip. I started to protest but decided I didn't want to get between a werewolf and liquor. I probably shouldn't drink it anyway since I was technically still working.

"Wanted to see what my favorite little vampire was up to."

I arched an eyebrow. Really? Sure, I'd buy that. Not. I hadn't heard anything from the werewolves since I'd saved their alpha's ass.

Sondra and I hadn't exactly been bosom buddies in the short time we'd known each other. At least on my end. Who knew with the werewolf?

"Uh huh." I'd play, but only to find out what she was really up to. "So how is the pack getting along after Victor's plot to overthrow Brax failed?"

A shutter slammed down over her face. "That's pack business."

Outsider's not welcome, huh? I shook my head and got to my feet. I so didn't have the patience or time for their cliquish bullshit.

"Great. Well, it's been not so nice seeing you."

"Wait. Where are you going?"

I gave her a look. One that said 'what world do you live in?'

She stared back at me as if she didn't quite understand the look or why I would give it to her.

After a beat where she was clearly not getting it, I said, "I'm not in the mood to play whatever game you've got going on. You want to pull the pack business card? Fine. I don't really care, but I don't plan on sticking around to get shut out again."

With that, I walked away.

"That's not what I was doing." She prowled next to me, keeping pace easily.

"You said 'that's pack business.' What else is that supposed to mean?"

I pushed open the door and walked out, pissed that Dahlia had put me off so I could talk to the werewolf when I didn't really have anything to say to the werewolf and when the werewolf had nothing important to say to me.

It wasn't Sondra's fault. Not really. The thing with Rick had freaked me out more than a little bit and Sondra had simply approached at the wrong time and pushed one of my many buttons. Hence my feeling of being done with this conversation.

"Will you slow down?" Sondra positioned herself in front of me, blocking me from getting my bike. "After what you did for Brax last year, that was a shitty statement."

Some of my anger abated. None of the wolves had ever acknowledged I had done anything for them. The vampires either. I wasn't expecting a thank you from those control freaks, but a simple chin nod of acknowledgement would have helped.

"Uh huh."

I wasn't willing to let this go yet. Especially since I still didn't know what she wanted. And she did want something. She wouldn't have chased me down otherwise.

"We're having some internal problems after what went down with Victor. There's also been a few weird things happening that has us all on edge."

Oh? Tell me more. Their weird happenings wouldn't happen to be werewolves freezing in place only to wake up paranoid and trying to answer a summons from an inkblot with a thousand eyes? Because that would mean that whatever had happened to Rick was affecting the wider supe population of Columbus.

"Yeah, I heard about that," I bluffed.

I'd heard no such thing. The werewolves kept things tight, but I was hoping that Sondra would assume I had heard something and maybe let something important slip.

The skin around her eyes tightened though her face didn't shift.

"I hadn't realized Brax had already contacted you." Her voice held a hint of suspicion.

I shrugged, not wanting to chance telling another outright lie. Not with their ability to scent deception.

"If you could just keep an eye out for us and report back if you find any wolves acting suspicious, the pack would appreciate it."

Something was going on with them. I wanted to ask questions, see if her problem had anything in common with the hobgoblin in Dahlia's store room. I kept my mouth shut.

She gave me another assessing glance, her eyes nearly glowing yellow at the shift of the light.

"I've got to go. If you find something, call me first." She handed me a business card.

I took it, reading the front. It said Sondra Banter and then a number. I flipped it over and found it was black with a crescent moon on it. Cute. And oddly elegant.

She strode off, leaving me staring after her.

This evening just got weirder and weirder. Starting with the homicidal hobgoblin, followed by a bartender acting all mysterious and then the werewolf wanting help with a problem she never bothered to finish briefing me on.

This sounded like the beginning of a joke. It felt anything but.

Chapter Five

My phone rang as I unlocked my bike chain. For a split second I thought about ignoring it and letting it go to voicemail. I disregarded that notion almost as soon as I thought it. Janice would rain fire and wrath down on me if she found out I let a client go to voicemail. Jerry wouldn't be far behind her.

I stood up and fished the cell out of my bag. The screen made me want to pretend I never heard it ring.

With a sigh, I touched the answer button.

"Liam."

"Where are you?"

What kind of question was that?

"I don't see how that's any of your business."

"As the client paying a lot of money for your undivided attention on this job, I suggest you answer the question."

I sighed, looking up at the sky. There were too many clouds to see the stars tonight.

Patience. Just because you wanted to snap back didn't mean you had to.

"Nowhere in my contract does it say I'm supposed to be at your beck and call," I said, struggling to sound reasonable and businesslike.

"It also didn't say you were going to make zero progress on our problem."

"I just got this case a few hours ago. Like literally three hours ago."

His sigh suggested he was speaking to a child. "We have very little time before the selection. That is why I wanted your full attention on this matter."

"I don't even understand why you're doing this for him. It seems like an awful long way to go just to make sure he gets to be the grand poo bah of Columbus."

"You don't need to understand. You just need to get this done."

I bit my tongue. Don't antagonize the client. Especially don't antagonize the big bad vampire who is capable of making your life hell and destroying everything you ever loved.

"Of course, Liam," I said, injecting as much toadying as I could into the words. "I'll make sure to give this my full attention as you requested."

"I have no doubt." His voice rumbled over the phone. "I need you at Asylum in the next twenty minutes. I have some leads I want you to run down, and I plan to personally supervise your progress."

What? No. That wasn't happening. I was not working closely with him.

"Sounds great. Be there as soon as I can," I said.

The phone clicked. I looked at the screen. He hung up on me. Bastard. Guess we weren't saying goodbyes.

*   *   *

The last time I visited Asylum, I didn't know it was owned by vampires. I only found out when I was dealing with the draugr incident and Liam had tried to order me to turn myself in for my personal safety to Asylum. I hadn't been back since. It was too bad. They had great drinks and the atmosphere wasn't bad if you went when it wasn't busting at the seams with people.

Even though it was well after midnight, there was a crowd waiting to get their dance and drink on. I slipped through while the bouncer was intent on checking the ID's of a trio of college girls who definitely didn't look old enough to be in here.

The bouncer didn't look too concerned, finding himself more inclined to pay attention to the revealing cleavage than their obviously fake ID's.

The club had many different sections, allowing a partier to drift through a maze of rooms and themes. The entrance was an outdoor oasis complete with tropical plants, a few fountains and a couple of high tops with no seats and a tiki bar. There was even a few hammocks and benches attached to the ceiling with long chains.

A cobblestone path led the way inside where there were two more bars on either side of a gaping maw of dark punctuated by flashing lights. Music spilled out of the room as a sea of bodies writhed under lights designed to highlight their frenzied movements.

I headed for the bar on the right. It seemed a little less crowded than the bar next to the dance floor, but it was still standing room only.

I had to elbow my way to the counter and slide between two inebriated men. I rolled my eyes as they kept up a running commentary about all the 'bangin' bodies' walking around.

I flagged down the bartender.

"What can I get you?" he shouted over the music.

I leaned over the bar. "I need to speak with Liam."

"Who?" he tilted his head as if he hadn't heard me the first time.

"Liam," I shouted back.

He shook his head.

"Liam. I need to speak with Liam."

He shook his head. "Sorry I don't know any Liam."

He moved on without taking my order, leaving me standing there wondering what to do next.

I was going to be pissed if I'd interrupted my night only to be kept cooling my heels by the bar because Liam couldn't be bothered to let anybody know I was coming.

I dug out my phone. I could try calling him again from outside. It'd be impossible to conduct a conversation in the din of this place.

A hand landed on my shoulder. I spun and was confronted by Kat, looking none too pleased to see me.

Kat had the face of a model, with pouty lips, high cheek bones and a graceful jawline. Her brown hair was perfectly styled, and her glare was hot enough to burn a hole in the fake wood bar behind me.

The two douches next to me fell silent as they took in the ten in front of me.

"Kat, what a surprise."

Just not the good kind.

"What are you doing here?" she asked.

How much to tell her? I didn't know if Liam had told anyone what role I had to play or if he wanted this to be kept totally below the radar.

"This is clan territory." Her grip on my arm tightened. She leaned forward to hiss, "Clanless rejects are not welcome on our hunting grounds."

Guess that solved that question then. She was still sore about how I'd ditched her last year. I wonder how much trouble she'd gotten in for my little stunt.

I looked down at her grip on my arm and put one hand over hers, digging my nail into the spot right above her thumb's nail. She grimaced and let go of me. I fought the urge to shake my arm. The woman had a grip like a python. I was pretty sure I'd have had bruises tomorrow if I'd been human. As it was, my advance vampire healing abilities would fix it way before then.

"I was asked here," I finally said.

She folded her arms over her chest.

"Oh? By who?"

I didn't see any way around this. If I didn't answer, she had every intention of kicking me out. Liam would just have to deal with the consequences.

"Liam wanted me to meet him here."

She arched an eyebrow, the corner of her mouth tilting down.

Thought that might stick. She couldn't kick me out since an enforcer was the one who requested my presence. I still didn't know exactly what an enforcer did or why they seemed to have such pull. All I knew was that his name opened doors that would have otherwise remained closed to a baby vamp.

"Why would he want to see you?"

I smirked. "That's really none of your business. Now, are you going to take me to him, or am I going to have to find him myself?"

Her eyes narrowed. "Follow me."

I waited until her back was turned before giving a sigh of relief. I didn't know what I'd have done if she had told me to pack sand and do it myself.

She led me to a door on the far side of the club. Once it closed, the sound disappeared as if the hundreds of people on the other side weren't making as much noise as they possibly could. I couldn't even feel the bass.

"Are you coming?"

I came unstuck from where I'd stopped to marvel at the soundproofing.

She gave me a once over as I walked towards her. "Try to keep up. I don't have all night to babysit."

Yeah, yeah. I got it. Don't fall behind.

She led me down a twisting corridor. What was it about the supe community that made them turn their businesses and homes into places that defied the physics of the universe? The last club I'd been in, the one where I'd met Kat, had also used magic to increase the size of the place, adding more rooms, higher ceilings and the like. Theoretically it could be a whole world unto itself.

For all I knew an entire clan lived here.

How Liam expected me to find my way to him was beyond me.

Without a guide, I would be lost.

Kat opened a door and gestured me inside. "After you."

I hesitated before proceeding her into the room. It was like stepping into a whole new club. One that had nothing in common with the public one. Instead of the tropical oasis of the normal side, this place was much more subdued.

Wood paneling covered the walls. Wooden beams made grid patterns on the ceiling and black lights completed the look. The small bar had a wooden top and the floor was covered in places by a cream colored rug. There was also a cream colored couch against the wall. Despite being a wood box, the place managed to defy the hunting cabin look gone wrong and pulled off an old world charm that said money, class, and taste.

There were several people decorating the chairs and couches, each more beautiful or handsome than the last. It was like standing at a convention for all the pretty people. I did not fit. I was pretty enough. Before becoming a vampire I had my share of guys trying their pickup lines on me, but I had nothing on the people in this room. When God was handing out looks, he'd wasted his best stuff on the people here. I mean, really, was the good looking trait a check box when these guys decided who to turn into a vampire?

Talk about boring.

A woman in a black dress beckoned Kat over. She was delicate, with perfectly arched eyebrows and a petite nose on a finely boned face. Her blond hair was swept up into a chignon. Her face was the sort great painters of the past would have had a brawl over to determine who got the honor of painting her.

Her earrings, amber drops on long chains, brushed her shoulder as she tilted her head.

"Kat, darling, it's so good to see you again. What is this you bring us?" Her low voice matched the rest of her, managing to sound both beautiful and superior at the same time.

I hated her instantly, not liking the way she looked me over like she was imagining what I would taste like. That may not have been far from the truth as I strongly suspected this woman was a vampire.

I had a feeling all of the people in this room were vampires. That was a cheery thought.

"Just a clanless looking for the enforcer," Kat replied.

I glanced at her, not surprised when she gave me a cool look. In retrospect, it probably hadn't been a good idea to follow Kat. I thought the threat of Liam would keep her from trying anything, but I'd been wrong. From the looks of it– big time.

The woman stood gracefully, circling me in a slow gliding movement. Her eyes had about as much feeling in them as a shark's.

"This is the clanless we've been hearing so much about?" she asked, no surprise in her voice.

My back twitched. I did not like news of me making the rounds.

"She's so young," a man in the corner said.

A woman seated at the bar closed her eyes. "I can barely feel any power signature on her."

Another power I was missing. I could feel power coming off someone but only if they were using a lot of it. Right now, the only power I felt in the room radiated from the woman treating me like prey. It had a cold bite to it, leaving me feeling an oily residue on my psyche where it brushed mine.

The woman took a seat and picked up her drink. The red liquid in the martini glass left a slight stain on the glass as she took a sip.

I took a breath, the smell wafting to me. Blood, but mixed with something. It had a slight burn to it that said alcohol. I was betting vodka.

A blood martini. How appropriate.

"I'm not seeing Liam in here," I finally said. "Did you get lost?"

The woman at the bar chuckled softly.

Kat gave her a look that should have bludgeoned her, but bounced off without phasing its intended victim.

"Darling, don't be so cross with our Kat. She was only trying to help you out."

Yeah, I believed that like I believed frogs were actually princes in disguise.

I decided not to take issue with her use of the word darling. This situation felt dangerous. It'd be best to be exercise a little bit of caution.

"I highly doubt that," I said. There, that was diplomatic, wasn't it?

Her laugh sounded like tinkling bells.

"You're probably right about that. Our Kat doesn't really like you. She was punished rather harshly after she misplaced you last fall. The enforcer was very irate. She's only recently been allowed out of her clan's isolation room."

Kat's face was politely interested, as if we weren't discussing her while she was standing right here.

I hadn't realized she faced any major repercussions from my

63

escape. I thought Liam would give her an ass chewing to end all ass chewings and that was it. Seemed like that wasn't the case. I strangled any urge to feel sympathy for her. That way lay monsters. She'd twist that sympathy and strangle me with it if she got the chance.

"Right. Good to hear. I'll be on my guard with her from now on," I said. I didn't know if this woman was warning me or trying to start something between the two of us. Maybe both. "I still need to find Liam."

"Don't rush off, little bird," the man in the corner said. "It would be to your benefit to make a good impression on Elinor. She's one of the applicants for the selection."

An applicant?

I looked at the woman before me, Elinor, with new eyes. Her power coiled around her. It was like standing next to a snow storm. One where only a thin membrane separated me from the subzero freeze.

Was she the one Liam suspected of hexing Thomas? Or was she just an applicant looking for an angle?

"How impressive," I said. Only those who knew me well would be able to tell I meant the exact opposite. "Still, I have places to be and roads to travel. I need to find Liam before I go."

"What interest does our enforcer have with you?" Elinor asked. Her eyes glinted dangerously. I had a feeling she'd been wanting to ask this question for a while.

I gave her my best businesslike smile. "I'm afraid that's between me and him."

The humor drained from her face, leaving a glimpse of the power hungry monster I suspected was behind the mask.

"You're refusing to answer your elder, girl?" Her tone made it clear there was only one right answer to the question that was not a question.

"Can't answer." I again gave her my professional smile. The one I practiced in the mirror to be sure none of my true 'fuck you' feeling shone through. "I'm afraid it's part of my job."

"And what job would that be?"

As if she didn't know. I'm sure if the rumors had tagged me as the clanless vampire they also tacked on that I was employed by Hermes Courier Service.

"I'm a courier for Hermes."

There was no humor in her laugh. None of her emotions reached her eyes. "Yes, I seem to remember hearing something about that."

The rest of them laughed on cue. I looked around, noticing that several had drawn closer. Before they had been spread out in the room with Elinor existing in her own oasis of space. Now I was the focal point of the room. It left me feeling like meat. Unliving, breathing meat. It was not comfortable.

I kept my breath even and the fear locked in a box in the back of my mind. Showing terror to a predator was about the worst thing you could do and despite their beauty, their nice clothes and seeming humanness, these people were predators. The type that sat at the top of the food chain and only feared those like them.

I was not like them. Not even by a long shot. I was willing to bet Kat wasn't like them either given the way she gave a few of them an uneasy look, as if it had suddenly dawned on her that she was in the line of fire.

"It's strange that you haven't been brought to heel yet," Elinor drawled. "Don't you think, John?"

"Very," a voice said next to my ear.

I twitched but kept myself from jumping. Must not show fear. Must not show fear even though my skin crawled and every instinct in my body said to make a break for the door.

"I find it curious that you've been allowed to run free, even though our laws state that a newly turned vampire must be claimed by a clan for the first hundred years of their life."

It was clear she expected an answer. I had no intention of providing one. Partly because it was an answer I didn't want her to have but mostly because she was starting to piss me off.

"No answer. That's good. It'll make this so much more fun if you insist on being difficult."

The power that had been slithering through the room struck, wrapping around me. It was like being dropped into a lake of ice water.

Have you ever experienced a change in temperature that was so drastic it was like your entire system shut down? It was like my brain got its finger stuck in a toaster. There was no thinking, just shock and pure, unrelenting cold. My heart fluttered, even my vital organs protested. My lungs locked, unable to breath, to suck down air.

Black ate at the edges of my vision.

Then suddenly that unbearable cold was gone. Well, most of it. I had a feeling my lips would still be blue. My body had been too shocked before to fight for warmth, but now it was trying to make up for lost time as I experienced a full body tremble so fierce that my muscles cramped.

Son of a bitch. What the hell was that?

The shark in front of me smiled.

"Now, shall we try this again? Why did Liam allow you to run loose despite being a yearling?"

My teeth clattered as I bit out, "Fuck you, lady."

Not the most eloquent of responses but it was all I could get out around the chattering.

Elinor's mouth tightened with displeasure though a spark of pleasure ignited in her eyes. She was enjoying this.

That wave of cold hit me again. I gasped and then couldn't get enough air in to breathe. With the iciness of death came a deep sense of despair and fear. Worse than I'd ever experienced.

It was the kind of despair that made me question what right I had to be standing before these perfect people who were so much higher up in God's good graces than me. The thought was so out of character that it jarred me out of the depression spiral.

I never thought like that. Sure, I had self-doubt, but I never brought the big guy into it. My mistakes were my own. Never once have I felt that he was responsible for my problems.

She was messing with my mind. It was different than a telepath's influence. That was more like a one way radio set on blast. The radio being my mind. This was more like she was creating the feelings she wanted me to have and then amplifying them in the worst possible ways.

The only time I'd felt anything like it was during my encounter with the draugr.

"Would you like to answer now?" she asked in a silky voice.

I closed my eyes, envisioning my forest around me. It was faint but the feeling of despair lightened just a bit. I added sunlight and imagined wild roses and bushes full of thorns. The fear lightened just a little more. Enough that I felt less like curling into a fetal position on the floor and more like killing the thing responsible for this feeling.

"I'll take no for a thousand," I said.

Her forehead furrowed as if she didn't get the reference, but then she shrugged. I braced, knowing this would be bad.

"I'm sure the enforcer would not like knowing someone was messing with his little bird," a voice said from the door.

Elinor gave the man behind me a superior smile. "Aiden, are you sure you want to interfere. It's not like you to make such a huge misstep when it comes to politics."

I couldn't turn to see what he did, not wanting to take my eyes off the monster in front of me. Whatever he did caused Elinor to frown in displeasure.

A pair of nice men's shoes appeared in my peripheral vision and a hand grabbed my arm and hauled me to my feet. I hadn't even realized I'd fallen to my knees during Elinor's little torture session.

"You're not the select yet," Aiden said.

"Being a Patriarch won't always protect you," Elinor warned.

"That's exactly what it means," Aiden said, giving her a cool smirk. "You forget, the select is not all powerful. You can only affect those less powerful than you." He paused, running his eyes up and down her. "And darling, we both know that you don't have enough power to force me to bow."

"We'll see." Her red tinged lips turned up in a self-satisfied smile that said she knew something he didn't. "There are always others around who can take your place."

Aiden didn't respond verbally. His hand tightened around my arm until it was a painful vise. I bit back my sound of protest and kept any hint of pain off my face. No way was I letting this bitch know that her barb had hit its mark.

"This has been fun and all, but I still need to see Liam," I said into the dangerous silence.

Both pairs of eyes landed on me. It was like being at the center of a hurricane or between a pair of boxers whose knockout punch was a simple flick of the finger.

"You know where he is?" I asked Aiden.

The skin around his eyes crinkled slightly. He gave a small nod. "He sent me to find you when it took you too long to show up."

"How thoughtful," I said. It would have been more thoughtful if he'd been waiting outside the club so I didn't have to go through any of this. "Lead on, buddy."

Those crinkles got deeper as if something I said had amused him.

He gestured me to proceed him out of the room. My legs were shaky, but they held my weight as I took the first steps to the door. I wanted out of here bad enough that I was willing to crawl, but was grateful when I made it to the exit upright.

"Aileen," Elinor purred.

I hesitated, shooting her a glance over my shoulder. Aiden paused beside me.

"Every vampire in Columbus is required to be in attendance at the All Clan later this week. I expect to see you there."

She gave me a sickly sweet smile. It was amazing how that smile hid the ruthless monster inside. One that liked throwing her weight around and torturing those less powerful than herself.

She didn't have to voice what would happen if I decided to miss it. I had a feeling her retribution would be nasty and very painful.

I didn't answer, turning back to the door.

"Oh, I almost forgot. There's a cocktail party tomorrow night. You should come."

Yeah, I'd clear my schedule. I had no intention of spending any more time with these people. If I never saw them again, I would count it a blessing.

I walked out the door without answering. Aiden paced beside me, one hand on my back.

I waited until we'd traveled far enough and had placed several hallways between us and them before I staggered away from Aiden's stabilizing hand and let myself sag against the wall.

My body trembled uncontrollably now that the danger had passed. I let myself have that freak out. I'd held steady in the moment, but now I needed to process.

That woman could have crushed me like a bug. It would have taken less than a thought to destroy me. And they wondered why I wanted nothing to do with the lot of them. I didn't like being scared and that seemed to be a common theme when I ran into a vampire.

Aiden waited patiently until I stopped shaking, seeming to understand how important it was to let me have that.

When I had pulled myself mostly back together, I said, "What the fuck was that?"

"That was Elinor."

"I got that," I snapped. "Do you people just go around torturing others for the hell of it?"

He shrugged one shoulder. "Some of us. If we think we can get away with it."

"More and more, I am grateful for this sorcerer's mark," I muttered.

"You would have avoided what just happened if you belonged to a clan," he said nonchalantly. "You would be protected."

"Except from whoever held my leash."

He gave a head tilt, conceding my point.

Thought so.

"Is that so much worse than now? Any vampire more powerful than you can take what they want from you and you can't stop them."

I had no answer for him. To me it was worse, but I doubted he would agree.

"Last time someone tried to take me into a clan, it didn't work out too well." I gave him a meaningful look. He should know; he'd been the one to try to establish the connection. That connection had nearly killed me and done some damage to him.

His lips twisted in thought. "I've been thinking about that. The connection should work if we did one of the older bonds."

I'd pass on that. I didn't want to risk my life on something that might work. Especially when I didn't really want to be claimed.

"Did Liam really send you?" I asked.

His face went carefully blank.

"He didn't, did he?"

"I'm sure he would have if he knew you were going to happen on one of the applicant's."

I wasn't so sure about that. I'd been thinking.

Liam was the sort to orchestrate that whole scenario to help motivate me to get to work on locating the descendants. It was diabolical, but Liam struck me as someone who thought and strategized on several levels.

"You know where he is?" I asked.

"He's probably in one of the back rooms working on plans for the selection."

Did I really want to find him? Sir Grumpy Pants was probably going to give me a bunch of orders that I had no intention of following.

I looked Aiden over. He didn't look like he was just going to let me walk away.

"Don't suppose you could pretend you didn't see me?"

He smirked. "Nope."

I thought so.

"We'd better get started on tracking Sir Grumpsalot down then."

Aiden gave me an appreciative smile. "Accurate, but I dare you to call him that to his face."

Not in this lifetime. Maybe on the phone when we had a few land masses between the two of us, but not when he had a chance of making me pay for my snarkiness.

Chapter Six

Liam turned out to be easy to find. He was in the first place we looked, giving a briefing to three very dangerous looking men. Aiden and I waited just inside the door as he finished up.

The men looked me over as they filed past us. They were all tall and had the look of soldiers. Fanged soldiers capable of tearing your head off with their bare hands.

Their eyes filled with humor as they took me in, and they shared a look. It made me curious about what they'd heard.

"Aileen. Come."

I couldn't help looking like I'd just bitten into something sour.

"Woof, woof," I muttered under my breath.

"I heard that," he said, not looking at me.

Louder, I said, "You were supposed to."

"She had a run in with Elinor," Aiden interjected.

"Did she?"

"Elinor was in rare form. When I walked in, she was trying to interrogate your little bird."

I gave Aiden a dark look that said I'd appreciate it if would keep his mouth shut about things that didn't concern him. His look responded that it did concern him. Also that he just liked messing with me.

I don't know what I'd done to draw his interest, but I wished I could undo it.

"Elinor was surprised at how resilient the birdy was. She wasn't expecting her to resist the fear once, let alone twice," Aiden continued.

"Did she use full force?"

"Felt like it, but only Elinor knows."

They both looked at me with considering expressions.

"You're just full of surprises," Liam said. He sounded like he was mentally reevaluating my place in the order of things.

I didn't know if that was good or bad.

"What did you call me here for?" I asked, tired of them staring at me like they were trying to figure out what made me tick.

"I wanted to go over your plans for the investigation." He leaned back on the table and folded his arms across his chest.

He was an ass, but a good looking one. The woman in me took a minute to admire the way his shirt stretched nicely over his muscles.

I gave Aiden, who walked to the table and poured a glass of water, a quick glance. He didn't look like he had any intention of leaving, and Liam hadn't made any effort to usher him out.

"He knows," Liam said, confirming what I was beginning to suspect.

That surprised me. Aiden didn't strike me as the sort to take interest in these kinds of political maneuverings.

"It's in his best interest that the wrong person isn't put in power."

Aiden toasted me with his water and took a sip.

Vampires. This was one thing the books got right. It seemed like they couldn't get enough of the Machiavellian politics. Not me. I was too strait forward, with no patience for this type of thing. I wanted my part done so I could go back to my simple job and simple life.

"Has she found anything yet?" Aiden asked.

"Of course not. I'm not a miracle worker. I got this job tonight. I haven't even had a chance to get in touch with my contacts, let alone find anything." Not strictly true since I knew Thomas sired me. I kept that thought very quiet as Aiden was a mind reader. A powerful one.

Aiden glance at Liam. "I don't have to tell you what's at stake here if she fails."

How about telling me what's at stake? And not talking about me like I'm not even in the room.

"I am well aware," Liam said.

"You're all in agreement that I need to make progress," I said. "Instead of calling me here for a pointless conversation, how about next time you let me do my job and stop getting in the way?"

Liam stared at me, his eyes intense, as if he was trying to see to the very core of my being.

"Why is it that I sense you're hiding something?" he asked.

Aiden's gaze fastened on me and suddenly it was like I was a bunny in front of two apex predators. It was not a comforting feeling.

How to play this? The crux of the matter was that I was hiding something. Something big. That something would solve all of their problems. It was also something I would prefer to keep under wraps until I knew the lay of the land a little better. Once that bell was rung it would be impossible to unring it.

From the statements both Liam and Thomas had made about my sorcerer's mark, it seemed that it wasn't the full protection I had thought. I had to make myself seem important enough to keep alive and happy but not so important that they would feel I was better off under the clan's watchful eyes.

Worse, I suspected if Thomas found out he could turn little ole me into a vampire, he might get it into his head that he wanted other ankle biters running around. What better way to test his new found ability to sire vampires than by using those who share genetic material with me? Like my sister. Or her daughter.

I needed to pacify them enough that Aiden didn't try to take a little peek inside my mind. I could keep him out with my forest visualization defense for now, but I didn't know if that'd hold up if he put in a concentrated effort.

"How would I have had the time to find anything to hide?" I asked. "I'd just begun visiting some of my contacts when you called me in."

Lucky for me, I counted Dahlia as one of my contacts so I wasn't lying. Entirely.

His eyes narrowed. I kept myself loose and relaxed and didn't go overboard with keeping eye contact, but I didn't avoid his gaze entirely either.

He seemed to buy it when he reached for a sheet of paper on the table.

"I've added a few names to the list of witches and other spooks that might have had a hand in the hex. We'll visit the people on this list to see if any might be involved in this."

I shook my head before he finished speaking. "Nope. Absolutely not. We are not working together."

He got that pissed off look that said he found me very trying. "We are."

"We aren't." I held up a hand to forestall the storm I could see brewing. "You came to me because you needed someone the witches and the rest of the community didn't fear. Someone they could talk to without thinking they're going to be drained of blood at the end of it. That someone is not you. How is it going to look if I show up with the big bad enforcer dogging my every step? You think they're going to talk? Because I sure don't."

Aiden snorted. "I like her."

73

"Gee. Guess I can die happy," I said in a dry tone.

I looked back at Liam who appeared none too happy with the interruption.

"You came to me for a reason. Trying to back pedal now is only going to be more suspicious to these supposed enemies."

His face was reserved as he studied me. I tried to project as capable a look as I could dressed in a pair of jeans and a t-shirt.

"Fine. You have two days. If you've shown no progress at the end of that time, I'm stepping in and you'll just have to figure out a way to make this work with the big bad enforcer." He gave me the smile of a tiger. The one that said he was on to me but was willing to play with his food for a little while before gulping it down.

His smile did nothing for my peace of mind.

Two days wasn't a lot of time, but I'd take it. I just needed to figure something out. No way was I letting someone else fall into Thomas's clutches if I could help it.

The hell of it was, I wasn't seeing a lot of options.

Elinor struck me as one of those who didn't need absolute power to be absolutely corrupted. If the rest of the applicants were anything like her, it would be like choosing your shade of evil.

"I'll just be on my way." My smile was more of a baring of teeth than an indication of happiness.

Liam's voice was silky and smooth. "Aileen. I know you're hiding something. I will get to the bottom of it before this is over."

My gaze shot between the two of them as my lips quirked up. "You're welcome to try."

Yeah, it wasn't smart bearding the dragon in his den, but sometimes you had to take a stand, if only to say you weren't as tasty as you looked.

His laugh was husky when it came and his eyes half-lidded as he watched me turn and leave.

So soft that I might have imagined it, he said, "I look forward to the hunt."

*   *   *

After the visit to the club, I needed a shower and some comfortable clothes to wash away the stench of fear and stress. I didn't see much point in visiting any of the names on Liam's list, not without doing some research first.

It would also give me a chance to see what I could dig up on Thomas's descendants.

Showered, fed and in a loose pair of capri pajama pants and another oversized top, I settled onto the couch with my computer and the file Liam and Thomas had given me. I set a notepad next to it and logged on to my computer.

The problem for me was where to start.

Typing in 'researching family history' led me to a ton of sites that touted being able to do the search for you. The problem was that I was starting at the top of the tree and trying to work my way down. Most of these sites worked the opposite way.

Thomas had lost track of his descendants back in the early days of the city when it was first being settled in the 1800's. It looked like he'd tracked them for over a hundred years prior to that. All the way back to before they'd left Europe for this country. From what I could make out in the chicken scratch handwriting on the notes, a Thomas Bennet and his wife, Martha Bennet, bought five lots in what was now the west side of Columbus. From a small painting included in the file, this Thomas Bennet was not my sire, though he looked enough like him that I could tell they were related. I wondered how old my sire was. Older than two hundred, that was for sure.

It looked like the Bennet family had a run of bad luck in that century with many of them dying under suspicious circumstances. Two of their children died before hitting their double digits. The cause of death in the obituaries was listed as unknown.

The oldest son married but was murdered shortly after the wedding. Lucky for him he left a widow behind who bore him a son six months later. None of the other children married or left behind children.

After hours spent researching, I sat back. It almost felt like this family was targeted from the get go. Like someone was systematically wiping them out of existence. Nearly every member was murdered or died under suspicious circumstances, the exceptions being those who married into the family.

I traced their history all the way to 1913 when the family and its descendants disappeared. A quick search found that was the year of the great flood. Pretty much all of Columbus and Ohio, and parts of Indiana, were underwater. I remembered reading about that in a history class in high school. It looked like the flood claimed over four hundred lives with ninety six of them in Columbus alone.

I saw a couple of Thomas and Martha's grandchildren's names listed as deceased, but that didn't mean anything. Records were notoriously bad back then. If his descendants suspected they were being hunted, they might have taken the confusion as an opportunity to disappear while letting the folks back home think they perished.

I leaned back and looked up at the ceiling. If I was a vampire and had placed a hex on my competition and knew that only a descendant could break that hex, I would have made damn sure there were no little rug rats left to ruin my plans.

But why take so long to systematically murder all of the direct line? Why not just do it in one go? Pay someone to burn their house down.

Maybe they needed to make their movements undetectable. Hide what they were doing until the hex was firmly in place so their victim couldn't figure out a way to reverse it. My limited knowledge of hexes said they took time to set. That for a brief window its victim could reverse the hex if they found a skilled enough practitioner.

That might explain things a little more. It would definitely explain why this hunt took place over decades rather than months. A vampire, or something similarly long lived, would have had that kind of time and patience to pull this off.

This made my task more difficult. If that family figured out something was hunting them, they wouldn't have made it easy to be found again. They probably covered their tracks and covered them well to avoid their hunter.

It would probably be easier figuring out the witch or spook who had performed the hex. It would also make me feel less guilty should this go sideways and a descendant was found because of something I did. Thomas seemed desperate to me. If trying to turn one of them would break the hex, he'd probably turn them and not care one bit if it upended their entire world. Or worse, he tried to turn them and ended up killing them by accident as it seemed he'd done to others he turned. I didn't want to be responsible for that.

Either way, this was as far as I could go at the moment with this line of research. Time to switch over to the spooks.

Finding information on the spooks was surprisingly easy. Especially any of the ones who tried to integrate into the normal world. Seemed even witches had a use for social media.

It took no time at all to cross off three names since the owners were dead. I found mention of them using a simple search that uncovered their obituaries. Now, they could have laid the hex but that wouldn't help us at all. We needed a live witch or spook to fix what got broke, which meant I was going under the assumption that person was still alive.

One of the names had since moved out west and another had moved to Russia according to their activity on social media. I moved both of those to a lower priority. I didn't think I had enough time to go all the way to Russia to question a witch.

Four of the names had no ties to the witch community, which I assumed meant they were some type of spook incapable of masquerading as human. I'd have to reach out to Dahlia or one of my other contacts to see if they knew where I could find those four.

I was betting the rest of the names belonged to one of the covens in town. Unfortunately I had no way of knowing which.

That might be a sticking point. I'd had a bit of a run in last fall with a couple of the witches and had no idea if we'd left things on a good footing. Not to mention I was pretty sure I couldn't trust anybody Miriam called friend as far as I could throw them.

It was too late to go on a wild goose chase across the city, but now that I had a plan of attack I felt more comfortable with this job.

I'd take the rest of the night to relax before the craziness that was sure to follow.

I set the computer on the end table and turned my music on very low before grabbing a beer and opening my front door. It was rare that I got to totally relax, and I was going to take advantage.

I sat on the top step, just enjoying being outside, sipping my summer ale. It was one of those perfect nights, not too hot and without the bitter chill of winter. A breeze rustled the trees out front.

My eyes closed as I let myself just exist.

I've always liked nighttime. There's something magical about that brief period when most of the world slumbers. Where one day ends and the next begins. There are so many endless possibilities.

As a vampire, tied to the sunrise and sunset, I experienced a lot of these but rarely do I get to stop and put myself fully in the moment.

A scrape of movement. Faint, like the sound of a shoe against pavement, drew my attention to the base of the stairs. My neighbor stood partially in shadow.

I started to look away when his eyes caught the light oddly and a green sheen washed over them.

I nearly dropped my beer in shock. The green disappeared and the shadows swallowed him before I heard the open and shut of his apartment door.

That answered that.

My neighbors weren't exactly human. It made me wonder what happened with my previous ones. Did they choose to leave or did something make that decision for them?

Wasn't my business. I'd leave them alone as long as they left me alone.

I was beginning to think I was cursed to draw trouble like a magnet.

With my quiet enjoyment of the night gone, I headed back inside.

*   *   *

My alarms blared, pulling me from a great abyss.

I groaned and pulled my pillow over my head.

"You do realize that's super annoying, right?" an irate voice asked from the other side of the bed.

I stilled, closing my eyes and wishing more than anything that I'd imagined that voice.

"Well? Aren't you going to turn them off?"

Damn. Looked like I wasn't that lucky.

I sighed and sat up, not bothering to turn off the three alarms.

A pair of bright green eyes in a teenager's face glared at me. The teenager attached to them had grown since the last time I'd seen him. He'd been standing on a grave cursing my name then. Now he had the beginnings of a scruffy beard. This was surprising given I knew he couldn't age and was, in fact, way older than his looks suggested.

"Turn it off." His voice echoed in the small room, the deep barrel bass thumping in my chest. It had way more power than it should, considering I'd slapped a genie cuff on him, which should have kept him from accessing his powers. I narrowed my eyes at him.

His wrist still held the copper bracelet. I breathed a sigh of relief. I didn't want to think about how much worse things could get if he had managed to get out of it.

"How did you get in?" I asked, propping myself up in the bed.

He gave me a dirty look and slapped each of the alarms. The last one switched over to a local rock station instead of turning off. He yanked the plug from the outlet. It died mid song.

"How can you stand that noise?" he asked, glaring at the now silent alarms.

78

I shrugged. "They have their purpose."

He gave me a sly look. "Like waking you before sunset?"

I didn't answer. Flipping the covers off me, I was grateful for my modesty. I'd slept in a pair of shorts and t-shirt last night, so he didn't get a full frontal. He backed away as I advanced on him, grabbed the door and shut it in his face, locking it in case he didn't get the point.

Concerned he wouldn't stay out for long, I grabbed the first pair of jeans I could find then pulled out a blue v-neck shirt. I paired the outfit with boots and my rust colored, leather jacket.

Since I was going to be interviewing people, I didn't want to dress like the bike messenger I was. Appearances and first impressions meant something, no matter how much we told ourselves otherwise.

Sometimes I went against the norm just to yank people's chains, but I didn't want to have to fight that stereotyping when I was on such a tight deadline.

Besides, it was easier to hide the holster for the judge under this jacket than in my bike outfit.

Dressed, I opened the bedroom door and went straight to my fridge. I had a feeling I'd need my hunger sated to be able to deal with the sorcerer over the next few minutes.

"Enough games, Aileen. I want this off now," he said, waving his wrist at me.

I didn't respond, grabbing a glass from the cabinet and tipping the wine bottle over. My mouth filled with saliva as my world spiraled down to that life sustaining ruby liquid.

I needed that first sip more than my next breath. I'd do anything to get it. Crawl through glass. Kill. Anything.

My desire for it was worse than any human inspired addiction, and it was one I could never walk away from. I might get better at controlling myself, but the need would always be there. Worse than crack. Worse than meth.

I bolted the drink, nearly choking as I guzzled it down. I gasped as I lowered the glass. A bead of blood slid from the corner of my mouth. I caught it with a thumb and sucked it off. Mustn't waste any. This stuff cost a pretty penny to get from the local blood bank.

"Do you have any idea how gross that is?" the sorcerer asked.

I had some inkling.

"How did you get in my place?"

He sighed. "Why must you waste time asking such pointless questions? Weren't you listening to anything I said?"

Not really. I'd been laser focused on the blood and had lost track of everything taking place around me.

He didn't wait for my response, holding his wrist up and shaking it. "Get rid of this abomination. You've had your fun. Time to fix this."

A tall and gangly teenager, Peter Barret was the sorcerer who owned my mark. His plan to make me hunt down the draugr and claim its treasures had backfired when I decided to give its possessions back to it, ensuring the mark stuck around for the next hundred years.

That was partially my intent as the mark prevented the vampires from claiming me for a hundred years. It was fortunate that I'd already slipped the cuff onto Barret, or I'm pretty sure my ass would have been toast after I pulled my little stunt.

To say he wasn't pleased was a bit of an understatement. He'd been blocked from his powers, courtesy of the cuff, for the last few months. I was pretty sure removing it without having some type of leverage over him would result in my prolonged and grisly death.

His eyes were chips of green as he glared at me.

I tilted my head. Something was different.

I stepped closer and ran my fingers down his cheek. Stubble. Scraggly stubble.

He smacked my hand away and ducked away from me. "What are you doing?"

"Feeling your beard. I've never seen you with even a hint of one before. It's cute. A little sparse but cute."

"Don't be absurd. I don't get beards." He rubbed his chin. A thoughtful look came over his face as his fingers paused on the few hairs.

"Whatever you want to tell yourself, pipsqueak."

His eyes flared. If they hadn't belonged to such an annoying pain in my ass, I'd say they were pretty. Beautiful even. But then I could say that about him as a whole too. The sorcerer was caught in that weird time between puberty and adulthood where his parts didn't quite go together right.

Eventually, if he had the opportunity to grow older, he'd probably break a few hearts with his looks. I couldn't imagine being stuck in that awful phase for decades. Guess he had a reason to be so grumpy all the time.

"Are you going to answer my question of how you got in here?"

The information was important. I wanted to make sure I discouraged any future urges to visit me while I was sleeping by him, or anyone else. I was totally defenseless when asleep. Someone could come in and cut off my head, killing me true dead. I'd like to prevent that.

He rolled his eyes, looking every inch the teenager in that moment. "I used an unlock charm."

Magic. I came alert, my hand moving to my holster in reflex. How? He shouldn't have access to any of his magic.

Seeing my movement, he gave me a nasty smile. "Oh, did you think I couldn't do any magic? Guess again." He held up his arm again. "Might as well remove this before things get nasty."

I studied him. Contrary to popular belief, accomplished liars often give away very little in terms of nonverbal cues. They are just as likely to meet your eyes as a non-liar. Most are versed in the nonverbal indicators of a liar and have practiced avoiding those traits when lying.

Nothing about Peter said he was lying. There was a slight tightness to his shoulders but other than that he looked calm. As if butter wouldn't melt in his mouth.

I wasn't buying it.

"Bullshit. No way you can do magic. Maybe charms other people brewed or one you had on hand already, but not stuff you did yourself."

If he'd had access to magic, I would have woken up in a lot more pain. I was willing to bet my life on that.

He folded his arms and glared at me.

Heh.

"Hand it over," I told him, making a give me motion.

He looked at me as if I was speaking gibberish.

"The charm. I know you have it on you. Give it over."

He dug it out of his pocket and passed it to me. "Not like I can't get more."

"But you won't be using this one."

No reason to make it any easier on him than necessary.

I turned the charm over in my hands. A medallion with strange etchings around the edge, it was attached to a black ribbon. It looked like the sort of thing found in a hipster shop, not something used to commit a B and E. It was such a simple thing to have opened my locks as if they weren't even there.

I stuffed it in my back pocket. Might come in handy later.

"As fun as this has been, it's time for you to go."

"Take this off and I will."

Erg. The guy was like a dog with a bone.

I folded my arms over my chest. "I take that off and what do you think the first thing you're going to do is?"

He opened his mouth but caught my expression and closed it, having the decency not to tell a lie so obvious that even astronauts in orbit would have been able to see it in glaring neon letters.

"Yeah, that's what I thought."

"So you're just going to leave it on."

Pretty much. That was the plan.

"What can I say? I'm pretty attached to my life."

"What if I promise not to kill you?"

I laughed. "I'm not fond of torture either."

"You can't do this." He sounded every inch the teenager after mom told him he was grounded.

"Sorry, guy. Until I can find a way to protect myself from whatever you've got cooking up in that brain of yours, you're stuck wearing that very trendy bracelet. Congrats on your fashion accessory."

"No, this isn't fair. I need access to my power. I'm a sitting duck without it. I've already had to fend off a pair of harpies wanting to steal a sixth century manuscript."

I blinked. That was a new one. What would harpies want with a manuscript?

"Welcome to how the rest of us live," I told him, not feeling a lot of sympathy. He'd pretty much described my everyday life.

His face twisted in anger, his eyes becoming an emerald green so vivid they glowed. His anger was a tempest in a teakettle.

"I'll figure a way out of this and when I do, you're going to pay." He shook his head. "I'm not even going to kill you. I'll make you beg for death, wish for its sweet release. These next hundred years are going to be hell on you."

With such sweet promises as that, was it any wonder I refused to remove the genie cuff?

"As fun as that sounds, I'll have to take a rain check. I've got places to be and people to see. None of whom include you."

His nostrils flared like an angry bull about to charge, and he shook his head then kept right on shaking it.

"No, I'm not going anywhere. I'm staying right here until you remove this."

That could be a problem. I didn't want him lingering in my apartment while I took on the rest of the supernatural world. Being worried about what traps or charms he was planting while I questioned witches was not how I wanted this evening to go.

"You're not staying here," I told him.

He lifted his chin. "I am. I'm not moving until you give me what I want."

"This isn't a demonstration. It's not a tree you can hook yourself to protest the unfairness of the world. This is my home and if I say you're not staying, you're not staying."

"Try and make me."

What was he? A child? Oh, I forgot. He was a grown man in a teenager's body. Perhaps his mind had reverted to the age of his body. That might explain this little game of his.

He smirked at me, confident that I was out of options.

My eyes narrowed; I smirked back.

He'd picked the wrong opponent. My sister would attest to that. I was the queen of bad decisions when someone tweaked my tail on my own territory.

I advanced on him, his smile disappearing quickly.

Heh, heh. Want to pull this stuff in my house when he didn't have access to his power? We'd just see who came out on top.

He backed away. "What are you doing? Stop."

Not so tough without those powers. No lightning bolts to send blistering pain down all of my nerve endings. No green lights to nip at me when I didn't do what he wanted.

"I'm warning you."

He jumped over the coffee table, putting it between the two of us. I walked one way and he walked the other. I switched back and he circled in the opposite direction.

What were we? Children playing ring around the rosy? Enough of this.

I stepped up and over, grabbing him by the arm before he could run. I hauled him to the door with him batting at me and struggling to get away. For a big bad sorcerer, he wasn't overly good at the physical stuff. It was kind of refreshing to be the one with all the strength for once. Usually I was so outclassed in terms of power both magical and physical.

He jerked hard, ripping his arm out of my hold. "Alright, I get it. What's your big rush anyway?"

"I told you, I have places to be and people to see."

He got a crafty look on his face. "This wouldn't have anything to do with those spooks going missing all over the city."

"What makes you say that?"

He shrugged. "Your penchant with involving yourself in trouble."

I narrowed my eyes. "I recall last time that trouble could be laid right at your door."

"You would have gotten involved anyway. I just sped up the process."

Sped up the process? He's the reason I almost got eaten by a dead man, not to mention he was the driving force behind the vampires finding out about my existence. If not for him, I wouldn't be in my current predicament of having to locate an heir for my sire to turn. I was guessing at my sire's goal but it was an educated guess.

"Let me thank you for that kindness." I flicked his ear.

"Ow." He covered the abused ear. "What was that for?"

"For being such a good Samaritan."

I flicked the other ear.

"You're very violent, you know?"

I bared my fangs. "Vampire, remember?"

He grumbled, looking almost adorable, cupping both ears to protect them from being flicked. Too bad that innocent face hid someone who'd just as soon rip my throat out as spit on me.

I yanked open the door. "Out."

To make sure he didn't try to come back in, I wheeled my bike out after him and used it to herd him down the stairs. Swiping my phone and keys off my kitchen table, I stuffed them in my messenger bag and put the strap over my head. I propped the bike against the wall as I finished getting ready.

The sorcerer watched with his arms folded over his chest. "I'll just wait here until you get back. You can't make me leave."

I wonder what the police would do with a trespasser. Taking in his surly teenage face, I had to ask myself if they deserved having to deal with him. Probably not, but it was sure nice to imagine.

My phone rang.

I answered without checking the screen. "Hermes Courier Service. We come to you."

"Get over here right now."

"Caroline?"

The sorcerer dropped his arms and edged closer, doing a pretty good job of pretending not to be interested.

I grimaced at him. Short of jumping on the bike and riding one handed down the street there wasn't a lot I could do about my eaves dropper. I was pretty sure he would just jog after me.

"Get over here right now, Aileen." Stress threaded through her voice. "I don't know what I'll do."

"Ok, I'll be right there. Are you at the OSU library?"

"Yes. Hurry."

I hung up, my stomach a mass of knots. She wouldn't have called me if she wasn't in trouble. From the amount of stress in her voice it had to be bad.

Perhaps supernatural bad. My stomach pitched.

No, no. It couldn't be that. I didn't need to jump to conclusions. What I needed was to get over there. Fast.

I threw my leg over the bike and pushed off. Peter stepped in front of me and grabbed the handle bars. I jolted to a stop.

"Move. I have to go."

"That was Caroline, wasn't it?"

The two had met after I asked Caroline to do some research for me after he set me on the draugr's path.

"Move."

"She sounded like she was in trouble."

I didn't ask how he knew what she sounded like. I had no time for this.

"Move."

He ignored the command. "I can help. Let me come with you."

Not happening. He had shown a level of interest in my friend that I was not comfortable with. I wanted the two kept as far from each other as possible.

"I don't think so."

I shoved the bike forward a step. He threw his weight against the handle bars, and I was forced to awkwardly dig one foot in, trying not to lose ground. Straddling the bike made this back and forth awkward on my end. I did not see good things for me if we kept up this shoving match.

"I can be an asset to you."

"How do you think you can do that? You have no powers."

"If someone would remove the cursed genie cuff, that wouldn't be a problem."

Push.

"Like that'll help. Your first move would be to kill me. You'll either forget about or torture Caroline."

Shove.

"Not true. I think Caroline has a brain in her head worth preserving. Unlike you."

He pushed the bike hard. I hopped back, trying to keep it from banging into me.

"Not happening."

I shoved the front wheel into him.

"I could be your backup."

"Again, you have no power. You'll just be cannon fodder."

He and I reached an impasse. He glared at me over the bike's handlebars.

"It'll take you at least twenty minutes to get there by bike."

This was true.

He saw the acknowledgement on my face. He played his trump card. "I have a car."

"Let me put the bike away."

Chapter Seven

The Ohio State University campus was a sprawling monstrosity that intertwined seamlessly with the city of Columbus. Although there is a campus district, it is only called that because it houses the majority of the buildings that make up OSU. Most of the students live on the edges in homes and apartments that were at times historic or falling apart. Sometimes both.

In the center of it all is the William Oxley Thompson Memorial Library. The name was a mouthful but matched the intimidating four story beast made of glass and metal. Despite the huge size it wasn't the only library on OSU, there were actually fifty four others, but it was the one that housed the rare book and manuscript collection, which is where I was willing to bet Caroline would be this late at night.

I didn't have a student ID to get in so I had to trail another student while silently castigating them for holding the door for me. It wasn't safe behavior. It didn't matter how updated your security protocols were if you've got people ignoring those protocols.

He probably thought I was a decent looking woman with no signs of mental illness or inebriation. There was no way I could have anything up my sleeve, right?

The bad guys know how people think. If you look like you belong, then you must belong. They use that kind of thinking to their advantage. Next thing you know you have a security breach at best. If you're really unlucky, you've got a murder or something worse on your hands.

The kid's inattention worked to my advantage, and I was in too big a hurry to give him a lecture on safety. Not that he would have listened. Kids his age all thought the bad things happened to someone else. Never them.

I headed for the escalators, the sorcerer tagging along at my heels. I took them two at a time until I got to the floor containing the archive section. My pace was fast, worry eating at me with every step. From Peter's silence, I could tell some of my worry had infected him. Maybe he did care about Caroline. Just a little bit. I still wasn't letting him around her if I could help it.

The customer service desk was empty and banging on the little bell didn't bring anyone running. Not even when the sorcerer pressed it and then kept right on pressing it, making an annoying cacophony.

I hopped over the desk and peered into the back room. No one there. I was relieved to see no bodies on the floor, but it didn't untie the knot that had taken up residence in my stomach.

"No one is here. You can stop pushing the bell."

Peter held the bell down for another long moment.

"You can keep pushing the bell, or we can try to find Caroline," I said, showing my fangs.

He was a distraction, and worse, he was wasting time that should be spent saving my friend. If he continued to waste my time, I was going to show him why vampires had fangs. He could be my first victim.

My eyes darted to the veins in his neck. I licked my lips. Come to think of it, I was kind of hungry. Power rushed below the surface of his skin. I took a step toward him. Power that could be mine. It'd probably be a hundred, no a thousand times better than the bagged blood I normally survived on.

He grabbed some papers and threw them at my face. I batted them away, losing sight of him.

"Do you have control of yourself now?" his caustic voice asked.

I blinked at the empty space in front of me and looked around. He stood by the open doors of the archive, more than ten feet away. How did he get over there so fast?

"Are you coming?"

Annoying little brat.

I stalked towards him.

"You really should get that hunger under control," he said as I passed.

"It is under control."

"Didn't look like it to me."

I gave him a fake smile, one that was more of a grimace. "Looks can be deceiving."

I'd like to think I wouldn't have snarfed him down like a chocolate shake, but stranger things have happened. It worried me that I'd been temporarily consumed by blood lust. I didn't have the same excuse as other times this had happened. I'd drunk my morning supply of iron yesterday before turning in and gotten my dinner's share when I woke up.

If hunger wasn't what sparked this episode, what was? And could I handle the answer?

I didn't want Liam and his merry band of psychos to be right. That I needed to be watched and monitored and controlled because I was a danger to all those around me. Not after fighting this hard for this long to stay free.

It was an aberration, brought on by worry. I needed to shrug this off and focus on what was important. Caroline.

The large, empty room was filled with stacks upon stacks of manuscripts, most of which were pretty old. Each had their own bin on the shelves and either lay flat in that bin or, for oversized papers, were rolled into a cylinder.

The controlled environment kept the temperature cool in here with little humidity. The lights were lower intensity to protect the fragile paper and ink, so there were no windows and only a few desk lamps.

It was easy to see at a glance that the room was empty. No sign of Caroline.

"She should be here, right?" Peter asked. He looked as uncertain as I felt.

I didn't like this. She said the library. This was where she could normally be found.

"Yes."

"Then where is she?"

"I don't know."

But I'd find out.

I'd already tried calling her several times on the way over here, but Caroline hadn't answered.

I had so few friends in this world; I couldn't afford to lose any of them.

"Let's check the rest of the library. Perhaps she's studying or tutoring someone."

Caroline wasn't much of a people person. I couldn't imagine her signing up to tutor someone. She didn't have the patience and her sarcasm would be more deconstructive rather than constructive.

It was worth a shot. Especially since I didn't want to consider something worse.

The door to the archives slid shut.

There was a sound. Slight, almost undetectable to a human's ears. But for a vampire it was as loud as a shout.

I checked the area in my peripheral vision, seeing nothing. Keeping my motions as nonchalant as possible I turned toward the sorcerer, getting a look behind us. Then I acted like I was looking for the exit and turned in the opposite direction.

Nothing.

Movement, so small I thought I imagined it. Could just be a trick of the light.

Something shifted in the shadows.

We were being watched by someone who didn't want to be detected. I was betting he or she was supernatural in nature given the way they'd wrapped those shadows around themselves.

I nudged Peter and flicked my eyes to where I knew someone waited. He caught on quick and tilted his chin down once to indicate he saw.

The watcher lurked behind the stacks closest to the exit. We'd have to pass him when we left. I'd planned to search more of this floor before heading to the next floor. Perhaps the watcher could help expedite my search.

I tapped Peter on the shoulder, hoping he'd take it as a signal to follow my lead.

"Guess she's not here after all. We'll try again tomorrow."

He nodded. "I think you're right. Yes, let's try again tomorrow."

I paused, giving him a look with widened eyes that said 'what the fuck?'

He shrugged, looking sheepish. He'd sounded stiff as if he was reading lines in a book. I had totally misread his ability for subterfuge. That, or maybe he was so nervous that he wasn't able to bring his normal talents to bear.

Naw, not the sorcerer. He had to have encountered much more dangerous situations than this.

Or maybe he knew something I didn't.

We headed to the exit. Just as we passed where I had first spied our peeping tom, I lunged into the shadows. My hand grabbed an arm and I yanked, dragging my watcher into the light.

A hiss and yowl, like something a cat would make, assaulted my ears. I grabbed a wrist and then twisted and yanked, contorting the arm into an unnatural position behind the person.

It was a man with short, yellow hair and slightly pointed ears.

Go Army combatives training. I hadn't been certain I remembered that move until muscle memory took over. I guess all that repetition paid off.

"Who are you?" I yanked the arm I was holding higher.

The man yowled again. Not a sound I'd heard a human ever make so he was definitely some type of spook.

"Why were you watching us?" Peter no longer sounded like a teenager, rather his voice was that of someone much older. One used to interrogation and who had no problem doing what had to be done to get the information he needed.

"Stop, please. I meant no harm."

I yanked the arm higher. "That's what everybody says when they're caught."

"Do you know who we are?" Peter asked, every inch the arrogant sorcerer I first met.

"Yes. You're the sorcerer. The one they call Barrett."

Peter's eyebrow twitched but otherwise he gave no reaction. Barrett was technically his master and Peter was his apprentice before he became a fully-fledged sorcerer.

"And her?" Peter indicated me.

"The vampire. The one without a clan."

Peter's face turned thoughtful. "Let him go."

Say what. I hadn't caught him in a surprise attack to let him go so he could then kick my ass.

"He's weaker than us. He won't try anything. Will you, sphinx?"

"No. I won't. I swear. Just let me go."

Peter leaned forward, thrusting his face close to the man's. "She's going to let you go, but you're going to stick around to answer some questions. Otherwise, I'll hunt you down and use you as ingredients in my spell work."

It was a good threat. One that had incentivized me to track down a deadly monster last year. One that I would face again if the sorcerer ever got free of the genie cuff I'd trapped him in.

"I won't run. I swear."

"Like I'd trust a sphinx's promise," the sorcerer sneered.

Then why was I letting him go? If you couldn't trust someone to answer a simple question, how were we going to trust that he had no plans to attack?

Noticing my hesitation, the sorcerer shot me a look.

I sighed and released the arm, shoving the sphinx away from me.

Peter had done me the favor of trusting me when it came to catching our watcher. The least I could do was return the favor until it became evident that our interests didn't align.

The sphinx looked like a professor, or maybe a grad student, one with a fashion sense that was a few decades older than him. He wore wireframe glasses and his golden hair stuck up in tufts. He was dressed in khakis and a dress shirt with a plaid vest over it. His ears were barely pointed and were partially covered by his hair. I probably wouldn't have noticed if I wasn't so close, and he hadn't been contorting to prevent his arm from breaking.

He looked scared out of his mind.

I hardened my resolve. If he had something to do with Caroline's disappearance, I didn't care how scared he looked. I'd make him tell me where she was. If he'd harmed her... Well, I had an extensive knowledge of torture techniques gleaned from years of reading and a friendship with an interrogator in the military, along with the will to use them.

"What's your name?" I repeated.

"Demetri," he said.

Sounded Greek, which fit. If I remembered my high school English class, there were stories about the sphinx in both Greek and Egyptian mythology. The Greek version made the sphinx out to be treacherous and murderous. The story I could remember was about Oedipus Rex who became king after killing a sphinx who lured travelers and killed them when they couldn't answer its riddles.

The Egyptian's cast the sphinx as a wise and benevolent guardian who protected the entrance of tombs and the like.

These were just stories of course, and I was walking proof that the myths weren't always true. I wasn't a soulless killing machine, so I couldn't assume the sphinx lived up to either version of its mythology.

"Alright, Demetri, let's try this again. Why were you watching us?"

He looked hunted, his eyes shifted from left to right as if he was determining his best escape route.

"Demetri." My voice lowered to a threatening growl as I stepped closer. "You don't want to test me right now. I can't guarantee I'll be as gentle as last time."

He slumped, the muscles in his body relaxing as if he realized how fruitless escape was. I didn't drop my guard, afraid this might be a trick.

"Now, why were you watching us?"

He lifted his eyes to mine and for a moment it felt like I was falling as a voice muttered incomprehensibly next to my ear.

I shook my head, shutting that voice out. I grabbed him by the collar, yanking him up to my face, and my exposed fangs. "Enough of that unless you want to be dinner. I've never had sphinx before. I might like it."

I was proud I didn't lisp once. Or spit on him. Talking around extra-large teeth had been difficult at first but I'd gotten the hang of it after a while.

"Please, not that. I'll tell you but just don't bite me."

My grip didn't loosen, but I did draw back a little and close my mouth gently around the fangs. They were pointy, indenting my lower lip. Usually I retracted them if I wanted to close my mouth. Otherwise I risked poking a hole in my lip.

"Hurry up. Our patience is growing thin," Peter inserted. "Don't try to draw either of us into a riddle again. You won't like the consequences."

I gave him a wry glance. He quirked one corner of his mouth as if acknowledging the fact that he sounded like a B movie villain.

"Ok. I wasn't watching you. Not really."

"Then what were you doing, because it seemed awfully like watching to me," I said.

"I was hiding," Demetri admitted. "I thought you were it and I was your next victim."

"It?" How very descriptive. No wonder he thought we were it. Anybody could be it.

He looked at the two of us, it just dawning that we had no idea what he was talking about.

"You mean you haven't heard? Everybody in the community is talking about it."

"Talking about what?" Peter snapped. His frustration echoed mine.

"The creature. The one that has been paralyzing people all over town. When they finally wake up, they're so convinced they need to be somewhere that they end up attacking anyone who gets in their way. Nobody has been able to find any of those who were able to run off after becoming unstuck. Whatever it was claimed three near here in the last week."

That sounded an awful lot like what happened to Rick in Dahlia's storeroom.

"Do you know what it is?"

93

Demetri shook his head. "No one does. You can't ask any of the victims because they just start howling and throwing themselves against things."

Shit. Peter and I shared a glance, for once on the same page. Neither of us liked an unknown spook running around town and using its mojo to paralyze and then summon its victims. It put our entire community at risk of discovery.

Not to mention it's easier to fight something when you know its weaknesses. In this topsy, turvy shadow world, the simple logic behind the laws of physics and the world didn't always apply. For instance putting three bullet holes in Liam's chest had only been a slight annoyance to him. He didn't even break stride. There was a possibility that this thing wouldn't be phased by normal weapons either.

Seeing that the two of us were uneasy at his words, Demetri threw in some extra information, "It got my cousin last night. That's why I'm here. To pick up his stuff."

Using the grip I had on his collar, I pushed him down the stacks. "Show me."

I wanted to see if he was telling the truth. If he was, there might be a clue if this thing had done something to Caroline.

We didn't have far to go. His cousin had worked at the customer service desk three rooms down from the archive room.

Demetri held out a bag. "This is his book bag. I don't think he had anything else."

I took the bag and upended it on the table. Peter picked up a notebook and paged through it. Demetri took a step back.

"I wouldn't if I was you," Peter cautioned without looking up. "She's a vampire. They're faster than a sphinx."

"She's practically still got her milk teeth," Demetri said scornfully. "I've heard of her. The clanless vampire, not even in her hundredth year. I doubt she could beat a medusa hopped up on snake venom."

I gave him a charming smile, being sure to flash my fangs. "Want to bet your life on that?"

"I wouldn't," Peter said in a sing song voice. "She's very motivated right now. I doubt you'd make it to the end of this table."

Demetri eyed the table and then glanced at me. I gave him my at peace expression, the one that said I was ok with whichever choice he made.

He blanched. Maybe that expression didn't say what I thought it said.

"I don't see anything in here," Peter said, riffling through some pens and a – was that a set of stamps?

I agreed. Most of this stuff was typical in a college student's book bag. Besides a bunch of papers, a book and a few notebooks, there wasn't much here.

"Can I go now?" Demetri asked.

"No," Peter and I said in unison.

"Come on. I proved that I wasn't lying."

"All you've proved is that some kid left his book bag here." I lifted said bag and felt along the seams. Maybe there was a secret pouch. Unlikely, but so were all of the things that go bump in the night.

Again, nothing.

I threw the bag on the table in frustration.

"What are you guys doing here?"

I jumped and spun around to find Caroline watching us with her arms folded over her chest. She was not far away. I'd miss her approach because I was so absorbed in questioning the sphinx and searching the book bag. I really needed to work on my situational awareness.

"Caroline, you're here," was my surprised response. Yeah, that wasn't suspicious or anything. "Actually, what are you doing here?"

"I called you, remember."

Yes. I remembered. It's why I was panicking because I thought something had happened to her. Judging by the slightly irritated look on her face I was going to say she was safe and unharmed and possibly pissed, though I didn't know why.

I handed the bag to Demetri. "You can go now."

"Demetri." Caroline's forehead furrowed. "What are you still doing here? Your classes ended hours ago. Did you have student questions to take care of?"

I gave the sphinx a sideways glance. So he was a professor. My initial assessment of him wasn't far off.

Demetri's wide eyed gaze went from me to the sorcerer to Caroline.

"Uh, yes." His voice rose, making the yes almost a question.

Judging by the suspicion on Caroline's face she heard the question in his voice too.

"Really. You took questions in the library rather than your office?"

Demetri shot me another panicked glance as if he didn't know how to respond. Considering all the trouble he gave Peter and me, I was having a hard time believing his panic. On the other hand, this was Caroline, queen of making you second guess yourself and stutter like you were giving a presentation to the president. Hell, she'd even put me off balance a time or two.

Taking pity, because I'd been in the same situation more than once and I needed to get to the bottom of why she called me here, I interjected, "Demetri was good enough to show Peter and me up here when we got a little lost. When we couldn't find you, he offered to help us look."

Caroline arched an eyebrow, "You got lost? Really."

I shrugged. "It happens. Let's move on."

"You had no trouble finding this place last time."

Ah, I'd forgotten about that when making up my lie. I decided to insert a little of the truth into my story. "You sounded like you were in trouble. I got a little turned around in my haste."

She had sounded like she was in trouble, but even worried I wouldn't have lost my way. I had an almost perfect sense of direction and remembered how to get to the places I've visited even years later. It's what made me a good courier.

I was hoping she didn't remember all of that. Or at least that she didn't push me on it.

"Uh huh." Her tone said she didn't quite believe me but couldn't think of an alternate excuse.

I released an internal sigh of relief. Caroline had never been easy to fool. I was rusty.

"Thanks for all the help, Demetri," I said, warning him with my expression to get gone.

He nodded like he'd caught my message. "No problem. Happy to help. I'll just be going now."

He gathered the contents we'd dumped on the table in one arm and stuffed them into the book bag, giving us an awkward smile before he hurried off. The shadows swallowed him almost as soon as he reached them. Only Peter and I realized those shadows acted unnaturally, bending against the laws of physics and reaching out to envelope him several steps before he reached them.

Caroline's gaze sharpened on the sorcerer standing next to me. "Peter, right? What are you doing here?"

We both looked at Peter, caught between us, unaware at being put in the spotlight.

"I was with Aileen when she got the call. It sounded worrisome enough that I decided to tag along to see if there was anything I could do."

Heh, he'd stuck with the truth. Would wonders never cease?

"Isn't there a curfew for teenagers? What do your parents think of you being out at night?"

Peter stiffened next to me. I knew through painful experience he didn't like to be reminded of his apparent youth.

I said, wanting to keep the blow up I could feel brewing from happening, "His parents are friends of mine. They said he could be out as long as he's with me."

Peter glared at me, not liking my response. I shrugged. What was I going to do? He did look like a teenager. They did have curfews. I was only going along with Caroline's expectations. My story was reasonable and more importantly wouldn't raise questions we didn't want asked.

Caroline's mouth tilted down as her eyes narrowed with suspicion. "Wait, you brought a kid into a situation that you thought was dangerous?"

It was clear from the outrage in her voice what she thought of this.

"Hey, I'm not a kid. I'll have you know I'm—"

"How dangerous could it be? It's a library," I said, speaking over Peter. No way did I want him revealing his actual age.

"The better question is why you thought I was in danger in the first place?"

"Oh, I don't know, maybe because you called me out of the blue sounding stressed out of your mind and ordering me to get over here with no explanation as to why."

"That's it?" Caroline asked, her face looking pinched and weary. "That's very thin, Aileen. It makes me wonder what kind of life you're leading that your mind jumps automatically to the worst case scenario."

I held silent. Her words were closer to the truth than she knew.

Caroline rubbed her forehead. "I called you here because Mrs. Jackson passed away this afternoon. I thought you would want to know."

I took a deep breath at the unexpected words. Mrs. Jackson. She was young, only in her forties. She'd been our History teacher in high school. Somehow she'd managed to make a topic that was usually a snooze fest into something exciting. She was the reason Caroline went into the field she did. Hell, she was a driving factor in me doing as well as I did in high school. Her and Caroline anyway.

I hadn't heard she was sick.

"How did it happen?"

Now that I knew, I could see the grief behind Caroline's façade, a slight redness to her eyes and nose.

"They don't know. They said she just kind of dropped where she stood."

"That's too bad, but something I could be told over the phone. Why am I really here?"

Caroline shrugged one shoulder. "Maybe I just wanted to see you, considering you disappeared after I helped you last year."

"And you waited until now to make your move?" That wasn't the Caroline I knew. If she had really been upset at my vanishing act, she would have called me much sooner.

I hoped my parents hadn't put her up to this. I didn't think I could bite my tongue if they tried another intervention. There was only so much my patience could take.

"Yes, Aileen. I waited until now. I thought if I gave you space you might reach out again, but I see now that was a stupid hope." Anger throbbed in her voice.

"Yeah, freaking me out and making me think you're in danger is a good way to get my attention."

"You're something else. It's not me hiding under a rock."

"I'm doing no such thing. If you wanted to talk, you could call like a normal person."

"Why should I be the one to reach out? You're the one who ran off."

"Wow, you guys sound like an old married couple," Peter said, looking between the two of us.

My mouth clicked shut. We did. We always had. Our friendship was as much about sniping and fighting with each other as it was about supporting one another. When we were younger, my mom had called us sisters of the soul. We fought like sisters too. Or we used to before I decided to leave for the Army and she took exception to my decision.

When someone attacked one of us, the other was quick to retaliate against that person. We might fight between ourselves but give us an external threat, and we united into a terrifying team with few boundaries.

The cracks in our relationship were probably mostly my fault. She shared some of the blame, but I was the one who refused to make amends. After college, she knew exactly what she wanted to do and went about achieving her goals.

Me, I was as lost as ever, with no clue what came next. I figured the Army would help. And it did. At least until I became a vampire.

What I had a hard time getting past was the crap she'd said to me when I informed her of my decision. Everything from how irresponsible and thoughtless to how selfish and cowardly I was. Not really the reaction I thought I'd get. I'd expected her support, as I'd given her mine in every harebrained scheme she proposed over the years. It's probably why I was still angry with her. When the dust cleared, I was on my way to basic and we were no longer speaking. I didn't contact her again until last fall when I needed her help with research.

We both turned to look at Peter, no doubt thinking the same thing– that we had forgotten he was there.

"He looks older than the last time I saw him," Caroline noted. "Is that a beard?"

"I think it's his attempt at one."

She snorted. "It's pretty scraggly."

"There's nothing wrong with my beard. It's the first time I've grown one. The hair just needs to learn how to grow."

"More like it's decided to grow in patches," Caroline said.

My lips quirked and I reached over to tug on a patch. Peter ducked and batted my hand away.

"What do you think you're doing?"

"Ah, come on. What's the good of a beard if you can't tug on it?" I teased.

He flushed and put more space between us. "Talk to your friend," he ordered.

I wasn't sure, but I thought I heard him mutter under his breath, "Impossible vampire."

Caroline watched us. She didn't look happy. A part of me regretted that. As mad as she had made me, I didn't wish for her unhappiness.

"I'm sorry to hear about Mrs. Jackson," I said. "I know the two of you were close."

It would sting knowing she was gone.

"Thank you," Caroline said. Her tone made it clear the thank you was a grudging one.

I nodded. There was an awkward silence.

"Ok, if that's all, we'll be heading out." I tugged on Peter's arm. This was getting into deep emotional waters. I wanted to keep things simple, especially with all of the other craziness taking place.

"Wait, Aileen. Come on. Don't be like that." Caroline looked fragile, her normally assertive demeanor showing a glimpse of vulnerability. "We were best friends. Can't we get some of that back again?"

Despite my resolve to stay distant, to protect the people I used to care about from the craziness in my life, I found myself questioning that decision. I would have to have a heart of stone to crap all over her, especially with the loss of Mrs. Jackson weighing on her.

So I did something I had a feeling I'd eventually regret. I was going to offer an olive branch. Damn it.

"I couldn't have finished my job if I hadn't had your research. It was a big help."

There. That wasn't so bad. She knew I appreciated her. That should be enough.

I pulled Peter by the arm and started to head for the exit.

"I'm glad it could help, though I'm not sure how that information could help with a delivery."

"That's because she's not just a messenger," Peter volunteered.

I cuffed him lightly upside the head.

He ducked, holding his hand to the spot I'd tapped and giving me a scandalized look. I narrowed my eyes at him, my expression saying I didn't appreciate his help.

"I thought you were just a messenger. What else do you do?" Caroline asked.

I could see she was trying to rein in her imperiousness. She used a question rather than a demand. Maybe she had changed in my absence. Just a little.

I sighed and gave her a half answer. "Just about anything that a client needs."

"Like what?" For once she sounded interested, not censorious, just interested.

I decided to give her a little bit of what I was working on now. "Right now I'm trying to track a family that disappeared during the great flood in the 1900s."

"How's that going?" she asked.

This was the longest conversation we'd had since our parting of ways that hadn't ended in argument.

I wasn't willing to shut her down quite yet so I admitted. "It's not. They're ghosts after the flood. I haven't been able to find anything on them."

"Could be they died in the flood."

"I hope not or my client is not going to be happy."

"Why don't you give me some of your information?" Caroline suggested. "I know a couple of people who specialize in that area of history. They might be able to find records that you don't have access to."

I tapped a finger against my leg. It was a tempting offer. I'd hit a dead end that I wasn't sure I could overcome. Who better to find this family's lineage than a historian?

Did I want to chance putting her in danger? It was one of the reasons I let our argument stand rather than trying to reach out sooner.

"I would need something from you in return," Caroline said nonchalantly.

Ah ha. Now we got to why she was trying to be so helpful.

I didn't want to be curious, but I was. "And that would be?"

"You attend the gala with me at the Columbus Art Museum tomorrow night."

Uh no. I didn't go to galas. That wasn't my scene at all. Give me a dingy bar with a dart board or pool table any day of the week. It didn't even have to have the stuff to make fancy cocktails. If it had beer, I was good. Galas? Nope. Not going there. She'd have to find someone else to be bored out of their mind.

"I don't think so."

"Come on. I don't want to go alone again."

I scoffed. She was known as the ice queen for a reason. "Since when? You've never had a problem with it in the past."

She rolled her eyes. "Since one of the professors in the sociology department has taken to hitting on me. Normally I wouldn't care, but last time he kept popping up to ask me out when I was talking with the dean of my department."

"So bring a date. Not your friend."

She looked a tad uncomfortable. "I can't. The last three guys I asked said no."

Caroline was good looking in a girl next door turned sexy teacher sort of way. I couldn't imagine that many guys turning her down. One maybe, but three?

"You acted like you were doing them a favor didn't you?" I accused.

She had a way of speaking sometimes that made you want to rip her hair out by the root. Especially when she was doing something she didn't really want to. She'd start speaking as if the other person was a few cards short of a full deck. Then she'd make assumptions. Next thing you knew the person she was asking the favor of responded with extreme hostility. Even if they would have been perfectly happy giving her what she wanted in other circumstances.

I'd seen it happen when her mom told her she would either have a date to the prom or not be able to attend a summer space camp. She drove off four guys, two of whom planned to ask her out before she opened her mouth.

She gave a grimace. "Ok, yes. I did. In my defense, they should be flattered I even offered to go to the gala with them."

"I'm sure they appreciated that sentiment."

She shrugged. "I don't know why they wouldn't."

Of course she didn't.

"The answer is no."

I wasn't going to that gala.

She gave me a Cheshire cat smile. "I think you are."

I frowned at her. I did not like being on the receiving side of that smile. It usually meant I wasn't getting my way.

"Nope, I don't think so."

"I had an interesting conversation with your mom."

I stiffened. No. She wouldn't.

"I was kind of surprised when she said you agreed to go to a clinic where they helped people with addictions and PTSD. Imagine my surprise. Especially when I met you after you supposedly agreed to go."

Bitch.

"You wouldn't."

She arched an eyebrow. "Wouldn't I? You know how I dislike lying to parents."

Bullshit.

Of the two of us, she was the one who'd gotten away with the wildest of deceits. She used that innocent face to fool people into thinking she wasn't capable. I, for some reason, always aroused their suspicion. That's why she was always in charge of lying to our parents when we decided to stay out late or do something they wouldn't approve of.

She gave me a grin that said 'I've got you.'

"I, for one, think it's a great idea," Peter said, giving me a meaningful look.

I didn't understand. Did he have an itch on his face? What was he trying to signal? I gave him my lost in the sauce expression, the one I perfected on officers when they gave an order that made absolutely no sense.

He stomped on my foot and drove an elbow into my side.

Little brat. Fine. I got it. Not like I had a choice anyway. Not if I wanted to stay off my mom's radar.

"Guess we've got a deal. Your contact had better get me the information I need," I said, rubbing my side. The brat had sharp elbows.

Chapter Eight

I gave Caroline everything I dug up last night, including some of my thoughts on where to look next.

"One more thing," she said once she'd written everything down and verified she received my email. "I won't be starting until you fulfill your end of the deal."

"You do realize I have a time limit on this."

She shrugged. "I know you too well. If I give you what you want before you come through on your end, you'll figure out a way to wiggle out of it."

Hmph. She did know me. Damn it.

"Fine." I didn't have much choice. "But your source had better make some progress tomorrow while we're at this ridiculous dance."

"It's not a dance."

"Oh, whatever."

Dance, gala. I didn't care what this thing was. This source of hers had better come through for me.

I gave a head jerk to the sorcerer. "Let's go."

He shook his head. "I think I'll stay."

"I don't think so."

"I do." Under his breath where Caroline couldn't hear, he said, "And there's nothing you can do about it."

Want to bet.

"She's right. You should probably head out. Your parents will get worried if you're out too late. I'm planning to be here a few hours longer."

Heh.

I gave him a victorious look. See.

He sneered, careful to keep his head turned away from Caroline.

To her, he said, "I was actually thinking I could hang around for a little bit. I'm considering pursuing a career as a historian, but my parents wanted me to talk to an actual historian to make sure it's a feasible career option. Considering your concentration is in medieval manuscripts and you're a recipient of a Mellon Fellowship, Aileen volunteered to introduce me to you."

That sneaky little bastard.

Caroline seemed flattered by his attention. She'd always liked having her accomplishments listed. She was also rarely chosen as a mentor for potential students. She was too cold and precise. She tended to scare them off rather than encourage them to join.

"I'm sure that can wait until later," I said, seeing my control of the situation slipping.

"If you don't mind, I'll hang around and ask a few questions until my parents pick me up later." Peter gave her a shy grin. Even though I knew exactly what he was and how he was lying, I felt my heart strings being tugged on.

Caroline didn't stand a chance.

"I suppose it wouldn't hurt to show you a few things and answer some questions while you're here."

"Caroline!"

"What? You're the one who brought him here. If he says his parents will be ok with him hanging around until they pick him up, then there's no harm in it."

No harm except that he was a dangerous sorcerer capable of pretty much anything. Including convincing my obstinate friend of his apparent harmlessness.

I knew I'd regret letting him come with me. I was outmaneuvered and judging by Peter's superior smirk, he knew it. I couldn't object too strenuously or Caroline would get suspicious. I also couldn't tell her he was dangerous because she wouldn't believe me.

That left one option. If he was staying, I was staying.

I folded my arms. "So what do we look at first?"

Caroline looked at me like I'd grown a second head. "You plan to stay."

"Yup."

"You?"

"That's what I said."

"You, who can't stay still for more than five seconds."

"I've been in a library before. I helped you with research last time."

"Yeah, but that was only because you needed something. Last time you hung around the library, just because you wanted to keep me company, you almost burned it down because you got bored."

That was an exaggeration. I'd only singed a few tables and caused a little bit of smoke damage.

I opened my mouth to defend myself.

She held up a hand. "No, you're not staying. Yes, he is. You said you had things to do. Go do them. We'll be fine here."

"But—"

She made a shooing motion, then compounded the insult by actually saying, "Shoo."

The sorcerer grinned and started making the same motion.

I was the big bad vampire, damn it. At least one of them should be wary of pissing me off.

I found myself standing on the sidewalk outside the library. Evidently I could be shooed away like a recalcitrant sheep.

I dug in my pockets for my phone and paused at the feel of cool metal against my fingers. Grasping that metal, I pulled it out of my pocket and gave a wicked smile.

Well, wasn't that nice? The sorcerer left his keys with me. I had no problem taking advantage and appropriating his vehicle for the evening. I might even put a few dents in it just to vent some of my anger at being outmaneuvered.

I pulled out my phone and brought up a few jobs Jerry had thrown me, scanning until I found what I was looking for.

Time for the other part of my plan for the night, delivering some ingredients to a witch.

*   *   *

The package was on the bench seat like always. Goodale Park was not as empty as you would assume this late at night. A small group of teens or twenty somethings gathered at one end and there was more than one homeless person sleeping under the big trees.

I grabbed the package and stuffed it into my messenger bag. It was no bigger than a small postal box so it fit easily. I left a piece of licorice in its place.

Technically, I didn't have to as the package's owner was the one to request my service but it never hurt to court favor with the fae. They loved candy.

The package's destination was only a few blocks from here, but I still headed to the car. This area got kind of dicey after dark on the human side, which wasn't that much of a concern since it took more than a bullet or knife wound to kill me. The more concerning part was that it was on the edge of vampire territory, and after my run in with Elinor and her lackeys at the club, I was hoping to avoid anything to do with vampires for a few days.

For once there was parking in front of the Short North tea shop that was my destination. The Short North was considered the art district of the city and had galleries lining the small strip on High Street. Over the years it had transformed into a mecca for trendy shops that attracted huge crowds on the first Saturday of the month for the gallery hop. It was the only night of the month where all of the shops, galleries, restaurants and bars were open late. In summer, you practically had to murder someone to get a parking spot.

Being a Tuesday, I was able to secure a spot with a minimum of hardship.

The name of the tea shop, Tranquility, was written in calligraphy above the door. It had photos of tea harvesting on the walls and traditional Japanese tea pots in display cases. It also had an eco-friendly thing going for it. It was exactly the type of place I'd imagine a witch owning.

A number of the seats were full of women sipping tea and chatting among themselves. Pretty good for a Tuesday night.

"I'm sorry, we're closed," a pretty woman with dreads told me.

My eyes went to the women sipping tea.

Seeing where my gaze went, the woman volunteered, "They're just finishing up. We stopped serving fifteen minutes ago."

Did they now?

One of those tables had a plate of untouched scones that smelled like they were straight out of the oven.

"That's ok. I'm not here for tea," I said.

How they wanted to run their business was up to them. Perhaps it was a private party or maybe they were friends of the owner.

Her face was politely inquiring.

I pulled out my cell phone and tapped on the screen. There it was. "I'm looking for a Sarah Temper."

The polite expression dropped from her face, leaving something fierce staring back at me.

Now it was my turn to smile politely.

"Who wants to know?" a woman sitting near the back asked. Her brown hair was piled in curls high on her head and had a gold ribbon threading through it. She looked like one of those Greek sculptures.

The group went from a bunch of soccer moms discussing the kiddos to one ready to act with the violence of a mother bear when her cubs are threatened. Power crackled through the air.

I kept my polite smile, though it was difficult. I'd been on the receiving end of similar power one too many times.

"I have a package from Hermes for her."

The woman who'd asked rose and glided toward me. Even her dress had that Grecian theme going for it as it fluttered behind her.

"I'll take that."

I gave her a sideways look, considering my options. If she wasn't Sarah, it was going to get awkward. On the other hand, I suspected she was a witch who could hex me or do something equally unsavory. Choices, choices.

Really there was only one choice. I pulled out my phone and hit the app for Hermes, navigating to the acknowledgement screen. If she wasn't Sarah, the screen would flash red and the shit would hit the metaphorical fan. For her at least. I'd heard more than one account of what happened when someone other than the intended recipient tried to receive a package. Those stories had not sounded pretty.

The app had some magical component to be able to recognize the real recipient. Someone tried to explain it one time, and I tuned them out before they could get too far into their explanation. Kind of like I had with my physics teacher once she started going on about electricity and electrons. To me, telephones were just as magical as real magic because I had no clue how they could send a voice out into the ether and have another device pick that voice up and make it sound like an actual person speaking.

If these people were really witches, they would know the consequences of committing fraud with a Hermes courier. Everyone knew. Though that didn't mean a few idiots wouldn't try to game the system.

I prepared to take off at the first sign of trouble. I had a feeling I'd be the one blamed if this woman got herself turned inside out, even if she was the one who tried to lie about who she was.

I could be wrong. Making mountains out of mole hills. They all seemed to act like she was their leader or at least someone important. Maybe she was Sarah Temper.

I held out the phone as she approached. She reached out to press her thumb against the pad.

"That's enough, Nadine." A woman spoke from the back of the

store. "She is who she says she is."

My eyes were drawn to the blonde woman who looked like a sorority coed enjoying a cup of tea late at night. Miriam. I didn't know if I was relieved that she had stepped in or if I wanted to drop everything and head for the door.

She was a witch. A powerful one. I still wasn't convinced she hadn't tried to kill me last fall. Her apprentice might have laid the trap, but she could very well have known and let it go for her own reasons.

I didn't trust her, but I couldn't flee either because of the damn penalty clause built into the delivery contract. Knowing witches, it probably had something to do with being used for parts. I might not survive whatever it was they intended to take out of me if I didn't make my delivery.

Nadine, the woman dressed like a throwback to the ancient Greeks, gave a small nod to Miriam and stepped back.

"Come along, Aileen. The person you want is through here," Miriam said, before turning into a back room.

Great, heading off alone with a person who may or may not have tried to kill me. This would end well.

Not seeing another option, I followed.

The back room was just a room. An office where the owner could pay bills or whatever a tea shop owner did, but still just an office.

Judging by the way Miriam watched me, it wasn't always just an office. Last year I saw through some of her enchantments to what she kept hidden. Either whatever boost in power the sorcerer's mark had given me was gone or this place's enchantments were better.

Miriam's face was thoughtful as she watched my lack of surprise.

An old woman with skin the color of an aged oak watched me with ancient eyes that were almost milky. I'd guess cataracts, but I didn't know if witches suffered from human ailments. Her hair was piled into a graying bun at the back of her head. Her hands were knobby and covered in raised veins.

"I hear you have a package for me." In contrast to her appearance, her voice was smooth and lyrical, not even a hint of her apparent age coming through.

"Sarah Temper?"

She inclined her head, the movement that of a queen bestowing acknowledgement on a subject.

I held out the phone, holding my breath as she pressed her finger onto the screen. Green. This was Sarah Temper.

"This was good work, Miriam," Sarah observed, her gaze on the phone but seeming to look past it as if she could see something that the rest of us couldn't. "I'd guess some of your best."

"Thank you, elder." Miriam's tone was deferential, as was the way she kept her gaze downcast as if she revered the person before me.

Elder? I was willing to bet this woman was a major player in the community. This could be good or bad. She would probably have the information I needed, but she could also swat me down with such strength I might not get back up again.

"You're the clanless vampire running around getting into all sorts of trouble," Sarah said, her gaze coming to rest on me. Her eyes did that unfocused thing as if she was seeing pieces of me that weren't normally visible.

A chill ran down my back.

This person could be dangerous. Perhaps more than any I've faced before.

My body instinctually braced for fight or flight as adrenaline flooded my system. Blood pumped harder, my vision sharpened until everything seemed to come at me in ultra-high definition. My body temperature rose sharply.

For most people, their flight or fight response causes them to freeze or to flail about uselessly. Once upon a time that instinct is what kept our ancestors alive and kicking. Now after thousands of years of civilized living that instinct is often an obstacle. Courtesy of the U.S. Army, I've been trained to act through it. To not let it take control and shut me down.

Over the last few years, this training has been reinforced. So instead of reacting with unwarranted aggression or fear as my body wanted me to, I took a deep breath and kept my natural instincts under control.

"You have a question for me. What is it?" Sarah gave a slight smile as if she knew what had just happened and my lack of response amused her.

Yup. Dangerous. Very dangerous.

My gaze darted from her to Miriam, who watched with an inscrutable expression. There was no help or guidance from that quarter, not that I expected there to be.

"There have been some odd things going on around town," I finally said. It wasn't the reason I was here, but I had a feeling leading with that would be better than just blurting out my real question. I've learned to trust my feelings since becoming a vampire. "Would you know anything about them?"

She tilted her head as if I'd surprised her. I got the feeling that wasn't the question she'd been expecting. Made sense. I hadn't expected to ask it.

"There are many odd things going on right now. You will need to elaborate."

Now I wanted to know more about the odd things she was talking about.

I needed to stay on track.

"Several people have disappeared after a bout of paralysis followed by raving madness."

"Ah, that odd happening."

I fought my impatience. I had a feeling that showing her any attitude would not end well for me.

"Why are you interested?" Miriam asked from her corner.

I blinked at her. That was a good question.

I shrugged. "Just curious. I've run across a couple of the victims and wanted to make sure whatever this is doesn't get any worse."

Sarah smiled, her face amused and full of knowledge gleaned from years, perhaps centuries, of experience. "You tell the truth or some version of it, but not your whole truth, I suspect."

I shrugged again, not wanting to examine my motivations any further. Right now I was curious, that's all they needed to know.

I turned the question back on them. "What does my reasons have to do with anything?"

Suddenly Sarah's expression made her seem ancient, as if she'd seen the passing of countless ages and had distilled that knowledge down into one expression. "The reason makes all the difference."

Reason, huh? I didn't have a reason for wanting to know. At least not one that made sense and could be shared with them.

"Just call me a concerned citizen."

That might work. It sounded good at least.

Miriam's smile was wry. "Somehow I think it's a little more than that."

I shrugged. It was and it wasn't. I couldn't help but remember the sphinx's desperation when it feared I was the monster. Something about that experience didn't sit well. If I could ask a few questions and get some answers for him, it cost me little and would mean a world of difference to the sphinx.

Sarah's gaze was assessing as she cataloged my features. I wondered what she saw when she looked at me. Did she see the monster that was sometimes closer to the surface than I'd like? Or did I look like a normal twenty six year old whose life hadn't turned out the way she planned? One of the boomerang generation? Someone's whose life didn't live up to its promise?

I stared back, keeping my thoughts to myself and my expression polite.

She cackled, her laugh sounded like sandpaper.

"Very well, little vampire. I've heard of the sowing."

The sowing? I'd never heard that term.

Sarah sighed, seeing the confusion on my face. "You know so little of our world. It should not be that way."

I fought the urge to roll my eyes. Another vote for the vampires conscripting me into one of their clans.

"It is what it is," I said, some impatience threading through my voice despite my best efforts. "I've got to live with the world as it is, not wish for a change that is never coming. You mentioned the sowing. What is that?"

Miriam and Sarah shared a long look. It felt as if they were having an entire conversation just by a slight shift of expression.

I let them have their argument and sat back, watching, cataloging their communication cues. I imagined I could almost hear the conversation they were having.

Sarah's tightly pressed lips said 'that information is on a need to know basis.'

Miriam's eyebrows lowered seeming to say, 'I think we're past that don't you?'

Sarah flared her nostrils, clearly saying, 'We're never past that.'

Miriam blinked. I took that to mean, 'do what you want. You always do.'

Sarah focused back on me, their conversation on pause for now.

"How much experience have you had with demons?"

I blinked, not sure I had heard her correctly.

"Can you repeat that?"

She sighed, looking at me with all the patience of a teacher with a student who wasn't particularly bright.

"You heard right the first time."

I still wanted her to repeat it.

She huffed at me, a sharp burst of sound.

"A demon. What do you know?"

"Uh. Demon as in the opposite of an angel? The ones that come from hell. That demon?"

I'd always assumed those were myth. Kind of like angels. Or if not myths, something I would never ever encounter.

If she said it was a demon causing this, I was out. Out of the city. Out of the state. Possibly out of the country. I wasn't dealing with a demon. No how, no way. Especially if said demon could make off with my not so mortal soul.

"Those are human concepts meant to reflect their concept of good and evil."

Oh good. I've seen a lot of weird things in this world. I don't think I wanted to see a human's concept of a demon. Some things are just not meant to be experienced or seen.

"Angels are just as vicious as demons," Miriam inserted.

Ah ha. That cleared things up.

"So you're saying a demon like what's in the bible has come to Columbus to paralyze people with fear?" I said, not sure I could say that without bursting into laughter.

"Of course not," Sarah said in a crisp voice. "That would be nearly impossible. A demon hasn't walked the earth in nearly one thousand years. If one did, it would make its presence felt with more than a few victims here and there."

Oh that sounded much better. Not.

"Then it's not a demon?" I wasn't sure what they were trying to tell me.

"Demons need to be summoned, but even then they're mostly non-corporeal. In history, only a handful have been recorded as taking a physical body on this plane of existence. That's much harder for them."

Despite my initial disbelief, I found myself interested in the conversation. This was the kind of stuff I'd been hoping the book could teach me.

"If they can't take form, then why are there so many stories in human religion?" I asked.

Sarah's bony shoulder moved up and down in a shrug. "Humans fear many things and tend to embellish the smallest things, creating monsters where shadows exist."

I conceded the point. We tended to vilify that which we didn't understand. We also had a habit of seeing fire where it didn't exist.

"Ok, so how does this relate to what's happening now?"

"Demons can't take form here, but they can still make deals."

The penny dropped.

"You think whoever's doing this made a deal with a demon."

Then why was it just causing fear and paralyzing its victims then leaving them there only to return once they'd reawakened. It didn't make sense.

Unless some of those affected weren't the intended victims. Maybe they just got too close to this demon and got caught in the magical crossfire. It would explain why some were left where they stood.

Still didn't explain why whatever this is then summoned the affected to it once they came unstuck.

The two watched me as I puzzled this out.

Sarah leaned back. "You'll have to give up a favor if you want anything more."

Oh no. I wasn't getting sucked back into that. The last favor I'd given Miriam had resulted in Angela escaping the consequences of using the draugr as a weapon of mass destruction. Any favor I gave either of these two would just come back to bite me on the ass.

They had at least pointed me in the right direction. I would just have to muddle through it from here.

"Would you like to discuss why you're really here?" Sarah asked with a knowing gaze.

I stilled. That was the second time she'd acted like she knew my real purpose. Either she was incredibly adept at reading body language or she really did know why I was here. I wasn't sure which would be worse for me. Though if it was the second, I had to wonder how she knew so much about my business.

I gave her a sharp smile, the one I'd perfected when a guy did that mansplaining thing that used to drive me crazy when I was younger.

"I have a friend with a problem. He thinks he was hexed at some point in the distant past. Since I occasionally do jobs for your faction, he thought I might know someone who could tell him how to lift a hex."

Sarah's dark eyes remained focused on me with a hawk like intensity. I had a feeling I wasn't fooling her, but that was alright. I didn't need to. She just needed to give me a hint.

"There are two ways to lift a hex. One is to find the witch who placed the hex and have her lift it. The second would be to locate a descendant to help him break it."

"How will having a descendant help?" I wanted to be very clear on what would happen to the descendant.

She gave me a dark smile. "A descendant carries his blood and can be used to circumvent the curse."

"How?"

"Blood recognizes blood. If your friend was to attempt to turn someone who shares the same bloodline as him, he might be able to circumvent the hex. This of course depends on how diluted the bloodline has become. If the descendant is too far removed from the family tree, the hex will kick in and they will die."

I fought the urge to growl. Even if I found this descendant, how could I hand them over to Thomas knowing exactly how dangerous he was?

"You guys don't have a default spell that could remove it?"

"Not for one as powerful as what is on your friend."

Sarah's peaceful smile told me she knew exactly why I was here. I hadn't fooled her at all with my questions about the victims.

"Don't suppose you could tell me who placed the hex."

"Not without—"

"Owing you a favor. Yeah, yeah."

Same song, different dance.

This wasn't worth owing the witches a favor. Especially not one with Sarah's obvious power.

Miriam's face was carefully blank as she watched the two of us. She'd never been particularly expressive in our interactions, but there had been something. Even if it was only amusement at my expense. It made me wonder what she thought of this conversation, or if she might have more to add if Sarah wasn't around.

It left me with something to think about. Perhaps this avenue wasn't as much of a dead end as I thought.

"This has been fun, but I have other things to do tonight."

I stood and adjusted my bag.

"Before you go, please try some of our tea. It's new. Just arrived." Sarah gestured to the table where I hadn't noticed three cups of steaming tea.

I controlled my expression of disgust. Tea. Not my favorite drink. I'd liked it well enough as a human but after my transition to vampire I couldn't stand the stuff. It tasted odd, like lost opportunities. Or maybe that was just the taste of pond water.

I wanted to say no. It always seemed like the taste of tea lingered hours after it was long gone. From the implacable expression on Sarah's face, I had a feeling it wouldn't go over well if I refused.

I gave her a strained smile and picked up one of the cups. The smell made my eyes water. It smelled like no tea I'd ever tasted, and that was not a compliment. The closest I could get to describing it was a cross between a sewer and unwashed socks. Not something I would put in my body if I had my preference.

Before I could talk myself out of it, I took a large gulp, trying not to taste it. Tea was meant to be sipped, not chugged like beer at a frat party. The taste made the promise of pain worth it as the heat burned the roof of my mouth and tongue. I didn't slow down, wanting it gone.

When the cup was empty, I set it down.

Why would anyone want to drink something so disgusting? It felt like my insides were trying to purge what I'd just put in my system. My stomach roiled, triggering my gag reflex. I kept the tea down by sheer dent of will, but it was a close thing.

Sarah held her cup in front of her, arching an imperious eyebrow at my empty cup. I mentally shrugged. I drank the damn thing. She'd just have to deal with the how.

She breathed in the steam before taking a sip.

My taste buds quivered in sympathy.

I noticed Miriam hadn't picked up her cup yet. She watched me with an assessing gaze. In fact, both of them watched me intently as if they were expecting something any moment now. I shifted uneasily. It occurred to me that they might have slipped something in the tea and stupid me just gulped the entire thing like it was the first liquid I'd tasted in days. If it was poisoned, I got a full dose.

When I continued to feel fine, I relaxed slightly. If they meant harm to me, I'd have felt something by now. Right?

"Interesting," Sarah said, her mouth half hidden by her uplifted cup of tea.

"Very," Miriam said, her eyes intense on me. Her tone said she wasn't entirely pleased with this assessment, whatever it was.

They were beginning to freak me out. It was time to go. "Thank you for the tea, but I'm going to be late if I stay any longer."

When I reached the door, Sarah said, "If you change your mind about that favor, you know where to find us."

I gave the two of them an uneasy look, noting how Sarah seemed like she was a cat who had cornered the canary. Miriam was stoic, as if she was just marking time until she could make her move.

I gave them a nod and walked out. Once again I was the center of attention as I made my way to the exit.

I wasted no time heading for Peter's car, walking the short block to where I'd parked.

The car was gone. The space it had been in featured a small, beat up bike. I stepped closer. My bike.

A note was attached to the handlebars.

Next time you take my car, I will run over your bike before returning it. – P

I crumbled up the note and frowned. The car had been nice while it lasted, but it looked like I was pedaling from here on out.

I had no set destination in mind so I just followed the road, taking turns when needed as I went over the conversation.

I got the feeling Sarah was extremely powerful. The scary part about that was I couldn't feel much power wafting off her. Nothing more than a mildly psychic human might present. She seemed like any other sweet grandmother. My gut told me she was anything but.

For now I was saved from having to deal with her again. Miriam had looked like she had something to say. I just needed to get her on her own to get it out of her.

I had no intention of ever owing Sarah a favor, but maybe I didn't have to. This wasn't my problem. It was a job. Any favor owed shouldn't come from me, but from the client. It was an interesting idea. One I would have to ask Liam to put before Thomas. If he wanted this problem solved bad enough, he would deal. Then I would just have to figure out if it was possible.

I'd save that option if Miriam didn't pan out and if Caroline came up with nothing. It would be my backup plan to the backup plan.

That settled, I allowed myself to enjoy the night as I pedaled just to feel the breeze in my hair.

Chapter Nine

It was rare for me to get time to just relax. Usually I spent my time working and surviving.

The road tilted and I leaned forward, picking up speed as I started down the hill. Faster, faster, repeated like a mantra in my head. When I was a kid, I believed if I could just pedal fast enough I could actually leave the ground and fly for a time.

The bike bounced under me as the wheel hit a series of potholes, bringing me out of that fantasy fairly quickly.

A blur darted in front of me. I braked hard and jerked the handlebars to the side, not quite dodging as I clipped the creature. A yelp followed as I slid, nearly going over the handle bars.

I climbed off the bike, hoping I hadn't killed the animal.

I turned back and froze. My heart climbed into my throat and took up residence there, beating out a tattoo of panic.

A wolf stared back at me, an intelligence in its eyes that had nothing in common with an animal. Werewolf. I'd bet a month's paycheck on it. I'd only seen a werewolf in its wolfy state twice, but this looked a lot like those.

It was big. Bigger than any dog I've ever seen, its head nearly reaching my chest. Its body was graceful and lean, a lethal power to it that made you realize how your ancestors must have felt confronted by its wolf cousin, before civilization made such encounters rare. It had a wild, untamed air that no dog, even a feral one, could hope to replicate.

Its ears were pricked forward, which I hoped meant it wasn't getting ready to pounce and tear my throat out. The wolf had reddish brown hair over most of its body and darker markings around its face and legs.

It was beautiful, a force of nature that could kill as easily as I breathed, perhaps more fascinating because of it.

We shared a moment that seemed to stretch through time, never ending, as I waited for it to decide on its course of action. I'd helped Brax, its Alpha, last year but that was no guarantee it wouldn't rip my throat out for nearly running over it.

I noticed its back leg was pulled up under it. Looks like I hadn't imagined that yelp.

"I can help you if you change back," I told it.

I had no intention of approaching those sharp teeth. A normal wolf's bite has twice the strength of a German Shepherds. A werewolf's bite is even stronger. It could rip my arm off, and I had no idea if my vampire regeneration was strong enough to fix a wound like that.

The wolf dipped its head at me and limped away.

Guess it didn't want help.

I watched it disappear into the night, half expecting it to change its mind and come flying out of the shadows.

Strange that it was running in the city. This bike path was near the river and wasn't busy this time of night, but I knew the wolves owned a rather large stretch of territory southeast of the city where they could run and not worry about humans panicking and calling animal control.

It made me wonder if Brax knew his wolves were running around the city in their fur. It seemed strange that it still needed to limp away. I thought werewolf healing was better than mine. Brax and the other wolves I'd seen injured healed almost magically before my eyes. This wolf didn't seem to have that same advantage.

Maybe it was new to the werewolf world, much like I was to the vampire one. That could explain some things like the sluggish healing and running somewhere that was normally off limits to werewolves.

I didn't like the idea of a new wolf running this close to humans. If this one was new, it might not have obtained the control needed not to infect another human.

Brax should probably be informed. Fitting that I'd be the one having to report the wolf, especially since I was convinced I didn't need anyone holding the end of my leash. Now that the shoe was on the other foot I was aware of the irony, but I didn't think I could live with someone else's life being turned upside down because I hadn't take the time to make sure a wolf didn't get all bitey on them.

I could follow the wolf to make sure it didn't bother any human. From a safe distance of course. It would absolve me of any guilt and let me see what it was up to if it had other intentions besides a night run.

There went my evening.

I turned the bike and pedaled after it, keeping my eyes peeled for any movement. If I couldn't find it, I'd have to go with option one where I reported it to Brax.

This would have been easier if I hadn't wasted time thinking about what to do. Werewolves were fast. Faster than I was on this bike. It could be anywhere by now.

I sped over the trail, growing more convinced I'd missed my opportunity when I spotted a small movement near the trees on the side of the path. I squinted. The reddish colored wolf loped toward a culvert and disappeared.

I pedaled faster, stopping at the edge. There was no way I could get the bike down the steep drop and across the rocks and boulders littering the bottom without risking breaking my neck. I'd have to leave it behind.

I threw my leg over and set the bike in the bushes. There was no time to get the chain and lock it to a tree. I had already lost sight of the wolf again.

I hid it as best as I could before ducking down the side of the culvert and splashing through the water pooled at the bottom. My gaze was constantly moving, checking the shadows and my periphery. The werewolf probably knew I was coming, given its hearing while in wolf form was a hundred times better than mine, but I didn't want to walk right into an ambush.

There was probably a way to go all ninja vampire and follow it without making enough noise to announce a battalion's presence, but I didn't have those skills. Maybe if I had joined a clan I would have been able to move a little more quietly but all I had was my human military training.

I cursed silently to myself at the light swish my feet made as I picked my way through the water. This was a bad idea. I should have chosen option one. Brax could have accepted any possible consequences for his wolf's midnight run. In fact, he should shoulder the responsibility. He was the alpha.

The only comfort I had was that a human would probably not be wandering around down here. The only exception might be a homeless person who had decided to camp beside the river, but most of the homeless tended to stay closer to the downtown area.

A murmur reached me from ahead. I paused. Guess I had spoken too soon. Looks like someone was out here after all.

Could be the wolf. It could have decided to change back to human. I shook my head. Why would it choose to change back here, in the middle of some bushes, instead of somewhere convenient? Maybe somewhere that had grass which would be a little more comfortable on human feet.

I softened my footsteps, being careful to pick places that would allow me to creep as silently as I was capable of, though with my vampire hearing each step sounded painfully loud.

Light flickered in the darkness. It was steady, bobbing up and down slightly as if someone was walking with one of those lanterns you took on camping trips.

I paused, making sure the light wasn't moving in my direction, before carefully slipping past clinging branches. At one point I had to drop and crawl as the underbrush grew too dense to walk. At least not without making a racket fit to announce my presence to any and every one.

The bobbing light paused and then lowered, as if someone had set the lantern down. Now I was curious what anyone would be doing out here at night. Columbus didn't have many areas overgrown like this, but every once in a while I happened on a small slice of woods that hid a surprising amount of wildlife, including deer, skunks, and ground hogs.

It wasn't surprising this one paralleled a popular bike path. My hearing picked up the gentle gurgle of the river so we must be close to that as well.

What was surprising was that a human would venture out here in the dead of night. It didn't seem like safe behavior in a day and age where parents wouldn't even let their kids walk to the park across the street without adult company.

I edged to a spot where I could see.

I blinked. The lamp wasn't a lamp so much as a—well I didn't know what to call it—maybe a sphere. A white sphere of light the size of my head hovering right above the grass.

So, not a human. That answered the question of what someone would be doing out here.

It wasn't just one person either. There were a handful gathered in the clearing, faces wiped clean of emotion as they stared sightlessly into the distance. It was like a bunch of sleepwalkers had somehow managed to walk in the same direction and then stop in the same little clearing.

Something told me magic played a big part in whatever this was.

Even from here I could tell some of the people weren't human. One looked like a naiad, essentially a water sprite that usually resided in a body of water like a river or a lake. I didn't even know naiads could leave their waters. I kind of thought they would dry up and suffocate like a fish.

This one's hair had whatever the freshwater equivalent of seaweed was threaded through it, and her skin was a brownish green. She wore no clothes and her limbs were a little less human than I was used to seeing, way longer and ending in webbed hands.

A few in the gathering looked entirely human and my only clue that they weren't was the company they kept.

There was also a figure, the shortest in the group with the hood of his sweatshirt up to hide his face from view.

A reddish brown wolf trotted into the clearing and sat down at the hooded person's feet like a well-trained dog.

"Change." The voice whispered through the leaves, dry and crackling, like sandpaper against wood. I hated the sound of sandpaper. My ears nearly turned themselves inside out whenever I heard the scrape and slide of it. The voice gave me that same cringe worthy feeling. The kind that sent my skin trying to crawl down my back to get away.

The wolf's fur peeled back and the sound of bones cracking and popping as the skeleton reshaped itself made my body twinge in sympathy. This wasn't the graceful transition I'd seen from Brax. This was painful and long and hideous.

For once I was grateful fate had decided to make me one of the fanged instead of a shapeshifter. Going through that at least once a month, and probably more, would have been enough to drive me insane. It was a wonder there weren't pain crazed wolves running amok

A woman with wild hair knelt at the hooded man's feet, her head bowed and her body clenched against the pain.

"Stand."

She unfolded, wobbling on her feet.

Sondra.

What was she doing here?

The red in the wolf's coat made sense now. Her hair had a reddish tint to it as it curled around her face in a mane of tangles.

Her face was as blank and expressionless as the rest of those in the clearing. Something that struck me as unnatural. Her face always had an intense alertness to it as if she was just waiting to act. The feral, untamed air she usually carried with her was muted, almost gone beneath that blankness. Her face had less expression in it than some dolls I'd seen, as if someone had molded a person into flesh and bone but forgot to include the soul.

One of the men in the clearing suddenly started hissing, the sound similar to what a very pissed off cat sounds like. A pair of fangs glinted from his mouth as the sound rose and fell.

"Quiet."

The tangled snarl cut off as if someone had muted the volume. The man's throat continued to work as though he was still trying to hiss, though no sound emerged.

This was wrong, whatever this was.

Sondra standing next to a vampire and a naiad. It was almost as if they were emotionless zombies being compelled to do the hooded person's bidding.

This city kept getting stranger and stranger.

I settled down to watch, knowing the chances of me sneaking out of here undiscovered were very small. The only reason I could think that I'd made it this close was that the compulsion, as I was calling it, interfered or disrupted the spooks' senses. Or maybe Sondra knew I was here on some level and the hooded person just failed to ask about it, secure in their assumption that this was a secret meeting.

It would have been if not for my run in with Sondra, the wolf on the bike path.

It made me question how much of that run in had been coincidence and how much of it had been her rebelling from this person's compulsion. As a wolf she would have heard my bike coming from miles away. Even under a compulsion she should have been able to avoid getting hit and drawing my notice.

Or maybe not and I was assigning motivations that weren't there.

It made me wonder if it had anything to do with the disappearances in the city. Whether I was looking at the reason for those disappearances. My first instinct said yes, but there were many things in this world I didn't understand. It could be something else.

My surveillance would have been boring if not for my rather intense fear of discovery. As far as I could see the group just stood around, not speaking. The only one who occasionally moved was the hooded man as he muttered to himself and occasionally referred to a notebook he pulled out of his pocket.

I remained motionless as he did, fighting the urge to shift my weight from one leg to another. Any movement could draw attention my way.

The puppet master held his hands out and shouted a word. Black smoke drifted out of him, threading its way to each of the people in the clearing, searching and feeling each of the victims.

I tensed as one of them made a sound. A groan of pain was wrenched out of him. The smoke spun, demonstrating an almost sentient alertness. Its tendrils withdrew from the other puppets and converged on the man who groaned.

He was one of the ones who looked human, with sandy brown hair and bland features. They didn't look bland now as they twisted in agony. Before my eyes, the man appeared to age as the smoke pulsed around him.

I wanted to fly forward, to help, but I didn't. I stayed pinned to my spot, shaking with fear and disgust. My logical self knew acting now would be fool hardy and beyond dangerous. I had no idea what that smoke was, but given the witches assumptions, I was guessing it was a demon. The non-corporeal type. I knew next to nothing about how to fight it or get it to stop doing whatever it was doing.

My other self, the one who ran on emotion and feelings, the one who was inspired to join the Army so I could serve my country, hated staying where I was. Loathed knowing that I was going to save myself even as I watched a demon suck that man down like a slurpy straw.

The demon finished, its shadows unwrapping from the man as he sagged onto his knees looking like he'd had something vital yanked out of him.

The smoke meandered back to its host, its movement lazy and indolent now that it had fed. It coated the man and gradually melded into his skin.

The man gestured and the group broke apart, leaving only Sondra and the hooded man. He gestured sharply and she fell to the ground with a sharp cry, her shift repeating in reverse and no less painful looking.

When the process was complete, the wolf lay panting on the ground as the hooded man knelt by her side. He bent down and even with my vampire hearing I couldn't hear a word he whispered to her.

He stood and walked out of the clearing. The wolf struggled to its feet, wobbling as it headed in the opposite direction.

Even when there was nobody left, I waited, not wanting to chance someone returning for something they forgot. Not that I thought the puppets were likely to even remember or care if they had forgotten something, but the hooded man might have and that was enough to keep me pinned in place.

I did not want that black smoke touching me. Some primal instinct warned that it would not be a good thing to be caught in its grasp.

After what I felt was an eternity, but was likely only twenty minutes, I shifted and took a step back, wanting out of there.

It didn't take long to make my way back to the bike. I kept as quiet as I could in case any of the people from the clearing were hanging around.

Grabbing the bike from where I had stashed it, I took off wanting to put as much distance between myself and this place as possible.

I didn't know what I had witnessed, but I had a sinking feeling that if the hooded man caught me, I'd be dead before I could open my mouth to say 'fancy running into you here.'

*　*　*

I waited until I was several blocks from the bike path before pulling out my phone and dialing the number I'd saved as Brax's last year.

The phone rang. I wanted this report done and over with so I could find my way home. Whatever that was had freaked me out, and I wanted to be somewhere enclosed where I could see anything that approached. Somewhere I viewed as safe.

"Hello," a young male's voice said. I didn't recognize it.

"Is Brax there?"

"Who's calling?"

I switched the phone to the other hand as I leaned into the corner before righting the bike again. The bike and I coasted down the deserted street.

"It's Aileen."

"Don't know you."

I gritted my teeth. Figures he'd have someone answering his phone for him and screening his calls.

"He does. Please give him the phone. I have information he needs."

I wasn't too sure about that, but I figured he'd want to know one of his wolves was running around like a puppet with that hooded man controlling their strings. Sondra had struck me as being in his inner circle. If it was my pack, I would want to know.

"How about you give me the information and I'll pass it along."

I debated that, tempted. It would be so easy to pass off the responsibility. I could head back home or make progress on the job Liam had given me.

Something stopped me. Perhaps it was the memory of last year when one of Brax's own pack plotted for his death, or maybe it was the memory of Sondra asking me to keep her updated on anything strange.

I didn't know if the hooded man had compelled anyone else or if he could compel them to act normal at times. Whatever the reason, I needed to give this message to Brax and only Brax. Anything else would nag at me.

"This isn't the kind of information passed through an intermediary."

"Then I guess Brax won't get that information."

"Look, just tell Brax to call Aileen. He'll know who you're talking about."

There was a snort of disbelief. "Right. I'll get right on that."

There was a click and then a dial tone sounded in my ear.

I held out the phone looking at it with disbelief. He did not just hang up on me. What kind of message taker was that? This was an emergency or at least had the possibility of being one. This seemed like a crappy way of managing your phone calls.

I somehow doubted he planned to let Brax know I needed to speak with him, which left me back at square one.

I took a sharp right and then wound my way through another street until I pointed my bike in the opposite direction.

I'd just have to track Brax down myself. He was going to get an earful about his phone management when I finally caught up to him.

*　　*　　*

Lou's Bar was harder to find this time. I probably wouldn't have managed it if I hadn't caught sight of a man I remembered from my last visit, leaving an unassuming building and heading to his car.

They must have increased the strength of their 'don't look here' spell. Even knowing it was there my eye kept wanting to skip over it.

Located in an area where Clintonville ended and Worthington started, the bar was in that transitional border that wasn't quite nice enough to fit into either. The area had improved in recent years from the sort you wouldn't be caught outdoors in after dark to one where you needed to keep your eyes on your valuables and walk quickly.

It should be a popular waterhole with the locals, but I imagined the spell kept anyone who wasn't a wolf from wandering in and sitting down.

Through several quick glances, where I had to fight against turning away the whole time, I noticed the lit sign above the door had the name Lou's Bar highlighted. This was definitely the place.

On my last visit, there had been two wolves guarding the door against any normal who somehow got past the spell.

I didn't see anybody standing there tonight, but that didn't mean they weren't there. It was getting increasingly difficult to focus on the bar. Almost like the spell knew I was trying to get inside and had doubled its efforts to keep me out.

My feet took me a few steps beyond it before I brought myself back under control by sheer willpower.

Whoever had boosted it had gone a little overboard. Especially when other people might need to get ahold of a wolf.

I could kind of understand their paranoia. A wolf had been killed in a back room last year. Right under their noses. It seemed to have made them a little sensitive.

No hope for it. I'd have to make my approach and hope I could talk my way past the door.

I headed toward where I assumed the entrance was, leaning forward even as my feet tried to take me in the opposite direction.

I summoned my visualization of my forest, hoping that the same trick that worked on a telepath would work here. Both affected the mind. If I could keep my mind hidden behind my little forest, maybe the magic would bounce off it or at least be slowed down enough for me to get in the damn door.

It might have been my imagination, but I thought the pull of the 'don't see me' faded just a little. Not enough to make a big difference, but enough that I could continue forward. Each step harder than the last until I stood at the door feeling like I'd been on a military ruck march with a fifty pound pack on my back. I wanted to drop where I stood. Forget finding Brax, I needed a place to lay down and maybe sleep for a thousand years. As a vampire, I could do that now.

I pulled open the door and stumbled inside, nearly collapsing as the spell suddenly shut off. Like someone had slammed a wall between me and it. The sudden release of pressure was almost as overwhelming as the spell.

The din inside didn't come to a screeching halt like you saw in the movies, but it definitely got a lot quieter until one by one I found myself the focus of a dozen eyes, some already shifted to the amber or ice blue of a wolf's.

I straightened and gave them a radiant smile, praying they didn't suddenly shift for an all you can eat buffet of messenger. Growls echoed from throats that should never have been capable of that sound.

Suddenly my plan to barge in here didn't seem like such a great one. I probably should have tried to get through on the phone a few more times or given the person who answered the message and hope it made its way back to Brax.

A man stood up in the back. Nothing was said but the growls cut off as if they'd never been, though I remained the focus of attention.

A pair of ice blue eyes pinned me in place, observing and assessing. Brax never missed much and this time would probably be no different. I waited for him to decide whether to speak with me or set the watching wolves on the hunt.

I lifted my chin and gave him my best 'make your move' look. I saved his ass last year, and he knew it. Clay would have led him directly into that trap. He might have stood a chance against Clay, but he wouldn't have been able to take out both the traitor and the draugr. Not without taking significant damage.

He made a small movement. Almost imperceptible to anyone not fully in tune with him. Just a twitch of the shoulders and the men and women turned back to the conversations they had been engaged in before I barged in.

He summoned me with a crook of the fingers. I took a deep breath and walked to him, not looking left or right but knowing that despite all appearance to the contrary, the entire room watched me, willing and ready to rip me apart at the slightest misstep.

He sat at a table with his back to the wall and indicated the chair across from him. It would place my back to the rest of the bar. Not my preferred seating arrangement. Strategically, it was the worst seat in the place, but I had no choice but to sit there or risk insulting the alpha.

I took a seat and leaned back, hooking one arm over the back and forcing myself to relax. My skin might be itching with the number of stares aimed in my direction and every instinct I had might be calling for me to flee, but I would appear relaxed and at ease if it killed me.

I hadn't anticipated he would want to talk to me out in the bar like this. It had been my assumption we would speak in a back office where no one could hear what was said.

I had no idea how I should start or what information I should share. My earlier reasons for not giving my message to the phone keeper held true. They were perhaps even more relevant with half the pack eyeing me like I was a tasty morsel of vampire delight.

I turned my attention to Brax. He was the sort of guy that was difficult to overlook. Not handsome. He was too rough around the edges for that, but there was a magnetic quality to him, one that would draw women and men alike.

I knew from watching him shift last year that his body was the kind that fanatic gym goers worked themselves into a grave trying to get. He looked good with clothes on, women no doubt hit on him all the time, but he looked even better without them.

His hair was dark and cut close to his head. He looked to be in his thirties. He wore power like other people wore coats. It was a bonfire on the coldest of winter nights. Almost painfully warm, and you knew if you got too close you'd go up in flames.

He wasn't the kind of person you took lightly. I'd seen him rip apart an undead wolf with his bare hands.

"For someone so intent on getting hold of me, you're awfully quiet," he said. One hand rested on the table, his finger tapping as if he was thinking very hard about something.

"You're a hard man to get ahold of."

"Maybe there's a reason for that."

I narrowed my eyes. Perhaps I hadn't given the message taker enough credit. Maybe he had given my name to Brax and the alpha had just decided not to call me back.

"So I guess you don't care that I bumped into one of your wolves running in their fur on the bike path near the Olentangy River."

My words fell like a bomb and had nearly the same effect as one. Chairs scraped as people came to their feet. I tensed, expecting biting teeth and ripping claws. Brax's eyes shifted to the people behind me, he gave one sharp jerk of his head.

Chairs were pulled back in and the sound of people sitting reached me.

They hadn't liked my statement. Guess I was right that running so close to the city wasn't allowed unless you had the alpha's permission. My words caused enough of a reaction that I suspected it was forbidden and possibly even carried a death sentence.

Brax's intense stare found mine. "Explain."

Although I didn't appreciate being barked at and ordered around like one of his wolves, I didn't say anything sarcastic. This was what I was here for. Taking umbrage with his manners could come later. When I wasn't surrounded on all sides by potential hostiles.

"I ran into her on the bike trail. I think I hit her. She was limping when she ran off."

"How do you know it's a werewolf?" A voice challenged from behind the bar. "Could have been a dog."

I didn't take my eyes off Brax. I was here to see him. Not the peanut gallery.

He arched one eyebrow.

I sighed.

"This was too big to be a dog, and its eyes had human intelligence behind them."

"You could be mistaken. Night can be disorienting and all that," Sondra said, stepping in from the back.

I tensed at the sight of her. I hadn't thought she'd be here. This wasn't good, especially since I didn't know what that man had said to her. If she was being compelled, she was a time bomb waiting to happen.

Brax noticed, his eyes sharpening at my small movement. I forced myself to relax, not wanting Brax to figure out it was Sondra by the river just yet. Something told me I needed more proof than just my word if I wanted to convince him.

"I see perfectly fine in the dark. Vampire, see?" I flashed my fangs at her, my voice sharper than I intended.

"Some vampire," she snorted. "You don't even drink from the source."

"That's a personal preference."

"It also makes you weaker than you would be otherwise."

This from the woman possibly under the compulsion of some guy in a hoody. It was that or she was willfully breaking Brax's rules. I didn't know which was worse.

Nothing seemed wrong with her at the moment. It almost made me think she was a willing co-conspirator except for how painful that change had been. It looked like it had been forced on her. I didn't see her conspiring long with someone capable of doing that just for kicks.

"What else?" Brax asked. He had a strange look on his face, like he suspected something. I gave him my best dumb private look, the one that said I could follow orders but wasn't too bright if left to my own devices.

He made a sound in his throat that sounded like a scoff and a snort. "I know there's something else, Aileen. You would have just left a message otherwise."

I held his gaze. True. I didn't like that he knew me that well. I guess I should expect it. He was a hunter. He observed everything and formed opinions and assessments that were probably incredibly accurate. They would have to be for him to be a good hunter.

This was the part I didn't want getting out to the rest of the pack. As much as Brax might think he controlled them, I'd been in the military too long to have faith in his underlings blindly following orders.

He might order them to silence, but there was always at least one person who felt the need to share. Gossip was like wildfire. Once you told one person, it wasn't long before the rest knew. I really didn't want it getting back to hoody guy that I'd taken the opportunity to spy on him.

It also didn't seem wise sharing what I knew with Sondra standing right behind Brax's shoulder.

There were too many unknowns. The problem was I couldn't see a way out of giving up my information. The growing impatience on Brax's face said he wasn't going to wait much longer before trying to shake the truth from me. He might even refuse to let me leave until I gave up what I knew.

On one hand it would give me a legitimate excuse not to fulfill my contract with Liam, but on the other it would probably cause more tension between the wolves and the vamps. Not to mention I had been in their basement cage before. It had not been my favorite experience.

"Don't suppose you'd be willing to talk privately," I said. I didn't have much hope, but it couldn't hurt to ask.

A chorus of growls greeted my request. Guess it could hurt to ask.

"Talk," Brax ordered.

It was on the tip of my tongue to tell him what he could do with his orders when the front door flew open, banging against the wall, and a trio of vampires, led by Liam, stalked into the bar.

Chapter Ten

Their faces were set and hard. The male equivalent of resting bitch face.

Liam's eyes landed on me sitting across from Brax and something flared in them. Could have been happiness or joy, but I was betting on one of the darker emotions like irritation or rage. Maybe exasperation if I was lucky.

The wolves flowed to their feet, moving with almost impossible speed as they prepared to attack the intruders.

The two vampires at Liam's back spread out as they eyed the wolves, some of which were beginning to sprout fur, their skeletons twisting closer to that of a wolf's.

"Hold." Brax's power spilled into the room. Where before it was a warm bonfire on a winter's night, now it was a raging inferno threatening to burn and destroy.

I took a shaky breath, struggling under the pressure of all that power. Sitting so close, I got a full dose of what it meant to be alpha and it gave me an idea of just how much he was keeping under wraps.

His power was vast like the ocean and could probably crush me with barely an afterthought.

Liam's power rose to meet Brax's, a cool breeze on a sweltering hot day. Immense in its own indefinable way. The two powers met and I was surprised when no weather event marked the area where they clashed, evenly matched. I expected a storm front or tornado to form.

I suddenly had a better appreciation of Sondra's statement about my weakness. Compared to these two juggernauts, I was an insect. So powerless that I might be destroyed by accident simply by standing too close to the epicenter of the blast.

I took hold of the glass in front of Brax and threw back the drink, savoring the burn of (was that bourbon?) as it hit my stomach. I didn't know much about bourbon, despite spending time on an Army base in Kentucky, but I thought this might be some of the good stuff. Definitely not meant to be guzzled like a shot.

Both Brax and Liam paused their stare off to look incredulously at me.

I held the glass up to the bartender, who looked like he was torn between hiding and attacking. "Got any more of this?"

His gaze shot to the blazing inferno on the other side of the table from me. Brax gave a small nod. "For our guests as well."

The barkeep pulled several glasses from beneath the counter and a bottle of amber liquid from the top shelf. Fancy. I never got to drink from the top shelf. Usually I stuck with the beer on draft or if I was feeling frisky, a rum and coke.

"What are you doing here?" Liam asked, without taking his eyes from Brax.

The blond vampire on his other side shot me an assessing glance before focusing back on the wolves. He and the other one looked familiar. Like I had seen them before, and recently.

Ah, they'd been in the club last night when Aidan had shown me to the room Liam was in.

From their body language, I was willing to bet Liam was their boss or commander.

I gave the bartender a big smile when he set the glass in front of me. He set another glass in front of Brax. The glare Liam was currently aiming my way caused him to bobble the rest of the glasses.

"You can hand those to me," the blond said.

The bartender gave up his burden. The vampire gave him a lazy smile while managing to hold his companions' glasses in one hand before taking a sip of his. He made a pleased expression as if to say it was good stuff.

"Aileen." Liam's voice took on a threatening edge.

"Oh, were you talking to me?" I asked, taking a sip of my drink. Bourbon wasn't my alcohol of choice. "It's so hard to tell."

"You try my patience."

Good. That was my goal.

Brax shifted and my attention shot back to him. His face was closed as he gave off all of the life signs of a rock. His eyes found mine and held a warning.

I got the strange feeling Brax didn't want me sharing about the wolf.

I agreed. At least for now. He would have to know eventually as I was pretty sure a vampire was in that clearing with the werewolf, but that information could wait until there weren't quite so many people listening.

I doubted Liam would believe I had just stopped by for a drink. I needed a lie he would believe. Preferably something that wasn't an out and out lie as I had a feeling he'd catch me in it.

Things would have been so much easier if Brax had agreed to have this discussion in the back room.

Liam looked expectantly at me, as if he had no doubt I would eventually answer his question. The arrogance of the man made me want to challenge him. Withhold information just to prove a point, but I wasn't a child anymore. As an adult I was expected to be the bigger person. To not escalate a situation.

Sometimes being the adult sucked.

Some of my thoughts must have shown on my face because the blond vampire looked like he was fighting a grin. His stoic mask breaking for a small moment. Enough for human emotion to be glimpsed if someone looked closely enough.

I shrugged. "Other business. Of which you don't need to know."

His eyes shot sparks at me, telling me he'd get the information out of me one way or another. I gave a smirk that said, fat chance of that happening.

I gave Brax a sharp look. "You sure you want to continue this conversation out here?"

My tone made it clear that would not be a good idea.

I half expected the alpha to go all stubborn male on me, intent on sticking to his previous statement despite the change in circumstances. Color me surprised when he stood and gestured for us to follow him.

I popped up, leaving my drink behind and following Brax before Liam could stop me. My main mission hadn't changed, even if that pain in the ass vampire had decided to show up.

As soon as we were in the hallway, Liam grabbed my arm and yanked me to a stop. I didn't bother trying to jerk my arm out of his vise-like grip. Nothing like taking a hit to the dignity and being made to feel like a child when engaging in a tug of war over my arm.

"What are you doing here?" Liam said, his breath whispering against my ear.

"My job."

"The job I gave you didn't involve confronting werewolves in their den."

"Perhaps we're not speaking about the same job."

"We'd better be speaking about the same job since you have very little time left on the clock. Do you need another reminder of what's at stake here?"

Ah ha. I knew he had something to do with that confrontation at the club. Manipulative bastard.

Brax paused in front of a door and looked back at us. Liam's hand didn't move from my arm, but he did change his grip from that of restraining a recalcitrant child to something closer to holding my arm in a courtly manner.

"We can talk in here," Brax said before entering.

Liam pulled me sideways, allowing the man with dark hair to precede us into the room. The man was expressionless as he slipped past us, as if he witnessed Liam taking someone to task on a daily basis. The blond took up position at the rear and shot me a wink.

Liam used his grip to guide me through the door. I tested its strength and found that while the hold had gentled, I wasn't going anywhere until he released me.

Great. Now I really did feel like a child. One that was on the proverbial leash.

Liam waited until the door closed behind us before rounding on me.

"What are you doing here? The truth. Now."

I shouldn't have left my bourbon on the table. I had a feeling I was going to need it for this conversation.

"I told you. It's none of your business."

He watched me with narrowed eyes, thoughts turning behind their blue depths.

"Does this involve a job for Hermes?"

Just like him to hone in on the heart of the matter.

"Yes," I tried.

"You are a horrible liar," the blond observed as he took a sip out of one of the glasses he held.

"I'm an excellent liar," I snapped. Then thinking about it, I added, "When it counts."

The blond snorted, making it clear he didn't believe a word out of my mouth.

"Aileen."

Again with my name said as a threat. Did he really think that would work?

"Liam."

I couldn't help it. I knew it wasn't a good idea to antagonize him.

It made me seem closer to the petulant child he viewed me as, but there were some things in life too good to pass up no matter what they cost you. Yanking Liam's chain was one of them.

The look he shot me said I was treading on thin ice.

"If it's not Hermes business, it is my business."

Now it was my turn to narrow my eyes.

"I don't think so."

"You're a vampire, which places you under my jurisdiction, hence whatever is your business, barring your job with Hermes, is also my business."

"Sorcerer's mark, remember?"

He gave me a humorless grin. "That only means you can't be claimed by a clan. You still have to follow vampire law."

I didn't know if that was true. This was where knowing about this world would really come in handy. I hated my ignorance. Knowledge was power, and I was seriously unarmed in that arena.

"And you say I'm irritating," I said.

He gave me a roguish smile. He thought he had me right where he wanted me. We'd see about that.

"Suddenly my memory is feeling kind of spotty. Must be all that bourbon. Alcohol just goes right to my head."

"You do know we can't get drunk drinking this stuff straight, don't you?" the blond asked. "It has to be filtered through blood before we get a buzz."

I did now.

"She doesn't," Liam said. "It's best if you assume she has less knowledge than an initiate applying for the kiss for the first time."

I resented that statement. Even if it was kind of true.

I gave Brax a long look, hoping he'd take it as his cue to step in. He arched an eyebrow at me. No help from that corner then.

Fine. I had questions for Liam about the vampire in the clearing anyway.

"I felt Brax needed information about some events I witnessed earlier this evening," I said.

"Oh? And you didn't feel that one of us could answer your questions."

I shrugged. Truthfully it hadn't occurred to me.

"This wouldn't have anything to do with a wolf running in their fur close to the city," Liam asked in a silky voice.

I stilled.

"Who was it?" Liam asked without waiting for my confirmation.

Moment of truth. Did I give Sondra up to face whatever punishment the action warranted or did I cover for her and keep that little tidbit to myself until I knew more about the circumstances that led to the action?

I shrugged one shoulder. "No clue. It's not like I've seen every one of Brax's people shift."

The second part of that statement was true at least.

"You're hiding something."

It didn't take a genius to figure that out. I decided to give him something to distract him.

"I saw a vampire too."

Liam's head jerked, a small movement that I almost didn't notice.

"I also saw a naiad and some others, but I couldn't figure out what they were. Looked human mostly."

"What are you talking about?"

"With the wolf. They all kind of seemed like zombies. It was actually a little creepy. They just stood there while this other guy in a hoody chanted a bunch of stuff. There was some black smoke-like thing that seemed to be feeding off some of the people."

Liam's gaze turned inward and I gave myself a pat on the back for distracting him from the wolf's identity.

"Did it look like the guy in the hood forced a change on the wolf?" Brax asked, his face intent like he was bracing for bad news.

"It kind of did, actually. The wolf approached and the guy said some words. Next thing you know the wolf was in the middle of a transformation. It looked painful. Never seen anything like it."

Even thinking about it made me hurt in sympathy.

Liam and Brax shared a long look. The kind that said they both knew something but didn't want to share with the group.

"You know something. What is it?"

"Did you see the face of the man in the hoody?" Brax asked, his voice grim.

I shook my head. "No, he kept the thing up and he wasn't facing me for the most part."

"Did you feel anything? Hear anything?" Liam asked.

"You mean like him chanting?"

"She would know if she had," Brax said to Liam.

"I agree. It's not the type of thing that can be mistaken for something else."

They definitely knew something.

"What's going on? Does this have anything to do with people freezing in place all over the city?"

Liam glared at me. "What makes you think that?"

"Maybe something to do with those people all acting like they were under a compulsion once they came unstuck. The people I saw looked like they were compelled too. They just stood there staring while that smoke did whatever it did to its victim."

Again the men shared a round of looks, a whole conversation taking place. One that seemed determined to stay a boy's club.

"Thank you for the information, Aileen." To the brown haired guard, Liam said, "Escort her to the vehicle and ensure she doesn't leave. We still have things to discuss."

What the flipper?

"I don't think so," I said, dodging the grab for my arm. "You know something, spill."

"As you so eloquently put earlier, this really doesn't concern you."

"Bullshit. I'm the one who brought this to you, remember? People are disappearing all over the city. You know something, so share."

"He's right. Thanks for the heads up, but the matter is closed," Brax said.

"Eric." Liam nodded and turned away as his goon grabbed me in a grip every bit as confining as his had been.

With no choice but to go or risk being dragged, I followed the guard, shooting a glare behind me. The two men who thought it was appropriate to send me away without even a pat on the back for giving them information had their heads bent together as they discussed whatever it was they were meeting for. Neither looked up as the door closed behind us.

I quickly found myself sitting inside a black escalade with the brunette guard beside me. Every time I shifted, he tensed as if he was getting ready to tackle me.

"How long have you been a vampire?"

No answer.

"You been in Columbus long?"

It was like listening to crickets.

"So you kidnap women often?" I asked.

He didn't respond, not even to shoot me a glance.

"I'll take that as a yes."

My conversational gambits tapped out, we lapsed back in silence.

The time passed slowly as we waited. Liam and the blond appeared from around the corner.

The man next to me climbed out and the three conferred before the blond slid into the passenger seat and the man who'd been guarding me headed for the driver's. Liam climbed in next to me.

"Find out anything useful?" I asked in a fake chipper voice.

"I learned plenty."

I liked it better when he and Brax had been at each other throats.

"You planning to share?"

"Not really. It's better if you focus on the task I gave you."

Because that was likely to happen. Arrogant, arrogant man.

It was tempting to hold back what the witches had told me. I meant to say this in front of Brax as well, but I'd been hauled out before I could get the words out.

"The witches think what's happening in the city might be the cause of demon taint."

I still wasn't too sure what exactly that meant, but it seemed important.

Liam stilled, as if the world had hit pause on him. There was no movement. No breath. He was like a painting. Only a lot more 3D. I eyed him. Was this a natural response as a vampire? If so, that was another thing I hadn't quite got the hang of.

"That is helpful information."

How? How was it helpful? It was like I was blindfolded in the dark and being directed by someone who said to turn right, no left, no straight. I kept barking my shins on things I couldn't see and all I needed was for Liam to untie the damn blindfold.

"Don't suppose you'll tell me what's so helpful about it."

"No." His voice was crisp and invited no argument.

I thought as much.

"You make it incredibly hard to trust you," I said. Not to mention all his secrets frustrated the hell out of me. I was curious by nature and having this mystery hanging just outside my reach was driving me batty.

"Why? Because I won't tell you everything you want to know?" Liam asked, his lips twisted in a superior smile. "You were in the military. You're familiar with need to know. This is information that you don't need to know because you're going to stay far, far away from what's causing this. You're going to stop sticking your nose where it doesn't belong and concentrate on the mission I gave you."

Yeah and that whole need to know thing hadn't gone over so well even when I was in the military and had no choice but to swallow the company line. It didn't go down any better this time. Just made me want to knock that smug look off his face.

"Who's to say following your mission doesn't lead me right to this thing?" I argued.

It was a legitimate question. This had witch and vampire written all over it and this task he gave me would take me right into their backyard.

"If you do your job right, it won't be a concern."

His response caused me to pause. Sounded like he knew more about whatever this was than I had previously thought.

"You know what's going on." My voice was flat.

He gave a nod. "I have an idea."

"And you're not going to do anything about it."

"It's not that easy. There are things going on that you don't understand."

"Then explain."

"I would if you were to join one of the clans."

"Not happening."

"Then that information will continue to be something you don't need to know."

I narrowed my eyes at him. What were we, three? Don't do what I want and I'm going to hold this stick over your head?

Vampires.

"Now, what's happening with the job I gave you?" he asked, ignoring my frustration.

I wanted to put my foot down and demand answers, but from the implacable look on his face, I knew that probably wouldn't work, and would most likely result in a screaming match. On my end at least.

I gave the two in the front seat a meaningful look.

"I trust them and they already know most of it," Liam said.

For a super-secret mission, he clued a lot of people in on the details.

"I'm working the problem."

I didn't have much to update him on.

"What does that mean?"

"It means I've talked to the witches, and they haven't been very helpful."

Liam's face was stony as he said, "Perhaps you need to go higher in their organization."

"Sarah seemed pretty powerful to me." My mind flashed back to the coiled power I felt surrounding Sarah and the avariciousness in her gaze when she looked at me. I wasn't sure I wanted to tangle with a witch more powerful than her.

"Sarah?" Liam's voice turned sharp. "Sarah Temper."

"That would be her."

"She's their crone."

"Is that so, Grandpa?" I asked with a sarcastic tone. I hadn't liked the woman but there was no reason to refer to her in such ageist terms.

"It's a term for a position of power."

Oh.

"She confirmed what you suspected," I said. "She said the only way to break the hex is to find the witch who cast it or a descendant of the vampire who was hexed."

At least we knew we were on the right track now.

"That's not new information."

Well excuse those of us who are playing catch up.

"She didn't give you anything on who cast the hex."

"About that. I got the feeling she suspected who had the juice to cast something like that, but getting the information out of her will be pricey. She wants a favor."

"No, not even if the sun were to fall out of the sky."

I shrugged one shoulder. "That's pretty much what I told her but figured you could bring the proposal to your guy. It's his life. He may have a different notion of what he's willing to risk."

Liam's face turned thoughtful before his jaw firmed and he shook his head. "Not unless we're desperate. What have you been able to find out on the descendants?"

"I was able to track them to the great flood of 1915 but lost their trail after that."

"You think they're dead," he guessed.

I hesitated, not sure if I should share what I suspected. "Not necessarily. I can't be sure, but it seemed like Thomas's descendants were being hunted. Most of his direct line died in suspicious circumstances. They may have used the confusion of the flood to disappear."

His face looked like it had been chipped from granite as he turned my words over, examining them, making his own conclusions.

"That would make sense. Whoever commissioned the hex would have known his descendants would be the only loophole. It would make sense to eliminate them."

"Why not do that immediately after the hex took affect? Why wait for them to multiply and spread out?" I asked, playing devil's advocate.

"Hexes take time to set. He may not have wanted to alert his prey to the problem while there was still time to reverse its affects. It could also be that he didn't realize there was a loophole until much later," the blond volunteered from the front seat.

"Thomas also went by a different name back then," the brunette said. "Records weren't like they were today. They would have had to hunt for that information. It would have taken time and money."

"This is interesting, but we still need the descendants," Liam said. "Focus on them for now."

I had planned to anyway. I didn't want to approach the witches again without something to trade for information. Something told me I'd gotten off lightly. I might not be as lucky next time.

"How are you conducting the search?" Liam asked.

"Computer mostly." That and Caroline, my secret weapon when it comes to all things research.

"You can do that as easily from our hotel as home. You're coming with us."

I'd walked right into that.

"That doesn't really work for me."

"I don't care. I'm not going to chance you running off and getting yourself killed or kidnapped before this is over," Liam said, sounding annoyingly autocratic. "You can do that after you've finished the job."

There was a snicker from the blond in the front seat.

Think. Think. I couldn't be tied down. Beyond the fact that I didn't want them to discover that Caroline was helping me with the research, I also had other avenues I could try, ones that didn't involve my computer.

"I said I'd be using the computer mostly. I still have a few other things I need to check out that involve boots on the ground."

"Eric or Nathan can be your eyes and ears."

"I don't think so."

"That's ok. I do."

"My contacts won't speak to them. They hate vampires."

The blond turned around. "You're a vampire."

"Yeah, but I'm more vampire-lite. You're the full fat, nothing held back type of vampire. They won't speak to you."

His face showed outrage. "There's not an ounce of fat on this body."

He pulled up his shirt, showing an eight pack of abs. He was right. There wasn't a speck of fat on him that I can see.

"I don't think my contacts will be impressed by your abs," I said, keeping my voice bland. Caroline might, but the sorcerer would probably try to curse him.

"Everyone is impressed with my abs," Nathan said.

I didn't doubt that. They were impressive.

"Then you're planning to run around without your shirt for the next few days?" I asked, arching an eyebrow.

"Enough," Liam said, before the blond could reply with the innuendo I could see brewing behind his eyes. "Give him your contact's name, and Nathan will see about getting the information you need from them. If he can't get someone to talk, you can step in from there."

He had an answer for everything. It was a reasonable plan, and I hated it on the spot.

"That doesn't really work for me."

"I don't care if it works for you. You're going to do what I say so I can keep your stubborn ass alive."

Nope. Not happening.

"Thought you said this job wasn't dangerous," I said. I didn't remember if he had or hadn't but it sounded good.

"Things have escalated. It's no longer safe for you to act alone."

He should have thought about that before he handed me this job. I didn't even know why I was arguing with him besides the fact that I didn't want to be pinned down. I had a feeling if I went back with them to the hotel, they would put me under lock and key until their selection took place.

While I was fine with that when it came to Thomas not finding his descendants, I was less fine if it meant letting this demon tainted monster affect the rest of the city.

No one had given me any assurances that this thing only went after spooks and it had already attacked someone at the library. Caroline worked there. With no knowledge of the supernatural world or how to protect herself from it, she'd be easy pickings if this thing switched its focus to humans or if she stumbled on something she shouldn't see.

I rolled up my sleeve and flashed him the mark, a lion with thorns entangling it. "I'm pretty sure this thing says you can't tell me what to do."

His face turned hard. His hand flashed out, grabbing my arm over the mark. It felt like I was being burned by the cold emanating from his skin. It sunk deep, tangling with the lion and shooting sparks into my bloodstream. I gritted my teeth against the scream of pain. I wasn't giving the bastard the satisfaction.

It was over quickly, the icy feeling retreating and leaving raw nerve endings behind.

Liam removed his hand, leaving a mark behind. When the sorcerer had first placed the mark on me, it had been a silver tattoo with glints of a metallic purple making up a stylized lion with thorns wrapped around it. Now in addition to the purple were streaks of green with an oak tree growing behind the lion.

"What did you just do?" I couldn't keep the horror out of my voice.

"Oh boy," Nathan said, twisting to face forward.

"What the hell did you just do?" I shook my arm at Liam wanting to slap that non-expression off his face. If he'd done what I thought he had, I was going to shoot him. Damn the consequences.

Liam gave me what I was learning was his patient look, the one that said, I will answer all of your questions even though I think they are silly and a waste of valuable time.

Yup, I was probably going to get myself dead before the night was over, but it would be so worth it to bring the arrogant man down a peg or ten.

"Your sorcerer's mark is still there," he assured me. "I just supplemented it with another mark."

"Explain," I barked.

"You now have two equal claims on you. One is the sorcerer's and the other is mine."

"I thought I had to give consent in order to have a claim laid on me."

After what had happened with the sorcerer and my accidental mark, I had gone and asked a lot of people questions in order to have a better understanding of these marks and what they meant. Everyone had said the same thing. A mark could only be placed with your consent.

"That is the usual method, yes."

"I know I didn't give you consent. How did you do this? On second thought, I don't care. Take it off."

Liam's jaw moved. I knew his answer before he said it.

"No. You wanted to do this solo; this is the price. I'll know if you're in danger. It'll also let me track where you are."

"I've changed my mind," I declared. "Nathan can do all the legwork."

He gave a negligent shrug. "Too late. The mark can't be removed."

"Bullshit, otherwise you'd all be walking around with half a dozen marks."

I didn't believe his excuse for a minute.

"Nathan," Liam said.

Nathan turned in his seat and pulled up his sleeve, showing a green and blue tattoo of an oak tree, similar to mine but in much greater detail. It looked similar to other tattoos I'd seen done that had a Celtic origin.

"Liam is my sire. His mark is the only one I've ever worn. I'll wear this until I am strong enough to remove it myself."

Staring at that mark, so similar to a tattoo, I felt my life slipping from my control. It was a feeling I didn't like and one I had not felt since the night I woke up sporting a brand new set of fangs.

I might have a mark, but that didn't mean anything. That's right. It didn't change anything. I was still master of my own destiny. I was still the one calling the shots when it pertained to my own life.

My homicidal urges started to fade. As they did, something occurred to me.

"You planned this," I accused Liam.

He lifted an eyebrow as if to say 'so what if I did.'

"It occurred to me that this step might be necessary if you decided to be as stubborn as you have been in the past."

I gritted my teeth against words I wanted to say. Words that might back me into a corner I would have trouble getting out of.

I started to say something several times. Each time thinking better of it before uttering the words.

I took a deep breath. Then another.

"This is not ok. Not by any stretch of the imagination."

"You'll feel differently if it ends up saving your life."

Not bloody likely. He'd essentially micro chipped me like I was a damn dog that might get lost.

"You'll need to attend a gathering tomorrow night. The applicant's will all be there, including the one who may have placed the hex. I want you there in case you see something we don't."

Guess we were through talking about this subject.

I was glad I had a reason to duck out of his plans.

"Can't. I have to meet with a source tomorrow."

"Where?"

I saw no harm in telling him. "There's a gala at the art museum. My source is meeting me there."

The corner of his lips lifted in a partial smile. "I can't imagine you at a gala."

I shrugged. Neither could I to tell you the truth.

"Do you have a dress?"

I froze. Shit. How could I have forgotten about that? I knew without even having to check that there was nothing appropriate in my closet. Mostly my clothes consisted of jeans and gear suitable for riding a bike for hours on end. Nothing that could be worn to rub elbows with whoever was attending this thing.

My face must have shown some of my consternation because Liam gave a warm chuckle. I glared at him, still pissed about the unwarranted marking. Like I was property or something. I'd find a way to get this thing off. It might take me a minute, but there was a way. I just had to find it.

"As fun as this has been, I think it's time for me to head home," I said. It was pretty late. Dawn was only a couple hours off, and I still had to bike home.

Speaking of bike, I took a look in the back. No bike.

"I don't suppose you'd take me back to Lou's," I asked.

"No."

"You left my bike there."

"How do you expect to go to a gala on a bike?"

Fair question. One he didn't need the answer to.

"How do you expect me to get anything done if you leave my bike where it can get stolen?" I returned.

"The wolves won't let anybody steal it," Nathan said. "The 'look away' will keep any humans from seeing it and spooks won't have any use for a bike, except maybe as decoration."

"We'll drop you off at your place and then Nathan can go retrieve the bike for you," Liam said, forestalling the argument he could see brewing.

It would have to do.

I gave a nod. The car took a left turn. We weren't that far from my apartment, confirming my belief that Liam had anticipated this ending all along.

I'd have to be more careful in my dealings with him from now on. He was a manipulative, sneaky bastard used to getting what he wanted. It meant I'd have to step twice as quickly if I had any hope of staying ahead of him.

Chapter Eleven

Home was exactly as I left it. I had only been gone a few hours, but it felt like days. Leaving my keys and messenger bag on the table, I headed for the book I'd been tricked into taking from the bookstore.

It didn't have any relevant information on vampires in it, but maybe it had a section on demon taint and what exactly that meant.

The book had moved again. This time it was on the coffee table instead of in my bedroom where I had left it.

I flipped through the pages, reading some of the entries before passing over them. It took longer than expected to find something as the topics weren't in alphabetical order, but finally I came across a section titled "Bargains with Daemons."

I read further.

A full Daemon has not set foot on the mortal plane for one thousand and sixty five revolutions around the sun, due mostly to the protections set by a no name sorcerer that prevents them from crossing the veil unless directly summoned in a three circle ritual. The exact ritual to summon a daemon with its corporeal body was lost during the European witch hunts when many witch and sorcerer bloodlines were stamped out. Today, a supplicant can only summon the daemon's essence. Though this may sound better, it's not. A daemon can strike a bargain with its supplicant to lend some of its powers in return for something of the daemon's choosing. This usually ends in massive bloodshed for all involved. My best advice for you is to avoid daemons and any who may be carrying their taint.

So the demon taint they were talking about was part of the bargain struck by the summoner. Interesting, but it didn't exactly tell me what that taint meant or how it was causing the symptoms people displayed.

I tossed the book on the coffee table, making a sound of frustration. I needed more information.

I headed to the bedroom, changing into my pajamas before heading to the kitchen for my nightly snack.

Dawn was coming, though it was still an hour or so off. There wasn't time to go anywhere or gather any information. I'd just have to go with what I had and see if I could glean anything from Liam next time he was around.

My reaching hand encountered nothing but air. I looked into the cupboard, standing on my toes. Where were the wine glasses? There should have been at least two clean ones left.

A flash of jewel toned wings appeared briefly in the darkness before disappearing. Pixies. Son of a gun. Not again.

I stepped back and reached into my spice rack, pulling out the cinnamon. Armed with the spice, I sprinkled some in the cupboard where I saw the wings. A soft sneeze greeted me; a blur of color attached to a small body flew past my nose.

Definitely a pixie. I should have caught on the first time something of mine was in a place it didn't belong.

Pixies were the annoying cockroaches of this world. Pranksters and mischief makers who could make life difficult for anybody whose house they infested. Where there was one, there were usually more.

They made my life a nightmare when I first came back to Columbus. At the time, I had no idea they even existed. I just thought I was losing my mind when things kept turning up in places I had no memory of leaving them.

How did the beast even get in here? I'd lined every entrance with cinnamon after I discovered how effective it was during my last infestation of the pests. I refreshed it regularly too. It should have been enough to keep my current guests out.

"Where are you, little pest?" I said in a sing song voice.

One of my framed photos fell over in my living room. Gotcha. I moved into that area, looking closely for any small flutters of movement or a brief glimpse of jewel toned wings.

The book flipped open, the pages turning one after another. I madly waved the jar with the cinnamon, leaving the room smelling like Christmas as half of the spice landed on me. There were no discreet sneezes.

These guys were fast. I'd give them that.

I crept close to the book, feeling the need for subterfuge despite the fact it was unlikely I would be able to sneak up on a pixie and outweighed one by quite a bit.

I bent over the book, thinking maybe it was hiding behind one of the pages. The words caught my eye, making my mission seem unimportant for the moment.

Ways to recognize Daemon taint

It is not easy to recognize those who consort with daemons, but there are signs for the observant. The best and most common sign is the smell of basil and anise. This isn't a common combo so it is a dead giveaway when you come across it. Despite human myths, daemon's rarely smell of sulfur or decay. Another sign that only shows in about sixty percent of summoners is a slight discoloration to their fingertips. Usually a color close to purple or blue.

Once again, if you see these signs it is best to take a big step backward and then run as fast as you can in the other direction. These individuals are extremely dangerous and not to be trifled with unless you have serious power at your back. There is no shame in living to fight another day.

It wasn't much to go off, but it was more than I'd had before. I wasn't even sure how accurate this book was or when it was written. Things could have changed or whoever wrote this might have been way off base. Either way, it was something to keep in mind.

"Little vampire," a high pitched voice sang. "Was that helpful?"

I stood, the cinnamon clutched in my hand. That voice had sounded close.

"Well was it?" a second voice said, right in my ear.

I spun, flinging the cinnamon in a circle around me. There was a brief movement as something flew into my curtains.

Heh. Not so smart after all.

I stalked closer, holding the jar at the ready. Time to evict these pixies. No freeloaders in this house.

A sharp sting in my hand loosened my grip on the jar. It fell, hitting the sofa before rolling to the ground and spilling half of the cinnamon in the process.

"Now that's not very nice after we helped you," a female voice said close to my ear.

There were two of them. Great. Knowing my luck they'd procreate and then I'd have a whole clan of them making my life hell.

A small body hovered in front of me at eye level. It was a female with wings of iridescent green and yellow that stole my attention. The fore wings had large green circles surrounded by a thin outline of yellow on a black background, making it appear like a dozen eyes were looking out of one wing. A spidery network of veins the color of every type of green imaginable were woven throughout. When the light caught them just right, they sparkled with a metallic sheen. The hind wings were a smaller, no less beautiful, version of the fore wings.

It was a good thing the wings were so beautiful because the rest of it was not. Its eyes were a little too large for its face and had the same intense green of its wings. The mouth was thin and when it spoke I could see razor sharp teeth and a pointed tongue.

The pixie is a carnivore. Its primary diet consisted of bugs or small mammals, though I'd heard stories that they could take down a human if their clan had enough numbers.

The female's head was shaved on both sides, with the top braided into one long tail. Her clothes were a series of scales in every color imaginable. I thought I recognized a wing pattern that belonged to a couple species of butterfly.

"Help? Not likely," I scoffed. "You're the one who keeps moving all my stuff around."

She shrugged one tiny shoulder. "It's entertaining watching you stomp around muttering to yourself."

Maybe for her.

"Not the kind of help I usually ask for."

"Harmless fun," she assured.

Unless it was happening to you, then it was just a giant pain in the ass.

"You've had your fun. Now it's time to go. This is your eviction notice."

"You would never have found the information on the daemon taint if we hadn't led you to it."

I paused, my eyes going to the book. It was pretty convenient that the book flipped to the exact page I needed.

Seeing an opening, she said with a sly look, "We can be helpful to you. We know things. Our kind go everywhere and no one ever suspects unless we want them to."

Sounded tempting.

She played her trump card. "We can tell you about vampires. You want to know. It's why you took the book, right."

I did, but you know what they said about things sounding too good to be true.

"I think I'll pass."

She sighed, the sound a high pitched squeak.

"Not an option. We've been here forty eight hours, which leaves us free to claim squatters' rights." She gave me a sharp toothed grin. "Bet you wish you'd taken the deal, huh?"

I gaped at her. She couldn't do that, could she?

"No, this is my house. You can't stay."

She shrugged her tiny shoulders and flew away, her wings a green blur as they flapped. The pixie hiding in the curtains chose that moment to make a break for it, darting in the opposite direction.

No, this wasn't happening. Not again. I was a vampire, by all that was holy. Top of the food chain. Supposedly. They should fear me. Or if not fear me, at least be wary of pissing me off.

I grabbed the cinnamon jar, scooping as much of the spilled spice back in as I could. They were not staying here. I didn't care what they said about squatters' rights. I'd teach them to mess with my home even if I had to stay up all day to do it.

*   *   *

My take no prisoners, hunt the pixies down, spirit lasted until five minutes after the sun rose. I ended up collapsing on the couch after ransacking half my apartment in search of the pests. My will power disappeared, leaving me with no energy to make it to my comfortable bed.

I woke with a crick in my back and drool on the couch cushion under me. I sat up, wincing as my hair caught painfully on something behind me. I reached back, feeling with hands what my hair was caught on. The bastards had braided my hair and somehow tied it to the lamp.

A small body landed on my nose, the oversized eyes looking like that of a bug as he glared at me.

"Bet you wish you'd taken the deal." Without waiting for a reply, he fluttered off, his purple and blue wings glittering in the light.

"I will figure out a way to get your tiny ass out of here," I yelled at him.

"Fat chance of that, meat bag."

Meat bag. What kind of insult was that? Upstart little pest. Just wait. I'd figure something out right after I hit up the grocery store for another jar of cinnamon. I emptied the last one chasing the pixies down last night.

I worked my hair free, though it took a bit of doing and left several strands behind.

"You better run. Your time's coming," I muttered.

My doorbell rang.

From my seat on the couch, I twitched the curtain open just

enough to peak through. If I craned my neck just right, I could catch a glimpse of the landing in front of my door. A view of a blond with shoulder length hair and wearing a long sapphire blue dress greeted me.

Caroline.

What was she doing here? I thought we were meeting at the Columbus Museum of Art at nine pm.

The bell rang again.

I looked down at what I was wearing and frowned. I was still in my pajamas from yesterday. No time to change.

The bell rang for a third time.

I sprung up and yanked the door open. Caroline had her hair pulled back into some type of fancy low bun. I saw I'd been wrong before. Her gown wasn't sapphire so much as a cross between sapphire and teal. It had a v neck with spaghetti straps that were covered in a lace cap, giving the illusion of sleeves.

"Hey, what are you doing here?" I asked with a bright smile.

She looked me over skeptically. "Are you still wearing the clothes from yesterday?"

"Ah. Yup. Got a problem with it?"

"No, no, just not used to seeing that," she said.

I noticed her arms were full of boxes.

"What's that?"

She looked down then frowned up at me. "I knew you didn't have a dress so I brought a couple of mine over for you to try on."

Ah. That explained why she had shown up unannounced. When we were still good friends, this had been normal behavior. Not so much after our falling out. That's why it was so unexpected finding her standing on my doorstep.

"That looks like a lot of dresses," I observed. She must have been holding four or five boxes. Did each box represent a dress? If so, how many of these galas had she attended? It made me wonder if it was considered tacky to show up in the same dress more than once. I was glad this would be the one and only one I attended.

"Yes, and they're very heavy. Are you going to invite me in?"

I stood aside, making it clear she was welcome to enter.

She stepped inside, her silver heels tapping across the wood as she crossed to my coffee table to set her burden down. She turned around, heading back toward me.

"I have several more dresses and shoes in the car. Why don't you get a shower and then get started with those to see if there are any you like while I get the rest?"

She had more? Good lord. How many fancy dresses did she need?

Grumbling to myself, I advanced on my coffee table with all the enthusiasm of someone approaching a rattlesnake. It wasn't that I didn't like dressing up. I did. Just because I spent time in the military didn't mean I was against looking feminine or wearing dresses. In fact, I found during my time in the service that the women were just as likely or even more likely to enjoy pampering themselves and wearing nice things. I think it came from having to wear the same uniform over and over again.

No, I just wasn't looking forward to having to go to a stuffed shirt event like a gala. I didn't even know what gala meant. All I knew was that I was going somewhere I knew no one and would be as out of place as a bird under water. Not something I particularly enjoyed.

I picked up the first box, made of a creamy white material that felt like money under my fingertips, the name Francois written in script letters on the top. Never heard of it. Might as well try it.

I carried it and another box, this one black with no name on it, to the bedroom. I pulled off my clothes and jumped in the shower, hurrying through my routine but paying close attention when it came to shaving. I skipped washing my hair, knowing I wouldn't have time to dry it before we had to be at the gala.

The military had given me the gift, if you want to call it that, of being able to shower and dress quickly. I was out within ten minutes and wrapped in a fluffy towel, as I pulled each dress out of its box and laid them on the bed.

The dresses were beautiful, and unless I was completely out of touch, very expensive.

The first was a cream sheath with a tulle like substance layered over it. A black and red lace detailing decorated the bust and sheer sleeves. That same appliqué decorated where the waist met the full skirt.

I pulled it on and turned to my full length mirror. Oh my. I looked like a girl. Like a fairy tale princess who had just an edge of badassness to her. I liked it.

Caroline stepped into the room carrying several garment bags and shoe boxes. She nodded once when seeing me.

"Nice. Turn around."

I twirled, the full skirt rustling around me as I moved.

"I like it, but it's a little much for tonight. Try the other one."

I took one last look at the gown. It was probably the last time I'd ever wear something like this. My life wasn't the sort that lent itself to ball gowns, no matter how pretty they were.

The next dress was as simple as the other had been complicated. A silvery waterfall of fabric that slithered over my head. This was not the dress for a fairy princess. This was the sort of dress a woman with utter self-confidence wore to tell the world that 'I'm badass and know it, so just fucking deal.' I absolutely adored it.

The silver was the perfect shade to set off my skin tone, which tended to wash out with paler colors, and highlighted my body while still allowing me to move and run if I had to. The skirt flowed around my legs but the slit over one leg gave me freedom of movement. I could probably hide a weapon in there if I needed to.

Caroline gave me an assessing gaze. "I like it, but let's try on a few more to make sure."

"I think this is fine. If it works, there's no reason to waste any more time trying a bunch of stuff on."

"If I took the time to drag all this shit here, you're going to try some of it on."

Ah, there was the Caroline I knew and loved.

I set the silver creation aside and pulled on a few other dresses at her direction. These seemed on the lower end of the cost spectrum. I should probably go with one of these in case of damage. Lately I seemed to be drawing all sorts of trouble to myself. I didn't want to ruin one of her expensive dresses just because I liked the way it fit.

"I'll just wear this one," I said, turning my back to the mirror to see how the black dress fit.

"No, you were right," Caroline said, looking over the mess we'd made of my bed. "The silver one looks best. Everyone wears black. No point in following the crowd. The silver will make you stand out."

"I don't need to stand out. I'm just going so you don't look like an idiot in front of your coworkers."

Her glare could have singed off my eyebrows. "In that case, you're going to look like the very best version of yourself. That means the silver dress."

I gave a shrug. It was her dress. If she wanted to risk it, that was her business.

I changed back into the silver one, taking a seat on the bed while Caroline got her curling iron and other hair styling implements ready. Given how nice her hair looked, it was obvious she'd gone to a salon. I knew arguing and saying I could just wear mine straight wouldn't fly.

"It's been a long time since we've done something like this," Caroline remarked, wrapping a section of my hair around the curling iron.

"You mean let you play dress up with me as the doll?" I asked.

She paused and leaned forward so she could meet my eyes. "I mean spend time together without arguing."

Chastened, I fell silent. It had been a long time. I didn't count the time I'd shown up asking for her help with the draugr incident.

"This could be fun. If you let it, that is." A thread of wistfulness came through in her words.

I shut my eyes and let go of some of my frustration, the hurt, and unsaid words between us. Even though I'd chosen to live my life this way, I was lonely and from the sound of it, so was Caroline.

I could put some of my snarkiness away for the night and just try to enjoy the evening. Even if it was an event I normally wouldn't be caught dead at.

A short time later, Caroline stepped back, squinting at her handiwork. She gave a firm nod. Evidently, I'd passed her exacting standards.

"Done. Have a look."

Caroline had achieved her goal. The person in the mirror was the nicest put together version of me that I'd seen in a long time. The makeup accented my eyes and cheekbones without being overwhelming. She'd curled my hair and then pulled it back into a soft twist, giving my face an almost dreamy quality and offsetting the fierceness of the dress perfectly.

"You do good work," I told her. Better than good, if I was being perfectly honest. I didn't think I could replicate this look. Not without several hours and even then I would only approximate a poor imitation of it.

She handed me a pair of silver shoes with a decent sized heel. Not as high as hers but higher than what I normally wore. "Luckily I was able to find a pair of shoes in the boxes that were sitting in front of your door. I didn't have anything in my collection that would go with that dress. Good thing you thought to have these included in the delivery with your dresses."

My hands froze where they were fixing the strap around my ankle.

"What boxes? What are you talking about? I thought you brought this dress."

She gave me a puzzled look. "No, I found the first set of boxes on your door step. I thought you had ordered some stuff and had it delivered."

I held my hand away from my dress, "Does this look like the sort of thing I would buy on my own? Let alone be able to afford it."

She shrugged. "I thought it was a little out of character."

"You didn't think the boxes were delivered to the wrong place?" I asked, my voice approaching a screech.

"It had your address on them." She held up a hand to forestall my next question. "And your name. I checked. Three times."

A pair of green wings appeared in my periphery vision near one of the boxes. The one that held the dress with the interesting bodice.

My eyes shot back to Caroline who was in the process of turning back to the boxes, intent on showing me the address and name she said she saw.

"That's alright," I said, my voice sharper than I intended. "I believe you."

"Ok." Caroline studied me, suspicion on her face, like she knew something was off. Like she knew I was trying to hide something. She knew my tells better than most and even a four year gap in our friendship didn't change that.

The fairy disappeared into the box.

"I should probably change out of this though since I don't know where it came from," I said, giving her a stiff smile.

She picked her phone up off the bed and grimaced.

"No time. We should have left fifteen minutes ago."

"It'll just take two seconds."

She latched on to my arm and hauled me behind her, grabbing a black lace clutch, my phone and a set of keys off my dresser. "Nope. You look awesome. Just be grateful someone sent you a dress that works on such short notice. That's like trying to find a pair of shoes that fit comfortably and also look great. Possible but highly unlikely."

"As great as that sounds in theory, I don't want to be on the hook for this dress if something happens to it. It feels expensive."

What I didn't say was that I didn't want to be beholden to the person I thought likely to have been responsible for it showing up when it did.

She paused and gave my dress a critical look.

"Don't spill anything on it or trip and rip it and you'll be fine."

With that final statement, she dragged me out of the apartment to her car.

"Wait, I need my bike." I thought about it. "And a change of clothes."

I had a few witches I wanted to see after the gala and it would save time leaving from there rather than coming all the way back here.

"You don't need either. You agreed to give me your full attention this evening. I'm not letting you sneak away early because of some emergency."

She gave me a look that asked if I understood and agreed. I had a feeling if I balked she would tell me she could no longer work on the research I needed her for.

"Fine."

She gave me a beautiful smile, happy now that she had gotten her way, before climbing into her car.

I cast my eyes up to the sky and shook my head before following.

Chapter Twelve

The Columbus Museum of Art was located on one of the main streets that ran through the heart of downtown Columbus. From the front, it had the same look as many museums, complete with oversized stone steps leading up to a grand building. The front façade was made out of white stone meant to imitate marble and came complete with columns framing either side of the entrance. There was even a stone lion staring down any who dared walk up those majestic steps.

We didn't bother trying to park on Broad Street. It was one of the busiest streets in Columbus and during an event like this, street side parking would be impossible. Caroline drove around back to where several parking lots for adjacent buildings had been set aside for event parking.

Viewed from the back, the museum had a much more modern look. Weird angles intersected each other and the walls were made entirely of windows.

The parking lot was nearly full as Caroline pulled in and gave her ticket to the attendant. He waved her on. She parked in one of the overflow lots and we climbed out.

The heels were surprisingly comfortable. A fact I was grateful for as we'd been forced to park at the very end of the lot in front of the adjacent Columbus College of Art and Design.

A long pathway, lined with sculptures in a mish mash of crazy shapes and colors, led to the entrance. I was sure there was a name for the style, but I couldn't have told you what that was to save my life.

Caroline handed our tickets to the usher at the door, who checked them against a clip board. He gave a nod and gestured us in. He gave me a sidelong, curious glance as I moved past him.

The entrance was a wide, open space with a raised ceiling that reached at least two floors above us. Sculptures hung suspended from it.

People milled around as waiters with appetizers circulated. Their conversation echoed in the large space, sounding like a dull roar.

Caroline paused and I stopped beside her, eyeing the gathering with skepticism. This was not going to be fun. I could already tell.

She took a deep breath.

"We could always blow this place and go get a hamburger," I volunteered.

"No. It'll be fine."

"You sure? Because you look less thrilled to be here than I do."

"It's just – a burger would be nice."

Now we were talking.

"But, I need this funding which means I have to go rub elbows and schmooze."

Damn. I was so close to being free of this obligation.

"Not what I would have chosen," I said. "Let's get this over with. The sooner we start, the sooner we can get out of here."

With the bearing of a queen going in to do battle, she advanced on a group of five holding champagne glasses and discussing a point of historical reference. I trailed behind her, snagging a glass on the way. If I was going to have to listen to a bunch of professors discuss the different schools of thought of historical study, I was going to go in well-armed with alcohol.

"Caroline, so good of you to join us," a man wearing wire rimmed glasses said. His words said one thing but the superior expression with which he regarded us said another.

"Wouldn't dream of missing this." Caroline's voice had that cool tone she used to get when she was dealing with someone who tried her patience. She gestured to me, "This is my friend Aileen."

"A friend of yours?" a woman asked. "I didn't realize you had friends outside of work. You never talk about them."

"She's been out of town for a while. She was in the military."

I took a slow sip of my champagne, not liking the small lie she had told but figured it was better than saying we'd had a falling out and were just recently back on speaking terms.

"Oh, is that so?" The woman cocked her head and gave me a false smile. "Thank you for your service."

I took another sip of my champagne before murmuring, "It was no trouble."

I've lost count of the number of times someone has thanked me for my service. I felt just as awkward being thanked now as I had the first time it happened. How do I respond to something like that? It's not like I joined up to be thanked. I got a paycheck the entire time I was there.

It was particularly awkward when the person doing the thanking made it clear that they were just saying what people expected them to say.

"What did you do over there?"

"I was a broadcast journalist essentially."

"I didn't know the military had such things," the woman said.

"They do."

"But you probably only released footage to military channels, right?"

"No, news stations back home picked up some of the footage too."

Especially given how expensive it could be to send a journalist in country. Not to mention dangerous. It was easier to pick up some of the raw footage shot by people like me and then overlay their own voiceover. It was the same with photos and news stories. A lot of my print friends had their stuff picked up in the local newspapers and magazines back home.

"You probably didn't go on any missions though. They would have sent real journalists for that," the man in the wire glasses asserted, almost like he had to discount what I did.

"Nope, I went on a lot of missions with the infantry guys. The patrols I was on even took fire a couple of times." I even had the Army CAB, Combat Action Badge, to show for it.

"I thought women didn't serve in combat roles."

"There are no front lines in combat anymore," I said. This was a common misconception civilians often had about the military. Just because women, up until last year, haven't been able to serve in combat roles didn't mean they were exempt from combat. It was rare to see a woman on patrol, but I'd encountered it several times while overseas. "Women go outside the wire on a regular basis, based on their MOS. My job required me to film events as they happened which meant I went."

"Fascinating," another man said. This one was in an ugly suit not at all common in this sort of event. "How did you find the dynamics between men and women in high stress situations such as you experienced?"

He, unlike his companions, genuinely seemed interested in my uncommon experiences.

I thought about it, trying to find the right words to express what

I'd seen and felt.

"I think the issue of gender in combat is a complicated one and not at all universal. In my experience, any resistance I encountered had more to do with the fact that I wasn't infantry than it did with me being a woman. As soon as I proved I could keep up and was willing to pull my fair share of the work, I had no trouble with my fellow soldiers. Other women may have had vastly different experiences."

I needed to get the attention off me before I said something that gave them the wrong idea about the military. Some of the small group had already drifted into side conversations. "Enough about me, what is it that you do?"

"I'm a professor of archaeology and Pleistocene geology. My focus is the study of the migration patterns of early man. Specifically the diaspora that led to the settlement of the Americas during the Last Glacial Miximum via the Beringian Land Bridge."

After that his words ran into a long line of incomprehensible babble as my eyes glazed over from the onslaught of information. He seemed only to require a periodic 'uh huh and that's interesting' to warm to his subject.

I took another sip from my champagne, noting Caroline was in an animated conversation with the woman who'd thanked me for my service and the man who made the comment about women in combat.

I turned my attention to the rest of the gala. Despite the name, there seemed to be little dancing. There was a string quartet in the corner with a wide, empty space surrounding them. Maybe the dancing came later in the evening, once people got a little more of the bubbly in them.

My gaze caught on a pair of intense blue eyes staring at me. Liam gave me a lazy smile from across the room as I almost choked on my champagne.

"Are you alright?" my conversation partner looked like he didn't know whether to break out the Heimlich maneuver or run for help.

I gave him a reassuring smile between coughs. "Quite fine. If you'll excuse me, I see someone I need to talk to."

I didn't wait for his agreement before heading across the room.

Liam straightened from his slouch against the wall and stepped forward, drawing my attention to the man next to him. Thomas's blond hair glinted in the light, a perfect contrast to Liam's darker looks.

Great. They were both here. Just what I needed.

I knew without looking that Caroline was still engaged with her coworkers. I couldn't rely on her continued preoccupation and the last thing I needed was for her to start asking questions about Liam or Thomas. Correction, the last thing I needed was for them to show any interest in her. I wanted to keep her as far from this world as possible.

"I thought you might choose that dress," Liam observed.

Ha. I knew he had something to do with this.

"What are you doing here?"

He looked around and nodded at someone. I followed his gaze, noting several familiar faces, including Nathan and Eric. Looking further I saw Elinor and John, laughing and talking with their own clusters of groupies.

Power moved through the room at a slumberous pace. Previously, I had attributed it to ambient magic, but now I suspected it had less to do with magic and more to do with a gaggle of vampires congregating in one spot. The buzz in my head ramped up now that I knew what it was.

Caroline's gala wasn't just a fundraiser's wet dream but also a meeting place for the vampire applicants.

We needed to leave. Now.

"You could have said something," I snapped.

He made a slight movement as if to acknowledge my statement. "I could have, but seeing the shock on your face was so worth it."

I snarled at him, spinning on my heel. I needed to find my friend.

His hand caught my arm. "Not so fast. You can't leave yet."

"Watch me."

"You'll just draw more notice to yourself and your lovely friend. Vampires are like sharks. Give the slightest whiff of blood in the water, and they'll be on you before you can blink. You might be able to defend yourself, but your friend will be helpless," he murmured in my ear.

I gave him a dirty look, even as I conceded his point. This right here was why I had made a point of keeping a distance between myself and the people I cared about.

Thomas glided up to stand beside us.

"Who is your friend, Liam?" Thomas asked, pretending that we had never met before. It seemed to be a theme with him.

I fought the choice words that instantly rose to mind. Hostility was all well and good but would do nothing for me right now.

I wished I'd taken the time to slip a weapon holster under the dress. It had been impossible with Caroline fussing over my hair and makeup. Now I was as defenseless as a lamb among wolves.

"This is the woman I was telling you about," Liam said, going along with the ruse.

"The clanless yearling. I assume that unfortunate set of circumstances will be taken care of as soon as the selection is settled," a voice as warm as honey said as its owner walked up to us.

He had the sort of good looks featured on the cover of a magazine. Hair perfectly styled, a roguish charm to his face. He wore a tux like he'd been born to it. Liam, by contrast, looked like an untamed warrior content to play a part for now. Handsome to be sure, but you knew just by looking at him, he wasn't meant for formal clothes. Instead he should be on a battlefield somewhere clutching a weapon as he hacked off his enemy's head.

"Stephen," Thomas said. His voice was carefully neutral. There was no warmth to it or hostility.

I was learning vampires defaulted to that bland tone when they were confronted by an enemy.

Stephen shot Thomas an affable grin and slapped him on his back.

"Thomas, old man, I was surprised to see your name on the list of applicants. Were you ever able to overcome your unfortunate tendency of killing every human you tried to convert? Or are you hoping for a last minute miracle?"

"I have a few options left to me," Thomas said.

Stephen's warm eyes landed on me. "I've heard a lot about you. Elinor is furious after she failed to break you. I'd watch your back if I were you, she makes a fearsome enemy. Has an unfortunate habit of killing her victims and all their loved ones."

He spoke of murder so easily.

I gave him a sharp smile. "Thanks for the warning, Stevie. I'll be sure to keep it in mind."

He grimaced. "Stephen. Please."

"Right, of course. I'll have to remember that."

"What was it like waking up as a vampire and not knowing what had happened?" he asked, his voice filled with idle curiosity.

"Educating."

Terrifying, lonely. At first, I thought I was going crazy.

"How did you figure out you were a vampire?"

I shifted. He asked a lot of personal questions for someone I had just met.

Liam's grip tightened on my arm in warning. Yeah. Yeah. I got it.

Play nice with the vampire who was infinitely more powerful than me.

"Someone in my unit had experience with this world and clued me in on what was happening to me."

He gave me an intense stare. His eyes somehow too intense. "Too bad they didn't also report you to the nearest clan. Your life would have been so much easier."

"Yeah, too bad."

"What was the name of this person who helped you?"

"Why?"

He shrugged. "It only seems right to thank him for all his assistance. A vampire is a very dangerous creature when we first rise to our new life. It could have been a blood bath."

"I'll have to think. That time is very hazy."

I knew his name. It was listed in my contacts on my phone under Captain, but I had no intention of ever giving that name to anybody. The captain had stuck his neck out keeping my secret and giving me enough knowledge to survive. I had a feeling the vampires version of thank you involved a lot more blood than mine.

"It doesn't matter much now," he said. "Your clanless fate will be decided by whoever wins the selection."

I stiffened. What did he just say?

"I'm afraid I don't understand."

"You're the first item on the agenda once the new select takes up their rule," he explained. "They will address the question of your existence once and for all."

"I'm surprised I'm on anybody's agenda. I would think the life of one clanless vampire, not even out of their first decade, would be fairly low priority in the grand scheme of things."

"Don't sell yourself short. You're the first vampire we've had in nearly one hundred years." He took a sip of champagne and inclined his head at someone across the room. "Besides, it wouldn't matter whether you were a unique existence or not. We can't have unclaimed vampires running around upsetting the order of things. If we let one do it, what's to say the next vampire yearling doesn't try the same thing. Next thing you know we'd have a massacre on our hands and the humans hunting us down in our beds."

Not to mention vampires who didn't take orders from people out of the dark ages, which I suspected was the bigger problem.

"Interesting take on the matter," I said, my grip tightening on my champagne glass. "It doesn't really matter what the new select decides.

The sorcerer's mark trumps vampire interests and will for the next hundred years."

His eyes dropped to the arm with the mark. The forearm was turned down, preventing him from getting a good look at the tattoo.

"Yes, it's inconvenient that you managed to get yourself tagged like a dog before swearing to a house, but marks can be erased." He gave me a smile that didn't quite reach his eyes. "You'll probably survive. Though your sanity may be touch and go over the next few decades."

"Kind of defeats the purpose of conscripting me into service if I'm a drooling imbecile before the process is done," I said lightly, not wanting to show how disturbed this conversation made me.

He gave a shrug. "Appearances must be maintained, and I'm sure every precaution will be taken to preserve your personality."

How kind.

Liam squeezed my arm in warning, as if he could sense my thoughts.

My smile bared teeth I would have liked to bury in his throat. "You're all heart, Stevie."

Anger flashed briefly in his eyes as he said, "My name is Stephen."

"Of course. I'm just so forgetful tonight."

His expression said he didn't believe me. He addressed Liam, "Enforcer, I trust you and your men have things well in hand. There won't be any surprises tonight, I hope."

Liam nodded. "My men are on hand to keep the events of the next few nights moving forward smoothly."

"Good. I would hate for you to be distracted due to worry for your brother." His eyes landed on Thomas meaningfully.

Wait, what? They were brothers? That explained why he was so hell bent on helping the man.

It was Liam's turn to stiffen. "I do my job. Even when it means upsetting another's schemes."

Stephen smiled. "That's what I like to hear."

I gave him a look. Did he not hear the double meaning in Liam's words?

"Excuse me. I have business to attend to."

The three of us watched him go in silence. Even when he was on the far side of the room no one spoke. Vampire hearing was tricky. In a crowded room like this, it was theoretically possible to hear every conversation. In practice, the words ran all over each other, making it almost impossible to cut through the noise to hear what a specific person was saying unless that person was relatively close to you.

That's how it worked for me anyway. With these guys, there was no telling what they were capable of. It seemed Liam and Thomas weren't taking any chances either.

"Dance with me," Liam said, his arm going around my back and ushering me closer to the string quartet.

There were no couples dancing.

"I don't think that's a good idea."

Besides the fact that I didn't want to stand out as the only one on the dance floor, I also had two left feet. Dancing had never been my sport of choice.

"Nonsense. I'll lead. You follow."

Advice I had heard before, and it was just as helpful now as it was the first time my dad tried to dance with me at my cousin's wedding. Which was to say not helpful at all.

"No one else is dancing," I tried.

"No one is brave enough to go first. As soon as we start, others will follow."

"I think I would prefer waiting for them."

He arched a smug eyebrow. "And here I thought you were a trend setter."

I snorted. "I don't know where you got that idea."

He set one hand on my waist and picked my other hand up, holding it at shoulder level.

"I don't think there has been a clanless vampire in nearly a thousand years."

"I'm not trying to start a trend. I just want to survive."

"Something that might be easier if you would just stop fighting us."

I scoffed. "Because being a vampire seems so great. One of you dumped me in a dumpster, another tried torturing me because I wouldn't answer her question, and another just threatened to turn me into a vegetable because I didn't follow your rules. Oh and let's not forget that you tried to kill me once upon a time."

"I also saved your life if you recall," he said close to my ear.

"Only because you nearly ended it."

"You were in a murdered man's house."

There was that.

"It doesn't matter. My encounters with vampires have convinced me that I made the right choice. I doubt I would survive very long in one of your clans."

"I don't know about that. You could be a valuable asset. You've already shown yourself to be quite resourceful in a pinch. You're stubborn and prone to taking stupid risks, but a smart leader can work with that."

Wow with compliments such as these I was surprised women weren't mobbing this guy in the streets.

"That sounds appetizing. Let me just sign right up."

"What if I could arrange it so you're with someone who could put your skills to good use? Someone that you wouldn't have any trouble working with."

"You assume you know me better than you do."

Staring over my shoulder, he turned us in another direction as we swayed to the song.

"I know you better than you think."

"I doubt that."

"I know you were at the top of your class in your military training course and that you advanced to sergeant in two years."

"You hacked my military records."

Why not? Brax had done the same last year.

He grunted in acknowledgement.

I shook my head in disgust.

"Your evaluations all said you were a leader who accomplished your mission even when under extreme stress. Your evaluator said you were one of the best soldiers he'd ever worked with."

Pressure from his hand on my back guided me in the direction he wanted as we glided across the dance floor.

I remembered when I got that evaluation. I had fully expected to get poor marks as my NCOIC, noncommissioned officer in charge, and I had never really seen eye-to-eye.

"It makes me wonder why someone who was so good at soldiering would be so opposed to joining us. We're not so different from the military."

I arched an eyebrow, giving him a 'get real' look.

"No, you're worse."

I could tell by the slight frown line between his eyes that he didn't like that statement.

"How can you say that? You haven't given us a chance. You took the word of some random stranger and decided you wanted nothing to do with us."

"That might have been why I stayed away for the first few months but not why I kept clear over the next two years." I needed him to understand though I couldn't say why it was so important. "Have you not heard of how your clans are spoken of by the rest of the spooks? The Maron clan alone is regarded with fear and terror. No one deals willingly with the Davinish clan because they're afraid of being cheated and no one wants to go against the combined might of a clan. You might not see it since you're part of the exalted elite, but from an outsider's perspective looking in, vampires seem like a bunch of elitist assholes used to doing whatever they please."

He was quiet a moment, the two of us swaying to the beat.

"They are the exception."

"Are you sure about that?" I asked. "Because from what I can see, their suspicion is warranted."

"I would have thought that as a child of this century you would know better than to paint an entire people with the same brush."

He had me there. I did know.

Serving in Afghanistan, I saw some of the worst things people could do to one another when they were caught up in hating those that were different. Improvised explosive devices that went off when a child walked too close to them, a man shooting up a market place and leaving scores of wounded and dead behind. Things that were not easy to think about even today. But I'd also seen the better parts. A man carrying a child to safety in that same market, using his body to shield his precious cargo. People making a genuine attempt to better their little piece of the world.

I knew people didn't fit into such tidy little boxes, but I also knew that the crowd mentality could lead a group to do things they might not otherwise have been capable of.

"I'm not saying I think every vampire is an evil creature bound for hell." That'd be depressing, as I was one of them. "But that doesn't mean I don't want to be in charge of my own destiny. It also doesn't mean I agree with the way your society is organized. This whole hundred years of service sounds a little too indentured servant to me."

There was also the little fact that I hated being told what to do. I was good at following orders, but I mentally cursed out my commander every time he gave me an order or instituted some ridiculous set of regulations.

"How typical of your generation to equate it with that." His blue eyes shot sparks at me.

"You forgot my generation is in love with counter culture. We hate being part of the in crowd. It's so ten years ago."

His bark of laughter caught me by surprise. I had kind of expected more growling and grandstanding.

We danced for several more minutes in silence. He had been right. Once we broke the seal on the dance floor, more couples joined us.

"Have you found anything else out about what's causing the victims in the city?" I asked.

"This again. I thought I told you to stay clear. I'll put you under lock and key if I think you're getting into things that don't involve you."

And he wonders why I'm so intent on staying out of the clans. Acting like I was a child who should be placed on timeout would be reason one.

"Don't worry; I haven't gone investigating." Yet. "I was just wondering if there was any new information."

"Why do you even care?"

"What do you mean?"

His sigh ruffled the hair on my neck. "You have no stake in this. It shouldn't matter what's happening to a bunch of spooks with no tie to you."

I gaped at him. What kind of question was that?

"It shouldn't matter if I don't know them personally. It's enough to know that it happened."

He grimaced. "You can feel bad without getting involved. You don't have to run off to try to save the city."

"That right there is what I'm talking about," I said. "It doesn't hurt for me to ask questions that just might save lives if I ask the right sort of questions. What kind of person would I be if I just sat around doing nothing when something so simple could help?"

I had to look at myself in the mirror every day. I wouldn't be able to do that if I knew there was something I could do to save someone.

"You're ignoring the fact that you're swimming in waters over your head. You're going to get yourself killed."

"It's my life to throw away." My response was more flippant than I intended.

"You can help countless people by simply completing the task I gave you," Liam said through gritted teeth.

He sounded very frustrated that I wasn't falling in line like all of the other vampires around here. Poor man. I think this experience will be good for him. Teach him that not everything revolves around his wants and needs.

"Don't get your tutu in a twist," I said. "I'm working that problem too."

"Progress?"

I gave a small shake of my head. "None yet but I'm expecting my leads to pan out soon."

My gaze went to Caroline. She gave me a questioning look as she caught sight of me dancing. Better than anyone, she knew just how bad a dancer I was. It had been her that had driven my date and me to Urgent Care when I sprained his ankle.

I looked away, pretending I hadn't seen the question. This was going to cause all sorts of interrogations later.

It didn't help that Liam had the sort of looks that made a woman, married or not, want to drop her panties and let him have his wicked way with her.

Too bad his personality was so bad.

It'd been a while since my last boyfriend. Years actually.

"I hope you don't mind if I cut in," a smooth voice said behind me.

Liam and I broke apart. A tall man with a thin face and a long nose regarded the two of us with a fixed gaze. He looked like a turn of the century undertaker forced into formal wear. His limbs seemed almost too long for his body and his face was frozen in a perpetually sour expression.

"Aileen, this is Robert Boone. He's an applicant for the selection." Though Liam's voice was perfectly even, it felt like he had added that last part for my benefit.

I started to raise my hand to shake Robert's when Liam's grip on my arm tightened in warning. I dropped my hand before offering it, making it look like I had tried to give him an aborted high five.

"This is the vampire everyone has been talking about." His tone made it clear his words weren't a question. "I wonder why."

I kept a pleasant expression on my face even as I felt my hackles raise. By Liam's utter stillness at my side, he wasn't happy with Robert's arrival.

"We will dance," he said, after a long moment spent studying my face. He extended his hand to me.

Liam's tension had become my own and taking that man's hand

was the last thing I wanted to do. I didn't see a way out of it without being rude, which might not bode well for my continued well-being.

Liam let me go, though he turned to watch as Robert stooped to place one hand on my waist and the other on my shoulder. It left me awkwardly placing my hands on his waist. Then we were off. Unlike the graceful dance Liam had somehow managed to lead me into, this one was jerky and full of hurt toes. This time it wasn't only me doing the stepping.

"You have not joined a clan. Why?"

Here we go again, and after I'd just finished discussing this with the other vampire.

"I saw no need to."

"Not very bright then."

I had a feeling he was talking about me.

"What does Liam want with you?"

Judging by the way he almost barked his questions at me, I was guessing this was an interrogation by dance. Let's hope my feet could survive the stomping they were taking.

"He's the first vampire I ran into after joining your ranks."

"He made you."

"No, I didn't meet him until last year."

Which was true. Just not the whole truth.

"The draugr incident."

"That would be the one."

"You seem very familiar. He cares for you."

Don't know where he was getting that one from.

"I doubt it. We can barely spend five minutes in each other's company before we start arguing."

"Then he wants something from you."

That was true.

"You ask a lot of questions."

He straightened. "I'm gathering information. Having the right information will give me a strategic advantage over my competition."

Couldn't' argue with that.

"How many applicants are there?" My meeting with Robert meant I'd met four of them, if you count Thomas.

"Five. Why?"

I shrugged. "Just curious. If you get to ask me questions, then turnabout's fair play."

He thought about it and then gave a decisive nod, accepting my assertion.

"What does Thomas want from you?"

"He wants me to join a clan."

"It would be safer."

"Safe's not always best."

"Agreed."

I was surprised the austere vampire agreed with me. I expected an argument. An assertion of how vampires needed to stick together.

Although he was a tad creepy, with his vibe of gloom and doom, he didn't seem like such a bad guy. There were no threats, no coercion to join a clan or else. If this selection were a voting thing, he'd definitely have mine. He seemed like the most stable candidate I'd met so far.

The song ended and we broke apart.

He gave me a nod and then turned on his heel and walked away without another word. He wove through the other couples on the dance floor, which had filled up during the dance, leaving me standing in the center on my own.

A glance at Liam told me he was occupied with something Nathan was telling him. I couldn't see Caroline. I stood on my toes trying to see above the crowd and caught a glimpse of a woman in a teal dress disappearing down one of the corridors leading off the atrium.

I shot another glance at Liam to make sure he was still occupied and then headed after Caroline. I needed to check on her, make sure she was ok.

The corridor was large and empty. The lights had been turned to dim. There was no bathroom, which was strange as I had assumed that was what Caroline was looking for.

I came to the end of the corridor and turned left, noting an open door leading to a stone patio surrounded by a wrought iron fence. The patio had two paths leading to a level below. Kind of like those old houses with their double staircases leading up to the door. These were framed by a well-groomed flower bed that was just beginning to show the first blooms of the season.

A hand wrapped around my mouth and I was hauled into the shadows next to the fence.

Chapter Thirteen

I grabbed the hand, pinching the thumb and wrenching it back even as I sent a sharp elbow into the stomach of my captor.

There was a soft grunt but the grip didn't release.

I fought down my panic, continuing to struggle. Nothing I did budged the hold the person had on me.

A spook then.

I pretended to go lax, letting them support my weight.

The grip loosened slightly. It was what I'd been waiting for.

I sank my fangs into the hand over my mouth before ripping myself out of their hold and losing some hair in the process. I backed away, my hand reaching for a nonexistent weapon.

Thomas glared back, cradling his hand. A small trickle of blood oozed from where his fingers were trying to stem the blood. It didn't take long for the trickle to slow and then stop entirely.

He released his hand, opening and closing the smooth, puncture free fist.

It took everything in me not to punch him in his face or run screaming into the night.

"Was that really necessary?" he asked, holding up his hand.

Was that necessary? Was that necessary? The question got louder and louder in my mind until I was practically screaming it. Silently, of course, because I was too stunned for words.

"You shouldn't bite other vampires unless they give their permission. It can be dangerous for you," he said reproachfully.

My fangs lengthened as my temper awoke. Vampires, I'd learned, showed their fangs based on their mood swings. Hunger, anger or lust brought the pointy tips right out. Right now, an anger approaching rage coursed through my veins. I couldn't have retracted the suckers even if I'd wanted to.

"You know what else vampires shouldn't do," I said, my voice hitting a pitch that would have made cats flee. "Yank other vampires into dark spaces with no notice or warning."

"I needed to get you alone."

"Did you now?" My hands found my hips as I paced in the tight space. It was either move or deck him. "This isn't how you do it."

"I don't have time to listen to you complain."

I stopped and stared at him. He didn't have time.

"You don't? Then I'll just take myself back to the party."

"You're supposed to be helping me."

I shook my head at him.

"Liam hired me for a job, which I'm doing. He didn't hire me so you could yank me here and there at your convenience."

"You're obligated to help me become the selected applicant."

"In point of fact, my contract stipulates that I attempt to locate the witch who placed the hex on you. As a secondary component, it states that I'm to help you in the attempt to locate your descendants in the event that I cannot find the witch."

I gave him a sharp smile, flashing my fangs for added affect. He didn't look too impressed by my fangs. He probably thought his were bigger. "Now notice where it says attempt. That means all I have to do is put in a good faith effort. You didn't negotiate for guaranteed results. Also, nowhere does it say I'm to help you stage a coup or let you drag me off into the night."

It did, in fact, say all that. I'd made sure to have Jerry email me the full contract Liam had signed so I could have an idea of just how much wiggle room I had.

It wasn't our standard contract. Normally, Jerry put in a clause that came close to guaranteeing results. That clause was missing from this contract. My guess is Liam gave him the terms and Jerry hadn't bothered to include the one about results. Thomas's loss but my gain.

I whirled, pulling up the strap of my dress and flicking the skirt so I could walk without face planting.

"Bad things will happen if you ignore me," Thomas warned.

"Perhaps you should have thought about that earlier," I shot back over my shoulder.

My feet stuttered to a stop.

Robert, the vampire I'd danced with before going searching for Caroline, stood on the other side of the patio from us, his face mostly in shadows. I only knew it was him because of our dance and his taller than average height.

"Robert, I've been meaning to talk to you since I learned you had thrown your hat into the ring," Thomas said smoothly, stepping around me.

Robert didn't answer. He didn't move.

Something struck me as off, but I couldn't place my finger on it. I grabbed Thomas's arm before he could step closer.

He shot my hand a scathing look. "What do you think you are doing?"

"Something's wrong."

There was a feeling emanating from Robert, one that was full of dark and despair. The kind that sucked everything good into it and ground it into dust.

I stepped out of my heels, wanting the freedom of movement.

Thomas's face took on a focused look, like that of a hunter who had finally caught the scent. His pupils widened, turning his eyes mostly black. His fangs snicked down.

He hissed, the sound that of a pissed off cat warning another off its territory.

Robert didn't respond. He didn't move even as the feeling grew stronger.

"Robert, what are you doing?" It wasn't Thomas talking, or at least not the Thomas I had come to expect. This was a darker version of himself. One whose voice was full of terrible things.

I saw why he was on the short list of applicants.

No answer came from Robert except a deep seated feeling of terror. Nothing in my short life compared. Not being shot at by insurgents. Not the whistle of an incoming rocket. Not my drill sergeant discovering my stash of granola bars.

I whimpered, the feeling crushing me. Weighing around my neck like a hundred pound anchor.

I would have fled if I could get my limbs to respond. I was anchored in place as Robert took a step forward, the light a slash across his face.

His eyes were entirely black with no white showing. A substance the color of night oozed from them with an oily consistency.

"Robert." Thomas's voice deepened into a threatening growl.

"The master says you're next," Robert said, no emotion in his words. His voice echoed in my bones and mind, reaching to my deepest depths. The ones that I kept secret from everyone.

I didn't think it was possible, but I tensed further, until it felt like my tendons would snap from the pressure. Robert held up both hands, showing us machete type blades.

"Don't. Think about this," Thomas said.

"Fear me. For I am what waits in the dark of night."

Blade in each hand, his arms crossed over his chest to place a knife on each side of his neck. There was no sign of him in his eyes. It was like he was in a deep sleep, his body acting without conscious thought. Thomas leapt forward. Robert yanked his hands in opposite directions, the blades cutting through flesh until there was nothing left. Blood spurted from the severed arteries as his head sagged backward, attached only by a thin ribbon of skin.

Thomas reached him a second later, catching him before he fell. He lowered the lifeless body to the ground.

The terror released me from its grip as suddenly as if it never existed.

"He cut off his head." My eyes went anywhere but the body. "He cut off his own head."

"So it would seem," Thomas said grimly.

"Could he survive that?" I asked still looking up.

"Probably not."

I chanced a look at the body. Nope. Definitely not a good idea. I fought through the light headedness, giving myself a pep talk about how badass vampires did not faint at the sight of a little blood. Except it wasn't just the blood. It was that head attached by only a thin strip of flesh. It was the sight of his spine and the idea that a few minutes before he had been interrogating me on the dance floor and now he was dead.

"Is this normal behavior for vampires?" I asked. I needed to concentrate on the problem at hand or I was going to lose my shit in a way that would bring all of the humans and spooks out here with us.

"Not in my experience."

"Have you seen anything like this before?" I didn't know whether I should mention the terror I felt. It could have been a product of my mind.

"Never." He sounded grim as he squatted over the body.

"I felt something from him. I could have just been imagining it, but it felt real." I didn't like how shaky my voice was as I tried to explain.

"I felt it too."

But he'd been able to act. To talk through it. I had frozen like a rabbit in front of predator.

"How'd you keep moving?

177

"I'm several hundred years older than you with a lot more experience with these sort of things. They would have needed a lot more power behind their compulsion to affect me."

"That was a compulsion?"

It hadn't felt like one. It hadn't made me want to act in a certain way. If anything, the opposite.

"There are different kinds of compulsion. Some force you to act based on a specific command. Others pull a veil over the victim' eyes so they experience things, but it's hazy, like they're walking through a dream. This one put an emotion in your head and then amplified it to the point where you could think of nothing else."

That seemed right.

My eyes fell on the body. I couldn't think of it in personal terms. I needed to distance myself from the reality of what just happened.

"Was Robert known for that ability?"

Thomas's face was grim as he glanced at me. "No, this is something he has never shown an aptitude for."

"Was he the type to take his own life?" I asked quietly.

Thomas shook his head.

I stared into the night. It didn't sit right. Deaths are always sad and leave intangible marks in their wake, but for whatever reason suicide has always struck me as something particularly tragic. It's the type of action to leave scars on the living, making them question if something they did contributed to the death. As if they just reached out sooner or made more of an effort, it might have been prevented.

During deployment, two of our soldiers committed suicide within weeks of being due to deploy back home. It devastated the command teams they belonged to, leaving twin feelings of grief and anger that someone could do this to themselves, especially when others who had lost their lives would have probably given anything to trade places with them in the land of the living.

I didn't want Robert to have killed himself. If it was compulsion, it was murder, which meant there would be someone to punish. Someone to seek justice from.

Thomas wiped his hands on the body's pant leg and stood. "This is going to cause a problem."

My eyes shot to him. "What do you mean?"

"The other applicant's will try to pin the blame on one of us. His children are the type to seek revenge."

"The forensic evidence should clear us," I said.

"That may not matter. Politics are a game of perception. Elinor and Stephen are not the type to let this pass without trying to turn it to their advantage."

I wanted to argue, but I'd seen the truth of it enough times in the human world.

"Get Liam; bring him here," Thomas ordered. "Don't tell him what this is about. I don't want anyone overhearing you. He should be able to verify how he died, which will give us an advantage when others discover the death."

I could do that if it meant getting away from the head staring at me with accusing eyes.

I moved with a purpose, careful to keep my pace down from an outright run. There was no need to let the entire party know that something was hideously wrong.

Backtracking down the long, empty corridor was an exercise in bravery. Before, this had been just another hallway with nothing sinister about it. Now it felt like the set of a horror film with the bad guy just waiting to appear.

Outside the party, I took a deep breath to compose myself. I needed people to think nothing was wrong, which meant none of the tension I was feeling could show on my face. I could do this. Just pretend it's a simple security matter.

I stepped into the atrium, my heels clicking across the slate tiles. Liam wasn't anywhere close. I wove my way through the crowd, keeping my eyes peeled for Liam or one of his underlings.

"Aileen, where have you been?" Caroline appeared from the crowd, looking irritated. "You disappeared. The whole purpose of you coming was to act as a buffer. You can't do that if you're going off into the shadows with a stranger."

"I didn't. I was looking for you." It was the truth. Mostly. I had been looking for her before witnessing a man cut off his own head.

"Alright, then. Let's go mingle."

She didn't wait for my reply before diving back into the crowd. It wouldn't hurt to follow and this way others wouldn't suspect my real purpose. I could look for Liam while humoring Caroline.

She found the group she was looking for, latching onto my arm and drawing me into the circle.

There were a few sidelong looks, the owners no doubt wondering who I was and what I was doing there. I smiled awkwardly and flagged down a passing waiter. At least with a glass of champagne in my hand I wouldn't feel quite so out of place.

I tuned the conversation out as I scanned the room, not remotely interested in the politics of the college set given the body sitting not too far from this gathering. Where was Liam? He was always turning up when he wasn't wanted and when I finally need him, he's nowhere to be seen.

There. The back of his head appeared briefly when the crowd parted.

"Where are you going?" Caroline asked sharply.

I fumbled for an excuse. "I see someone I need to speak with."

I could tell she wanted to say something, but the others in the group forced her to hold her tongue.

She gave me a gracious smile. I was the only one who saw the anger behind it. "I'll talk to you later then."

I gave an apologetic nod. As soon as I turned, Caroline and the shit storm she was saving for me dropped to the back of my mind.

I forced my way through the crowd, almost shoving people out of the way when they didn't move fast enough. I left a trail of apologies in my wake.

"Liam," I called when it looked like I would lose him again.

He turned and frowned at me.

I gave him a bright smile. He blinked and frowned harder.

"I'm so glad I found you. There's something I need to show you."

"It'll have to wait. I'm in the middle of a conversation," he said, indicating a man standing next to him.

The man was my height and looked Asian. His cheekbones could have cut glass and his eyes had a sharp intelligence that told me he wasn't one to be messed with. At the same time, he looked perfectly at home with this crowd, wearing his suit with a suave sophistication that contrasted with Liam's rough and tumble air.

The wattage on my smile turned up another notch. My cheeks were beginning to hurt with all this smiling.

"It concerns our mutual friend," I said. That should give him a clue.

His frown turned into a glare.

"Later."

Arrogant, insufferable vampire.

He turned back to his companion. "I apologize for the interruption."

The man inclined his head.

Liam began to speak before turning to stare at me.

I stared back pretending I didn't see the clear dismissal in his eyes. He wanted to ignore me after I made it clear there was an emergency? Fine. He had more to lose in this whole mess than I did. Thomas was his friend. That didn't mean I was going to make things easy for him.

"Aileen."

"Liam."

He grabbed my arm and hauled me a few steps away. "This isn't the time. I'm busy."

"I'm so sorry to bother you," I said in a sweet voice, though the look on my face was anything but sweet. It was closer to homicidal rage. "It's not like I have anything better to do."

"You may think you're cute, but I can assure you that you aren't," he hissed. He jerked his chin at Eric who nodded and stepped forward to talk with the man watching us through narrow eyes.

Liam dragged me a few steps further into the crowd, placing it between us and them.

"What is it you want?"

"It's something that would be better seen than retold."

His face reflected irritation. "Just tell me whatever it is."

"Trust me. You need to see it." I added a 'catch the hint' raise of my eyebrows.

The frown lines on his forehead said he finally caught the hint.

"This really isn't a good time," he said, looking back at Eric and his companion.

"Hey, this is your show. You want to ignore this; I can't stop you, but don't blame me when you get screwed later."

That was probably more than I should have said. A secret agent I was not.

Nathan appeared beside us. "She needs to get out of here. We can't afford for Tse to get upset."

He pronounced the man's name using the Ts from the word Tsunami and the e sound from the word bed. I knew without trying I would probably butcher the name by trying to repeat it.

"There seems to be a problem," Liam said in a grim tone of voice.

Nathan's eyes shot to mine. For once, there was no humor in them. Gone was the joking man I'd met yesterday.

"This should wait."

"Can't," I said.

I had a feeling they would want to know about the headless body even if they were being difficult at the moment.

Nathan bent closer, his face growing intent. "It. Should. Wait."

I said through gritted teeth, "It. Can't."

Nathan's gaze shot to Liam whose jaw locked. Liam looked no happier about the situation.

"I'll go," Nathan volunteered.

I thought about it. Nathan probably had the knowledge we needed. That might work. On the other hand, if he saw the body and needed Liam he'd have to come back here and risk drawing more attention to us. I shook my head. Thomas had wanted Liam. Better to be safe than sorry.

"What is so important that it can't wait?" Nathan asked in frustration.

I gave him a fake smile and gestured at the crowd saying between my teeth, "Do you really want to discuss this here?"

He looked around and acceptance registered on his face.

Liam said, "Lead the way."

I released a sigh of relief. Finally.

He caught hold of my arm saying so only I could hear, "This had better be as important as you've indicated. You will not like the consequences if it's not."

I met his eyes and indicated I understood.

*   *   *

The three of us rounded the corner and stepped outside into the crisp night. The patio was empty.

I took two big steps forward. Where was the body?

I opened my mouth to curse when suddenly the blood slick pavers blinked into view. I stood on the edge of the pooled red, the toes of my shoes just barely touching. I jumped back.

Thomas dropped into view. Literally, he dropped. As if he'd been perched high above us on the roof and had suddenly stepped off to join us on the ground.

I swallowed my yelp. If it was possible for vampires to have a heart attack, these guys would figure out a way to give it to me.

Liam ignored my jumpiness, but Nathan gave me a long look. I looked back and raised an eyebrow daring him to say anything.

His lips twitched with humor. So glad he found my agitation amusing.

"It took you long enough to bring him," Thomas said. His voice was neutral but lurking beneath was a thread of disapproval.

"What can I say, the appetizer tray was just irresistible."

Liam squatted next to the body, careful not to touch anything. I stepped to his side and leaned over his shoulder.

The wounds at Robert's neck were clean and precise. His blades had been very sharp. They had done their job efficiently and effectively. There had been no hesitation.

"Severing the spine is what killed him," Nathan said crouching on the other side. "He would have survived if the blade had missed his spine."

"Severing the carotid and jugular arteries wouldn't have killed him?" I asked.

Liam shook his head. "Vampires can heal wounds such as that fairly easily. It'll slow them down, cause them to be susceptible to the sun, but for the most part it's just a nuisance. We'll heal as soon as we get new blood in our system."

It was a little odd to think of myself as being able to survive a wound of this magnitude. Liam had helped me heal a few major injuries, including significant damage to my spine, but it still shocked me when I was confronted by the possibilities.

He shifted and pointed to the spine. "Severing the spine, on the other hand, is fatal in all but the very oldest of vampires. Even the ancients will need significant time to heal a wound of that magnitude. Robert was far from an ancient."

He looked up at Thomas and me. "Did you see what happened?"

I folded my arms across my chest.

Thomas looked no happier than I felt. Guess I wasn't the only one disturbed.

When it appeared he was lost in thought, I said, "We were there."

Liam stood, his face intent. I paused, not knowing how to explain the rest of what we'd seen. Hell, there was every chance Liam wouldn't believe any of this. I certainly wouldn't if I hadn't witnessed it firsthand.

"What did you see?"

My eyes dropped to the headless body. My voice was haunted as I said, "He did it to himself."

Nathan's head popped up as his eyes swung to me, "What are you talking about?"

"He cut his own head off," I said.

"Bullshit."

"It's true," Thomas said coming out of whatever fog he was in.

"How is that even possible?" Nathan asked in an incredulous voice.

Liam bent back to the body, examining it. He picked up the blade with a cloth, holding it up to the light. The blood was still wet and slid down the steel. He set it back in the body's hand before reaching over to do the same with the other.

"Describe exactly what you saw," he ordered.

Thomas explained what we'd witnessed, starting with Robert's appearance and the words he spoke before committing the deed.

I squatted next to Liam, careful to wrap the lower half of my dress around my lap to avoid getting it in the blood.

Despite how the movies make it appear, beheading someone is not easy. It takes a considerable amount of strength, precision and the proper tool. It's actually a pretty messy business. There are stories in history about executioners who needed three or four whacks before successfully beheading their victim. That Robert had done it as quickly and efficiently as he had was more than a little unbelievable and I'd been there. He should have hesitated once he got through the first few inches. Barring that, he should have stopped once he began to lose consciousness.

"His eyes were all black," I said, looking at the corpse. "Before. I mean."

Liam's eyes rose to mine.

"The other applicants are going to be like sharks in a feeding frenzy once they get a whiff of this," Nathan said to Liam.

"You never make things easy," Liam said to me.

I took exception to that. "Don't blame me for this. It's not my fault he decided to off himself right in front of us. Keep a better hold on your vampires and maybe problems like this won't happen. Besides, this was a message for your boy over there. I just happened to be an innocent bystander."

"What were you even doing out here?"

I stood, stepping back and letting the skirt of my dress fall once I was out of danger of the blood. "Ask your brother."

"He's not my brother," Liam said. "Not by blood anyway."

But I thought- I could have sworn the man had referred to them as brothers.

"Vampires often refer to others sired by the same master as

brother," Nathan volunteered.

All eyes swung to Thomas, who looked annoyingly unflappable.

"I needed to speak to her in private."

"I told you to limit your contact with her." Liam didn't sound happy about Thomas's excuse.

"This was important."

"Not this again. I told you that avenue was a dead end."

"I disagree," Thomas said. "Finding him would solve many problems."

"And open many more. The rules state that you must demonstrate the ability to sire other vampires. Having sired one isn't enough."

"Wait, are you telling me he has already sired a vampire?" I asked. Why hadn't they told me before? It would mean I wouldn't have to turn a possible descendant over or bargain a favor to a witch. This was information I should have been told.

"Yes, William. He was remade before my hex took hold."

"And you didn't think this was important enough to tell me?" I accused Liam.

"It's not important. William is unlikely to help us. He holds a grudge for actions taken in his first century. The rules state you must be able to replenish our ranks in time of strife and that those vampires must be mentally sound. The other applicants will assert the man is insane."

"That's not an archaic rule or anything." It sounded like something out of the middle ages. Ensure you have an heir and a spare.

"We must explore all avenues. William is a possibility that might turn the tide in our favor," Thomas said.

"We'll speak of this later," Liam warned. "We have more important matters to address at the moment."

Thomas didn't look too worried about the prospect. More like he welcomed the chance.

Nathan leaned closer and took a deep sniff. "It's faint but I smell anise, the same scent I found on the other victims."

Other victims? What other victims?

"You've encountered this before?" I asked sharply. Where?

"Not this exactly," Nathan said.

A suspicion occurred to me.

"Is this related to the other strange things in the city?"

Nathan and Liam shared a long glance. Liam gave a slight nod.

"Possibly. We're not sure. The pattern isn't clear. Different people react in very different ways so it's hard to tell if the source is one thing or many. This is the first that was compelled to commit suicide."

My eyes dropped back to the body as I turned his words over in my head. I was willing to bet the source for the odd behavior affecting spooks in the city was the same. Maybe the difference in reactions could be attributed to different species or different levels of powers.

If that was the case, Robert shouldn't have been affected as heavily as he was. As an applicant for the selection, he should have been among the more powerful in the city.

"How powerful was he in comparison to the other applicant's?" I asked.

Nathan looked like he was thinking my question over. "I'd say he wasn't the weakest, but he wasn't the strongest either." He looked at Liam for confirmation. "Thomas is probably the strongest by a large margin, followed by Stephen, then Robert and Elinor. Robert held the advantage there as he had considerably more experience in battle. He's had a lot of practice using his abilities to their maximum potential. He could probably give Stephen a run for his money; he was that good at the finer details of control."

"Could everything that's been happening lately be aimed at fixing the applicant selection?" I asked, my question falling into a sudden silence.

I saw grim expressions on the men's faces. I was taking that as a yes, which meant we had a roomful of suspects inside.

"What are we going to do with the body?" Nathan asked.

"That's a good question," an accented voice spoke from the doorway. "What exactly is your plan, enforcer?"

This time I controlled my jump, converting it into a quick turn.

Nathan looked like a little boy caught with his hand in the cookie jar as he met Liam's eyes in a silent apology.

Eric stepped from behind the short vampire, his eyes landing on the body. He grimaced and mouthed a choice word before his face turned expressionless.

Liam stood and inclined his head in a slight bow to the other man.

"Elder Tse, we are still gathering evidence. Once we have all of the facts, it will be time to decide."

The elder's eyes lingered on me as he joined us on the patio. His eyes fell on the body. They reflected a brief moment of sorrow before a mask slid over them, hiding any feeling he might have had at the loss of life.

"If your friend is right and this was an attempt to influence the selection, it will have to be addressed. We have not had a death in a selection for a very long time."

That surprised me, given the behavior of the vampire applicant's I'd met. They struck me as the type willing to do anything to gain power even if it meant killing their opponents to ensure victory.

"You witnessed this?" Tse asked, his eyes pinning me in place, the weight of a thousand anvils behind them.

I didn't like being the focus of all that attention. It made me feel small and helpless, as if my life balanced on the thin precipice that was his good will.

Not knowing what answer would damn me or save me, I chose the truth. "I did."

"Do you believe he took his own life or that he was compelled to do so?"

I looked at the others, finding no help in their carefully blank faces. Whoever this Tse was, he was dangerous. The rest guarded their expressions and body language, making it impossible to guess which direction led to safety.

"There are easier ways to kill yourself," I said, thinking my answer over carefully. "Even for a vampire. I can't imagine this was his will. I'm willing to bet there was a compulsion that forced his hand."

Tse's black eyes were intent on mine. It felt like that intensity was trying to burrow into my soul and see what made me tick. It took everything in me to hold his gaze. Weakness, I felt, would only lead to bloodshed.

His unblinking eyes left mine. "Find out what did this, enforcer. There is no reason for your existence if you cannot do the job you were entrusted with."

None of us spoke as Tse gave one last look at the body and then turned back the way he came. Liam indicated Eric was to follow.

He waited until long after the two had disappeared to speak.

Thomas crossed his arms over his chest. "I would not want to be in your shoes right now, old friend."

"Who was that man?" I asked. The others treated him as someone to be feared and respected.

"He's part of the council," Liam said. "He's one of two conducting the selection."

"So not someone to mess with then," I said, looking down the corridor.

"That would be the wisest course of action," Liam said.

"I'm surprised you would view him that way as you haven't demonstrated an abundance of caution to this point," Thomas said.

I gave him a long look. "Perhaps you just haven't demonstrated a reason to respect or fear you."

Thomas's fangs showed. I gave him fang back.

Liam whirled, grabbing my arm and dragging me several steps away. "Enough baiting him. What is wrong with you? He's a possible candidate. If you had any sense in that thick head of yours, you'd be bending over backwards to get on his good side, not giving him reasons to destroy your life."

"Perhaps I just don't like his face," I returned.

He studied me, his eyes seeing way more than I wanted. "No, you're reckless, but not usually this reckless. There's more to this than you're telling me."

He'd nailed it.

"How would you know?" I said. "You've met me a handful of times and read a few reports on me. That's hardly enough information to form a reliable judgement on my actions."

His sigh was angry, a sharp expulsion of breath.

"Go home. Do the job I'm paying you for."

I stiffened. He wasn't shutting me out of this investigation. I wasn't a child to be sent to her room when the adults were working

"I don't think so. Whatever is doing this is affecting the rest of the city."

His voice was calm but deadly as he said, "This doesn't concern you. This is vampire business and you've already decided you want no part in that." He arched a smug eyebrow. "Unless that's changed. Has it?"

I glared at him, hating the smug arrogance that said he had me trapped and he knew it.

"I didn't think so. Run off, little girl. We have business to attend to."

He did not just call me little girl. The wicked grin on his face said he knew exactly what affect those words had on me. It made the blood rise to my head and steam practically pour from my ears.

Fine, if he wanted to be an asshole about it, two could play that game. We'd just see who the little girl at the end of this was.

I walked backwards. "You have fun with that, grandpa, but you may want to tell your boy over there that the basil and anise he keeps smelling is a sign of demon taint."

I gave him a victory smile as the smug look dropped from his face before whirling and strutting back inside. Let him chew on that.

Chapter Fourteen

The smile dropped from my face as soon as I stepped inside. I hurried back to the rest of the party. I needed to find Caroline and get her out of here. It was too dangerous.

Caroline was involved with a different group this time. How many people did she know here? And how did she meet them? It wasn't like medieval history professors had a lot of chances to rub arms with the city's wealthy elite.

Unlike the other groups, this one held a vampire dressed in a wrinkled suit. His curly brown hair gave him a charming, innocent look. The way he was eyeing my friend made him seem anything but harmless. No, that made him seem more like a wolf in a dinner suit. It was the first time tonight a vampire had triggered that thought in my mind. It made me even more intent on getting her out of here.

"Caroline, I've been looking all over for you," I said, giving the group a big smile after making sure my fangs were retracted. No need to terrify the art lovers.

"I don't know why as I've been here for the last half hour," she said somewhat acerbically.

My smile didn't falter. "I need to show you something."

"Later. I'm talking."

Why is it that my excuse never seemed to work when I needed it to? Perhaps it said more about the people I spent time with that they didn't respond well to being interrupted.

The curly haired vampire's attention shifted to me, his eyes lighting as if he saw a tasty snack he'd like to gulp down. Not in this lifetime, buddy.

How to get my friend out of her current conversation without destroying our relationship forever. We weren't in active danger quite yet, though I could feel it lurking right around the corner, so I hesitated to do something I knew might take our relationship back to the arctic tundra days. She wouldn't forgive me if I embarrassed her in front of these people, especially if they turned out to be potential benefactors.

Hearing the current conversation begin to wrap up, I latched onto Caroline's arm and pulled her away. "There's someone I need to introduce you to. He's been asking to discuss some fourteenth century manuscript with you all night. He's a huge benefactor to the university."

"Really?" Caroline asked me skeptically.

"Uh huh. Huge." I was going to hell for lying to my friend like that.

I led her through the crowd, keeping an eye on our rear for anyone following us. I breathed a sigh of relief when Curly watched us go with interest. At least I had one less obstacle to deal with.

"I'm surprised you know anyone who'd be interested in that sort of thing. Don't your friends tend more toward an interest in studying different ways to kill people?"

"What are you talking about?" I asked, surprised out of my surveillance. "What kind of people do you think I hang out with?"

She shrugged. "I don't know. People who own guns and think the second amendment should justify owning enough weapons and ammo to start a third world war."

"That's some opinion you have of me," I said. "It's a wonder you asked me to come at all. I would think you'd be too ashamed to have your violent, unintelligent friend in the same room with all these intellectual giants."

Caroline flinched. "That's not what I meant."

"I think it was exactly what you meant," I returned in an even voice.

It might not have been in her thoughts when she invited me, but it had certainly occurred to her by the time we walked in here. Maybe after that conversation with the group who had stared at me like I was an animal from the zoo, here to entertain them with my experiences of war.

It's why she hadn't really introduced me after that or tried to include me in any of the conversations. It was why she'd left me to fend for myself in the conversational jungle. She might not want to admit it to herself but some part of her thought I didn't fit with these people and it embarrassed her.

"Aileen," her voice had a soft, pleading tone to it.

As much as that realization stung, it actually helped. It gave me an excuse to get us out of here.

"Come on. We're leaving." I used my grip to keep her moving, making sure it wasn't tight enough to hurt her. Just firm and unyielding.

"What? We can't. I still have potential donors to talk to and the chair of my department will have my head if I leave this early."

I tugged her closer to the door.

"Aileen. Are you listening to me?" Caroline's voice was no longer apologetic. It had the firm confidence that made her such an unstoppable force.

"Not really."

"Didn't you have someone to introduce me to anyway?"

I gave her an 'are you serious' expression, arching both eyebrows and widening my eyes slightly.

Her mouth clicked shut as she got the message. It made no difference that I had never intended to introduce her to someone. If I had, I wouldn't have wanted to after her statement. She wouldn't have deserved it.

Lucky for me she put her foot in her mouth, saving me from having to fess up to the lie.

Somehow I didn't feel very lucky right now.

By now we were outside and half way to the car.

"This is completely unnecessary. You're over reacting."

I didn't respond, keeping my attention on our surroundings in case of an attack. I doubted one would come, but it never paid to let your guard down.

"I'm beginning to see why your family staged that intervention," she said in frustration, yanking her arm from my hand.

I stopped and turned slowly, the look on my face making her back up a step. Remorse flashed in her eyes.

"Keys."

She hesitated, glancing back at the gala.

"Keys, Caroline. I'm tired and in no mood to talk to your friends. You can either leave with me, or I can go back in there and create a scene sure to get you fired. You pick, but either way I'm going home in the next few minutes. Up to you how that happens."

"You wouldn't."

"Try me." Right then, I meant it. I didn't care if it could possibly cost her career.

She must have believed me because she dug in her purse and flung the keys at me before stalking to the other side of the car. I caught them easily and unlocked the vehicle.

I gave one last scan of the parking lot, stiffening when I caught site of Curly watching us from the end of the lot. A figure, coming no higher than his chest, stood beside him with his back to me. I couldn't be sure but it looked an awful lot like Tom, the gnome.

It was possible he had a delivery in the area, but the two didn't act like it was a delivery. More like they knew each other.

Strange. I'd been under the impression Tom didn't like anyone who wasn't a gnome or Jerry.

"Are we going or not?" Caroline asked.

Curly smiled at me and waved. He could probably hear across the parking lot, which meant he'd heard our argument. I didn't like that.

I slid into the car and slammed the door shut. Backing out of the parking spot and driving away.

"What can you tell me about the man with brown, curly hair you were talking with earlier?" I asked.

Caroline glanced at me. "Who?"

"He was in the group you were speaking with when I came out."

"I don't know who you're talking about."

"The man with curly hair. Kind of looked like a car sales person despite the nice suit."

Her forehead crinkled as she thought. "Doesn't ring a bell."

Hm. Did she honestly not remember him or did she have help in forgetting?

I let the matter drop. Maybe Liam could clue me in on the mystery guy. Wait. I forgot that Liam had sent me away like a child off to bed so the grownups could talk. I'd have to find a new source for vampire information. Damn it.

*   *   *

I pulled up to my apartment and put the SUV in park.

"Do you need anything else to get started on the research for the descendants?" I asked.

"No. I have everything I need for the moment. If I have questions, I'll call you."

I was surprised at her response. I had expected to have to fight her over this. Do a little threatening, maybe some wheedling, possibly some outright begging. Her acceptance threw me.

"Ok. That sounds fine."

She got out. Guess that meant the conversation was done. I left the keys in the ignition and stepped aside. She climbed back in without speaking to me, avoiding my gaze as she drove away.

I watched her go. If I'd been a good friend, I would have apologized. Told her I knew she didn't mean those things, even if a part of her had.

I didn't do any of that. It was better this way. There was a reason I'd distanced myself from my nearest and dearest, and tonight had proven my decision correct. Even something as simple as a gala at an art museum ended with a body on the ground when I was involved.

It worried me to think of what could have happened if Caroline had decided to go looking for me and stumbled across that scene. The vampires may have killed her or barring that, tried to wipe her memory. Neither option left me with warm, cuddly feelings.

I clattered up my steps. A woman stepped out of the shadows onto my landing. I nearly twisted my ankle trying to flee. I only ended up stumbling and clutching the railing to keep myself from tumbling down the steps.

"Miriam," I snapped, fear making my voice harsher than I intended.

"Vampire." She watched me struggle upright, amusement twisting her lips.

"That's a nice trick," I said, advancing until I stood next to her on the landing.

She inclined her head.

I'd like to know how she did that. It would come in handy the next time I had to hide a body.

"I suppose you want to come inside," I said.

"It would be preferable to standing out here all night, yes."

I unlocked the door and opened it, kicking off my shoes as soon as I was inside and making a bee line for the fridge. Miriam could follow or not. Her choice.

My fridge, I found, was in serious need of restocking. There was little besides my bottle of blood masquerading as wine and a wedge of cheese. Guess I wasn't going to be offering my guest a snack.

"I have water if you're thirsty," I said, closing the fridge.

"I'm fine."

I turned and placed my hands on the counter. "Sorry about that. I wasn't expecting guests and it's been awhile since my last store run."

"I wasn't really expecting edible food in a vampire's house to begin with," Miriam, said looking around. She didn't seem overly impressed with what she saw. "Your living conditions are very different from others of your kind."

I snorted. What a nice way to say I lived in a dump. The paint was peeling, the ceiling was drooping in places, and I'd picked all of my furniture up at garage sales or thrift stores. It was a long way from what I had grown up with, but I loved it because it was mine. It might not have been the nicest furniture in a decent apartment on a nice side of town, but it was home.

"I take it from your living space that you are sticking to your edict of remaining clanless."

"Hm." I made a noncommittal sound that was neither affirmation nor a negation.

Her eyes fell on the counter by my hand. I followed her gaze and bit back a curse. That damn book had popped up where it didn't belong again. It was like a clingy puppy always wanting attention at the worse times.

"I see you've visited the bookstore," she said neutrally.

"You recognize the book?" I asked. Maybe she could answer some questions.

"Not this particular one, but others like it. I recognize the aura around it." Her head tilted as she examined the book. "May I?"

I slid the thing over to her. The bit about the aura sounded a little new agey to me, but then she did own a store that catered to that set. Maybe witches were able to see auras like the humans who claimed that good chi or chakra could improve your health.

She laid her hands to either side, just shy of touching it. To me it just looked like she was staring at it. There were no fireworks or colorful sparklers. She frowned and drew her hands away.

"You keep strange company," she told me. "It is very odd how one so young and powerless can attract such trouble."

"So it's dangerous." If it was, I was returning it first thing. If the book keeper wouldn't take it, I was burning it. Fire was a purifying agent in all sorts of religions. Books and fire were notorious for not mixing well. Chances were fire would destroy it, ending any potential trouble it could bring me.

"Not necessarily." She thought about it before coming to an internal agreement. "At least not at the moment. Not to you, anyway."

That wasn't cryptic or anything.

"It can move on its own and the text changes sometimes," I told her.

She nodded but didn't seem particularly surprised. "It's sentient and powerful. It's learning you. What makes you tick, what motivates you, what interests you. That's why the information seems to change. It's parsing what it thinks you need to know and feeding it to you."

I looked down at the book. If I'd wanted a roommate, I would have moved in with my sister, Jena, and her daughter.

"Why not just give me all the information?"

"Knowledge is power. In the wrong hands, it can do an untold amount of damage."

"How very conscientious of it," I said in a dry voice.

"Not necessarily. Items such as these rarely have a conscious in terms that human's understand. At the moment, you fit in its plans and it's your on side. For now." She cocked her head. "I'm actually surprised you drew something of this power. You're still too close to your human self to normally be attractive to such an item. There must be hidden depths to you."

Just what every girl wants to hear. That she's a magnet for weird and supernatural items of power.

I rubbed my head. At least I had an answer now. The book wasn't outright dangerous and could wait to be dealt with until the current events had resolved themselves.

"I'm guessing telling me about that book isn't why you're here," I said.

"No, it is not."

"I'm surprised to see you. I kind of thought you planned to avoid me after the conversation with Sarah. What brings you to my part of town at this time of night?" I asked, stepping back to lean against the fridge and fixing Miriam with an intent stare. I was curious to see what she had to say.

"What friend were you making inquiries after regarding the hex?" Miriam asked.

I straightened. "Why do you want to know?"

"I may know something, but I need more information before I know if it will be helpful."

"Tell me what you know, and I'll decide that."

"I can't do that. This information is dangerous. I would prefer only to speak it if the matter at hand can be directly impacted by it."

I studied her, weighing the wisdom of revealing what I knew. There was a reason for my secrecy, but if she did have the answer to my problem it might be worth taking the risk.

"How much do you know about the selection?" I asked.

"Not much. They're quite secretive about the process."

"I'm guessing they're not quite so secretive about the results."

Her lips quirked in a half smile. "Yes, they think they have the power to act as the presiding authority over the rest of the community."

"Bet that goes over well." I'd had enough interaction with spooks to know that they didn't take orders well, especially when those orders came from someone who didn't have authority over them.

"There have been skirmishes in the past. Vampires are powerful so their hold over their territories vary depending upon whether that power is stronger than those who live in it."

"And this territory? Are there any who can challenge the power grab?"

She thought about it. "The werewolf alpha is uncommonly powerful. His pack has grown in recent years. He would be one. The witch coven is another."

It sounded like the position was powerful in theory but in practice had little influence on the rest of the spooks.

Good. It meant the outcome would be limited in its impact. The fate of the city didn't rest on my shoulders.

"Of course, if the selected is smart and strikes an alliance with enough of the factions, it could tilt things in their favor."

"Can you tell me anything about how the applicant is selected?"

She shook her head and frowned. "They guard that information very carefully. All I know is there are a series of tests to determine the best candidate."

Which meant it was possible the witch hadn't known the side effect of her hex. That indicated there was a strong possibility that she'd been hired to do the job for one of the other applicants.

"The vampire in question is named Thomas. He said the hex would have taken place a few hundred years ago."

There was a shadow of an expression that crossed her face. She recognized the name.

"It would be wise not to trust Sarah," Miriam said.

"As opposed to trusting you," I said, letting the skepticism show in my voice. "You never did explain how that spell you cast managed to backfire so badly."

"You were there. Angela must have done something to the spell."

"Funny that you, as the more experienced witch, didn't catch what was going on before it was too late."

Miriam gave me a humorless smile that said she pitied my ignorance. "Spells are incredibly delicate castings. One wrong ingredient or word said the wrong way can drastically alter the outcome."

"If it was my spell, I imagine I'd be a little obsessed with attention to detail. I might double check and triple check everything to make sure the spell went off without a hitch. That means I've either underestimated your abilities as a witch and you're incredibly inept, or you knew something was going on and decided to let things play out to expose the snake in your house."

Her face closed down, and her hands flattened against the counter.

"I'm willing to bet it's the second one," I said. It wasn't a bad play. It was just too bad she put my life in danger to make it.

"This was a mistake," Miriam said. "I shouldn't have come here."

"Does Sarah know about Angela?" I asked as she turned to go. She paused and turned back to me, her body braced like she was preparing for battle. "I didn't think so. Tell me what you came here to tell me."

She took a deep breath and stepped back to the counter. "There are few witches with enough power in the time frame you're concerned about to cast a hex of that magnitude. We live longer than humans, but we are still considered mortal."

I hadn't thought of that, just assumed from the way Liam and Thomas had talked that witches were just as immortal as vampires.

"There were only a handful witches in the entire states at that time capable of that hex who are still alive." I waited with baited breath. "Sarah was one of them."

"You're saying Sarah cast that hex."

She shrugged one shoulder. "All I know is that she was around and was one of the few with the power."

"But by your own words there were others capable of that spell. An ability to cast it doesn't mean she was the one responsible," I pointed out.

"She is the only one I know of who had a relationship with Thomas that ended badly. She could very well have taken her wrath out on him."

Or had the very raw feelings taken advantage of by someone who wished Thomas harm, which I thought was the more likely reason. A woman scorned would have chosen something much more painful, something that would have had a definite and immediate impact.

She flicked her hair behind her shoulder and gave me an arrogant look. "I trust that is enough information to go on."

I nodded. If it was true, it gave me a definite place to start. Thomas could confirm the relationship, and Liam could do the interrogating.

"It was very helpful."

It made me question why she had given it up. There was some motive influencing her actions that I couldn't see. Yet. I would need to be cautious in how I handled this. I didn't want to get bitten in the ass by whatever plot she had simmering under the surface.

"I'll see myself out," she said, casting another distasteful glance around my apartment. "I trust you'll keep the knowledge of where you got this information to yourself."

"I won't run down the streets screaming 'Miriam told me Sarah did it' if that's what you're asking," I said. "But I also won't conceal it if I feel it can help in my investigation."

She didn't look happy at my comment, but she inclined her head and left. I locked the door behind her and turned back to my apartment.

"The witch obscures the truth of the matter with other truths," a high pitched female voice said next to my ear.

I swatted at the pixie. It dodged and flitted through the air, its wings casting multicolored lights over the walls. It settled on the arm of my couch and took a seat.

"How would you know?" I asked.

She shrugged her tiny shoulders. "Nobody sees us, and when they do they forget that we are intelligent too. They disregard what we may hear or see, thinking we are unable to relay it to anyone who matters. As a result, we go many places unnoticed. It lets us learns things."

"And have you heard anything about the witch?"

The pixie lifted a finger. "Ah, ah. That would be telling."

"And we wouldn't want that, now would we?" I said, giving it a nasty smile.

She leaned back on one hand. "Of course, if we had an agreement in place, it would mean I'd be bound to share information that might help you."

"What sort of agreement?" I asked suspiciously.

"You let us stay here for the next few days and I'll tell you everything I know."

"Why here?" I asked, not understanding why they'd want to stay here. "There are thousands of houses out there for you to make your home in. The mortals won't even suspect you're there."

"We have our reasons, which are not part of the bargain," she said.

It would be useful having some background on the events taking place. I was in over my head and I knew it. The only way I was going to get out of this in one piece was by knowing all the moving pieces.

"Leave my stuff alone and promise not to play any of your pranks on me and we have a deal," I told her.

She gave me a smile, one that was crafty and smug. It made me question my decision to let her stay. I had a feeling I would end up regretting this before the end.

"Now tell me what you meant."

"So impatient." She gave me a fake frown of disapproval.

"I can still change my mind, you know," I said conversationally. I wouldn't. I'd already made the deal, but she didn't know that.

"Fine, fine. You don't have to get all huffy about it."

I was not being huffy.

"Get to the point, pixie."

"My name is Inara," she said. "You might as well call me that instead of referring to me by my species. It's rude when you do that. Vampire."

"Fine, Inara. Get to the point."

"Much better."

I briefly imagined hitting her with a fly swatter. Would she go splat or just be a little bruised?

"The witch spoke true enough. Word on the street was that Sarah had a brief romance with Thomas a few hundred years ago, and it's true the relationship did not end well. What your little witch friend failed to mention is that she was also around back then."

"You mean Miriam?" I asked, crossing my arms over my chest. "You're trying to tell me she's also a few hundred years old."

The woman looked no older than twenty five.

"Is that what she's calling herself these days?" Inara grimaced with distaste. Judging by her expression I could only assume she wasn't a big fan. "Sarah and your buddy Miriam had a bit of a rivalry back in the day."

"Wait a minute. If that's true, why does Sarah look ancient while Miriam looks like a coed?"

"Witches and others of their ilk are different than other immortals. With a vampire like yourself, you're locked into your age for the rest of eternity. The fae grow over centuries before their aging stops at the optimum age. Witches rely on their inner spark to extend their life into the centuries. A weak witch might only gain a few years. Maybe a decade. Most live to be about three hundred or four hundred years old. A truly powerful one can live for a millennium. You can never tell how long one will live until they exhaust their spark."

"You're saying Miriam is more powerful than Sarah. That her spark hasn't worn out yet."

The pixie rubbed her lips with her thumb in thought. "Perhaps that was a bad explanation."

"Not bad, just simple," the male pixie landed on the couch next to her. He touched her shoulder in that way lover's had. As if to say, I'm here. I see you. It was a touch that spoke of long familiarity.

"In your human media, witches are often portrayed as crones, yes," the male pixie had a slight accent as if English wasn't his first language.

I thought on what he said. Maybe in some versions of our stories they were crones but in many they were young, nubile women who had made a deal with the devil.

"There can be consequences for wielding your power in certain ways. One of those is aging before your time. Certain powers twist the physical form. Sarah may be a victim of such a power. There is also the possibility that she was hexed in turn or that she is casting an illusion to make her appearance different to what it is. Witches are tricky. It's best to avoid them whenever possible."

Casting an illusion that altered her appearance could set her up to move unseen around the city when not meeting with her coven. Only those who knew her when she looked younger would ever guess.

None of their explanations had convinced me Miriam was outright lying, but they had placed enough doubt in my mind to be doubly cautious going forward.

While I was thinking the two disappeared, leaving me standing in my living room alone. I hadn't even notice them go. Sneaky little pests.

I headed for my shower. It was early still, but I was ready to call it a night. I had no plans to venture outside, not with some demon-tainted thing running around causing all sorts of problems. Knowing my luck, I would happen on the creature and end up getting killed or seriously injured.

As for the pixies, I wasn't happy about my new house guests, but as long as they kept their pesky little hands off my stuff I would endure them. Their information had only bought them a few days in my apartment. I had every intention of kicking them out at the end of the time they'd bargained for.

Showered and clad in a robe I headed for the fridge and the blood. Since I was staying in tonight, I wanted to test a few things. Specifically my healing abilities. The blood would help.

As a clanless vampire, I had no one to teach me the things other vampires took for granted. Like healing, or compulsion. Every time someone surprised me with a new ability it was like being confronted with all the things I didn't have access to. It meant I had to be resourceful. And dedicated. It was a slow process that felt more like beating my head against a wall over and over again, only to get deliriously happy whenever I made some microscopic advancement.

This time I wasn't challenging my sunlight abilities. I was doing something much more painful.

I drew a knife from the drawer and took a deep breath. I'd found that healing abilities weren't automatic. At least for me. Maybe it was because of my relative youth or my bottle diet, but I had to concentrate to heal myself.

I set the knife against my forearm and drew it across the skin in a quick, sharp movement, leaving a thin line of blood. Setting the knife down, I concentrated, trying to imagine the power coursing in pathways beneath my skin.

Liam had made this seems so easy when he showed me how to use it last year.

For me, the power slipped and slid, avoiding every attempt to force it to the cut where it could heal the surrounding flesh. It was like trying to pin down a grape with a fork. Every time I thought I had it, the path rolled away. Even when I managed to pin it, the power moved sluggishly as if it were a teenager being dragged from bed.

After several minutes, the wound began to close, the skin around it itching with a mad intensity. The cut healed but left behind a raised, angry, red welt that I knew from experience would remain for a few days before healing all the way.

The effort left me feeling weak and lightheaded. It wouldn't do me much good in a fight if at the end I passed out from exhaustion.

"You're doing it wrong," a high pitched voice said next to my ear.

I jumped and the pixie flared his wings, gliding down to the counter top. He held a piece of cheese the size of his head in his hand.

"Is that my cheese?" I asked.

He ignored me. "You're trying to move the whole line when you should be summoning only a thin tendril."

I see we weren't going to talk about his thievery.

"Try again, but this time instead of shifting the line to the wound, envision you're trying to open a small channel that routes to the wound."

"Wouldn't more power work better?"

"It's not how much you have but how well you wield it. You're flooding yourself with everything you've got and your body doesn't know how to deal with it." He broke off a piece of the cheese and ate it, his sharp teeth making short work of the hard surface.

Anything was worth a shot at this point. I hadn't shown progress in my healing ability in months.

I made another cut and set the knife down. Staring at the wound, I imagined the spidery pathways. Every attempt to pull any of my power from the source failed to take ahold.

"You're trying too hard," the pixie said. "Relax."

I gave him a look. That was the most unhelpful advice he could have given me. How could I relax yet pull the power to me?

When I was in high school a friend had been into tai chi and meditation. I'd thought it was a waste of time before I tried it. Meditation had never really caught hold with me, I found it impossible to think of nothing while sitting still, but tai chi was different.

I could let the flow of the movements distract me from my thoughts. It was like being part of a river where one form just flowed into the next, until you found yourself moving with little conscious direction on your part. Your body taking advantage of muscle memory as your mind let go.

It never worked when I struggled to capture that mindset though. It had to come naturally, my mind sinking into that mode with little effort on my part.

Instead of thinking, I watched as the power circled in a clockwise motion through my body.

Slowly, like a spider seeking a new anchor point for its web, a thin tendril reached out and a cool sensation washed over my arm, right before the skin around the wound began itching again.

"Not the fastest healing time, but better than before," the pixie said. His wings flared and he leapt into the air before buzzing off with his spoils.

I touched the skin. It was smooth and, besides a ravenous hole in the pit of my stomach, I felt fine. None of the wooziness that characterized my prior attempts.

Still wouldn't be much help in a battle, but it was progress.

I grabbed the wine bottle and poured myself a glass of the red liquid before pulling up a movie on the instant streaming service.

At this point there wasn't much to do, the city was sleeping and I'd already laid all my plans. Now the only thing to do was wait and hope that something came of all my hard work tomorrow. I had a feeling I was running out of time. Tomorrow would be the night when things happened. Good or bad.

Chapter Fifteen

The ringing of my cell phone woke me from a weird dream of a shirtless Liam featuring a few interesting tattoos and a wicked grin that just begged me to let go of my dream inhibitions.

It took me a moment to remember where I was and to identify the annoying music blaring right next to me. The phone went quiet, the music stopping. I closed my eyes. Good, maybe I could get back to that dream.

The music started again.

I sat up on the couch, knocking the book off the coffee table as I groped for my cell.

"Crap."

My fumbling hands knocked the phone away, and I had to extend my reach. In that weird logic that makes perfect sense when you just wake up but your brain hasn't caught up entirely, it made sense to prop my shoulders on the coffee table while keeping the lower half of my body on the couch. This resulted in an awkward flailing that ended with me bumping my elbow hard on the corner of the table.

After way more effort than it should have taken, I grabbed the phone and rolled back onto the couch, managing to leave another bruise on my ribs in doing so.

"Hello," I croaked.

"Where the hell have you been?" Caroline snapped. "I've been calling you for hours."

I sat up, biting back a groan as muscles protested my choice of beds. I thought being a vampire meant I wouldn't have problems such as achy muscles anymore.

I twitched the curtains aside, blinking rapidly like a mole suddenly confronted by the light. The sun was still up. Not by much. Judging by the red tinge, it was in the process of setting.

I glanced at the clock on my DVR. 7:35. Full sunset wasn't for another thirty minutes at least.

"Aileen, are you still there?"

"Yeah. Yeah. Sorry. My phone was dead. I just plugged it back in an hour ago."

There was a brief silence as I imagined she was debating on whether to confront me about the lie.

"Why'd you call?" I asked, hoping to avoid having to make up any more lies.

Her hesitation was clear in her voice. "I made progress on your search."

"Already?"

She would have only begun work on it after the gala last night.

"I gave it to one of my TAs the night you gave it to me. He's pretty good at family trees. He's writing a dissertation on the migration patterns to the west during the mid to late nineteenth century so he had plenty of sources he's familiar with," she explained.

My eyes started sliding close. I was so tired.

"Your friend Peter was also helpful today in compiling that information and finding a few other sources for us to check.

Wait a minute. My eyes popped open. "Peter is there. He's been helping you?"

Her pause this time seemed a bit wary. "Yes. I assumed you'd be ok with that. Is there a reason you're not happy about that?"

"No, of course not." I was going to skin that sorcerer and make a rug of his flesh when I saw him next. "I just wasn't expecting he'd be that interested in helping you. He has a bit of a short attention span."

"I don't think I could have done it this fast without him. He's got an amazing knack for research, especially in one so young."

If she only knew. His research ability was probably refined over centuries.

"What did you learn?"

"It wasn't easy, but I found out the family you were tracking lost most of its members during the flood. Only two survived. A girl, aged three, and a boy of fourteen. The siblings left the state at that time."

I was afraid of that.

"How were they able to leave?" Normally orphan children would have been remanded to whatever orphanage was open at the time.

"Family friends took the children under their protection and relocated to California."

I didn't know if that would help us. I got the feeling Liam and Thomas were relying on his descendants being local.

"Ok. Send me the names, and I'll take it from here."

"Wait, don't you want to hear the rest?" Caroline asked.

"There's more?"

She laughed. "I wouldn't be much of a researcher if I didn't look below the surface."

"Don't leave me in suspense," I said.

"Hold on, someone just knocked. Tell you what, head to my house. What I have to tell you is pretty big, and all this research has made me hungry. You spring for pizza and we can discuss the rest when you get here."

Pizza. I hadn't had that in a while.

"That sounds good. I don't think I have your new address though."

She rattled off the address as a doorbell rang.

"What the?" Caroline said, angrily.

"What's going on?"

"Some jerk did a ring and run. There had better not be a bag of shit on fire on my front porch."

A warning niggled at the back of my mind.

"Don't open your door. Wait until I get there."

"It's probably just teenagers playing pranks."

"Let's be safe. I can be there in minutes."

I still didn't know where she lived or how far it was from my apartment, but in this situation I planned to break all sorts of records getting to her house.

I heard the sound of locks being undone.

"Caroline, listen to me."

"It's fine. I'm just going to make sure there's nothing on the porch."

I stood and ran to my bedroom, pulling on the first pair of jeans and t-shirt I could find.

"There's no one here," Caroline said.

"Do not go outside," I ordered.

"Wait, I think I see something."

"Stay inside."

"I'm not letting some idiot damage my property," Caroline snapped.

She was going outside and there wasn't a damn thing I could do about it. What I wouldn't give for the ability of compulsion through cell phone connection.

There was a pause where I could hear movement.

"What is that? What are you doing?" Caroline sounded freaked out like she had just seen something she couldn't explain.

"Get inside. Stop asking questions and get inside." I struggled to sound calm.

A door slammed shut and then Caroline yelled, "I'm calling the police."

There was a loud crash and the sound of splintering wood followed by a short scream. The phone cut off and I was left with a cut connection blaring in my ear.

"Damn it. She never listens." I dialed the phone. It went to voice mail. I dialed again and again. Same result.

Kneeling by the safe in my nightstand, I inputted the code and pulled out the Judge. Chances were if you shot someone with this, they weren't getting back up. At least if they were human. With the spooks, you could never tell. It might slow them down long enough for us to run away or they might shrug it off.

After a brief hesitation, I grabbed the special rounds I'd researched how to make on the internet. Filled with silver nitrate, I was hoping the silver would be powerful enough to slow down a vamp or a werewolf since both were highly allergic to the metal. This would be its first field test. If my measurements for the homemade bullet were off, it would result in a misfire, rendering the gun useless until I could clear the chamber and reload the magazine.

It was a risk I was willing to take. The last time I used normal rounds on a spook he had shrugged them off like they were no more than an irritating bee sting.

I should never have asked Caroline for her help. I should never have involved her. When it was clear what sort of party that gala was, I should have dragged her out of there whether it permanently damaged our friendship or not.

I just hoped she was still alive when I got there. The nasty feeling in the pit of my stomach didn't give me much hope. These weren't the sort of people to take prisoners.

*   *   *

The city sped past as I reached speeds not even a professional biker in the tour de France could achieve.

I spotted a house with the door kicked in and veered toward it. I didn't have to look at the address to know it was hers. Throwing a leg over the seat, I hopped off while the bike was still in motion, letting it fall as I ran.

I darted up the front steps, vaguely taking in the bench swing and the white painted posts and railing, in favor of focusing on the destruction to her door.

That splintering crash I had heard was the sound of something bursting through. Normally when someone kicked in a door, they concentrated on the weak point next to the handle. Whatever had done this went straight for the middle, using enough force to break a solid oak door in half.

I drew my gun from the holster, holding it in a two handed grip as I stepped inside. Or at least that's what I intended to do. A force stopped me at the threshold.

I tried again. Nope. Didn't work.

I backed up to the edge of the porch and took a running start. The force stretched like taffy as I made it one step, then two steps inside. I dug deeper, trying to put enough strength behind that third step to get me further in.

The force rebounded like a sling shot, flinging me outside. I sailed through the air, landing on my back. My hand didn't let go of the gun, though I made sure my finger wasn't on the trigger.

I sat up and glared at the door. Turns out that old wives' tale about vampires not being able to enter a human's home uninvited was true. Great time to discover at least one superstition had merit.

Wait, if I wasn't able to get in, that meant Caroline had to be alive. I'd been able to get into other homes after the owners were dead so the handicap was tailored to the living.

"As entertaining as this is, just what exactly do you think you're doing?" Peter asked next to my ear.

I yelped and spun around, bringing the gun up to point at the sorcerer.

He lifted an eyebrow and smirked. "I doubt your toy will have any effect on me."

"You ever been shot before?" I asked, lowering the gun.

He thought about it. "I don't think that I have."

"Then how do you know it won't hurt you?"

He gave a slight shrug as if to concede the point. "Fair point. That brings us back to my question of what you're doing. As entertaining as it is to watch your flying lessons, I'm sure Ms. Caroline will not like it when you crush one of her rose bushes. She's quite fond of them."

209

"I'm sure she'll understand when she finds out I was trying to save her," I said, wiping dirt from the seat of my jeans.

He frowned, his gaze going to the door. He rushed up the steps and inside, leaving me standing by myself.

"What do you see?" I asked, walking up the steps and stopping at her threshold.

"There's blood."

I bowed my head and shut my eyes.

"I don't think there's enough to signify death, but she was hurt when they took her."

Hold on Caroline, I urged silently. I'll find a way to save you.

"Can you invite me in?" I asked, my voice thick with repressed emotion.

The sorcerer appeared in the doorway, his face serious. I thought he looked a little older since I'd left him with Caroline in the library. It wasn't much, just a slight maturing around the eyes and mouth. I could have been imagining it, though.

"Aileen Travers, I bid you welcome."

I pushed against the threshold. It resisted a moment before breaking. I stepped through, the scent of blood permeating the air. My eyes went to the bright liquid that was already drying. The freshness told me I hadn't missed them by much.

There was more of it than I had assumed based on Peter's assessment. The wound was serious.

I squashed the urge to throw stuff. Losing my cool wouldn't help my friend. I needed that calm in a storm the military attempted to teach its soldiers.

First, assess the situation. You can't act effectively without the facts.

The room was a shambles. The sofa overturned. Books yanked from the built in shelves and thrown around the room. Her computer was in pieces on the floor. It looked like a twister had been through.

"They were looking for something," I said.

"I agree." Peter bent next to the coffee table and picked up several books, laying them gently down in piles next to him. He grabbed ripped papers and smoothed them out before setting them in neat stacks next to the books.

"It's impossible to know whether they found what they were looking for," I said.

The entire room was tossed so it was hard to say for sure. I would assume if they'd found what they were looking for their destruction would have stopped at that point. The fact that nothing had been left intact led me to believe they hadn't found whatever that was. At least not in here.

"I'm going to walk through the rest of the house."

Peter nodded and flapped a hand at me as if to say get on with it. He didn't look up from the papers. I took that to mean he was planning to stay and find out what he could.

I headed deeper into the house where the destruction wasn't quite so pronounced. The kitchen was left virtually untouched, as was the sun room. Her office shared the same fate as the living room. Again, the computer had been torn apart and the books pulled off the shelves. Someone had taken claws to her desk and chair, leaving deep gashes in the wood and leather seat.

Her upstairs was also left mostly untouched. The faint smell of animal and something more tickled my brain. I knew that second smell. What was it? I inhaled filling my lungs with it. I'd smelled it recently. If only I could place it.

Ha. Basil and anise. That was it. The same smell that was on Robert.

Why had the smell stayed here rather than in either of the offices? I hadn't caught anything but the faintest whiff down there.

The scent was concentrated around her walk in closet. Someone had lingered here, but nothing was disturbed.

I didn't think it was a good sign that someone with demon taint had paid my friend a visit. It confirmed my suspicions that there was a link between the trouble throughout the city and the vampire selection. I just needed to find out what that link was.

I headed back downstairs to find Peter had gathered enough piles of books and paper to be in danger of running out of room on the coffee table.

"Her office looks like this," I said. "The rest of the house is relatively undisturbed."

"Hm." Peter didn't look up, consumed by whatever was on the paper in front of him.

"What is that?" I asked.

"I can't be sure, but I think it's what they came here for."

I moved quickly, settling down beside him and trying to get a glimpse of the paper. It made no sense to me, looking like a bunch of squiggly lines with names at odd intervals. I tried to grab it from Peter for a closer look. He elbowed me and yanked it out of reach.

"Unless you've been working with her over the last several days on this matter, I suggest you let me finish looking at it. I doubt you would understand what you were seeing anyway."

I settled back and gave him a flat stare. "Then impress me, oh wise one."

"We weren't able to do a normal genealogical search as we were starting at the beginning and trying to extrapolate down through the years," he began. I made a motion signaling he needed to speed this explanation along.

He rolled his eyes. "The records are sparse and you have to eliminate possibilities to find the needle in the haystack. Unless someone stays in the same area from birth to death, it can be quite challenging tracking down records. Until we found a mention of the family friends in the last will and testament left by the children's parents, we were stuck."

"She said the friends took the children to California."

"They did." He paused and turned to look at me, "Did you know humans have compiled most of their historical records online in state archives? It's quite convenient if you know what you're looking for."

I raised my eyebrows and said with a straight face, "Did they now? I had no idea."

"It's quite impressive. I've decided that the preservation of even the minutest detail in their records is one of the few redeeming traits of humanity."

"Ah hah." That was an interesting observation. One I didn't know what to do with it. "What does this have to do with what you found, or Caroline's abduction?"

"I'm getting to that."

"Get there faster. The clock's ticking."

"We came across mention of them and the children in a church roster that had been uploaded to the California archives. Took us hours to find the mention and then it was only luck that we checked through some of California's records," he said. "I think during her research she may have stumbled across something besides those names that her attackers didn't want us to know."

"Do you know what that is?"

He shook his head. "Given enough time, I could probably recreate her work, but as it stands several pieces are missing. Without them I'd only be guessing."

I sat back.

"It may not be important anyway," I said, thinking carefully. "My primary objective is to find Caroline, not complete her work. This can wait. Right now it's enough to know this probably has something to do with the vampires."

I needed a way to find her. The witches. They'd been able to track the draugr based on a picture. They just needed an item with some kind of tie to Caroline.

"What are you doing?" Peter asked as I started sifting through the piles.

What would Caroline have considered important? The item needed to have enough sentimental value that it could make the link.

"I'm looking for something we can take to the witches. They can cast a spell that'll pinpoint her location."

She loved books, but I couldn't tell which ones were her favorite. Same with the photos.

"It won't work."

"Of course it will."

Maybe this, I picked up metal key with the ornate initial C engraved on the top. I remembered it. She had hunted through several stores for the exact one she wanted during a school trip to Washington D.C. our senior year. When she was the only one in our group who didn't get a nasty case of a stomach virus, she'd sworn the key had acted as a good luck charm.

"No, it won't. The people who did this have magic of their own. The witches don't have enough power to counter dark magic on this level. Even if they did, what makes you think they'd help you? In case you haven't heard, they use their magic for their own interests."

He had a point. Miriam hadn't exactly been happy with me by the time she'd left my apartment last night. I doubted Sarah would walk across the street to spit on me if I was on fire, and from my encounter with the coven at the tea shop, I was willing to bet the rest of them were likely to follow her lead.

"I'll just have to take that chance."

"And while you waste time on a pointless endeavor, your friend is probably being tortured for information, or they may be just doing it for fun at this point."

"What do you suggest I do then?" I shouted. "Sit around doing nothing? I need to do something. Even if they don't help, at least I'll have tried."

"I want you to put that brain to use," he snapped back. "She can't afford for you to go off half-cocked."

We glared at each other.

He was right. I was letting my desperation and fear for Caroline influence my actions. Rushing off halfcocked wouldn't do anyone any good and might result in my friend being hurt or killed.

I took a seat beside him, cradling the key in my hand.

"You have experience with this world. Is there another way that doesn't involve the witches?"

He tapped the paper with his forefinger. "The wolves might be able to track by smell."

I shook my head. "I suspect one of them has been compromised."

"How do you know?"

"I may have hit one with my bike and then followed it to some type of meeting between it and a man in a hooded sweatshirt. Can't be sure but it looks like he was conducting a ceremony. Could be the one responsible for the demon taint."

Either way, I didn't want to chance any of Brax's other wolves working for the wrong side.

"There are other spooks capable of doing something similar," he said in thought. "None that I'm in good standing with."

As a vampire, one without a clan, it was likely I wasn't going to have any more success in convincing them to help us either.

"Keep thinking," I ordered. "There's a way. We just need to find it."

"What are you going to do?" he asked as I stood.

"I need to report this to the vampires in case we're successful. We may need reinforcements."

"Is that wise? If the werewolves are compromised, what makes you sure the same isn't true for the vampires?"

"Liam should be safe enough."

He was an ass, but he'd come through for me in a pinch before. What I didn't say is that if we couldn't trust someone we might as well sentence Caroline to her fate. I was pretty sure I wouldn't be able to win against the combined might of whoever had done this.

Seeing his acceptance, I pulled out my phone and clicked on his name in my contacts.

"Do you have news?" Liam said, his voice sounding tense.

"Possibly. Well, sort of."

"What does that mean?"

I pinched the bridge of my nose. It seems like the very thing I'd tried to avoid, revealing my tie to Caroline, was the very thing I needed to blow wide open.

"It means that the person I've been using for research just got kidnapped."

There was a long pause.

"I thought our agreement made it clear that you were to work on this alone. If the wrong person found out about this-"

"Relax. The person is human. She has no ties to this world."

Another pause. I could almost feel the thoughts turning over in his brain.

"Your friend from last night."

Smart man.

"That's the one."

"How much did she know?"

"Not much. Just that I needed her help tracking the descendants of a certain family to present day." I gave the sorcerer a glance over my shoulder. Caroline had no ties, but the sorcerer did and technically he'd been there when I asked for help.

"Alone, that information would not be very useful," he said almost to himself.

"That's not all," I said.

The quality of his silence changed, almost as if its ears perked up.

"Oh?" was the soft response.

"I'm pretty sure the demon taint had something to do with this. I smelled basil and anise in her house."

"She could just be a fan of that combination."

"No. You know as well as I do what this is."

There was a long drawn out pause. I got the feeling he'd put me on mute and was conferring with someone on the other end.

I waited, summoning patience I didn't necessarily feel.

"Why is it that you're calling?" he asked.

My hand tightened on the phone until it creaked ominously. I relaxed my grip. "You know why I'm calling. I need to know what you know about the demon taint and where he might be keeping her."

"You want my help saving her."

Give the man a prize. He'd guessed the obvious.

"Yes."

He gave a long sigh. "Why should I help you? You've spurned every offer to join us."

"This whole thing started with you. If she hadn't been working on your project, she would be safe."

"I never told you to involve her. In fact, I think it was just the opposite. The fault lies more on you than it does me."

My grip tightened again, but this time I didn't gentle it when the phone creaked in warning. "You asked for something that even with all your resources you couldn't find given unlimited time. Then you gave me a ridiculous timeline that would be impossible to meet. Of course I went to an expert for help. Even if none of what I just said was true, you should still help me because my fault or not this mess is still your responsibility. I can promise you if you let her die when you could have done something, I will make it my mission to destroy your buddy Thomas and bring you down in the process."

I waited, hoping something I said had gotten through to him. I meant every word.

"You have the worst timing," he said. "I don't have any information on where they might be holding her. You'll have to figure that out yourself. The selection takes place tomorrow so there are things happening that need to be handled."

That sounded like he was going to refuse to help.

"Do you think she figured out where his descendants are?"

"Yes."

I was only half sure, but if it would get him to help me, I'd say anything.

"You'll need to get her location yourself, but I'll do what I can from my end once you do."

A whoosh of air left me. Relief filled me. I couldn't do this alone. Not against an unknown number of assailants. Liam's backup might mean we had a fighting chance.

"Aileen," he said softly. "You'll owe me after this."

The way he said that made it seem like it was a big deal to owe him. That it might have repercussions I was not aware of.

"Understood."

Some debts were worth the risk.

"Keep me updated."

"Will do."

He hung up.

I turned back to the sorcerer. "The vampires couldn't tell me where she was, but they should be able to help us when we go in to rescue her."

Peter's young face wore an expression often seen on someone his apparent age. It was full of skeptical disbelief. The teenage nonverbal way of saying I'll believe it only when it hits me upside the head.

"Any luck on figuring out a way to find her?"

"There is one way," he said, looking away from me.

"And that is?"

"You're not going to like it."

I watched him, noting how he avoided my eyes and fidgeted with the cuff around his wrist.

"You want me to open the genie cuff." My voice was flat.

"I can't think of another way." His eyes rose to meet mine. "I can do it faster than anybody else. My magic is better equipped to combat dark magic than a vampire's, and I've had experience with demon taint before."

"Have you?" He'd neglected to mention that earlier.

"It's the best way."

I watched him. He had demonstrated a liking for her. Everything about his demeanor said he would do anything to save her, even putting aside his dislike of me.

"You swear you'll do everything in your power to save her?" I asked.

"On my honor, I swear to stop at nothing to rescue Caroline Bradley."

I felt a spark of something, as if the universe had taken notice of his oath. It might have meant nothing, just a passing fancy of mine, but I believed him. In his desire to help Caroline, at least.

"Give me your hand."

He looked startled and stared at me as if he couldn't believe I'd agreed. He placed his wrist in mine and watched closely as I hit the sequence that would release him. The band popped open and dropped to the table. Its copper a dull sheen against the wood.

For a moment Peter sat frozen, then it was like he took a deep breath and power swamped the room, stretching and kneading like a cat waking from a long nap. His eyes took on a greenish glow.

My muscles locked in place as my instincts roared at me to run. It was like looking into a great yawning maw, one that intended to disrupt everything I held dear.

"Thank you, Aileen."

I drew a deep breath as green sparked along my vision. Pain seared my skin, diving deep into the muscle, straight for the bone. Pain so

217

great I couldn't even draw breath to give it voice.
The world clicked off.

Chapter Sixteen

I knew before I opened my eyes that something was wrong. Every muscle in my body ached worse than any 'take no prisoners' workout I'd ever conducted, and my head hurt in a way that told me that moving was going to be excruciating.

The events came racing back to me. Peter asked me to remove the cuff and like an idiot I had.

My mark blazed to life, sending white hot fire shooting down my nerves.

I whimpered, curling around the arm.

"The pain will pass," Peter said from above me.

I managed to crack my eyes open and stare at the room around me. It looked like a dungeon. Like an actual sixteenth century dungeon complete with dripping water and straw on the floor.

"It's from the buildup of magic over the last few months," he said conversationally, turning his back on me and walking to a wooden table loaded down with books and neon colored liquids. "Under normal circumstances, you would have gotten a steady trickle over a long period of time which would have increased your tolerance level. That process is now happening all at once. I'm told it can be quite agonizing." He sounded happy about that.

"I'm going to kill you," I said, my face pressed into the stone floor.

"Big words from someone who doesn't even have the strength to stand."

Very dead. I was going to kill him very dead.

"Dead, Peter. Very, very dead."

"Stop being so melodramatic." I could practically feel him rolling his eyes "The power rush should be slowing any moment now."

He was right. The pain was lessening from 'want to cut my arm off to get away from it' to 'wanting to curl up for the next few centuries to avoid aggravating it'.

"I thought we had a deal," I snarled, forcing myself to sit up.

"We do, but the power draw is a natural process of the mark. There's nothing I could do about it." He didn't sound very sorry about it. Quite the opposite in fact.

"Explain."

"Basically, that mark functions on a number of levels. The first is it marks you as my servant and binds you to my will." Yeah, I remembered that part. It's the reason I had left the genie cuff on him. "The second purpose is the part that's really important. It turns you into a deep well of power for my spells, essentially making it so I can filter magic through our bond."

"So what you're saying is you've turned me into a supernatural battery," I said.

He lifted his head from fiddling with the skeleton of a bird and nodded. "That's a good explanation for it."

"Why? I thought you were powerful enough without it."

He slammed something down. "I am powerful enough without it. This mark is just going to draw focus from where I need it. This was your choice remember? This thing was supposed to vanish after you fulfilled your part of the bargain. You were to give me the draugr's watch and locket, and you would go your own way. Instead, you ruined everything by giving back his trinkets. Now I'm stuck with you for the next hundred years."

He sounded enraged by my actions all over again. Strange behavior when the relationship so clearly worked to his benefit. It made me think there was more to this bond than he was telling me.

I remember Miriam telling me how marks of this nature often went in both directions. Perhaps it wasn't the power he could draw from me that was the concern.

He continued tinkering with the assortment of items on the table, measuring powder out using a tea spoon and dumping it into some noxious liquid that sent up a puff of foul smoke. It smelled like an infantryman's bag after a seven day mission outside the wire. It was disgusting.

"What are you doing?"

"What I promised, concocting a spell to locate your friend."

I closed my eyes in relief. At least one part of this crazy plan had worked out. I could take this pain if it meant he did as he promised.

He muttered to himself as he poured over his table, shifting items around to find the things he needed.

I drew my legs under me and stood. The mark was a steady burn, but nowhere near as bad as it had been when I woke up. I took a wobbly step toward him, as unsteady on my legs as if they'd turned to stilts.

My headed pounded in time to my heart beat.

"I need one more item," he said.

"That's it?" I asked.

"Normally, no, but I tagged Caroline with a strand of magic when I was working with her earlier. It should act as a locator."

"You did what?" My voice was a high pitched shriek.

"Calm yourself. It did her no harm and will probably end up saving her life."

"What is it with you people supernaturally microchipping human beings without their permission?" It seemed to be a theme with the spooks.

"Are we really going to argue about the ethical ramifications of my actions when we need to save Caroline?"

My mouth clicked shut, and I made a gesture that said by all means continue.

He nodded, pleased with my answer.

"How does this work anyway?" I asked.

"I'd explain, but I doubt you'd comprehend. It takes years of intense study to understand even the most basic of concepts."

I gave him a flat stare. "This insignificant mind will struggle with the basics."

He gave an angry sigh. "We don't have time, but I'll try to dumb it down for you."

How kind of him.

"Your description of a microchip is incredibly apt, but in this case it acts more like a beacon. When viewed on the proper plane, that beacon lights up like a Christmas tree and can guide us to its owner, that being our mutual friend Caroline."

"And how do we find the proper plane?"

"We change our perception of the universe."

Ah. Because that was so easy.

He stepped back from his concoction and turned toward me. Suddenly his eyes were the only thing I could see. His voice echoed in my head.

"Aileen Travers, give me your left eye."

The order repeated, over and over again, until it was a cacophony of sound in my head. Of its own volition, my hand rose. Horror filled me as my fingers dug into my eye socket. I screamed as I ripped it out. The voice never once stopped.

Wet coursed down my cheek. My hand rose and set the eyeball, my eyeball with its blue gray iris, in Peter's hand.

The compulsion disappeared.

I covered my socket and screamed again, the sound filled with rage and pain.

My fangs dropped down, and I lunged at Peter only to be brought up short, my limbs hung suspended as if I'd been caught in a spider web.

"Be a good girl and just stand there until I'm done with this," Peter ordered.

I had no choice but to obey, standing frozen, my arms outstretched, blood dripping down my cheek as he chanted over his mixture.

"If I did not want to find Caroline so badly, I'd spend the next few hours torturing you, making you beg, breaking your spirit for all that you've done," Peter said conversationally. "I have never been made to feel so completely powerless in the last fifty years. Being mostly cut off from my magic and incapable of defending myself is an experience I am looking forward to introducing you to."

I flexed my hands. He had no idea how much pain I was going to inflict on him once this was finished. He had the upper hand now, but I was patient and very, very motivated.

"Nothing to say?" he asked.

I kept my silence, glaring at him from my one good eyeball.

He mistook my silence for defeat. "A pity. Perhaps I misjudged you, and you're already broken."

I remained motionless as he went back to work, watching, waiting, letting my anger settle in my belly to keep me warm.

"Almost done," he said.

He turned to me and dipped his fingers in the mixture, chanting under his breath, his voice falling and rising a smooth cadence. It sounded like drum beats in the night, building and building in intensity until it was a pounding rhythm.

All around me I could feel something forming. Growing and becoming until the air felt thick with it.

He shouted the last words and it was like the world popped, all that power rushing out in an explosion.

He dipped his fingers in the mixture and drew a symbol on my forehead. Finished with the symbol, he dipped his fingers in it again before smoothing it over my eyebrow and down where my eye used to be. The stuff burned hot before deepening to a searing cold.

The pain ate at my consciousness until finally I passed out.

*   *   *

"This isn't what we agreed to," Peter snapped. His voice sounded like it was coming from far away.

"Do not speak to me of agreements. I told you what would happen to you if she was harmed," Liam rumbled.

He sounded furious. I was glad I'd never had that tone of voice directed at me. It might have made me do something crazy. Like obey.

"What do you care about one insignificant vampire? You can always make more to replace her if she gets a little broken."

I was betting he was talking about me. His assessment wasn't too far off the mark. Right now I did feel a little broken. Like I should lay my head back down and take a nap for the next hundred years. Oh right, my head was already down and my eyes closed.

I blinked one eye. The other refused to open. Pain radiated from it. Memory returned on the heels of the pain. That's right, he'd ordered me to give him my eye, and I had done it. Like I was a robot fulfilling an order.

"I have plans for that insignificant vampire." Liam's voice was calm but had a deadly undertow. The sorcerer would be wise to step carefully.

"I don't care about your plans, vampire."

Guess he wasn't all about being wise. He probably felt secure now that he had access to his power again.

Liam moved, his motions a blur I couldn't track. One second he was on one side of the room and the next he had the sorcerer by the shirt and was yanking him up to meet a pair of lethally sharp fangs.

Liam buried his fangs in Peter's throat. Peter struggled for all of two seconds before his arms fell limply to his side.

I levered myself up to standing, almost falling to the floor. The world was topsy-turvy, the floor tilting up to try to meet me. Whoa, guess I wasn't feeling up to running yet.

"Liam," I said, or at least tried to say. My throat was parched. His name came out in a croak.

Peter's blood perfumed the air, smelling like a rainstorm after a

223

long summer's draught. My fangs slid down.

I held a hand up to my forehead, wishing the world would stop spinning. For the smell of blood to go away. It was driving me mad.

"Liam." That was better. I didn't sound like myself yet, but at least I could form words.

Liam continued to drink Peter down like a man size big gulp.

"Liam, stop." This time I managed to put a bit of force behind my voice.

Liam raised his face, blood around his mouth and trickling down his chin. His eyes looked electric blue and his face had an alien hunger in it.

My heart fluttered. In my current state, I wouldn't be able to offer even a token resistance if he attacked.

"That's enough. I need him alive," I said. My voice was breathier than I'd like. I sounded like I might collapse at any moment, but the tone was confident enough.

He threw the sorcerer, who sailed across the room and landed limply on the stone floor.

"Stay," Liam commanded.

Peter lay like a ragdoll.

Liam advanced on me and it was only because I was pretty sure if I tried to run I would fall flat on my face that I remained in place. This wasn't the man I'd bantered with or needled simply because I could. This was the enforcer and he would roll right on over me if I got in his way.

He looked coldly dangerous, as if he was going to start sprouting icicles from his eyeballs at any moment.

I jerked when his hand slid around my neck and turned my face so he could get a better look at the missing eye. For someone so furious, his touch was surprisingly gentle.

If anything his face got even colder, approaching subzero temperatures. I was suddenly glad I couldn't see the wound. I probably would have thrown up.

"It's the newest style, I hear." It was a lame joke, but sometimes laughter is the only way you keep yourself together. It's why soldiers display such a dark humor. It's a coping mechanism, one that keeps us sane in insane conditions. This situation qualified.

"I do not believe it is one that will stick around," Liam said.

I snorted. He'd cracked a joke. Perhaps he wasn't a complete asshole after all.

There was a sound to our left. I jerked, trying to turn my head so I could see. Liam's grip didn't let my face budge.

"Holy shit, what did you do to yourself?" Nathan swore.

"I've never been a big fan of that eye." Some of the pain I felt radiated in my voice.

Liam didn't take his eyes off my face. "See to the sorcerer. Make sure he doesn't try anything."

Nathan moved across the room, finally coming into view of my good eye. It was strange being unable to see much of the left side of the room.

I felt a thin thread of otherness touch me, gently probing where my eye should have been. It withdrew as gently as it came.

"This is why we don't make deals with sorcerers," Liam told me.

"I'll keep that in mind for next time."

"When's the last time you fed?" Liam asked me.

"This morning." I thought about it. Caroline's call had woken me up. "Wait, no. It was last night. About two hours before sunrise."

Once I'd heard the break in I had rushed out of the house without bothering to fill up.

"You need blood."

"I'll be fine," I said. I knew I wouldn't be. I was still woozy, probably from blood loss coupled with hunger and pain.

"You won't. Your body is already showing signs of a deficit. It could throw you into a feeding frenzy."

His hold tightened on my neck. He drew me a step closer until I was pressed against him.

"What are you doing? This is hardly the time for any hanky-panky."

His chuckle sounded warm in my ears, totally at odds with the situation. "You need to feed. I'm the best source at the moment, though I'll take note of your desire for 'hanky-panky' at a later date."

I gave him the best glare I could with only one eye and my face a giant, throbbing mass of pain.

He didn't seem that impressed.

"What about the sorcerer?"

He shrugged. "Only if you want to drain him dry and chance killing him."

"Only because you got to him first," I accused.

"It wouldn't be a good idea drinking from him anyway. It'll only strengthen your mark."

225

"I don't want to," I said, leaning my head against his chest. The room was spinning and had gained a slight red tinge. I felt as weak as a kitten, and my fangs ached with the urge to bite something. Anything.

"Why?"

Because it'll make me a monster. I didn't say that out loud.

He seemed to guess at my silent thoughts. "When you were in the military, would you have hesitated to use a weapon placed in your hand to defend yourself and others?"

"That's different."

"Why?" His voice reflected no judgement, only security.

It was hard to put into words. "It wasn't about me, or not only about me. If I failed to defend myself, I left the person standing next to me vulnerable to the same fate. It was about the people back home, and what I stood for just as much as it was preserving my life."

"It is the same today. We use the tools granted to us to do the job we've chosen. Whether that's a gun or your fangs. You're a vampire. Not drinking blood from a neck makes you no less of a vampire. By not accepting this, you place everyone around you in danger. Starting with your friend, Caroline."

I sighed. I thought I'd accepted what I was, learned to live with it and overcome any obstacles. It was more difficult than I thought to achieve that inner acceptance. It was a series of choices, not just one. This was just another hill I had to climb.

"I don't know how."

"I will show you."

His hands cradled my head, guiding me to his throat. The nails on his hand thickened and lengthened. He used his thumb to open a small wound right next to the carotid artery. Instinct took over and I attacked.

My fangs sank through skin. It felt like biting into a grape, crisp and firm until you got to the juiciness inside. He moaned and his hold tightened.

Blood flooded my mouth. I lost control, my grip tightening as I pushed and pulled, trying to get closer to that amazing taste. Frenzied, I climbed him, wrapping my legs around his hips and holding on as tight as I could. He helped, lifting me and holding me to him just as tightly.

I'd never get enough. It was like liquid life pouring down my throat. The taste of dark delights on a wicked night. Bagged blood had nothing on this. It set my senses afire and suddenly I could hear everything and see everything, power the likes I'd never felt filling me up to overflowing. It felt like my skin would burst trying to contain it, that it might shoot out of my fingertips.

I came back to myself, my lips moving wildly on Liam's as I fought to get closer to him. At some point I'd stopped drinking and started kissing him. His hands held my ass in a bruising grip.

I pulled back, panting. That was—I didn't know what that was.

He pulled me closer, but I held myself away, trying to catch my breath and bring myself back under control.

"Let me down."

His eyes snapped fire at me. I stared back, letting him know I meant business. He'd have a raging tornado of claws and teeth on his hands if he didn't release me in the next few seconds.

He let me go, letting me slide down him with an agonizing slowness. I stepped back, wobbling momentarily before catching my balance.

"Blood from the vein causes lust," I observed.

"It can," Liam said in a neutral voice.

"You should have told me."

He arched an eyebrow. "So you could have refused?"

I shut my mouth. I wasn't sure if I would have refused if I'd known.

"It doesn't always have that affect," he said, his lips tilting in a sensual smile. "Usually that only happens when there are feelings of lust, as you called it, to begin with."

I flushed. "You're hot. Doesn't make you less of a jerk."

I walked away before he could say anything else.

"You'll change your mind."

"Not in this lifetime."

As I left I thought I heard him murmur, "Good thing we have several lifetimes ahead of us."

I stalked toward Peter, ignoring the smug vampire at my back. Nathan gaped at me as I moved towards him.

"Wow. Just wow." His mouth moved like a fish's. "That was just hot. I mean, like really hot."

"So glad you enjoyed it. Let's get back to business," I said.

"You can take blood from me anytime," he offered.

"I'll keep that in mind."

I knelt beside Peter and shoved him. "Wakey, wakey, eggs and bakey."

He came alive with a flurry of limbs, swinging at me way too fast for someone coming up from unconsciousness. I knew he'd been faking the sleeping beauty routine.

Nathan stepped forward, catching one fist and forcing it behind his back. "None of that now. It's just rude."

Power gathered in the air. Nathan hauled his arm higher. A pained whimper escaped Peter and the power dissipated.

"I wouldn't if I were you," Liam said. "Nathan can snap your arm and then your neck before you can draw enough magic to do more than tickle us."

Peter glared at us, uncowed by the threat.

I remained crouched right in front of him. The need to punch him, kick him or do something equally violent coursed along my veins just under the skin. I didn't like feeling helpless. I tended to react with extreme aggression whenever it happened, and Peter had brought that feeling out in abundance.

"I thought we had a deal, Petey," I said. "I release the genie cuff and you help me find my friend."

"That's what I was doing," he snarled.

"Really? Because to me it felt like you were exacting a little revenge."

He gave me a nasty smile, one at odds with his boyish face. "That was just an unexpected benefit."

Nathan twisted his arm harder and Peter screamed as his elbow contorted in an unnatural angle. With just a slight flex to his arm, Nathan could break the elbow, doing extensive damage to the tendons and ligaments that connected to it. On a human, it would be an injury that could take months or even years to heal, if it ever healed all the way. As a sorcerer, he'd probably only need a few days.

"I say we just get rid of him," Nathan said.

"You hear that, Petey. There's already one vote for your death," I said, ducking my head to meet his eyes.

He gritted his teeth. "You need me."

Nathan scoffed behind him.

"You do," he yelled. "You kill me and my death will rebound through the mark, likely dragging her with me."

"Which is why we'll break the mark before we take your head and burn your body," Liam said calmly.

Peter stared at him in shock. "You're bluffing."

Liam gave him a taunting smile. "I never bluff."

I contained my snort, but barely. Right. I doubted that. At least

Peter seemed to believe it.

"The shock will drive her insane."

Liam grasped my arm, turning it to show him the twin marks of the lion and the oak tree. "Maybe if she only carried your mark. The additional mark should take some of the stress of the break away. She's one of the most stubborn women I've ever met. I doubt her sanity will be affected."

I pulled my arm away, not sure how I felt about his talk of breaking the sorcerer's mark. I was betting that's why he'd forced the mark on me in the first place.

"Your chances of surviving intact are only fifty percent at best," Peter told me.

"Better than my chances of surviving you for the next hundred years," I said in a quiet voice.

His face closed, and he looked away from me.

"I wasn't lying. It wasn't for revenge."

Nathan tightened his grip enough to let him know his lie had been heard.

"It wasn't. Not entirely. The spell needed the vision of someone who walks the line between life and death."

"If that's true and we still don't know where she is, that would mean it didn't work."

Nathan glanced at me. "Are you really believing his lies? He is a sorcerer, you know? Adept at the art of deceit and subterfuge."

I didn't actually know, but I believed him. To a point. The best lies have a kernel of truth wrapped up inside them.

"It worked. I know it did."

"Then you can lead us to Caroline," I said.

His eyes shifted away from me.

I grabbed his face and turned it back to me. "You can lead us to Caroline."

"It worked. I think. I felt the spell close and take hold. I just don't know how."

My fingers tightened on his jaw. All that for nothing. I shoved away from him and paced to his work table.

Nathan hauled him up. "I've never killed a sorcerer before. I don't think anyone in our little family has. Hey, that'll mean I'm the first."

"Eric will not be happy to have missed this," Liam said in a bored voice.

"It'll work. I just have to figure out how it presents," Peter yelled, trying to escape Nathan's hold.

Nathan spun him and shoved him against the wall, stuffing a rag he'd yanked from the table in Peter's mouth.

"Less chatting. More dying," Nathan said in an upbeat voice.

"Not yet. We may still need him," Liam ordered before moving toward me. "We need to get that eye healed."

I touched my cheek in shock. I'd almost forgotten in the rush of sensation from the feeding. It didn't hurt anymore and if not for the lack of vision on that side I probably wouldn't have noticed.

His warm fingers touched the skin next to the socket sending tingles that spread in waves throughout my being, calling to my own power until it rose in a rush of feeling to meet his. The eye socket started burning, deepening into an agonizing pain that felt like a white hot poker was being shoved into the eye.

"There," he said, his touch lingering.

I blinked, looking from side to side.

"I don't think it worked," I said.

I closed my eyes before opening them. The world was a white haze that refused to come into focus. My right eye saw fine, but the left only saw blurs in the haze.

Liam's power shifted through me, searching and probing before withdrawing.

"It looks healed both on the outside and the inside," Liam said. "You should be able to see."

I squinted. It was still hazy, but I could see shapes. Sort of.

"Give it time," he said. "Some of the synapses may be adjusting."

I nodded, not feeling a lot of confidence in his statement.

Without my left eye I was clumsy, misjudging where the table was and bumping into it when I turned. I stumbled, my hands touching the paste Peter had used for the spell and upending the entire mixture onto the floor.

It reacted oddly. Instead of forming a puddle as a normal liquid paste would, it rolled into little balls before inching its way toward me. I stepped back, hopping away as it crawled faster until it met the wall, where it just stopped, the little balls joining to form one quivering blob.

To my right eye the mixture looked like the same grayish stuff Peter had smeared on my forehead and eye during the ceremony. To my left, it was a strange light purple, mixed with a sickly yellow. The colors were the only relief from the white haze, showing like a neon sign in that eye's vision.

Peter mumbled against his gag and gestured with his head at the paste in excited movements.

"I think he's trying to say that's how we'll find Caroline," I said, staring at the paste that bunched next to the wall.

Liam sighed next to me and nodded at Nathan who gave us an incredulous look. Finally he huffed and reached up to yank the gag out of Peter's mouth.

Peter started talking as soon as it was out.

"I told you the spell worked. It works like a dousing rod. It should lead us right to Caroline." Peter glanced around at the unhappy faces around him. "You'll let me help, right?"

Nathan threw the rag on the table and crossed his arms, glaring at Peter. "I suppose this means we have to wait to kill him."

Neither one of us bothered to answer Nathan.

"We should grab something flat to put it in," I said. "It'll make following its direction a little easier."

Liam nodded. "I agree."

Chapter Seventeen

We all ended up in Liam's black escalade, Nathan and Peter in the front, Peter holding the blob and navigating, Liam and I sitting in the back.

"Go left here. No wait. We're going in the wrong direction now."

"You said left," Nathan snapped.

"It looked like it was moving left," Peter defended.

"Someone else should have the blob," Nathan said, yanking the wheel right on the next street. "You obviously have no clue what you're doing."

Peter shielded the petri dish Liam had unearthed from Nathan. "It's my spell. I'm the best choice to decipher its signs."

Nathan's snort was derisive. "What signs? It moves in a direction and we go that way. We're like friggin homing pigeons."

It was an apt description. Getting a general direction was easy, but narrowing the area to a specific location had proven much more difficult. For the blob, street layout wasn't a factor. Unfortunately, the escalade could only drive in straight lines down streets that weren't always lain out in a perfect grid pattern. As a result we'd been circling the same area for over an hour and were no closer to discovering Caroline's location.

I stared out the window, ignoring the argument continuing in the front seat. We were in one of the less well-off neighborhoods on the east side. I hadn't spent a lot of time in this part of the city. Growing up on the west side meant most of my experience had been confined to that area and a few neighborhoods downtown and to the south of Columbus.

The houses were different here, built so close together they almost touched. They looked deceptively small, not being wide in the front but each went back quite a ways. Every single one had a porch. Some were falling down, windows boarded up and weeds overgrown in the front yard. Others looked well maintained, with painted trim and cut grass. The neighborhood must have been charming at one point, but now it looked like it couldn't decide between being part of the up and coming town or the part people didn't go to after dark.

My eyes caught on a figure creeping through the shadows in front of a house down the street. It was a flash of movement that I almost missed.

I peered closer.

There. The shadows shifted. To my left eye, a spark of green wrapped in threads of bronze coalesced in the darkness where I thought the figure was.

This time it was easier to follow the figure as it moved from house to house. I turned backwards to follow it. We were almost to the end of the street. Once we turned, I'd lose sight of it.

Come on, I urged. I needed to see what it was.

A large dog darted across the street, the faint light from the moon showing its sleek form.

Liam, noticing my focus, turned to look.

"Werewolf," he said.

I nodded. I was betting that werewolf had a reddish coat and white paws.

"Could be nothing," Nathan said. "A wolf out for a run."

"Brax has a strict policy about running in their fur in the city without a good reason. None of his people would flaunt his rule, especially so soon after the assassination attempt last year," Liam said.

"Remember me telling you about that wolf meeting the other demon tainted in the woods," I said in a soft voice. "I'm pretty sure that's the same wolf."

"You said you couldn't describe the wolf," Liam said sharply.

"I lied. I know exactly who it was. Just didn't know enough about the situation to reveal what I knew."

His breath hissed out in an angry sound. "This would have been helpful information before. Brax and I knew there was a mole in his pack. We just couldn't figure out who it was."

"I planned to tell both of you about it, but you're the one who showed up all huffy and butt hurt because I wasn't investigating your precious Thomas's problem. Since when do the vampires work with the wolves anyway?"

He had the look of a man dealing with something that tested his patience something fierce. "Since a certain annoying yearling can't keep her nose out of things that don't concern her," he snarled.

We glared at each other.

"Do you know the name of this wolf?" he finally asked, his voice making it clear he was holding onto his patience by a thread.

"If she's actually under a compulsion, her actions aren't really her fault."

"Aileen." That thread was fraying.

"Just wanted to make sure you'd thought of that."

"Who is it?" The thread snapped.

"Sondra."

He dug in his pocket, pulling out his phone and hitting dial.

"Go," Brax's voice sounded like it was coming from a distance over the speaker of the phone.

"It's Sondra," Liam said.

There were several creative curses spat from the other end of the line.

"How sure are you?"

Liam glanced at me. "Aileen saw her. She was the wolf running in her fur in the city."

"Nice of her to share that with the class," Brax said in a sarcastic voice.

"I've already made known my feelings on the matter." Liam's voice was wry.

"I don't envy you getting her to toe the line."

I grimaced. I wasn't a good little soldier any more. That life was over. Liam was drinking the cool aid and Brax with him if they thought I was going to fall in line with whatever rules they placed before me.

"You'll be there as backup when we locate the stronghold," Liam said, a statement more than a question.

"I take it you're calling in your marker," Brax said.

"The first part."

"We'll be there. Text me the address when you know it."

They both clicked off.

"Nathan, drive to the next street and park. Aileen, stay with the sorcerer while we follow the wolf."

I nodded, not liking being relegated to the car but knowing the two of them had a better chance of following her without getting caught.

Liam held the phone out to me. "If we don't return in the next hour, call Brax and tell him what happened and then drive straight to Thomas. He's staying at the Le Meridien in room 434. He'll offer you protection."

I took the phone. I had no plan to follow his instructions but figured it'd be quicker and easier to pretend to agree.

Nathan and Liam stepped out, slamming the car door behind them. I watched as the two disappeared, moving faster than any human could manage.

"You have no intention of driving off without them, do you?" Peter asked.

"None."

"At least you're consistent."

He put his head back and shut his eyes while I watched out the window. There was nothing to do but wait.

The sight in my left eye had lost some of the white haze, settling into a bunch of dark blurs. Shapes were still difficult to distinguish, though I had hope they would become clearer as my eye healed, but I'd noticed strange flickers overlaying some of those shapes.

For instance, the wolf wrapped in green and bronze vines. Peter with an emerald green at his core, his colors more vibrant than any other I'd seen.

I didn't know what it all meant yet. Just another thing in my life that inspired more questions than answers.

Time passed and Peter snored in the front seat while I kept watch. Liam's hour was almost up when the back doors opened and he and Nathan slid inside.

I turned, noting that both of them had different shades of blue threading through their bodies, creating a tangled spider web overlay. Liam's shades were considerably brighter, a blaze that flickered and beckoned.

"Find anything?" I asked, ignoring the temptation to just keep gazing at his blues and silvers. It felt almost intimate looking at it, especially when a spark leapt from him to my arm. I jumped as it meandered in a lazy circle that I swear I could just barely feel before it faded. It felt like a soft touch against my skin.

"Something wrong?" Liam asked.

"Nope. Nothing." I kept my face expectant and resisted the urge to close my left eye.

He looked like he didn't believe me but didn't press.

"We followed the wolf to a house. I didn't see your friend but there were several spooks in there. I'm willing to bet your friend is too."

I turned to the front and took a deep breath. Hope leapt inside even though he hadn't seen her.

"Could you tell how many were in there?" I asked in a steady voice.

"I counted seven, maybe eight," Nathan said. "That's just what I could guess from the windows. There could be more in other parts of the house."

"Did they have lookouts or guards?" I asked.

"At least two in the upstairs windows, one in front and the other in back. One on each door downstairs and two outside," Liam said.

Nathan nodded. "Heavily guarded. It won't be easy getting in there."

Not what I had hoped to hear.

I handed Liam the phone, watching as he texted Brax the address of the lair of the demon tainted puppet master.

If this was a military operation, we would create a distraction on one side, probably with the help of explosives, then go in the other with an overwhelming show of force, clearing each room one by one from bottom to top.

There were several problems with that technique tonight. One, there were only the four of us and whoever Brax managed to bring. Peter's loyalty was extremely suspect. He was as likely to hit one of us with friendly fire as the enemy. Not exactly the show of force I was accustomed to.

The second was that I had a strong feeling the others wouldn't be relying on guns, which meant any clearing technique that I was familiar with wouldn't work.

The last and most important was that the enemy would have heard us coming before we stepped foot over the threshold and have had plenty of time to murder my friend.

I sighed and rested my head against the seat. Sometimes it felt like fate hated me, like I had stolen her candy at some long ago point and she just kept dumping bad circumstance after bad circumstance in the hopes that I'd break.

She was a fickle bitch, that one.

War, as I'd already experienced, was nine tenths waiting and one tenth sheer gut wrenching terror, mixed with a deluge of adrenaline and motion. Waiting, for me, had always felt like the equivalent of having a root canal without any painkiller. I'd rather get whatever was coming over with so I could get to the next part—living with the consequences.

This time around was no different. Actually it was probably a hundred times worse than that entire year spent waiting for the next rocket attack or IED.

I tapped my finger against the seat. Tap, tap, tap. A rhythm that begged for action and the entire time knowing that Caroline's best chance would only be possible if I waited.

Peter was no better than me, moving restlessly in the front. The vampires had that odd stillness I'd noticed a couple of times before. Like that of a snake when it spots its prey. No movement disturbed them, even their chest remained motionless. No breath in or out that I could see. It was like someone hit the pause button. Normally it freaked the hell out of me, but at the moment I would have given anything to be dropped into a mental space empty of thoughts about what could be happening to my friend.

A tap came on the window. Brax's face appeared beside me, and he gestured for me to let him in.

I opened the door and slid over as he climbed inside, pressing me between the vampire and the werewolf.

"Where are the rest of you?" I asked, glancing behind him.

"Three of my pack are waiting in a car on the next block," he said.

Three was hardly the army of reinforcements I was expecting.

"That's it?" I asked. "What about the rest?"

With his three additional wolves, plus him, that only put our number at eight. Hardly the shock force I'd envisioned.

"It'll be enough."

"Are you high?" We didn't have time for his false conviction that one of his wolves were worth ten of the vampires or whatever bullshit had led to that statement. "We know they have at least seven. That's only what the vampires laid eyes on. For all we know they have a dozen more waiting in the basement for their chance to shine. These are creatures from all different factions of spook, including werewolf. How are the eight of us supposed to be enough?"

"Seven."

My head snapped to Liam.

His electric blue eyes found mine. "Seven. You're not going."

Everyone found somewhere else to put their eyes.

"The hell I'm not. That's my friend in there."

"You'll just slow us down. You're weaker than the rest of us and will be a liability."

My eyes felt like they were about to bug out of my head. I'm pretty sure if I was capable of it, steam would have been pouring out of my ears.

"We'll go in and get your friend," he continued.

"You're not leaving me behind."

He looked at Brax. I shot forward but not fast enough. Steel wrapped around me, trapping my arms. I struggled but it was like trying to move a mountain. Werewolves were strong.

I stopped fighting, figuring it was useless and wanting to retain some of my dignity. I settled for shooting daggers from my eyes at the bane of my existence. Pity they just glanced off his arrogant face.

"We'll be right back," he said.

"You're going to pay for this," I swore.

He shrugged. "Undoubtedly, you'll try."

He didn't look too worried about that.

"You don't think anything I do will touch you."

"Let's just say I look forward to your attempts," he said with a wicked grin.

I was going to wipe that grin off his face the first chance I got.

His attention turned to Peter. "If you'd be so kind."

"I've been waiting for this."

I could practically hear him rubbing his hands in glee.

He said a word and in my left eye green sparks with silver threads shot from him into the seat under me where it coiled and multiplied. Fabric darted forward and wrapped around my legs. The seat belts wove around my arms and across my neck like snakes, writhing and slithering as I struggled to escape.

Every single one had a core of emerald in it. Magic. I was seeing magic. The shock stilled my struggles.

The car doors slammed around me, leaving me sitting in the car by myself, chained by a seatbelt and the fabric from the seats. Galling for a vampire. I wrenched forward but was held fast.

I was weak, but I should have been strong enough to break through this. Again that emerald teased my vision. Struggling was useless. The fabric was probably reinforced by Peter's magic. I relaxed back into the seat.

All I could do was wait and pray.

The minutes passed as I came up with the various kinds of torture I planned to subject Liam to. I had no intention of letting him get away with this. Even if his words had the smallest grain of merit, that my presence would have weakened them, that didn't mean he had a right to literally tie me to the car.

Strength came in many forms. I might not have had the physical strength of a werewolf or a centuries old vampire, but I had other tools. Like a brain. And a gun.

The seat belts loosened, falling away from me as that emerald faded. I jerked free and scrambled out of the car, not wanting to chance them coming back to life and entangling me in their grasp again.

Nothing moved. Like they had never done their impression of a charmed snake. To my left eye, there was no trace of the emerald I'd come to associate with the sorcerer's magic.

It was odd that it just disappeared. Liam must know that as soon as I was released I would head for the house. I didn't have a good feeling about this.

Something must have gone wrong in the rescue.

I turned toward the house and started jogging. I knew where it was only by chance. I'd taken a look at Liam's phone screen when he typed the address for Brax. Now I was glad I had.

It was only two streets over and one block down. I covered the distance quickly, making sure to stick to the shadows as I crept up to a house next door. A cat started at my presence and then settled down when I clicked my tongue at her.

Her feline eyes watched as I crouched next to her and stared across the street. To my left eye, it was lit up like the antithesis of a Christmas tree, an oily inkblot coating the exterior. Under all that black were a few flickering colors as if the inkblot had tried swallowing them and now they glowed in its stomach like lightning bugs.

I did not want to go in there. In fact, every instinct in me begged to go in the opposite direction, bringing up the way I'd frozen the last time I'd encountered a sliver of demon taint. That had been nowhere as bad as this.

Staring at that inky blackness, my primal hindbrain screamed danger. It would be so easy to flee in a terrified mess.

I made myself take in the house, checking the attic windows and the entrances. No visual sign of people. Didn't mean they weren't there. Just meant they might be hiding. I couldn't trust my vision. Not if they'd managed to taint Peter.

I drew the Judge from my holster before I forced myself away from my shelter and ran across the yard, keeping low and moving fast. I placed my weight carefully on each stair as I made my way onto the porch. Somehow I made it to the door and inside without the house or its occupants collapsing in on me.

I stepped to the side of the doorway and took a deep breath as I listened. Hearing is an important sense. One that is too often overlooked in favor of what we see. What you heard could tell you so much. Like the racing of a heart or the click as a round was chambered.

For now, it was what I didn't hear that worried me. There were no screams or sounds of fighting. Both of which I'd expect if Liam and his men had stormed in here.

It was quiet. The silence before a storm when the world holds its breath, as if that would protect it from what came next.

I moved deeper into the house, pausing at the stairs. Nothing came from up there. I moved into the next room, peeking around the corner before entering.

I heard the faintest murmur of voices. I crept forward, holding the gun at the low, ready as I moved. A door separated this room from the next. Enclosed, small rooms were common in the era this house was built. No open floor plans here. It made each room a potential land mine of hostiles. On the other hand, it also allowed me to get much closer unseen.

Light came through the crack beneath the door, and the voices were slightly louder though I couldn't distinguish what was said.

I put my ear against the door and made out a woman's laughter.

I backed away from the door and eyed it. Opening it would instantly draw every person's attention. Without knowing what was happening on the other side or where my people were, it would be suicide to go bursting in.

I stepped away and moved back into the hallway, noting where the room fell in the house's layout. The kitchen was next, with a closed door leading into the room I needed to get into. Why in the world would they have shut both doors?

Couldn't anything be easy these days?

I continued through the kitchen and out the door before making my way around the side of the house. I edged up to a lit window and peeked inside, making sure to expose as little of myself as possible to the occupants of the room.

My heart nearly stopped at the sight of a person standing in front of the window. I froze, not daring to withdraw for fear the movement would draw their attention. My heart settled down when I realized the person had their back to me.

Not very smart to station the guards with their backs to the window.

Heart in throat, I took a chance and peered around the man. Liam and Brax knelt in the middle of the room, their faces blank masks showing no emotion. A woman stood in front of them, her head thrown back as she gave a throaty laugh. It was Elinor. I recognized that laugh and that hair.

I ducked under the window and crawled to the next one. This one gave me a better view of the room. There were three other people there, including Sondra. Bodies littered the floor. One of Brax's wolves looked like he'd had his heart torn out. Sondra's bloody hand made me think she'd been the one to do the deed.

Peter lay next to the dead wolf, blood on his shirt and pants. I couldn't tell if he was dead from this angle, but figured he wouldn't be much help given his motionlessness.

I fought an urge to curse. This was not good. The cavalry was dead or in the enemy's control. This was probably one of the worse scenarios I could think of.

One of the prone figures caught my eye. She had blond hair and was wearing a pair of comfortable looking flannel pajamas.

Caroline.

Her motionless body just lay there. Unmoving.

I sighed in relief as her chest rose.

I holstered my gun before I pulled out my phone and held it to the window, snapping several photos before crawling along the side of the house. I couldn't chance a call this close to Elinor, but I could still text. I pulled up Thomas's number and sent him the photos and the address.

Metal pressed against my cheek.

"What do we have here?" a voice I recognized said. "A little mouse scurrying about and poking her nose in places it doesn't belong."

The person holding the knife to my face stepped around me, his short figure coming into sight.

Tom.

I snarled, letting my fury come out in a sound that terrified even me. The knife drew blood. A cut opening on my cheek.

"None of that now." Happiness gleamed in his eyes when I flinched. He enjoyed causing me pain. "There's someone who wants to renew your acquaintance."

He nodded at someone behind me and I was hauled up.

"Tom, you're being controlled. You need to snap out of it," I said in as calm a voice as I could manage.

His laugh echoed in the night, a low rumble of sound.

"You think I'm like all these other poor slobs? Controlled? A shadow of myself?"

I had, but now I was having doubts.

He shoved me forward, his knife cutting through my shirt. I stumbled forward, hissing at the sting of pain from his blade.

"I leapt at the chance to be a part of this. The mistress has big plans. When she's done, we won't be hiding in the shadows anymore."

"Is that what you think this is about?" I infused as much surprise in my voice as I could. "I thought you were smarter than that. She's using you so she can win this selection thing. It's all so she can get a leg up on the competition."

"And what do you think she's going to do with all that power?" Tom snapped. "She'll use it to bring us out of the shadows."

"What do you think all of the other territory masters will do about that? I'm sure they'll have their own opinions. Even if she succeeds, I doubt she'll keep you around once your use has vanished. She doesn't seem like the type to reward her allies once they've fallen out of favor."

He shoved me and I tripped, falling up the stairs. "That's enough from you. Another word and you're dead."

I kept my mouth shut and preceded the two back into the house. My gun was still in my holster at my hip. If I could get to it, I might have a chance.

Tom shoved me forward again. Guess I wasn't moving fast enough for him.

I held my hands out before me as I entered the room. Elinor looked up, frowning at the interruption. Her frown changed to a wide smile, showing her fangs.

"You've brought my little friend," she exclaimed.

I looked to Liam and Brax. Their faces showed no reaction to my presence. Not good. I'd hoped their immobility was a feint, designed to fool her into lowering her guard.

Peter still showed no sign of life, and Caroline stared blankly up at the ceiling.

"Do you like what I did to your librarian?" Elinor said silkily as she came to stand at my shoulder. The skin on my arm closet to her shivered and crawled.

There was a darkness that brushed against me and clung. With my left eye, I could see the oily residue it left behind. I stilled the urge to brush it away. I had a feeling the type of taint that clung to me couldn't be so easily washed off.

Elinor grabbed my arm, digging hardened nails into the skin and leaving five crescent moons filled with blood.

I hissed.

"I'm going to do worse to you," she said. Her eyes found the blood and gleamed. She raised her hands to her lips and licked each red drop from her fingers, her eyes closing in bliss.

That was a picture I could have lived without.

My eyes flicked to the seething mass of darkness gathered behind her. It was faint, but I could almost imagine a shadowy figure standing there. Its tentacles disappeared into Elinor's body and every so often it looked like a little piece of her amber center was sucked into one of the tentacles and fed into the dark mass. Almost like it was sucking down her soul, one small piece at a time.

I glanced around the room, noting thin filaments attached to all of the people in the room. I fought to swallow as I noticed the gossamer thin strands attaching me to Elinor and then feeding into that shadowy mass. The demon I was guessing.

Elinor was the focal point; all threads led to her. If she was to die, perhaps they would all be cut.

"I've never tasted anything like you," Elinor said, her voice dreamy.

My eyes drifted back to the dark mass. For some reason I was more horrified at what I saw there than I was at the very real and present danger before me. Maybe it was the human part of me that still believed in a heaven and a hell, but the thought of that thing sucking down any part of me, my soul in particular, repelled me on every level.

You see me. The voice was like a thousand out of tune bells chiming at once. A sound to make ears bleed.

Fire raked down my arm. Elinor bent to take in the blood she drew.

The mass shifted closer. I kept my attention focused on the vampire currently lapping at my wounds. Her tongue was rough and dragged painfully on the flesh. I couldn't help it as a thin sound of pain escaped me.

The mass shivered. My pain pleased it.

Don't play coy. The thing sounded amused. I think. It was hard to tell as his voice was a discordant jangle in my ears.

The darkness shifted closer, its tentacles enveloping me. I fought against a flinch, knowing that's what it wanted.

A sharp line of pain opened on my other arm and a tongue slid along it, capturing every drop of blood.

The demon, for that's what I thought he was, moved against me. I could endure that. The sensation of its touch sent every instinct I had screaming, but I could endure. What almost sent me into a meltdown was the feeling of those tentacles reaching inside me, brushing up against my inner core.

I projected as much of my shields as possible, trying to protect the very essence of me from its taint.

That won't work, he crooned. *But keep it up. This is fun. It'll make my inevitable victory that much sweeter.*

His black smoke delved deeper, filtering through my mental forest as if it wasn't even there, leaving ruin and charred husks in its wake. Pressure built in my head as I struggled to hold onto the last scraps of my shields.

I haven't run into someone who could see me without a contract in place in centuries. What's your secret?

I kept my mouth clamped shut and concentrated on holding on.

Not going to answer? No matter. I'll just have to rip you apart to see if your insides can tell me. I prefer it that way.

His black smoke burned its way across my skin, leaving agony, like my skin was boiling. I screamed as the pain dove deep until it felt like all of me was burning, my insides, my mind, the core of what made me, me.

Elinor lifted her head and glanced at my face.

"Abdiel, you naughty thing. We won't be able to enjoy her if you burn her essence out."

The black smoke stroked her face. *Don't worry. I'll stop before she's too broken.*

My gaze drifted back to Liam and Brax. There was a faint tightening around Liam's eyes, but his face remained expressionless. I felt hope leap in me. If he could move, we had a chance.

The demon turned its attention back to me. I don't know how I knew, but some sense told me I was suddenly in his sight once again. It rushed me, latching onto me and trying to force open my mind. I resisted, throwing every piece of my will power behind my shields.

You're a stubborn thing, aren't you?

Pain consumed me, eating away at my vision. All, except my left eye and its view of magic. He drew harder on his link to Elinor. Power rushed from each person touched by the threads. One of the men at the window dropped, sucked dry by those same tentacles. The thread detached from the man, slithering back to its master.

The demon redoubled its efforts and another man dropped. The power sucked at me, making it impossible to draw a full breath. It felt like I was drowning and burning alive all at the same time.

The pressure abated leaving me gasping on the floor. In the midst of his attempt to crack me like a walnut, I'd collapsed, not even realizing I'd gone from standing to lying.

I rolled my head to look at Liam. If he was going to make a move, I'd prefer he get to it. I didn't know if I could survive another attempt to crack my mental fortress.

Sweat dripped down my forehead, sliding into my hair.

Hope died at the blank expression on Liam's face. Help wasn't coming from that direction. Not until I got that tentacle attached to him off.

If I wanted a rescue, I'd have to rescue myself.

Her defenses are stronger than I thought. If we had more time, it would be a joy to chip away at them over months. I could make you my next contract, the demon's voice offered.

Not in this lifetime.

He sighed, taking my silence as the refusal it was. *A pity. I think the two of us could have accomplished some truly spectacular things. Alas, my time to fulfill this contract is quickly running out.*

The mass was slowly turning into something more closely resembling a form. Not quite human, not quite beast, but something in between. It was still an indistinct shadow at this point, one that I knew I was going to have nightmares about for years.

He still flickered in and out of existence, as if a strobe light pulsed over him. There one moment and gone the next. Horns the size of my arm spiraled out in two tiers, the points sharp and deadly. His face was an indistinct blob, punctuated by a beast-like snout. He wasn't wearing clothes, his pot belly hanging in folds and his phallus erect under it. His legs were that of an animal's, the knee turning the wrong way to be human.

He stroked himself as he towered over me. I bit back my whimper. He fed off fear.

You must weaken her, he told Elinor.

"It'll be so much more fun to keep her as a plaything," Elinor pouted.

The demon drew her close, cradling her against its protruding stomach and rubbing his oversized appendage against her. She didn't flinch or show signs of distaste. It made me suspect that she couldn't see his actual appearance.

I agree, but you want power and the selection is tonight. Just think how much power she and the others will give you. We'll have enough sacrifices to draw from to put you above all the others.

She snapped, "I don't need power from some yearling not out of her first decade. Kill the alpha and the enforcer. The two of them should have plenty enough power between them to overthrow any challenger."

She's strong. I can feel it. Her power is just below the surface, waiting to be sucked down. Consider her my payment for my help over the last few years.

"You've already been paid in full, demon. There's no renegotiating now."

Ah, but you're not the one who paid me. That means the terms remain open.

Elinor's face turned ugly and she snarled, her face bestial in its rage.

I shifted back, inching closer to the sorcerer and Caroline. I belly crawled the few feet and touched Caroline's back. Her heartbeat was there, under my palm. I could barely feel it, but it was there.

I checked Peter next and was relieved when I felt his pulse. He might have been a pain in the ass, one who forced me to pull out my own eye, but he had led us to Caroline while putting his life on the line to do so. I could forgive a lot for that one act.

"Fine," Elinor snapped. "Have it your way, but you had better make good on your promises."

Careful, vampire. Your fangs can't touch me, but I can still affect you.

Her face twisted, but she didn't argue again, just advanced on me.

Don't worry, you'll get what's coming to you, the demon murmured. I got the feeling he hadn't meant that to be overheard by anyone, especially not the vampire looming over me.

I started for my gun, knowing that whatever came next would not work in my favor. Her hand darted forward, burying itself in my stomach. It withdrew, covered in blood and leaving a fist sized hole hemorrhaging blood.

I screamed, an animal sound of pain. My hands covered the wound, desperate to stem the bleeding. It gushed out anyways in great red spurts.

She must have hit an artery. Probably damaged the intestines. Cold crept in, sinking into my skin and down into my bones. My hands slipped away, the feeling in them fading. Too bad there wasn't anybody left with enough of their faculties to administer first aid.

I tried calling to my power, that ball of magic deep inside, but it refused, hugging itself tight. Not even trying to redirect some of the tiny streams as the pixie had tried to show me worked.

Black bit at the edges of my vision. I was losing consciousness.

The demon loomed in my vision, his face less man and more beast, his slitted eyes bright yellow and a pair of fangs on him big enough to make grandma run and hide.

Finally. Smoke poured off him to consume me, streaking toward that ball of magic inside my core. I struggled lethargically, trying to force my will to assemble some type of defense but it slipped and slid, refusing to catch purchase.

I grasped further, reaching deep, seeking out anything that would help.

As if pulled from my body, I was suddenly in my mental forest, walking through a dark and dangerous world. Storm clouds pregnant with rain above. Wind lashed the branches, whipping them into a frenzy and sending pain stinging across my nerve endings. At the core of my mental forest, I came to a large oak in a clearing. One of the biggest I'd ever come across. Its branches stretching out like a lover reaching for the sky.

I walked closer, even as the sounds of the demon's laughter echoed around me. Something in me compelled me to race for the shelter beneath its branches.

A large animal crashed in the forest behind me. I hurried. The branches stretched towards me as if they wanted to shield me from the monster coming for me.

I reached their shelter just as it sailed through the clearing and crashed to the forest floor behind me. It crouched, all traces of humanity gone from its form. A slavering, hairless beast, its eyes glinting with a mad lust.

Little vampire, what is this that you hide behind?

I took a step back, oddly comforted by the rough bark behind me.

He paced in a circle around the tree. I moved with him, keeping him in front of me.

Full of surprises. I've changed my mind. I'll take you home with me. You'll make a lovely piñata for the family.

247

"No, thanks," I rasped. "You're not really my type."

He chuckled, his voice sounding like gravel in my ears.

I do hope your humor lasts. It's always so much more rewarding breaking someone with a little gumption.

I wanted to assume this was another scare tactic, one meant to terrify me. He was non-corporeal whereas I was very much of the corporeal state. Taking me to his realm should have been impossible by the laws of physics.

Unfortunately, I'd learned in my short time in this world that very little was impossible.

"Why freeze people and leave them where they stand?" I asked.

I needed time to think.

I got the sense he cocked his head and looked at me quizzically.

Why not? It was more fun than just taking them with us while we slowly drained them.

"You wanted to make them afraid." He got off on it. Maybe even derived a power from their fear.

Ding, ding, ding. Give the woman a prize.

He could have made his victims, the human sized milk shakes, disappear with none of the spooks the wiser. Instead he'd left his victims in public places where they were bound to be discovered.

I can see those wheels turning, he said as he drifted closer to the invisible line under the oak's branches. *You're so close.*

It would have been safer and wiser to kidnap them rather than wait for them to wake and compelling them to his side. The witches and Inara both suspected the culprit was demon tainted. He was like a serial killer who felt the need to show off, wanting everyone to know what he'd done.

"You don't just feed off your victim's fear but the community's as well," I guessed.

He snickered. *Very good. It's not as sustaining as a direct feed, more like a delicate dessert. One that's meant to be nurtured and then savored.*

He pressed against the invisible barrier, pushing and pushing. Cracks started appearing, emerald and silver and electric blue.

Those were not colors I normally associated with my magic.

Something tugged at me. I remembered those colors. I stepped away from the oak and looked up at it. I remembered this oak.

Liam. Peter.

I had a link to them. One both had put on me without my permission.

I reached, trying to grasp their magic. Like mine had previously, they slipped and slid from my grip, stubbornly remaining just out of reach.

The cracks next to the demon widened and he advanced a step.

I reached again, pulling and pushing and insisting. They slid further away.

The demon reached for me. I backed away.

Once again. This time I didn't reach; I didn't coax. I yanked, forcing the powers up and to me. Peter's came first, pulling like a fractious horse. Mine was little better, acting like water draining from a sieve. Liam's followed mine, shadowing it and forming a barrier as it threatened to leak away from me again.

I growled. I would not die when I had the means to survive right within my grasp. I mashed them together, having no idea what I was doing, going off instinct.

Three was better than one, so I combined them, forcing them to meld and then pushing them out and away from me in an ever expanding arc.

What's this?

The magics hit the demon, yanking him up and away. He resisted, using his own black smoke to bat them away. They persisted. When one threatened to fail, the other two fell into the gap, gradually overwhelming him and forcing him back, biting at his smoke until little of him remained except a black spot on the ground.

His laughter trailed behind him. *Marvelous. Simply marvelous. We'll have to do this again sometime.*

I opened my eyes to fighting. Peter's face was above mine, his hand on my stomach.

Brax and Liam were up and attacking Elinor, who rebuffed their attempts with mad laughter. Brax was in half beast form and standing upright. His head was mostly wolf, with ears and snout and fangs. His arms a cross between man and wolf, longer than normal and tipped with lethal looking claws. He looked like a b-movie wolf man, only much more real.

Liam had vamped out, his eyes glowing a surreal blue, his fangs bared.

A small, reddish wolf wove in and out of Elinor's reach, snapping and trying to draw blood but being forced back before she could do any real damage.

The three of them moved in a blur. Elinor's hand flashed out, leaving strips of flesh hanging off Liam's chest. She glided away from Brax's lunge and shoved him, sending him crashing into the wall.

They were losing.

I could see the black tendrils draining their power and feeding it to her. As they got weaker, she got stronger.

My hand moved, grasping at my holster. I rolled to my knees.

"What are you doing?" Peter snapped. "We need to get out of here. Let the enforcer and the alpha take care of her."

I didn't bother responding.

I used him as a crutch and levered myself to my feet. My stomach was still bleeding but not as badly as before. Vampire healing to the rescue.

The reddish wolf darted in. Elinor turned, grabbing her by the neck and wrenching. I withdrew the judge and aimed. She dropped the wolf. It didn't get back up.

Elinor turned toward me. I pulled the trigger. Once. Twice. Double tap. Just like the Army taught me.

Blood splattered on the wall behind her. Her body slid to the ground, not much left to her head.

To the eye that could see magic, the black threads shriveled and dropped. I looked at Brax and Liam, noting with relief that theirs had detached as well.

"You're an idiot," Liam told me.

"You're welcome, asshole." My knees buckled. Liam caught me before I could fall.

"We had it under control."

"Sure looked like it from here too."

Pain radiated from my stomach. Maybe I had overestimated the amount of healing my wound had done.

"I can't heal all this damage," Liam said, his voice grim and sounding like it was coming to me from down a dark hallway. "Not when I'm this weak."

I closed my eyes. That was too bad.

Chapter Eighteen

"Don't you dare go to sleep." A sharp slap stung my cheek.

I blinked open my eyes, glaring at the teenager looking down at me.

"Is there a reason you're hitting a dying person?"

He snorted. "You're not dying. You're just healing. Very slowly."

It sure felt like I was dying. If I'd been human, I would probably already be dead. I touched the wound. It was still tender and bloody but not the gaping hole of before.

I glanced up at Liam. He looked exhausted, like he'd had his insides flipped out and then reassembled on the outside.

"I couldn't heal you all the way, but I've stopped the bleeding and you should be stable enough until your body can heal itself," he said.

He glanced in the corner of the room where Brax sat beside the wolf, stroking its fur. It moved slightly, making a pained whimper.

"Sondra was hurt pretty badly. Neck injuries are difficult to heal. If she'd been any lower in the pack, she probably would have died," he said softly.

I released a breath.

"What about Caroline?" I was almost afraid to ask.

He nodded to where Peter had gone after arguing with me. Caroline remained motionless.

She should have been waking up with the demon's taint gone.

I tried to sit up but collapsed back, fighting the urge to curl in around my stomach. Given the pain radiating from it, my wound was definitely nowhere close to healed.

"Careful," Liam cautioned.

"I need to see about my friend."

His cool hands reached down and helped me sit. He scooped me up before I could try to stand and carried me over to Caroline, setting me down so I lay next to her.

She was still, and when I touched her face, burning to the touch.

"What's wrong with her?" I asked.

Peter gave a small sigh and reached down and gripped her leg, turning it so I could see the blood soaked cloth.

"I don't understand," I said.

"A werewolf's bite can cause two reactions. The first does nothing but cause a mild cold and the victim can return to their normal life. The second," he trailed off.

"The second? What does the second do?" I grabbed his arm, gripping in tightly.

"Forces the change," Brax said from behind me.

My head swiveled towards him.

No.

That was not what was happening. Not Caroline.

"You're wrong. She's just taking longer to recover from the demon taint because she's human."

"Aileen," Liam began.

"She's fine," I shouted. She was. She'd be fine.

"You know she's not," Brax said, his voice gentle. "It's best this way. At least she has a chance to survive."

"What do you mean?"

They all traded looks.

My voice dropped to a deadly tone. "Explain what he meant."

This time it was Peter who spoke up. "Demons can drain the essence from their victims. With spooks, this can last for days depending on how big our pool of power. Humans don't have that same advantage. A demon can suck them dry in hours. She'd be dead if she hadn't started the transformation."

Silence fell between us as I stared down at my friend.

"You're telling me she can either be one of the monsters or be dead," I said in a flat voice.

Liam watched me with intense eyes. "Is that how you see yourself?"

I looked away, back at my friend. Sometimes. When it's the middle of the night and I'm all alone. Other times I can see that I'm not only what circumstances made me. I feel the same as I always have.

Will Caroline feel the same as I do? Or will she hate me for this nightmare I brought down around her?

"What will happen to her now?" I asked.

"If she survives the change, she'll be a werewolf." Liam's gaze burned the top of my head. "She'll join the pack."

"If she decides she doesn't want to be part of the pack?"

"Death," Brax rumbled.

"Werewolves need pack, especially in the first few years. They go crazy without it."

We'd see. I'd made it just fine. If Caroline wanted out, I'd move heaven and earth to get her out, even if I had to burn the world down around us.

Liam's phone rang.

He stood and answered it.

I was too tired and too consumed by my own thoughts to eavesdrop. I touched Caroline's arm again, flinching at the heat pouring off her. She felt like the sun.

"We'll be right there," Liam said. He turned to me. "We need to go. The selection begins in one hour and we must attend."

"I'm not leaving my friend," I said.

"This is not a choice."

He reached for me. I jerked away and pointed the gun in a lightning fast move that I would have sworn I was not capable of.

"I'm not leaving my friend," I said in an even voice.

His blue eyes spit fire at me. I gave him an implacable look. He could glare all he wanted. There was no way I was leaving my friend to wake up with strangers, afraid and alone. He could take all his vampire politics and stick them where the sun don't shine.

"You know what happened the last time you pointed a gun at me."

I gave a careless shrug. "I didn't have bullets with silver nitrate then."

His eyes narrowed further, and I felt a small feeling of triumph. That's right. The baby vamp just found a way to even the playing field.

"You are being ridiculous."

I didn't care.

"Your friend will be safe with Brax. She will be fine."

Fine was a long way from great.

"I don't even know why I'm trying to reason with you."

His eyes developed a strong pull, the blue deepening until it threatened to swallow me. I pulled the trigger. The gun barking in my hand. A thin slice opened on Liam's cheek.

"That was unwise."

I gave a smile that exposed my fangs. "I've never been particularly smart."

Anger coiled around him, charging the air with an almost physical presence. I tensed, my finger tightening on the trigger.

He relaxed, that rage that had been threatening to crush me under its pressure sucked out. He gave me the smile a wolf gives a rabbit he's cornered, full of wicked danger and smug assurance that he was going to walk away from this encounter the victor.

"Very well. You're welcome to stay here."

He was up to something.

"Of course, you'll be in breach of contract if you don't show up at the selection."

I tried to recall what penalty clause had been tacked onto the job. Nothing came to mind. I'd considered it irrelevant once I saw there wasn't a guarantee of success.

"What are you talking about? The contract mentioned nothing about a penalty if I didn't succeed in finding the witch or descendants."

"You didn't read far enough down," he said giving me a relaxed smile. He thought he had me right where he wanted me. "If you'd read past the guarantee of success section you would have seen the second part. The one where you must present yourself on the day of the selection if you haven't solved the case."

I couldn't pull out my phone to check the truth of his statement. Not without taking my eyes off him, which would mean instant death for me given how fast he could move.

"Unless you've found the witch who placed the hex or a descendant." His voice made it clear he thought that unlikely.

It burned that he'd guessed right.

"I've narrowed the witch down to two strong possibilities." I was guessing, but he didn't have to know that.

"Not good enough. I need the actual witch plus proof."

"There was nothing about proof needed in that contract."

He shrugged. "It's assumed. I can't just run around town killing any witches you might suspect."

He had a point.

"And the other part?" he asked.

I gripped the gun tighter. "If you would wait until Caroline wakes up."

"No, I don't have time for that. You reveal the names of a descendant now, or you attend the selection with me. Choose neither and you're in breach, which means you're effectively part of a clan for the next two hundred years."

Two hundred! That was outrageous.

"The claiming is only for a hundred," I hissed.

He gave me an unamused smirk. "Consider the extra hundred years interest for the difficulty it took dealing with you."

Arrogant, obnoxious ass.

I wanted to shoot him so bad. Make perfect little holes in his smug little face.

Seeing my frustration, his smirk widened. "Your choice. I'm good with either."

I was stuck, and he knew it. Now it was just a matter of which choice presented the least objectionable path.

Caroline groaned behind me. My grip loosened on the gun. It'd never been a choice, really. I would not leave my friend to face the same fear and confusion I had.

"You should go with him," Peter said, interrupting me.

I looked back at him.

"You should go," he said again, raising his eyes to meet mine. "I've got her. She won't be alone."

As nice as his offer was, I couldn't. He might not be a total stranger anymore, but he also wasn't her best friend.

"You're going to need to be a free agent once she's completed the transition." His eyes seemed to send me a warning. I stared back at him.

He was right. I wouldn't be able to help her if I was locked down by a clan. They could send me hundreds of miles away. I needed to stay clear of vampire influence in case Caroline needed a bolt hole.

"You don't leave her alone," I ordered.

"I'll stay with her until she wakes up."

I lowered the gun.

Liam was on me before I could finish, his hand around my throat, squeezing gently, and his face close to mine. His other hand caught my arm as I tried to raise the gun again.

"That will be the last time you point this thing at me," he warned.

We'd see about that.

"Didn't realize it scared you so bad," I said.

He pressed his nose against my neck and inhaled. "That's not what it does," he rumbled in my ear.

I could feel the press of a smile against the side of my cheek before he stepped away. His face was a neutral mask.

He addressed Brax, "You'll clean this up?"

Brax nodded and flicked his hand at him in dismissal.

He turned, expecting Nathan and I to follow. Like good little soldiers we fell in, leaving the house of horrors behind.

* * *

"Where are we?" I asked from the back seat.

Nathan was driving and Liam was in the passenger seat.

I didn't recognize this part of town or the big hulking mansion surrounded by houses that looked like they were about three steps up from being dilapidated. The mansion, one of those gothic ones out of the turn of the century, surrounded by its manicured lawn and wrought iron gate did not fit into this neighborhood.

With a sharply sloping roof and pointed buttresses, it was at least four stories tall and was everything I'd ever imagined as a clan home. It looked like it could fit dozens of rooms.

"We call it the gargoyle," Eric volunteered. "For now, it's home base."

I could see why he called it the gargoyle. It loomed over the surrounding neighborhood. I wouldn't go so far as to call it elegant or even pretty, but it definitely had substance and character.

"Why would you need a home base? I thought, as enforcers, you tended to travel a lot."

Nathan shot a glance at Liam before turning his attention back to his driving.

"We do, but it's always nice to have a place to call home and head back to after a difficult job."

Hm. I got the feeling that wasn't the entire story.

Judging by the rigid line of Liam's back, it was all the explanation I was going to get.

Nathan pulled into the drive and parked. The three of us climbed out and walked up the steps to double doors that extended well above our heads. They looked like solid oak, stained a dark brown.

This place would have cost a pretty penny, I was betting. Strange that the neighborhood wasn't nicer.

I gave my companions a second look. Or maybe not so strange after all. They'd certainly be able to come and go in a neighborhood like this at all hours of the night or day without rousing a single question.

The doors opened before we reached them and a young man who looked like he was barely in his twenties slipped out. He shot me a grin, a glint of fang denting his lower lip, as he caught the keys Nathan tossed at him.

He was a vampire. I turned to watch him saunter down the steps.

I blinked, trying to catch a peek of his power signature with my left eye. All I got was a faint haze. No colored veins of power threaded through him that I could see.

I turned, noticing the two had gotten ahead of me and hurried to catch up.

The furnishings in the entryway and the hallway matched the exterior. Dark, masculine and old. I'd bet my fangs that every one of them was an antique.

We stepped into a large room that was three times the size of my entire apartment. A raised ceiling created the optical illusion that it was bigger than it probably was. It was tempting to call the place a ballroom, with its ornate chandeliers hanging above us.

The people in their fancy clothes, some verging on costumes from a point far back in history, added to that perception. Not everyone wore clothes that would have been at home in some French court in the seventeenth century, preferring the simpler styles of today. Suits or slinky dresses were just as common.

It made me feel underdressed in my jeans and a simple top covered in blood, especially when heads turned to follow our progress to the middle of the room.

A small knot had formed there. Thomas and Stephen stood next to a trio that involved the Asian man from the gala, the one who had ordered Liam to solve Robert's murder. His eyes were nearly black as he watched us approach.

At his side was a woman who only came up to my chest. Her hair was pulled back from her face, revealing creamy skin that only the very young had. Her breasts were underdeveloped and her face so very youthful. She had to have been a teenager when she was turned.

The third in their trio was a tall man, with eyes a piercing amber and skin the color of deepest night. Three faint scars marred his jaw giving him a sinister look.

A space surrounded the trio as if the gathered were afraid to get too close. They wore their authority as another person might wear clothes.

Thomas's face was guarded, giving me no hint of his thoughts as he watched us stop in front of the three. I noticed Aidan at his side, holding a wine glass filled with a dark red liquid. His face was bored, but I could see the sharp interest lurking behind the mask.

Liam stopped in front of the three, giving a sharp nod and the faintest beginnings of a bow. Nathan's bow was deeper. I stopped a few steps behind Liam and Nathan, not wanting to draw more attention than I had to.

"Councilors Jabari, Tse and Sophia." Liam gave a nod to each one.

The woman's attention shifted to me. "Is this her, then? The little lost child."

"It is," Liam answered.

I found myself the center of attention, their regard almost a physical weight. I held still, feeling like I was the focus of a trio of apex predators. The sort that could end me without even meaning to.

Tse turned to Liam. "You smell of death and demon."

"We were able to track the one responsible for Robert's death. The one responsible had made a deal with a demon."

His interest sharpened. "A demon tainted vampire shouldn't have been strong enough to compel Robert to take his own head."

"Perhaps it would be best to take this conversation somewhere private," Liam said.

Tse bowed his head in agreement and turned to stride to a door. The crowd parted as Tse, the other two and Thomas and Aidan followed. Not knowing what else to do with myself, I stayed in place until Nathan grabbed my arm and propelled me after the group.

I shrugged him off and trailed behind, wishing I could be anywhere but here. Following a bunch of lions into their den didn't seem like the sort of life plan that guaranteed a long eternity.

They led us into an office, one with a heavy wood desk and dark furnishings. There were several paintings on the wall, the kind that said these people used to be important. And rich.

The door closed behind us.

Tse circled the desk and sat behind it while Jabari took up a position against a wall and Sophia found a seat on one of the chaise lounges.

I hung back, not wanting to get involved. These did not seem like the type of people I wanted taking an unhealthy interest in me. Flying below the radar was the best plan.

Liam and Nathan advanced to the middle of the room while Aidan, Thomas and Stephen spread out. Aidan lounged in a chair, his posture relaxed as he expressed a mild interest. Thomas chose to stand, taking a position against a wall and listening attentively.

Stephen took up a position just to the left of the desk, his focus intent on Liam. It was a position of power, one that said he was only second to Tse. It was not a position I would have expected from an applicant. Not yet anyway. To my knowledge they hadn't chosen the new master.

My left eye decided to act up, giving me a glimpse at what magic lay below the surface. Liam was his normal electric blue, the intensity stronger than that of Nathan and Aidan's colors. The three counselors, as Liam referred to them, looked to be just a tiny bit more powerful than Liam. It was kind of like staring into the sun too long, their powers nearly blinding my left eye and leaving black spots.

I looked away and blinked, fighting the urge to cover that eye.

Jabari's attention shifted to me and I stilled, not wanting to make myself seem any more suspicious than I already was. Something told me that revealing the fact I could see the magic resting in these people would be hazardous to both my health and my freedom.

I could think of a lot of scenarios where someone with that skill might come in handy. I needed to keep this new ability under wraps unless my life was in imminent danger.

I tuned back into the conversation as Liam explained how Elinor had been behind the contract with the demon.

"Her power always leaned toward compulsion," Tse was saying. "If she had made a deal, it would make sense that her ability would be amplified by the demon's taint. It might be strong enough to overwhelm Robert. Especially if she was able to override the will of someone close to him and gain leverage that way."

"You were able to overcome this compulsion?" Sophia asked in a lilting voice.

Liam paused before saying carefully, "With a little help from the werewolf alpha and a few others."

Jabari's attention hadn't wavered from me. "It is rather fortuitous that you had such powerful allies to draw on."

"As is always the case," Liam said.

Stephen's slight smugness at the announcement of Elinor's death struck me as odd. I knew they were competitors and her death only gave him another advantage in this selection, but it was more than that. It was almost as if he'd been expecting it. As if some plan of his was coming together.

I chanced a glance at Stephen using my other sight. Black, oily smudges ate away at his veins of power, as if he was rotting from the inside out.

Demon taint.

My attention shifted to the others. Should I say something? None of us had imagined there would be more than one person who'd entered into a contract with the demon.

We should have.

Things started making a little more sense. What better way to eliminate the competition than by having them eliminate themselves? Even better if you convinced one of your main competitors to make a deal so that when people came looking for the culprit, because no crime was perfect and people always came looking, the trail would lead them to the last person in your way.

He probably hadn't accounted for my seeing magic. A side effect of the spell the sorcerer had cast, no doubt.

"This changes things," Sophia said. "With Elinor and Robert's elimination through death, that leaves only two applicants."

Attention shifted back to Thomas and Stephen.

I didn't like the look on Stephen's face, smug and proud of himself.

"It's odd, isn't it? That Elinor never bothered going after you," I told Stephen. "You're supposedly her biggest competition, and she just left you alone."

I couldn't keep my mouth shut. Couldn't let him get away with this. If his actions had just affected the vampires, maybe. But they hadn't. They'd changed Caroline's life forever. Put me through having the horror of plucking out my own eye.

"I'm strong. She no doubt figured she'd work her way through the less powerful competitors," he said with a careless shrug.

Bullshit.

Even I could feel the lie in that one and by the looks on the faces of the vampires around me, they did as well. Tse looked like he wanted to disassemble Stephen and scatter him across the city. Sophia looked at him with distaste while Jabari kept his enigmatic expression, giving no clue to his true feelings.

"Doesn't matter why," Stephen continued. "I'm the last competitor standing. That means the position is mine by default."

"There's Thomas."

Sophia shifted. "Thomas has failed to pass one of the most important tests. That of proving he can sire vampires."

I knew I shouldn't keep drawing attention to myself. I should just let it go, keep my head down and hope Stephen forgot about me in the rush of assuming the mantel of leader of the entire Midwest.

"What does his ability to sire little, baby vampires have to do with being able to lead?" I've never been good at doing what was best for myself.

"A vampire can draw power from those he's sired. Without them his base of power is much smaller."

"Thomas seems plenty powerful to me. Doesn't much seem like he needs a bunch of little rugrats running about supplementing him."

It was the truth too. Thomas's power shone like the brightest sun, nearly eclipsing Liam's and two of the three in front of me. Jabari looked like the only one who had enough oomph behind him to present a danger to Thomas.

It was a risk letting them know I knew how powerful he was, but I was hoping they thought I had just been lucky in my assumption.

"The rules state that the master must be able to sire other vampires."

"Sounds like he already has," I argued.

"You speak of William," Tse said. "He was never confirmed as being of Thomas's line before he died."

Died? I thought he had just disappeared. Not that I blamed him.

"Thomas must prove he has sired a vampire or prove that he has the ability to sire them." Jabari smiled, a wicked tilt to his mouth. "You wouldn't happen to know where any of his descendants are, would you?"

Liam stiffened beside me. I sensed we were in dangerous water with that last question.

I gave a careless shrug. "Not at the moment. I'll get back to you as soon as I do."

It was the truth and flippant enough that I hoped they wouldn't pry further. From the slight smile tugging at Jabari's lips, I guess he knew exactly what Liam had been up to over the last week but had decided not to reveal it for whatever reasons.

Fricking vampires. Dealing with them was like dealing with politics wrapped in a hand grenade. My touch wasn't exactly delicate either.

"Then the matter is settled. Stephen will be the next master of the Midwest," Sophia said, her young face at odds with the formality of her voice.

Stephen's smile made my stomach twist, especially when he eyed me with the kind of look that said he was picturing what my insides looked like.

This was not a man I wanted in power. Unfortunately, I doubted anyone would believe me if I accused him of being demon tainted or that they would really care. It seemed like the vampires were fine with anything as long as you were the most powerful in the room.

I stepped aside as the others filed out.

He paused next to me and leaned close. "I'm looking forward to breaking you down. Maybe I'll even use you as the anchor for my next demon summoning. I'm sure he'll enjoy a new puppet especially when he learns what you did to Abdiel."

My hand twitched, begging me to go for the Judge. It would be so easy. Draw, aim, fire. It'd wipe that smug look right off his face. I'd probably be dead in the next minute, but it'd almost be worth it.

Liam came to my side, a calm, deadly presence as he stared down the monster in front of me. That's what Stephen was. A monster. One that got off on others pain. He and the demon must have got along really well. Two peas in a pod. The cheese to his wine.

We waited for the others to clear the room.

"You know he's the one behind all this. Probably even laid the hex on Thomas," I said conversationally.

"What makes you think he's responsible for the hex?"

"Something he said earlier." I thought about it. "And the fact that Elinor and the demon only made a halfhearted attempt for Thomas. As if they knew he posed no threat to them."

Liam looked as if he was weighing my words.

"It doesn't matter at this point. There's not much to be done."

"Can't you tell them what you suspect?"

He shook his head. "Not without proof, and you don't have any."

His last statement wasn't really a question, but I shook my head anyway. No proof, just a lot of unsubstantiated observations.

"If we'd had these suspicions even fifty years ago we could have done something, but it's too late now. Things have gone too far. If we were to accuse him now, it would be considered a challenge."

"So." That was the answer. "Challenge him or, if you can't do it because of this enforcer thing, have Thomas do it. He's more than strong enough to take Stevie."

Liam's gaze rested on me, making me uncomfortable.

"What makes you think Thomas is powerful enough to win against Stephen and his demon taint?"

I fought the urge to drop my gaze, knowing it would make me

look guilty. I shrugged, trying to affect a nonchalance that I didn't feel. "Just a feeling."

His eyes said he didn't believe me.

"It wouldn't work anyway. Not at this stage. The counselors wouldn't let an accusation or a challenge stand at this point. They need someone to take control of the Midwest and won't tolerate anybody who stands in their way."

"Not Tse. I bet he'd welcome someone taking the prick out."

"But Sophia wouldn't."

I noticed how he didn't mention Jabari.

"There has to be something we can do."

"You've lost your chance. If you'd managed to track down a descendant or even the witch who cast the hex, we could have asked for a delay. You failed. Now we have to deal with the consequences."

He stalked out of the room, leaving me glaring after him.

I followed, wanting to put my fist through one of the perfect walls. His words stung. I didn't like failure. Though I wasn't sure this could be classified as a failure, considering I'd had no intention of handing over the descendant if I'd managed to locate one.

I trailed behind him back into the ballroom, pushing past vampires not inclined to move out of a baby vamp's way.

I made it to his side and stopped, horrified at the scene before me.

A woman, her hair in a ponytail and wearing an OSU sweatshirt, hung limply from Stephen's grip. His face was buried in her neck. Blood dribbled down, staining the gray and blending into the scarlet letters of the O. She made a pained sound of fear, and her eyes rolled back and forth like a panicked horse.

He hadn't put her under. Hadn't used any of the compulsion I knew he was perfectly capable of.

The vampires around us watched silently. None moved to stop the feeding. Thomas watched with a look of distaste while Aidan seemed bored again. I was beginning to think boredom was his default look when he was unhappy with a situation.

Her struggles slowed and her arms went limp. Stephen's tight grip was the only thing keeping her standing.

I moved forward. Liam caught me by the arm, his eyes giving me a warning. I jerked free. If he wasn't going to do something, I would.

Surprisingly, he let me go.

I stopped a few steps from the pair. My strength was nothing compared to Stephen. I wouldn't be able to break his hold without killing the girl. Physically, there was little I could do against him. If I pulled the gun, I might kill him but it would most likely result in my death as well as the girl's.

"All Thomas needs to do is prove he can create a vampire?" I asked, my eyes on Jabari as I tilted my head at Thomas.

Out of the corner of my eye, I saw Stephen lift his head from the girl's neck, his face bestial as he focused on me. The wounds on her neck were savage as if an animal had been gnawing on the flesh, not someone who just needed the blood in her veins.

"That is correct," Jabari said.

I sighed. This hadn't been in my plans. I did this and everything could change. It would give the vampires a legitimate hold on me and nothing I said would make a difference.

Thomas watched me with a cautious look.

Stephen dropped the girl. She flopped to the ground, her head thudding against the wood floor.

"What is this?" he asked, his voice a hiss.

I ignored him. "He proves he made a vampire and you appoint him and not Stevie as the next master of the Midwest."

I needed to be sure this would have the outcome I wanted.

Jabari gave me a secretive smile and inclined his head.

My eyes went to Tse. His smile sent shivers down my back. Bloodthirsty and just a hint of cruelty. "Agreed."

Sophia watched me, sizing me up and cataloging everything about me. This was no piece of fluff. There was a highly intelligent woman behind that teenage exterior. One with a razor sharp mind. Her red lips tilted up. "Agreed."

Stephen reached for me. I stepped aside as Liam suddenly appeared between us, blocking Stephen's attempt.

"Stop this," Stephen said. "I am the master of the Midwest. You will do as I say or I will have you spend the next century praying for death."

"You're not the master yet, Stevie," I said, shooting him a glare. "Didn't your mother ever tell you not to count your chickens before they hatch?"

He gave me a glare, one that promised suffering and retribution. A lesser person would have withered and slunk into the dark praying not to be found.

I turned my attention to Thomas and frowned. I didn't want to help him. Not even a little bit. The only reason I'd spoken up was because I hated the thought of a person like Stephen getting that kind of power. It outweighed my dislike for Thomas.

"I may have been able to track down a vampire you created," I said.

He stepped forward. "You found Connor."

I shrugged. This was the tricky part. I didn't want to reveal too much before the right moment.

"Before this person comes forward and gives you all that your little vampire heart desires, they want some ground rules established," I said.

He waved a hand for me to continue.

I bit back my retort at his imperiousness. Something along the lines of telling him to go shove it.

Instead I said, "You're not to harm or allow any other vampire to harm anyone they consider a family or friend."

He narrowed his eyes. "Family, yes. Friend is too vague a term. Connor could claim any passing acquaintance as a friend if it suited him."

"You'll just have to run that risk," I said through gritted teeth.

He considered me for a moment, his gaze weighing. Judging.

I lifted an eyebrow.

"So long as the 'friend' has not posed a direct threat against me or mine."

Fair enough. I doubted Caroline or any of my other friends were likely to challenge this guy anytime soon.

My family and friends were safe. For now.

I hesitated before my next statement. This was the one that could be the deal breaker.

"You will not claim this person or try to force them into one of your clans."

Outrage showed on his face and Stephen started laughing.

"I cannot do that," he said. "Connor asks too much."

"Up to you. You're the one who lost track of a vampire you made. They're a little touchy about it and not sure they want anything to do with you. I'm sure ol' Stevie will be pleased with your choice."

"I can make you tell me," he warned.

I gave him a humorless smile. "Not before Stevie takes the crown."

I let him see I meant it. Every person has a breaking point. I was no different, but I could guarantee he wouldn't break me and get at my

265

secrets until he'd lost his shot at victory.

He looked at Aidan, asking a question with his eyes. Aidan shook his head.

"Her defenses are too strong. It would take too long."

I allowed myself a small smirk, knowing Thomas had asked him to use his telepathy to gain the vampire's name.

Stephen gave a pointy toothed grin, sure of his victory. Vampires, from what I'd discovered, were more possessive of the vampires they made than some sports parents were of a child destined for the professional leagues.

"I can't give up my claim. Invalidating the relationship would make me ineligible for the position of master of the Midwest."

Damn. I hadn't accounted for that possibility.

Now I had to ask myself how far I was willing to take this. How much I was willing to sacrifice to make sure the one responsible for what happened to Caroline wasn't in a position of power.

Everything. I was willing to sacrifice everything.

"You swear not to give any orders or place any responsibilities on this person. In fact, you promise not to have any contact with them."

He gave me a narrow-eyed glance. "No, I won't promise that. Connor will give me a chance to repair our relationship, and in exchange I will promise not to make any demands until then. That's the best I can offer."

Not what I'd wanted, but better than I'd hoped.

I turned to the three counselors. "I assume you have a way to prove the bond."

Sophia gestured to a table that I hadn't noticed before. It held a bowl with a sharp knife laid across it.

"This is ridiculous," Stephen sputtered, seeing his victory going down the drain. "If he had a child, he would have produced him sooner. This is just so he can buy time in a desperate attempt to turn things in his favor."

I ignored him and stepped closer, Thomas shadowing me.

"What needs to be done?" I asked.

Thomas picked up a knife, drawing it across his skin and allowing a few drops of blood to fall into the bowl. His wound healed before he could get more than a couple drops out. He made another cut forcing the blood to drip into the bowl. Enough so there was a thin sheet of red on the bottom. I was impressed in spite of myself. He healed almost instantaneously. Almost faster than he could bleed. Much different than mine.

"The child's blood will combine with mine. If this person was made from me, we'll know it."

I sighed. Of course it would involve blood. I should have expected it. We were vampires after all.

"You'll call this person," Thomas said. It wasn't a question. He fully expected my compliance.

I took the knife from him and slicing a cut, allowed my blood to dribble into the bowl. "No need."

Chapter Nineteen

Thomas's jaw dropped and he stared at me in shock. Jabari and Liam didn't look surprised, though the shock on the other's faces were worth it. I'd remember this later and have a good laugh.

For now, I stared at the blood in the bowl waiting for something to happen.

For a long minute, so long that I was a little worried that I'd been mistaken, that maybe Thomas wasn't the vampire I remembered from the night of my transition, nothing happened.

My left eye with its weird ability saw it first. It was subtle, just a wisp of smoke curling out of the bowl. Then it was like it caught fire, rose gold and a cerulean blue twining together as it consumed the blood and spread from the bowl to the table. I stepped back as the two colors flickered merrily together, each mirroring the others movements in flickering shades.

He was right. There was no explanation needed. That reaction said it all.

"That work?" I asked Jabari.

He nodded. "Indeed."

"This is impossible," Steven said, staring at where the blood still burned with our powers.

"How is it impossible?" I asked. "Isn't turning humans into vampires what you guys do?"

"He shouldn't have been able to turn you. There must be a trick somewhere."

"Every vampire has to get it right sometime."

"No, you're lying. You did something or the results are false."

"Are you questioning our honor?" Sophia's voice dropped to a dangerous tone.

A smart man would have changed lanes. Backpedaled and assured her he wasn't.

"There is no way she is his child," he yelled, pointing at me. "It's impossible."

The fire was still going strong.

"Looks like you're wrong."

He stared at the table as if he was trying to figure the trick out. The best part was that there was no trick. Thomas really had turned me into a vampire. How? I had no idea, but I'd choose vampirehood over death any day.

"The test shows she is his child. He is now master of the Midwest," Tse said, a deep pleasure in his voice.

Steven's eyes turned black. I stepped back, remembering the demon. His fangs dropped. They were different than other vampires. Instead of one set of teeth there were two on the upper row and another set of fangs on the bottom.

His hiss raised the hair on my arms. Spittle flew as the humanity drained out of his face leaving something straight out of a nightmare.

He leapt. I drew my gun and aimed in one smooth movement, pulling the trigger, once, twice.

This time my bullets had little effect, only causing him to slow before rushing me again. I leapt back, firing again, emptying the chamber in a blink of the eye. Thomas flew past me, tackling and raking claws across Stephen's face.

Liam caught the back of my shirt and dragged me out of the way of the battle. Placing one hand on mine, he forced me to lower the gun.

"It would be best to let Thomas handle this from here on out."

"It will be a good first act to his rule," Jabari said from beside me.

I jumped, not having noticed him move.

The two vampires flowed back and forth, their movements a blur. To my left eye, their powers met and clashed, the waves forcing the crowd back, leaving a circle of emptiness around them.

Thomas's power flared and suddenly he was holding Stephen by the throat.

Stephen batted at him, his power striking Thomas like a snake and leaving wounds on his arms and chest. Thomas didn't notice, bringing him close and ripping Stephen's throat out with his fangs.

"Your Change of Command Ceremony is a lot more violent than I'm used to," I told Liam.

Thomas didn't drink any of the blood draining out of Stephen, which for a vampire who held blood as the source of life was unusual. I could only assume it had something to do with the demon taint that was even now trying to breach Thomas's defenses.

Stephen still had some fight in him, digging his claws into

269

Thomas's side. Thomas shook him like a rag doll and laughed. He changed his grip, grabbing Stephen's neck in two hands and wrenching hard until his head separated from the body.

"It could have been worse," Liam said. "He could have ripped every limb from his body before taking his head."

Thomas wasn't done. He tossed the head aside and sank his hand into the chest cavity before yanking out a heart that he crushed into a bloody pulp.

He held the mess above his head and roared, turning to observe the crowd. They roared back, approving of the bloody display.

I stepped back as Liam advanced on Thomas. The two clasped each other in a hug before pounding the other on the back. I took another step back. Jabari noticed, giving me a half smile before turning back to focus on Thomas.

It was easy to slip into the crowd and make my way to the front door.

Once there I realized I had no bike, no car and no way to get back home.

Damn it, I was going to have to walk. Again. I was still weak from the wound Elinor had given me. I did not look forward to this.

I started for home, but only made it a few blocks before I stopped.

"You knew, didn't you?"

Liam stepped out of the shadows, appearing beside me. "I suspected."

"How?"

"I knew Thomas was still trying for a way around the curse two years ago. He was in the area where you were turned. It was simple to put it together from there."

I should have known he wasn't going to let the question of my maker go. I hadn't expected him to track the man down quite so easily.

"So this was all a setup."

He watched me, his eyes intense.

"Why didn't you just bring me to his attention at the beginning? Why go through all this? Put me on the trail of the descendants and the witch?"

His subterfuge made me feel like a trained monkey, compelled to dance at his whim.

"We both know if I'd forced you into revealing yourself you would have gone to ridiculous lengths to try to escape us. The simplest solution was for you to choose this path."

And because I'd chosen it, there wouldn't be any easy exit ramps. There would be no one to blame but myself. I'd have to accept things.

"I didn't expect you to negotiate for as much freedom as you did."

No, he probably hadn't.

"You manipulated me into the course you wanted."

He shrugged. "So I did."

"And you think that I'm going to dance to your tune now."

"Not at all." He gave me a smile full of sin and dark things. "I'm looking forward to our next battle."

Somehow, I thought he saw these little battles of the wit in a different light than I did. Where I saw it as a vital piece of my survival, he saw it as a game to be a won. A challenge to be overcome.

"Game on." I stalked off, anger providing fuel. At least for the first couple of miles. By the fourth mile my emotions had settled, leaving one thing clear. I'd have to steer clear of Liam in the future. That sleek and dangerous packaging hid a lethal wit inside. He was too sneaky and manipulative to play with.

*   *   *

Brax didn't answer any of my calls that night. Or the next. By the third night, I decided I wasn't waiting around for news any longer. I grabbed my bike and headed for Lou's Bar.

Unfortunately, he wasn't there. Sondra and Clay weren't there either and none of the other wolves would tell me any news of Caroline.

I stopped at the bar, figuring the bartender might be able to get a message to Brax. It was a different man than the last time. He was big and rough, looking like a biker after a five day ride. Tired and grumpy.

"He doesn't want to speak to you." The man set hands the size of dinner plates on the bar, the threat clear. "You're to forget about your friend and mind your own business."

I felt several wolves close in at my back. Their presence a looming danger.

I sighed. I'd been afraid of this, which is why I'd come prepared.

I looked down, seeing the smirk he shot at those over my head out of the corner of my eye. Yeah, the big bad wolf just made the vampire back down.

I whipped out a hand, grabbed him behind the neck and slammed his face into the bar, drawing a gun and pressing it against his forehead.

As a human, I would have never had the strength. Even a week ago, I would have struggled. Liam's blood had supercharged a few things.

He chuckled, the wolves behind me cackling. "Stupid bitch. Guns won't do shit to us."

I smiled. It must have conveyed the depth of my rage because he flinched, ever so slightly.

"They do when they're filled with silver nitrate. My own special recipe." It had to be because you couldn't buy bullets containing silver nitrate anywhere. I'd checked. "I've already seen what it can do to a vampire. It worked beautifully, by the way. But I haven't had the chance to test it on a werewolf."

The laughter disappeared and the air shifted to a wary hostility. They'd been playing games before, thinking I wasn't a threat. Now they weren't sure how much danger I presented.

I tightened my grip on the bartender. "Shall we test it on you?"

He jerked and I kept him down on the bar through sheer force of will. He was strong, but I was motivated. And pissed. Very, very pissed.

"I want you to pass a message to Brax. He's to call me by sunrise with news of Caroline. If he doesn't, I'm going to call my demolition buddies from the Army and tell them we have a few places to level."

"Bullshit, no soldier is going to put their neck on the line because some skirt tells them to."

I dug my nails in his neck, not particularly liking the term skirt. It was so fifties of him.

"He will, given the fact I saved his best friend's life, and his, if we want to get technical about it. He owes me one and his friend will go along with it because he's just a little bit north of crazy town." I bent down to say into his ear. "Make no mistake, if your alpha doesn't call me, I will burn down every building your pack owns. You don't believe me, watch me."

I flung him into the wall and raced past the wolves, digging for every ounce of the speed Liam's blood had given me. The sound of broken glass followed me from the bar. I didn't stop running until I was several blocks away and sure the wolves hadn't followed me.

I headed home and trudged up my stairs, carrying the bike. Setting it on the landing, I felt for my keys. My phone rang.

I snapped it up and hit answer without looking.

"Brax."

"Aileen."

"I want to see Caroline."

"That's not possible."

I punched the wall next to my door, not caring about the dent I left in the plaster.

"Make it possible."

"You don't understand what you're asking."

"I'm sick of you people using that as an excuse. You either let me see her, or I burn your world down."

"You don't want to threaten me, little vampire."

That's exactly what I wanted to do.

"It's not a threat."

It wasn't.

"Your presence could do more harm than good at this stage. Her transition won't be complete until the next full moon when she turns. She's at a very precarious time. It could still go either way. I will not chance your presence tipping the balance in the opposite direction."

"That's not good enough."

He sounded like a cult leader wanting more time with his disciple so he could continue brainwashing her.

"Her mind is unstable right now. Worse than usual with an attack victim. Probably due to the demon. Frankly, she doesn't want to see you."

"Bullshit."

His voice had a thread of sympathy as he said, "She's angry right now. Rightfully so. Her entire life has been upended and the person she thought she knew is part of this entire world she never knew about. She knows you lied to her about what you are. It's easier to focus on her anger at you than to focus on the fact that in a few weeks' time she's going to go through the shift."

Silence filled the phone as I stared at my door. I stepped forward and leaned my head against the wood as I fought not to cry. Vampires threatening to burn other people's businesses and homes down did not cry.

"You're a problem she does not need."

His words jabbed at me, opening wounds I'd rather not think about.

"Is the sorcerer still there?" I asked, my voice thick with emotion.

He paused. "We had to remove him when it became clear his presence was making her upset."

His hesitation made me wonder what he wasn't saying.

"I can't just leave her there."

273

He sighed. "You don't have a choice, not if you want her to have the best chance of surviving this. I can have Sondra give you regular reports."

"Sondra." Her name was an ugly curse on my lips. She was the reason Caroline was becoming a wolf.

"It's not her fault. She was under Elinor and the demon's control. If she hadn't bitten your friend, Caroline probably wouldn't have survived. Humans typically break easily when a demon is present. Their minds can't handle the strain."

He wasn't going to convince me that this was the best thing for Caroline.

"Send someone else. I don't want to see Sondra."

He murmured an agreement.

"You have until the full moon, Brax. Then I'm coming for her."

He didn't respond before hanging up.

I punched the wall again and then kicked it for good measure. My rage nowhere close to exhausted I took a deep breath and let myself into my apartment, setting my bike next to the door before heading for the couch.

I'd just taken a seat when the doorbell rang.

I thought briefly of ignoring it, not wanting to deal with any other problems for the night. In the end, I hoisted myself up and answered the door.

The landing was empty. I stepped out and caught sight of the vampire from the mansion, the one Nathan had given the keys to, disappearing into a black car that drove off before I could call out.

My foot brushed against something that crinkled. It was a white envelope with the name Aileen Travers handwritten in ornate letters. I picked it up and opened it. A set of car keys fell into my hand along with a note on thick card stock.

I stepped onto the landing, noticing a black escalade parked in my designated spot. A spot that had never had a car in it the entire time I'd lived here. I pressed the unlock button on the key fob and the escalade's lights flashed.

I read the note.

In payment for services rendered. I look forward to working with you in the future.

-Your Sire
Thomas

Discover More by T.A. White

Shadow's Messenger – Book one in the Aileen Travers series

Dragon-Ridden
Pathfinder's Way

Connect with Me

Twitter: @tawhiteauthor
Facebook: https://www.facebook.com/tawhiteauthor/
Website: tawhiteauthor.com
Blog: http://dragon-ridden.blogspot.com/

About the Author

Writing is my first love. Even before I could read or put coherent sentences down on paper, I would beg the older kids to team up with me for the purpose of crafting ghost stories to share with our friends. This first writing partnership came to a tragic end when my coauthor decided to quit a day later, and I threw my cookies at her head. Today, I stick with solo writing, telling the stories that would otherwise keep me up at night.

Most days (and nights) are spent feeding my tea addiction while defending the computer keyboard from my feline companion, Loki.

Excerpt for Shadow's Messenger

Coming home from Afghanistan was supposed to be something great. That ended when I met tall, dark and handsome in a bar and wound up in a dumpster sporting a nice set of fangs and my life flipped on its head.

Now I'm a messenger for Hermes Courier Service trying to make enough to support my ice cream habit while staying below vampire radar. When this newest job of mine goes disastrously awry, it puts me on the hook to be indentured to a sorcerer for the next fifty years unless I can find a way to fix things.

What's hidden can't stay in the shadows forever and my life will never be the same.

Chapter One

Late. And I fucking hated being late.

Even if this job hadn't been reliant on me delivering the goods on time, I'd still be pissed about missing the deadline.

Damn the accident on Fifth. When would people learn texting and driving just don't mix? The resulting fender bender backed everything up for miles. If I hadn't been on my bike, there would have been no hope of me making the destination on time.

I leaned forward and pedaled harder. Three years in the military had reinforced the habits of a lifetime. Fifteen minutes early; you're on time. You're on time, you're late. And if you're late, well, you might as well just start pushing.

These days being late carried worse consequences than muscle failure. That's why even with my thighs burning in protest and my chest heaving, I stood and pedaled faster.

A right and then a left and I'd be there. I could make it. No reason to tarnish a perfect record.

I veered around a stopped vehicle and narrowly missed an

oncoming car before jumping the curb and making the last turn. I braked hard, hopping off at the same time. No doubt I left several drivers in my wake, cursing my existence.

No time to put a lock on the bike. Not my first choice when in the Short North. Though a trendy, upscale destination just outside the Columbus downtown, bikes were still a popular target for kids and vagrants looking to make a quick buck. In high school, my boyfriend and his friends used to come down here and egg cars. Why was anybody's guess.

I was rushed for time so I had to pray that my beat up old bike would escape attention. I yanked the seat off the bike. Hopefully, that would delay a would-be thief long enough for me to complete my business.

Adjusting my messenger bag, I checked the name of the store against the one in my notes. Right where I was supposed to be.

Located in an old brick building off High Street, the name 'Elements' was etched in silver lettering complete with one of those flourish things at the end. The shop window had an attractive display of a skeleton in a top hat, holding a glass titled 'Potions' while sitting on a funky patterned sofa.

The brief ding of a bell announced my arrival as I stepped into a maze of touristy candles, gothic necklaces and other paraphernalia I didn't recognize. The small aisle was narrow and overgrown with items just waiting to be knocked over. I clasped my bag tightly. It would not be a good idea to break anything in this place.

A witch owned Elements. Getting on her bad side was something I'd prefer to avoid.

I made my way over to the woman next to a cash register. A skull candle sat next to the change tray. It was actually pretty cool. I wondered how it would look in my kitchen.

The girl wore all black and her face was coated in way too much makeup. Her blond hair was plastered to her head and pin-straight with a severe part in the middle. She didn't look up as I stopped before her.

"Delivery for Miriam," I said.

The girl flipped another page in her magazine, not acknowledging me. I didn't have time for this. There was less than a minute to get the package into its owner's hands.

As the girl turned the next page, my hand darted forward, stopping the page from completing its movement.

Slowly and precisely, I said, "Delivery for Miriam."

A pair of washed out blue eyes, rimmed in bright blue eyeliner, lifted to mine. With the disdain only the young could summon, she nodded at a door hidden behind a purple curtain embroidered with black and silver beads.

"Thanks."

I didn't know why I bothered. The girl had already returned to her magazine.

I moved as quickly as I could, without running, through the store. I'd learned on my first job for Hermes Courier Service that running would not be tolerated. Appearing rushed was a good way to get fired. I needed this job a lot more than it needed me so I was stuck moving at a snail's pace when every ounce of me screamed for speed.

The curtain led to a staff room complete with fridge, microwave and laminate table. Even with the time constraint I couldn't help blinking dumbly at the blond seated at the table calmly flipping cards.

Not what I had expected of a store owned by someone belonging to the Coven.

It was even less expected to find the proprietor playing what looked to be Solitaire.

"Miriam?"

"Yes?"

"I have a delivery for you." I stepped forward and pulled my phone from my pocket.

With a swipe of my fingers, I pulled up the delivery verification app and held the device out to her. She rested her forefinger lightly on the screen until it beeped. Before sliding it back in my pocket, I glanced down to make sure it said confirmed. Even more important, the words still showed green. It meant I'd made it in under deadline. If I hadn't, it would have turned red, and I'd have been screwed.

"You cut it close," Miriam said, already turning back to her game.

Pausing in the act of pulling the package out of my bag, I grimaced. No kidding.

"Another minute and I could have solved my ingredient shortage," Miriam said, eyeing my body with an appraising eye.

Oh. That would have been unfortunate. And probably painful.

I'd never had that as a consequence.

Hermes Courier Service was special. Its owner guaranteed satisfaction of service. Things like merchandise reaching its intended destination in one piece, and more importantly, on time. Failure resulted in a penalty clause kicking in, usually at the client's discretion.

279

This was normally something simple, like working as unpaid help for a predetermined length of time, but the penalty could be anything the employer wanted. The more expensive the job, the nastier the penalty.

I'd never been late so I hadn't bothered to inquire about this job's penalty clause. I may have also been more interested in the money.

"Right," I eventually said, handing over the small package. It was no bigger than a deck of cards and wrapped in brown paper and tied with red twine.

As always, I had no idea what was in it.

The witch set down her cards and took the package from me. Dressed in jeans and a bright yellow shirt, Miriam was different in almost every way from the girl watching the front counter. Except the color of her hair. Miriam's makeup was done with a light hand and flattered her large green eyes. If I met her at a bar one evening, I would have assumed she was a young professional only a couple of years out of college with a normal job, something like a graphic designer. Of the two, the girl out front seemed more likely to be a witch.

"Not all of us embrace the human's depiction of us," Miriam said.

I shifted back and eyed the witch warily.

Miriam looked up from her game with a sardonic lift of her eyebrow. "I didn't read your mind, if that's what you're thinking."

Since that's exactly what I was thinking, I didn't feel much better even with her assurance.

"Your face is surprisingly open for a vampire."

Crap. That was supposed to be a secret.

"Relax." Miriam turned back to her game and flipped another card. "I wouldn't be much of a witch if I couldn't tell if someone was supernatural or not."

While slightly more reassuring than the thought of Miriam being a mind reader, it didn't solve the issue of her knowing I was a vampire. I wasn't exactly in hiding but I also wasn't 'out'.

Miriam didn't give me time to dwell on what I should do or if I should even do anything. "What news do you bring me, courier?"

I settled down to the second half of my job. That of acting as a verbal news source.

One of the things I'd learned since my involuntary transformation to one of the fanged was that the different species of the supernatural world didn't play well together. It was kind of like the Hatfield's and the McCoy's only with many more families.

Information was a prized commodity. My job allowed me to go

anywhere as long as there was a package to be delivered. This gave me unique access that Hermes' clients were willing to pay for and pay well.

"Another human family was found murdered."

"I could have learned that from the human media. Tell me something I couldn't find out for myself." Miriam stared down at her cards with a frown.

"There's been talk of a task force being put together."

Miriam snorted. "There's always talk. Nothing ever comes from it. Everybody will want to be in charge but nobody will want to donate their people for it."

"I don't know. Fear does funny things. They might be willing to set aside differences to get to the bottom of the murders and disappearances."

Everyone was spooked. I could see it in their eyes, hear it in their voices. The last time I'd seen something similar I'd been in a war zone.

It had started with disappearances at the beginning of summer. Mostly from the smaller enclaves. The ones who weren't strong or under the protection of someone strong were the first to vanish. A few dryads from the Park of Roses gone in one night. From there the perpetrator moved on to the bigger groups. A sorcerer found smoldering in his bed. A few shifters torn apart like they were ragdolls. Shifters were strong too. Anything that could do that was not something you wanted coming after you.

It wasn't limited to the supernatural world either. Humans were being slaughtered in their beds. Police were horrified at the grisly remains but helpless to figure out who—or what—was doing it.

The only common thread in all this was that nobody knew anything about what was doing it. Not species, gender, or name. Nothing.

I lifted one shoulder. "If a few more disappear, it might give them incentive to work together."

Miriam propped her chin on one hand. "You're so young."

I mentally snorted. I hadn't felt young in a long time. Not since I'd come back from war. And not since my entire world view had been readjusted to include things that went bump in the night.

That was rich coming from her. She didn't look any older than I did.

"How old are you?" Miriam asked.

What could it hurt to humor the client?

"28."

"And how long have you been a vampire?"

I pretended to think about it. It was mostly for show. I knew exactly how long it had been.

"About two years."

Miriam turned back to her game. "Once you've been part of our world a little longer, you'll see we never really change. The different species will never successfully work together. Too much bad blood between us."

Right. I didn't agree, but it also wasn't my place to argue with a client.

Miriam waved a hand, dismissing me. "Ask Angela for your payment."

Guess my job here was done.

Before turning to go, I paused. "If you move the black nine to the red ten, you can clear a spot and move a king there."

I was through the curtain moments later, stopping only long enough to get my payment from the Goth girl, Angela.

My bike was right where I left it. Missing a seat of course, but that was easily fixed.

Pushing off, I headed home. It was just after midnight and that had been my last job. There'd been fewer deliveries to make than normal. I had hours of free time stretching before me. I'd miss the cash but it was nice to have the rest of the evening to myself.

Being a vampire had its advantages. Long life and near miraculous healing being among them. The hours? Not so much. Only being able to go out at night severely limited my free time. I'd always loved summer but found myself wishing the past few months would fly by. Having less than eight hours of dark to move around had been challenging both personally and professionally.

It's one of the reasons I worked at Hermes. The owner might be a complete troll but at least he understood my special needs. More than I could say for most potential employers.

With fall firmly upon us, it meant lengthening nights and more time to work and play.

Now that I had a rare night off, I planned to take advantage.

Hm.

What should I do first? Most stores were closed, so that was out. It was a weeknight so my old friends would be firmly asleep. Same with my family. I could go for a bike ride. But I did that most nights, all night. I wanted to do something different. Something I never had time for.

Who was I kidding? There was nothing to do at this time of night. It was kind of sad really. A rare chance down the drain.

Might as well head to the grocery store for my shopping before heading home. Maybe I could watch a few episodes of Firefly on Netflix before dawn.

Yeah. Vampirism was really paying off for me.

*　　*　　*

The grocery store was mostly empty at this time of night. Only students and the rare frantic parent walked its fluorescent lit aisles. There were maybe five people total in the store, including the stock boy, cashier and me.

I wheeled past the produce aisle and headed for the meat section.

Not all of the myths about vampires were true. Thank God. I could still eat, which considering my life-long love affair with food was a blessing. Never to taste chocolate or the black raspberry ice cream from Graeters? Might as well kill me where I stood.

Food didn't carry the same nutrients as it had before. Mostly it passed through my system doing nothing to help. Too much of it would make me sick, but in moderation I could still eat some of my favorites as long as I was careful.

The one exception was red meat. I could eat as much of that as my stomach could hold. I think it had to do with the blood and iron content, but I'd never had anyone to ask. All I knew was it hit the spot in a way even black raspberry ice cream didn't.

And the rarer the better. Yum. I think I drooled.

Two years ago I'd been returning with my unit from Afghanistan. I was a 25V, a combat camera for those in the civilian world. I, like so many of my fellow soldiers, was eager to hit the town after 362 days locked on a FOB where the closest I got to alcohol was what was in my mouthwash, and the height of entertainment was watching dust storms blow in.

That night was where my life took a serious detour from the path I'd planned for it. My night began like so many other young twenty somethings. I met a stranger. He was cute. I was horny as fraternization is strictly forbidden while in country and I've never been one to break the rules. I've always had an irrational fear of jail, and it didn't really matter if breaking the rules would actually lead to a jail cell. At least back then. Now, most nights I break three laws before midnight.

That's the only excuse I have for lowering my guard for some strange man when I'm normally extremely cautious. So cautious that friends have accused me of being unreasonably paranoid when it comes to men.

Not that night, though. That night I had to be wild and carefree and in love with being home. The world was my oyster and nothing could touch me. I'd survived a year in a warzone getting shot at, after all. The states were a cake walk after that, right?

Not so much.

It was quick when it happened. I didn't even see it coming. He'd isolated me from my friends without me even realizing it. Before I knew it, I was held tightly against him and his teeth were in my neck. Then I was discarded like so much trash. Woke up the next night lying on a gurney being wheeled to the morgue. I scared the daylights out of the attendee when I sat up in my body bag.

There were a lot of screams exchanged between the two of us before it was assumed the doctors had made a mistake in pronouncing me dead on arrival.

The authorities were called. My statement was taken and then they called my military chain of command.

Lucky for me, the captain on duty owed me big. Even luckier, he was part of this new world I suddenly found myself in. He's the one who got me put on profile, allowing me to stay in my room during the day and ultimately processed out of the military. That last one I'm still not too happy about, but it couldn't be helped. What good is a soldier who's useless from the time the sun rises to the time it sets?

He even got me the job with Hermes. Not that that's saying much, but it keeps me from having to move back in with my parents.

I pulled a tub of cottage cheese out of the display case and eyed it with uncertainty. I used to love cottage cheese, but ever since my change it tasted funny.

Shrugging, I put it in my cart. Just because I bought it didn't mean I had to eat it. People from my old life still stopped by now and then. They'd expect me to have some health food in the fridge. It's what the old me would have done. I was careful to show them what they wanted. It was safer for everyone that way.

The bottom of my cart barely littered with items, I headed to check out. Being in the grocery store was depressing me tonight. It reminded me of all the things I'd lost. I hated getting maudlin. What's done is done. Truthfully, most nights being a vampire wasn't so bad.

My sneakers squeaked against the linoleum as I wheeled my cart over to the cashier, bypassing the self-pay kiosks. The ones at this store tended to go a bit buggy after midnight. Even if they worked perfectly, I would have chosen the cashier. I needed human interaction.

I placed my groceries on the belt and wheeled my cart to the other end. The cashier's face was bored as he slid each item over the scanner. He was a college kid, his face all sharp angles and so incredibly young.

"That'll be $21.06."

I handed him a twenty and a five dollar bill. He took it, hitting the cash button on the register. It beeped but didn't open.

"What?" The cashier looked slightly more alert now. He hit the button twice more. "Come on. Not again."

He felt along the register, the boredom now completely gone from his eyes and his motions becoming slightly more frantic when he didn't immediately find what he was looking for.

"Oh no. No. No. No. My manager will kill me if I've lost the key again."

Out of the corner of my eye, I saw a pair of translucent wings disappear behind one of my plastic bags. Pixies. Great. I'd have to avoid this place for the next few weeks until the little bastards moved on.

Pixies were the magpies of the supernatural world. They tended to appropriate things that interested them only to discard them soon after. A lot of times when humans misplaced things, it was pixies at work. They love mischief and helping someone "lose" an item is right up their alley.

On one of my first jobs, a few managed to stow away in my messenger bag. I was new and still trying to figure this whole world out. I didn't know to guard against the pests. Hell, I hadn't even known what they were. They'd made life impossible in my home for nearly two months before they got bored and moved on. More than a year and half later, I still found things they'd hidden in the most random places.

I was not going to chance them hopping a ride again.

Taking pity on the cashier, I pointed to the bags. "Have you checked the bags yet? You may have placed it over there."

The cashier rounded on me, "The key never moves. It should be right here."

I held my hands up and motioned for him to calm down. "Hey,

just trying to be helpful. Obviously the key has moved. Might as well check the area thoroughly before panicking."

Rolling his eyes to make it obvious he was just humoring me, he rustled through the bags.

"I don't see-" His voice trailed off and he held up the key.

He looked at me suspiciously. I shrugged.

He didn't say anything as he unlocked the drawer and gave me my change.

I smiled and told him to have a nice day as I grabbed my bags and walked out. As soon as I was through the doors, I dumped everything on the ground and shook the bags out. I inspected every item thoroughly before putting them back in the plastic bag.

Groceries taken care of, I headed home. My apartment was a one bedroom walk up located right outside the campus district. I'm about eighty percent sure the rickety wooden staircase leading to the second floor entrance wasn't up to code.

My place was small, and while the area wasn't rough it also wasn't nice. Most of my neighbors were college kids or grad students.

Things went missing around here all the time so I hoisted my bike onto my shoulder and carried it up the stairs. A porch light illuminated the steps, not that I really needed it. Vampirism came with improved night vision. I'd say I had the vision equivalent of a cat if I knew what that equivalent was.

At the top of the landing, I propped the bike against the rail and reached into my mailbox. Pulling a cinnamon spice container out, I shrugged off my bag before emptying its contents on to the wooden landing. I liberally doused everything with the cinnamon and shook it a few times over my bag.

A soft sneeze, and then something darted past me, faster than my eyes could track.

Ha. Served the little bastard right.

Pixies disliked cinnamon. It affected them much like ragweed affected humans only about three times worse. They wouldn't linger long in an area that contained it.

It was one of the most effective, low cost methods I'd found for warding off pests. Much cheaper than a charm from a witch and just as effective.

Satisfied no other pixies lurked in my items, I dumped everything back into the bag and wheeled the bike inside, propping it inside the entryway.

My kitchen was small, just a fridge, stove and microwave, with barely any counter space. Since food was optional for me, I didn't really need counter space any more. It only took a few minutes to pack away my groceries.

I grabbed a wine glass out of the cupboard and fished a bottle from the fridge. The dark liquid was mesmerizing as I poured it into my glass. I unconsciously licked my lips, my stomach rumbling. I was already anticipating that first sip.

The blood tasted cool and crisp as it slid down my throat. I could practically feel the tissues soaking up the liquid. In seconds, it was gone.

I set the glass down, licking my lips free of any blood. God, I'd really needed that.

A stray spot of red drew my eye to the counter. I stared at it transfixed. I must have spilled a drop.

My eyes drifted to the clock. 1:07. I didn't have it in me to walk away from that drop, but I could wait. I had enough discipline for that. Five minutes. If I ever wanted to have full control of myself, I needed to start exercising will power.

I could do this. No problem.

My finger tapped against the counter anxiously. I let go and crossed my arms in front of me. My eyes never strayed from that drop.

Imagine the worst craving you've ever had. You know, the kind you get for that last piece of pizza after a stressful day at work. You've been thinking about it all day and remembering how it tasted last night and imagining the hot cheese on your tongue, the springy dough as you bit into it. Now take that craving and magnify it by a factor of about ten. That might give you some idea of what it's like to crave blood.

I'd be tempted to compare it to how a junky feels staring down their next fix, but I've never done drugs so I can't be sure of that.

Either way, blood was addicting and damn near impossible to resist. I was determined though. I was getting better at fighting temptation too. When I'd first been brought over, I would have licked that drop away almost as soon as it hit the counter. I also would have licked the entire glass in an attempt to get every speck of the life giving nectar.

These little exercises in self-restraint were torturous but oh so necessary. One day it might even save someone's life.

And time.

The five minutes were up. I forced myself to use my finger to swipe it up rather than just licking it. My tongue darted out to catch the drop. My eyes closed in bliss. So good.

I recapped the bottle, putting it back in the fridge where it had plenty of company.

Feeling good now that I'd had a top up, I changed into a pair of pink flannel pants and a loose t-shirt before grabbing a bag of chips and settling onto the couch.

What should I watch tonight? I'd just finished a sci-fi show last night and was in the mood for something different. Drama? Nah, I needed something a little more light hearted than that.

I navigated to one of the funnier shows on my list and sat back, prepared to follow Nathan Fillion around as he solved crime while keeping up a running stream of banter with his female costar.

Manufactured by Amazon.ca
Bolton, ON

35765282R00162